About

Justine Davis lives o... State, watching big shi... go by, and sharing th... wildlife, including a p... two, and a tailless raccoon. In the few hours when she's not planning, plotting, or writing her next book, her favourite things are photography, knitting her way through a huge yarn stash, and driving her restored 1967 Corvette roadster – top down, of course.

Publishers Weekly bestselling and award-winning author **Elizabeth Heiter** likes her suspense to feature strong heroines, chilling villains, psychological twists and a little romance. Her research has taken her into the minds of serial killers, through murder investigations, and onto the FBI Academy's shooting range. Her novels have been published in more than a dozen countries and translated into eight languages. Visit her at www.elizabethheiter.com

Debra Webb is the award winning, *USA Today* bestselling author of more than 150 novels, including reader favourites the *Faces of Evil*, the *Colby Agency*, and the *Shades of Death* series. With more than four million books sold in numerous languages and countries, Debra's love of storytelling goes back to her childhood on a farm in Alabama. Visit Debra at www.DebraWebb.com or write to her at PO Box 176, Madison, AL 35758.

Love Under Fire

Love Under Fire: Secrets and Lies

JUSTINE DAVIS

ELIZABETH HEITER

DEBRA WEBB

MILLS & BOON

First Published in Great Britain 2022
By Mills & Boon, an imprint of HarperCollins*Publishers,* Ltd
1 London Bridge Street, London, SE1 9GF

www.harpercollins.co.uk

HarperCollins*Publishers*
1st Floor, Watermarque Building,
Ringsend Road, Dublin 4, Ireland

LOVE UNDER FIRE: SECRETS AND LIES © 2022 Harlequin Books S.A.

Operation Notorious © 2017 Janice Davis Smith
SWAT Secret Admirer © 2015 Elizabeth Heiter
The Safest Lies © 2019 Debra Webb

ISBN: 978-0-263-30421-3

MIX
Paper from
responsible sources
FSC™ C007454

This book is produced from independently certified FSC™ paper to ensure responsible forest management.

For more information visit: www.harpercollins.co.uk/green

Printed and Bound in Spain using 100% Renewable electricity at CPI Black Print, Barcelona

OPERATION
NOTORIOUS

JUSTINE DAVIS

SAM

Sometimes the best things just end up on your doorstep...

One day a little puppy, lost and alone, somehow managed to pick the right house to show up at. He was a two-color pup, black-and-white fur, with one blue eye and one black eye. Irresistible, because when it became clear no one knew where he came from, the people at that house took him in.

They dubbed him Sam, sometimes called Perky because he was, and he became a member of the family. He took to life on a farm, with cattle, horses and chickens, grew to a nice medium size and functioned as buddy, playmate and, if necessary, protector. He loved them as only a dog can, and they loved him very much in return, for all the many years they were blessed with. And, as all dogs should be, he is remembered with love to this day.

To all who loved him, from Granny Thrasher.

This is the latest in a series of dedications from readers who have shared the pain of the loss of a beloved dog. For more information visit my website at www.justinedavis.com

Chapter 1

"I'm sending him to you. Make up something you need him for."

Quinn Foxworth blinked, and frowned at his phone. "What?"

"Fight info's en route. You've got six hours to come up with something. Good luck."

"What am I supposed—"

He stopped when he realized he was talking to dead air. He lowered the phone, staring at the screen that told him the call had lasted eighteen seconds.

Funny, it seemed shorter.

He turned to his wife, Hayley, who had come out onto the deck with two mugs of coffee and was now looking at him curiously.

"Charlie."

"Ruh-roh," she said with exaggeratedly widened eyes as she handed him his coffee.

"Yeah."

He wrapped his hand around the mug. It was due to rain by this evening, and he'd come out to scan the clouds. The warmth of the coffee was welcome against the chill of the shifting season.

"Dare I ask?" Hayley said after taking a sip from her own morning brew.

"Gavin's on his way here."

"Our Gavin? De Marco?" Her brow furrowed. "Do we need him?"

"No."

"Then why—"

He offered her his phone. "Call Charlie and ask."

She laughed. "No, thank you. So she didn't say why?"

He shook his head. "Only that it was life-and-death that he get out of there."

Her eyebrows rose. "Whose?"

"No clue. Maybe he's just driving Charlie crazy."

"Now that," Hayley said with a grin, "is a frightening thought."

Quinn laughed. "For you? I don't believe it."

And he didn't. The first time she'd met his fearsome sibling, and gotten that up and down, assessing, calculating look that intimidated less hardy souls, Hayley had never wavered.

So you're the one who thinks she can tame my brother?

I don't want him tamed. I love him as he is. And he loves me. So if you hurt me, you hurt him. Don't.

Charlie had blinked, stared, then burst into laughter. *She'll do, little brother. She'll do.*

Indeed she would. Forever.

"Well," Hayley went on after a moment, "if something's really eating at him, one of us should be able to get him to talk."

A quiet woof turned both their heads. And simultaneously, they laughed at their dog, Cutter.

"You can, is that what you're saying?" Hayley asked the clever animal.

Cutter's plumed tail wagged, and his amber-flecked dark eyes gleamed with amusement. Given the dog's history, Quinn wouldn't put it past him to have even the man who had once been the most famous attorney in the country spilling his guts to him.

And then the dog's expression changed, and his head swiveled around, looking north. Never one to waste time, he trotted off to investigate whatever had caught his attention.

"Good thing all the neighbors know him," Quinn said.

"And we don't live in a city of leash laws," Hayley added.

Once they'd realized what they had on their hands, they had introduced Cutter to all of those neighbors. Most were receptive to a trained watchdog who would look out for all of them as part of his home duties. The dog was respectful of the older neighbors, gentle with the young children, playful with the pets in the zone he'd mapped out for himself, and somehow realized that the rather reclusive residents on the corner didn't care for dogs and kept his distance.

"Maybe he can help Gavin," Hayley said.

Quinn grimaced. "Sure. Because Gav is so good about accepting help."

"Because he doesn't trust anyone. Except Foxworth. Cutter is part of Foxworth. Besides there's one thing he can be surer of with Cutter than anyone."

Quinn lifted a brow at her. "Which is?"

"Cutter," she said seriously, "will never, ever lie to him."

And that, Quinn thought, was the key to Gavin de Marco. He would tolerate much, never blinked at the grimness and unfairness he sometimes encountered in his work

for them but, with very good reason, he refused to put up
with liars.

And now he was going to get therapy from a dog. A
dog Gavin didn't quite understand yet. But he would. He'd
have no choice.

Quinn nearly grinned at the prospect.

Katie Moore drew her knees up tighter to her chest,
wrapping her arms around herself as if that could keep her
from flying into pieces. The nightmare hadn't been this
bad for a while, and she'd dared to hope it might eventually go away entirely. But last night it had returned with a
vengeance and now, three hours after waking up screaming, she was still shaken.

She sat on the floor of the small garden gazebo, amid
a patch of roses stubbornly refusing to admit it was almost November. She stared at one of the blooms, studying
each curving petal as if it held the answer. When she had
moved here, away from the city where life had turned so
ugly, she'd planted the roses around the gazebo with some
vague idea in her mind that someday when the worst was
over, she would sit here and breathe in the sweet scented
air and remember the good times. She'd never had a sister
by birth, but she'd found her sister of the heart, and since
they'd met in elementary school they'd rarely gone a day
without communicating in some way.

And still sometimes she had her hand on her phone
to call before she remembered she would never speak to
Laurel again.

Images from last night's horrific dream seethed just
below the surface, and her barricades seemed particularly
weak this morning. She wished it was a workday; losing
herself amid the books she loved would help get her mind

off this ugly track. Maybe she should go in anyway. Surely, there were things she could do.

Being the librarian in a town this small wasn't a difficult job, but she loved it. The new library was a beautiful, light, airy space that was a delight to the community that had worked so hard to make it happen.

Laurel would never see it.

That quickly, she was back in the morass. She felt so lost without the steady, loving friend who had always been there for her. If she hadn't been the one to find her body, maybe it wouldn't be so bad. The loss would be just as great, but she wouldn't have those horrifying images seared into her brain. Maybe—

"Woof?"

Katie snapped out of her grim thoughts, startled by the quiet sound. She smiled when she saw the dog sitting politely at the bottom of the gazebo steps. Cutter, Hayley's dog, from down the street. He was unmistakable with his black fur over face, head and shoulders, shifting to a rich reddish brown over his back down to his fluffy tail. She'd seen him often since her neighbor had come by to introduce him, and had been amusedly grateful he had apparently taken it upon himself to protect this entire block. More than ever now she needed reassurance of safety.

"Hello, boy. On your rounds?"

For an instant she could have sworn the dog shook his dark head. She laughed at herself. She'd never had the tendency to anthropomorphize animals, but it was hard to avoid with this one. Especially when he came up the steps, turned and sat down beside her, and leaned in. As if to comfort her, as if he knew how roiled her inner self was this morning.

As, perhaps, he did. Dogs did wonders as therapy animals, she knew. One of the most popular nonfiction books in the library last month had been the story of one such dog. But she wasn't sure anything could alleviate this kind of pain. What could possibly make this any easier to bear? She shuddered, her throat going tight, nearly strangling her airway. Cutter leaned in harder, and when instinctively her hand came up to stroke his soft fur, she found, to her surprise, that the horror receded slightly. Only slightly, but enough to allow her to breathe again.

She hugged the dog. And by the time he trotted off toward home, his rounds completed for the morning, she realized she was going to have to read that book.

Gavin de Marco shifted the backpack slung over one shoulder, and adjusted his grip on the duffel in his left hand as he walked through the airport parking structure to the rental car area. The crisp Seattle air was like a gulp of pure, clean ice water after the humidity he'd left in St. Louis, which was having trouble surrendering its grip on a muggy summer even two months into fall.

Two children in Halloween gear raced past him, shrieking. He'd almost forgotten the day of costumes and candy was nearly upon them. A man he'd noticed on his flight let go of the suitcase he'd been wheeling and bent to greet the two mini-superheroes, a wide, loving smile on his face. The woman with the children joined them, and the look the man gave her made Gavin turn away. It was personal, intimate, even here among the throngs of a busy afternoon at SeaTac Airport. That "you're mine and I'm yours" kind of look that meant a deep, irrevocable bond that might change over the years, but would never fade or break.

The kind of look Hayley gave Quinn, and more surprisingly, Quinn gave Hayley.

The kind of look no woman had ever given him.

Not, he thought wryly, that he'd ever earned it.

He let out a disgusted breath. The disgust was aimed, as it usually was lately, inwardly, not at Quinn Foxworth, one of the last few people on earth he trusted without reservation.

Unfortunately that few did not include himself any longer.

He made himself focus on the task of picking up the car. He'd refused Quinn's offer that they would pick him up—by car, plane or helicopter, whichever he preferred—and insisted on the rental car. He wanted to be independently mobile, because recently there were times when he just couldn't stay put.

He said he just felt restless.

Charlie said he was crazy-making.

So here he was, sent off to make the other Foxworth sibling crazy. Maybe that's all it was, Charlie getting him off nerves he'd trod on too often.

He hoped Quinn had something going on he could seriously gnaw on. Not that it hadn't been a challenging go-round last time. Taking down a governor was not simple, even when they mostly did the job for you. Gavin didn't want to admit he'd been exhilarated by walking through that minefield; it made him wonder if he'd become some kind of adrenaline junky.

He knew some had assumed he always had been, what with the kind of headline grabbing cases he'd been involved in during his career in criminal defense, but that hadn't been it at all. He'd been coolly analytical, helped by his knack for anticipating the moves of others. He'd been able to think on the fly and draw up almost any precedent-setting case he'd ever read about. He'd been—

Wrong. Don't forget that one.

He interrupted his own thoughts with the sharp, bitter reminder. For he had been wrong. Very wrong, and it had pulled the rug out from under not just his career but his entire life.

By the time Gavin's phone warned him he'd reached his destination even he had to admit his brain had eased up a bit, as if responding to the more peaceful surroundings. Just as Quinn said it did for him. Here on the other side of Puget Sound seemed a world away from the bustling city in feeling if not distance. He never would have thought he'd say it, but maybe Quinn was on to something here.

A light rain had begun just as he stepped under cover of the porch, and his hosts congratulated him on his timing. He was welcomed, his bags stowed in the guest room, and a drink poured and waiting for him by the fire crackling in the hearth before he recognized the luscious smell wafting from the kitchen was Quinn's famous spicy chicken.

"I'm honored." He tilted the glass of wine in a salute. "You cooked for me?"

"Don't get used to it," Quinn said.

Gavin managed a creditable grin before asking, "Where's that rascal dog of yours?"

"On his nightly rounds," Quinn said.

Gavin found himself laughing, to his own surprise. "Patrolling the neighborhood?"

"Morning and evening, every day we're not on a case," Hayley said.

"Strong sense of duty, that one," Gavin said, not really kidding.

Quinn nodded. "Like most good operatives."

Gavin had heard enough stories of the uncannily clever canine to know Quinn was dead serious. "Even Charlie has finally accepted that he's an integral part of your team."

"Speaking of Charlie," Hayley began, then stopped.

Gavin studied her for a moment, then let out a long breath as he lowered his gaze. Quietly, he voiced what he'd been suspecting since his plane had cleared the Rockies. "You don't have a case, do you?"

Hayley exchanged a glance with her husband. Quinn grimaced.

Quinn had never lied to him—one reason he trusted him—and Gavin knew he wouldn't now. But before he could answer there was a sound at the rear door that drew their attention. Gavin turned just as a hinged section at the bottom of the door swung open. A second later Cutter was there, looking a bit damp from the rain, which had picked up now. He had something in his mouth, some toy Gavin guessed.

"He has his own door now?" he asked as Hayley grabbed a towel clearly kept by the door for that reason and turned to the dog.

"It's easier," Quinn said. "He's got a mind of his own and—"

He stopped as the animal walked past Hayley and the towel, toward Gavin. He guessed that figured, given he hadn't been here when the dog had left the house. Cutter sat at his feet, looking up at him intently. Did he even remember him? Gavin wondered. He hadn't spent much time here last time, and—

His speculation broke off when he saw what the dog had in his mouth. It was not a toy. A cell phone? What was the dog doing with a phone? Whose phone? Where had he found it? And why the hell was he bringing it to him?

By the time he got through the string of mental questions Quinn and Hayley were at his side. Cutter allowed Hayley to take the phone from him, but the dog's steady gaze never left Gavin. He found it strangely unsettling.

"It doesn't look like it's been lying around and he just found it," Quinn said.

"No," she agreed. "It's not damaged at all. And it's on, so it's working."

"Is he given to stealing things?" Gavin asked neutrally.

Quinn gave him a sideways glance. "In the interest of a good cause, it's not unheard of."

Gavin didn't know what to say to that, so he said nothing as Hayley pressed a button on the side of the phone.

"Locked," she said. "Charge is at 65 per cent."

"Good. The owner will probably call it once they realize it's gone," Quinn said.

"Assuming they have another phone, and don't already know because Cutter snatched it right out of their hand," Hayley said, sounding a bit glum.

"Well, there's that," Quinn said, glancing at the dog. Hayley handed him the phone and went to work on the dog with the towel.

She had just finished when the doorbell rang. She put down the towel and looked at Quinn. "And maybe," she said, "whoever it was—"

"—followed him here," Quinn finished for her.

"I'll get it, shall I?" Gavin said lightly, telling himself a buffer between a possibly irate phone owner and the owners of the dog who'd grabbed it might be a good idea. Quinn didn't immediately answer him, but moved across the living room to where he could get a glimpse out the window to the porch, where a motion-sensor light had come on. Only then did he nod.

"Sometimes I forget," Gavin muttered under his breath as he reached for the door handle. Coming in as he did, usually after everything had happened and there was nothing left but cleanup, he did sometimes forget that Foxworth occasionally irritated people with minimal impulse control. People who could be dangerous.

He pulled the door open, revealing a woman who looked

a bit damper than the dog had. Rain glistened on hair pulled back in a wavy ponytail, and a couple of drops clung to long, soft-looking eyelashes. Lashes that surrounded eyes that seemed vividly blue even in the artificial glow of the porch light. Her face, with a slightly upturned nose and a nicely shaped mouth, was turned up to him since she was probably about five-four to his five-eleven. Her cheeks looked even wetter than her hair, and if it hadn't been raining he might have thought she'd been crying. Which would explain the distress he saw in both her eyes and her body language; she was hunched into herself against more than the chill.

"Is Hayley here?" she asked. "Or at least Cutter?"

Chill, he thought again, only this time in the nature of a self-command. Belatedly he realized she wore no jacket over her jeans and light sweater, as if she had come hastily. In pursuit of her phone? He shook off the strange sluggishness that had overtaken him.

"Sorry," he said, stepping back to let her in. Obviously she knew Hayley and she hardly looked like a threat, even if he'd been studying her as if she were one.

"Katie, isn't it?" Hayley said, coming forward. "Katie Moore? The blue house?"

"Yes," she said, sounding grateful.

Quinn had disappeared from his position by the window, but now reappeared with a fresh, dry towel, which he handed to the newcomer.

"Here, dry off. I'm Quinn, Hayley's husband."

"Thank you," the woman said, then applied the towel. "I'm sorry to intrude, but—"

"It's no intrusion. Neighbors are always welcome. Come in by the fire and get warmed up," Hayley said.

"Thank you," she repeated, folding the used towel. Gavin noticed, because it was what he did, that her hands trembled slightly. And again he was certain there was more to it than simply being cold. "I don't quite know what happened. I—"

She stopped then. Because Cutter the phone thief had stepped between them and stood at Katie's feet. And then he turned and sat, staring up at Quinn and Hayley.

"Ah," Quinn said, as if the dog's action explained everything.

Gavin had heard about this, although he'd never seen it in person. But even if he hadn't known, he could have seen that this was a signal.

Fix it.

That's what Quinn called it, the dog's "fix it" look. And eyeing the clever animal now, he believed it. What he found harder to believe was the thought that popped into his head then.

In the interest of a good cause...

That was a bridge too far, thinking the dog had stolen the phone specifically to get this woman here because she had a problem that Foxworth could fix.

Wasn't it?

Quinn and Hayley exchanged a glance. And then Quinn looked at Gavin.

"That question you asked, about a case? The answer just changed."

Chapter 2

"Sorry, I'm a bit scattered," Katie said, hands wrapped around the steaming mug of hot cocoa Hayley had fixed for her.

She was starting to feel warm again, thanks to it and the fire. And Cutter's presence. The dog had taken up residence at her feet, lying on them in fact, and his body heat was doing nearly as much as the fire and cocoa to warm her up. She felt miles away from the new pit of shock and despair she'd been cast into just a short time ago, and for the moment she let herself revel in the warmth.

"This rascal is good at distractions, when needed," Quinn said. His voice was quiet, steady, but it took nothing away from his formidable appearance. In fact it added to it. This was a man, she thought, who had nothing to prove to anyone.

"He's been visiting me a lot lately," she said. "He's really been quite sweet. I don't know why he did this."

Quinn and Hayley exchanged a look that was both know-ing and wary, but also seemed slightly amused. They didn't seem the type to take their pet's misbehavior as funny, not after Hayley had gone to the trouble of introducing Cutter to the neighbors, but maybe she was wrong. She hoped not.

As for their guest, introduced as Gavin visiting from St. Louis, he was something else altogether. When a complete stranger had answered the door, all sorts of crazy thoughts had run through her mind. She'd known she had the right house; she'd done her due diligence on the neighborhood before she'd moved in five months ago. But when the man who now sat slightly apart from them, as if he were in the room but not the group, had opened the door, her heart had slammed into her throat.

Hayley's husband was tall, looked strong, and his mili-tary background showed in his demeanor. This Gavin might be a little less imposing physically but there was some-thing about the way he looked, something in eyes so dark they almost appeared black, that she found even more im-posing—a bright, quick intelligence that to her crackled as tangibly as the fire she was sitting beside. And the way he'd stared at her, making her overly conscious of how wet and bedraggled she must look, left her feeling she had been thoroughly assessed and cataloged.

Could you tell I'm a basket case? About to fly into a million pieces?

"Katie runs our new library," Hayley was saying to their friend. "And it's become quite the success thanks to some of her ideas."

Katie found herself watching the man who'd opened the door, awaiting his reaction, half expecting some kind of joke or comment she'd heard too many times before. Somehow being a librarian came with certain judgments or stereotypes, many of them wrong, some of them very,

very wrong. But nothing showed in his expression, and he said nothing. She wasn't sure why she had reacted to him so strongly, with that startled leap of her heart.

"So, Cutter's been visiting you a lot?"

Hayley's quiet question snapped her out of her ruminations. "Yes. I haven't minded," she put in quickly. "He's been…quite comforting, actually."

"He has the knack," Quinn said.

"He does," Hayley agreed. "He can always sense when someone is in turmoil. Or pain. Or has a problem."

Well, all three of those fit her just now, Katie thought.

"And," Hayley said, her voice even softer now, "he'll do whatever it takes to get that person the help they need."

"Including making off with their cell phone," Quinn added.

Katie blinked. She stared at them both, then at the dog at her feet. Then she looked back to Quinn. "Wait. You're saying he took my phone on purpose? To…what? What are you saying?"

Hayley leaned forward, focusing on Katie. Her voice was gentle, encouraging, like a hug from a friend. "He can always sense when someone needs the kind of help the Foxworth Foundation can provide."

Katie frowned, puzzled. She remembered the name from when Hayley had come by, but she'd been too entranced by the charming Cutter to really focus on the brief mention of the foundation she and her husband—and the dog—were part of, other than to register she'd heard of it before. But while she appreciated the concern—and heaven knows she needed any support she could get—she doubted this foundation of theirs could help, even though she had only a vague idea of what kind of work they did.

"I'm afraid your foundation can't solve my problem," she said. "Because what I need is a really, really good attorney."

Neither Foxworth answered her. There was no sound but a loud pop from the fire. But Hayley, Quinn and even Cutter had all shifted their gaze. And they were staring at the man sitting in the chair opposite her. The man who had gone suddenly very still.

"Told you," Quinn said, breaking the silence.

Katie had no idea what Quinn was referencing, but Gavin muttered something she guessed she was glad not to have heard.

"Katie," Hayley said in a more formal tone that was no less gentle, "let me more fully introduce someone to you. This—" she gestured at Gavin "—is the Foxworth Foundation's attorney, Gavin de Marco."

She was so startled at the coincidence of their guest being an attorney, on top of their dog seemingly leading her here, that it was a moment before the name registered. When it did she gaped at him, she was sure gracelessly.

"De Marco? *The* Gavin de Marco?"

She'd known the name since before the scandalous downfall of the governor last spring, but once it was discovered that the formerly famous but now rarely heard from attorney was involved in sorting out the aftermath, his name had been included in every news story. And suddenly she remembered that was where she'd heard about the Foxworth Foundation before, in those stories. She just hadn't realized that Quinn and Hayley were *those* Foxworths.

But she doubted there was any adult in the entire country, except perhaps those who lived purposely in ignorance, who hadn't heard the name Gavin de Marco. Any criminal case that had hit the national news in the last decade, there was a 50 per cent chance de Marco's name was attached. After blasting into the public awareness at a young age when a senior attorney had died midcase and he'd had to take over—he often referred to himself as the understudy who made good—his record was so amazing that it had become, in the public mind, an indicator of guilt or innocence in itself. Not because of lawyerly tricks or clever dodges, but because he always seemed to turn up the evidence or get testimony or make an argument that exonerated his client so thoroughly juries could vote no other way.

And then there were the other cases. She'd read about them, back when she'd been living and working down in Tacoma, because they were hard to avoid as she shelved the newspapers patrons had still wanted in those days. The Reed fraud case, the Redmond murder case, and the others where he had withdrawn from the defense. By then his reputation was such that it was practically a conviction in itself, no matter what reason was given.

All these thoughts raced through her mind in the embarrassingly long moment when she simply stared at him. Along with a rapid recalculation. She'd thought he must be about her age, but he had to be older. College, three years of law school, however long it had taken to hit the national stage, all those famous cases, and then the three or four years since he'd dropped out of sight for reasons still a matter of wide speculation.

He didn't look like the pictures and video images she remembered. Gone was the exquisitely tailored suit and the haircuts that had likely cost more than her monthly food budget. Now he was wearing a pair of black, low-slung jeans and a knit, long-sleeved shirt that stretched over broad shoulders and clung to a narrow waist and hips. His hair was longer, with a couple of dark strands kicking forward over his brow. Outward signs of inward changes? she wondered. It all made him less intimidating…until you looked at his eyes. No one with those eyes could be anything less than intimidating.

She had no idea how long she'd been sitting there gaping at him when he said, in a level tone that told her he was familiar with her reaction, "And you need an attorney because…?"

No preamble, no "Nice to meet you" exchange. He'd cut right to the chase. But then, wasn't that what an attorney was supposed to do? Be objective, get to the heart of things, and not be distracted by such messy things as emotions?

Easy, when you're not the one whose life is being blown up.

The spark of emotion she felt at his cool detachment enabled her to pull herself together. And instead of saying the multitude of things piling up in her mind, she made herself answer his question simply.

"I need an attorney because my father is suspected of murdering my best friend."

Chapter 3

Well. He hadn't expected that, Gavin thought.

He'd wanted to cut through her obvious reaction to his name, even as he wondered yet again when it would at last fade from the public consciousness. He looked forward to that day with more longing than he ever had getting into a courtroom, even in the fresh, young days of idealistic fervor.

That it was likely going to take until an entire generation grew up having never heard of him was a thought he tried not to dwell on. For a guy who, unlike many of his fellow attorneys, had never wanted that kind of fame, he surely had acquired enough of it to last a lifetime. And he was likely going to be a crotchety old man before it faded.

And who says you're not a crotchety old man already, de Marco?

"No wonder you're scattered," Hayley was saying. She'd moved to sit next to the woman on the sofa, putting an arm around her. Cutter sat up and shifted so that he could rest his chin on her knee. The woman lifted a hand to stroke the dark head. He could almost feel some of the tension ease from her, even from over here.

That dog was…something. Then again, Gavin couldn't blame the dog for wanting to be stroked by this woman.

He blinked. *Where the hell had* that *come from?*

"Can you tell us the story?" Hayley asked gently.

"I wouldn't know where to start."

Gavin heard the husky tremor in her voice, saw the sudden gleam in her eyes, recognized the welling of moisture. She was on the edge of breaking. He knew there were usually two ways to go with someone who was teetering like this. Let them go, let it gush out uncontrollably and try to make sense of it after, or take the lead and control it for them. Both approaches had their benefits. An emotional flood sometimes netted information the person would not necessarily have revealed had they been in control. But it could also lead to confusion, because emotionally distraught people often saw connections where there were none, assumed cause and effect where it wasn't warranted, or at worst made no sense at all.

He decided on the latter approach, and told himself it was not because he simply did not want to see this woman break down in front of him. And it had nothing to do with that errant thought that had blasted into his mind as he'd watched her stroke Cutter's soft fur.

"Or," he said, intentionally rather briskly, "would you rather just answer some questions, in a logical order?"

Gavin saw her take a deep breath, as if to steady herself. Her mouth tightened slightly, and he found himself disliking the tension of it in a very peculiar way.

"There's no point." She glanced at Gavin. "I need an attorney for my father, but we can't afford Gavin de Marco."

Quinn stepped in then. "If we determine Foxworth can help—and that is a big *if*—you won't have to. Gavin works for us."

"In that case, I probably can't afford you, either."

"Not an issue," Gavin said. "Whether your case meets Foxworth criteria is."

"And if it does," Quinn said, "there's no cost for Foxworth's help."

"No cost?" She glanced at Gavin. "What's your billable rate? A thousand an hour?"

His mouth quirked upward. There had been some bite in the question, a sign she was steadying. Given even what little he knew of her situation from her stark explanation, he found it admirable. He doubted many could manage it.

"It was actually a bit more," he said. "Back in the day."

Her gaze shifted to Quinn. "So you have him on retainer, or what?"

"Actually," Quinn answered mildly, "we don't pay him at all."

She drew back rather sharply. Hayley put a hand on her arm. Cutter nudged her to keep petting. Between the two of them Katie didn't have a chance, Gavin thought, but he hid his amusement.

"Gavin," Hayley said, "works with us because he, like all of us, believes in what we do."

Katie's gaze shifted from Hayley to Quinn to him in rapid succession. "For free?" she said in obvious disbelief.

"I get compensated in…other ways," he said. *Like the easing of my soul.*

She looked genuinely confused. People always were, when first confronted with the idea of an organization like Foxworth. It just didn't seem possible these days that anyone would take up causes like this.

"What exactly is it," Katie said carefully, "that you do?"

Gavin glanced at Quinn, the man who had pulled him out of a quagmire of betrayal and self-doubt and given him a clear and bright path to follow. Were he not here Gavin might have tried to explain himself, but the Foxworth Foundation was Quinn's creation, his and Charlie's. Quinn walked over and sat on the edge of the coffee table in front of Katie, his elbows resting on his knees.

"When I was ten, my parents were killed in a terrorist bombing. I have never felt so helpless or so enraged as when the terrorist was set free and nobody would tell me the truth. Foxworth was founded to help people who are in that same boat, fighting injustice. Honest, good people in the right, who have fought but can't fight anymore, or who haven't been able to get help anywhere else."

Gavin watched with interest as Katie Moore studied Quinn. "And who," she asked after a moment, "decides they're in the right?"

Gavin registered the question that many didn't even think to ask. Ms. Moore was clearly not in the nonthinking category. He could almost hear the click in his mind as he checked off that box in his assessment. She would not be difficult to work with in that way. In other ways...

Again he had to slam on the mental brakes. Maybe Charlie had been right, and he really was going nuts.

"That's the joy of being a private enterprise," Quinn answered with a smile. "We do. We have our values, and our criteria are ours alone."

"We only take cases we can get behind wholeheartedly," Hayley added. "We can't help everyone, but those we do help get it all."

Katie seemed fascinated by the concept, and was now distracted enough that she appeared and sounded calmer than when she had arrived. Gavin knew he was right because Cutter settled back down at her feet, head resting on his front paws.

Her hair had dried now, and he saw it was a sandy sort of blond with strands of a lighter, golden color here and there. And her eyes truly were that blue. Even as he thought it she glanced at him, giving him the full force of that vivid color. Then she turned back to Hayley and Quinn.

"What kind of cases?" Katie asked.

"We've reunited long-lost families—my own included," Hayley said with a smile. "Recovered a kidnap victim. Helped some troubled kids, and adults, find their way. Gave a grieving family a reason they could bear for a suicide. And Quinn found a stolen locket that was the only memento a girl had of her dead mother." She looked at her husband proudly. "That's still his favorite case."

Katie smiled at that. It was a nice smile, Gavin thought, yet it was tinged with a sadness that made him wonder about her own mother. *Not something you need to know. Stop it.*

Katie only asked, "Even more than taking down a corrupt politician?"

"In a way, yes," Quinn said.

"And there you have it," Gavin said, speaking for the first time since this explanation of Foxworth had begun. "The reason Foxworth is what it is. It's in what they value."

Katie's head turned and she studied him for a moment. She clearly took her time, thought through things, processed them. He wondered if she ever did anything on pure impulse. Images flashed into his mind, of things Katie Moore might do on impulse. Heat shot through him, as if the fire they were gathered around had suddenly flared. He quickly shifted his gaze to that fire, wondering what the hell was happening with him, and if she'd seen anything in his eyes.

He looked up again when she spoke, but she was back to looking at Hayley and Quinn, and he could breathe again. He would analyze this later, far away from those eyes.

"I'm sorry," she was saying, "I didn't realize you were the Foxworths mentioned in all the stories last spring."

"We don't advertise it. We work mostly by word of mouth," Hayley said. Then, rather pointedly, she nodded at Cutter. "Although these days, he brings us enough work all by himself."

Katie blinked. Gavin understood. He was more than a bit bemused himself by how easily Quinn and Hayley accepted that their dog had not only sensed this woman needed their help, but apparently had engineered this entire meeting.

Quinn smiled. "I was as skeptical as you are, but he's proven himself time and again. I've learned to just go with it."

"We all have. Even Gavin," Hayley added with a grin and a sideways look at him, "and he's the least fanciful guy you'll ever meet."

"Thanks," Gavin said drily. "I think."

"I would think being fanciful wouldn't be a good trait for an attorney," Katie said.

Gavin found himself oddly curious. "And what traits would be?"

Katie studied him again, perhaps looking for any sign his question had been facetious or snarky. His curiosity was genuine, and apparently she sensed that. Once decided, she seemed to consider the question as thoroughly as she had everything else. After a moment she said, "Sifting. Through all the dross to the essentials, I mean. Empathy that doesn't cloud objectivity. Researching. An affinity for the facts."

Gavin stared at her. "That was very concise."

"I read a lot. Remember most. Was I close?"

"Very." His mouth twisted at one corner. "Except the objectivity and affinity for facts seem to be falling by the wayside these days."

"You asked what traits would be good, not which ones were common."

He blinked. Quinn laughed aloud. "She got you there, Gav."

He laughed himself, something rare enough to be appreciated. "Indeed."

Cutter's head came up, and Gavin found himself the object of the dog's steady gaze. He got the oddest feeling it was a look of approval. Then he almost laughed again, at himself for attributing such things to a look from a dog. And he was glad when Quinn turned things back to Katie's situation.

"It's up to you, of course, but if you tell us the story and Foxworth can't take the case, we can perhaps guide you to someone who can. We have a lot of contacts, people who'd be willing to help."

"That's the payment Foxworth gets," Hayley told her. "The willingness to help someone else down the line."

Katie glanced at Gavin again. He could almost read the question in her glance, if he was one they had helped who was now paying them back.

More than you could imagine, he told her silently.

She continued to look at him. Cutter made a small, low sound, drawing his gaze. The dog was staring at him again, and he felt oddly compelled to tip the troubled woman over that edge, get her to open up. He leaned back in his chair, as if settling in.

"What was your friend's name?" he asked.

"Laurel," she said. "Laurel Brisbane."

The pain that echoed in her voice jabbed at him. The old instincts still kicked in, but the old impartiality was struggling. He tried to ignore it and went for the easiest question that was likely to get her started. They'd get to the rest once she'd gotten used to the idea of talking.

"Tell us about her."

She drew in a deep breath, and he knew the ball was rolling.

Chapter 4

Katie was amazed at what a relief it was to talk about Laurel to people who hadn't heard it all before. People who neither wanted salacious details nor tried to steer her away from the painful subject. She knew her friends and even her family meant well, but the way they shied away from even speaking about Laurel or her death, as if the lively, clever and utterly loyal woman she'd been had never existed, only added to the hurt.

And yet she herself shied away from her death now, choosing to start at the beginning, when two girls had laughed at the same thing in a fourth grade classroom, and a fast, enduring friendship had begun. And they listened, these people she barely knew, even though this wasn't the story they were really waiting for. Even Gavin—she had to think of him by his first name because realizing she was sitting in the same room with the celebrated Gavin de Marco disconcerted her—listened quietly, not interrupting or prompting. That was unexpected to her; she thought he'd be more of a "cut right to the chase" kind of guy. At least, that was the impression he'd always given in news reports and video clips. He'd been renowned for his talent for reducing a case to its simplest aspect in a broadcast-worthy sound bite, succinct and pithy. Of course, the fact that the camera loved him didn't hurt, she'd thought back then when she'd seen him.

Now, however, she knew it wasn't the camera at all. He really was that good-looking, and more compelling in person than any recorded image could be. And that was a path she was not walking, she told herself sternly. But didn't it just figure that the first spark of real response she'd had to a man in a long time would come now, not only amid an impossible situation but with an impossible man?

Ignore it. It will go away. Or he will.

She jumped ahead to where Laurel had, temporarily, moved into Katie's apartment in Tacoma after a final breakup with her boyfriend of a couple of years, Ross Carr. Laurel had seemed both unsurprised and resigned, and Kate's role seemed to mostly be offering commiseration, ice cream and reassurance that she was better off without him.

Until that day a week later, when she had come home from work to find a bloody nightmare of a scene. Her fingers curled into fists as she fought to get it told. The words came out in compressed chunks, in between harsh breaths.

"They told me there was no sign of forced entry. She fought him, they said. Then…he used a kitchen knife. It wasn't mine. He…he slashed her. Blood everywhere. He cut—"

She broke off, nearly choking on what she couldn't, just couldn't give voice to, the horrifying carnage she'd walked in on. She was aware of Hayley putting a comforting arm around her. Cutter jumped up beside her and put his head in her lap. She automatically put a hand on his head, and the feel of the silky fur steadied her again.

"Is that why you moved here?" Hayley asked, and the gentle concern in her voice almost broke Katie. She was holding on to a hair of control when she answered.

"Yes. The opening at the library here came up, I knew the area because my father lives here, and… I wanted new surroundings. Quiet, peace. A place where I could soak in the tranquility, purge the…the ugly."

"Of course," Hayley said.

Katie nodded because she didn't dare speak anymore. This quiet, supportive concern, even from near-strangers, was somehow harder to cope with than the thoughtlessness of people who had no idea. That was another reason she'd moved here, to get away from those who couldn't resist speculating about the shocking murder, never realizing or caring that they were talking to or in front of the collateral damage.

"It's taken me a while, but I reached…tranquility, if not peace." She grimaced. "I wasn't sure of that until I went back to visit a friend and ran into Ross at the coffee shop."

"That must have ripped the scab right off," Quinn said with a grimace.

"Yes. Yes, it did. I couldn't wait to get back here. I could feel the…serenity, I guess, growing the closer I got."

"Sign of a good decision," Hayley said.

"Why isn't he the prime suspect?"

The question, the first time Gavin had spoken since she'd begun her sorry tale, was not quite brusque but close. It had the effect of a blast of cool wind, complete with the rain still falling outside. And it quashed the silly reaction she was having to him.

"He was. In the beginning. Especially since they'd recently broken up. They even grilled me, until they verified

I'd been at work late that night. The ones closest to the... victim always are the first ones they suspect, aren't they?"

"And they're guilty more often than not," Gavin said, in that same tone.

"I know. But Ross had a solid alibi. They verified it. Lots of witnesses."

Odd, she thought. It was somehow easier to deal with that brisk, businesslike tone. Or maybe it was the inexplicable comfort provided by petting Cutter.

"And," she added, "he was as devastated as I was. He genuinely cared for Laurel. He told me the breakup had made him realize how much he loved her. He'd even bought a ring, was about to propose, right before she was killed."

"Then why did they break up in the first place?"

Again, Gavin's clipped tone made it somehow easier to answer. As if they both realized this, Quinn and Hayley stayed silent. Cutter never moved, however, and she was glad of that. Still she hesitated, then said, "I know she's gone, but it still feels like betraying a confidence."

"Weigh it," Gavin said, "against finding out who killed her."

Put like that, there was no question. "*Cheating* was all she said. She hadn't been ready to talk much about it yet."

"And so she turned up on your doorstep, expecting you to take her in?"

Something jabbed through the pain of her recollections. "No," she said, rather sharply herself, "she turned up on my doorstep *knowing* I would take her in. As she would for me."

His expression didn't change, as if he hadn't heard the shift in her tone. She wondered then if he'd done it on purpose, to shake her out of the dreadful memories. Surely he hadn't gotten to where he'd been a household name without having more than a few tricks up his sleeve. And she had to admit this one had worked; she was steadier now. Before she had time to decide how she felt about that, he dragged her back to what she'd been dreading most of all.

"Your father," he said flatly. "He's now a suspect?"

"That's what they're saying. And they're talking like he's now the only suspect. The news, I mean." She gave herself a mental shake; she was sounding very scattered. "A friend heard it and called me."

"Let me guess," Gavin said, his tone sour now. "It was 'according to a source close to the investigation,' or some such."

"Yes, something like that. They didn't say who it was."

"Of course not."

She realized he'd dealt with the media a lot during his career. She saw him exchange a glance with Quinn, and although the other man didn't speak Gavin apparently saw some kind of signal and went back to his questions.

"Has an investigator called you yet?"

"Yes, although I didn't realize it was about this at the time. A detective contacted me about a month ago, said she was following up, and asked several questions they'd already asked. But one of them was if my father had a key to my apartment—he used to, but I got it back to give to Laurel—and if I'd seen him that day."

"That came in the middle of a lot of other questions, I'd guess."

"Yes. Why?"

"Less chance for you to realize that was the whole purpose. Hide that particular tree in a forest of them. So you couldn't tip off your father that they were looking at him."

Her mouth tightened. "Well, it clearly worked on Ms. Oblivious."

He shrugged. "If they're good, it works on most people. What did you say?"

"The truth, of course. I hadn't seen him or talked to him, not that day. Since there's no way he could have done it, it didn't matter. At least I thought it didn't. Until I heard he'd become their prime suspect."

The toxic combination of anger and despair threatened to rise and swamp her, and she barely managed to hold it at bay. She felt a bit like a bug—a helpless one—under a microscope, and wondered if that was what the people Gavin de Marco confronted in court had felt like. She wondered, as she had at the time, why he'd really quit. Cutter gave a low whine and licked at her hand. And again the dog steadied her.

She lifted her gaze from the dog to the man whose attention was so focused on her. "If they were so worried about keeping it secret, then why are the police talking to the media about it now?"

"Likely because they haven't got enough evidence, or it's all circumstantial."

She frowned. "Of course they don't, since he didn't do it. But why would they let it leak that he's a suspect now, after all this time?"

"They may be hoping to prod him into doing something."

Perplexed, she frowned. "Doing something?"

"The knife," he said. "Did they find it?"

"No. The killer took it with him."

"Then they may have wanted him to think he had to get rid of it, if he hadn't already."

Her frown deepened. "My father doesn't own that kind of knife, either." Somehow she was able to say it fairly evenly, and fight off the images that were piling up behind that barricade she'd built in her mind. She suspected it was thanks to his businesslike tone.

Again Gavin glanced at Quinn. This time she saw the

barely perceptible nod. It was odd, she thought, to think of Gavin de Marco having a boss. She would have thought he would call his own shots. And again she wondered why he'd walked away, wondered who left when they were top of the heap?

She remembered the stories after he'd removed himself from the Reed case, his request to the judge stating that there had been a breakdown in the attorney-client relationship that made him unable to provide effective representation. The congressman had later been found guilty of fraud, his political career destroyed by proof of influence peddling and graft. His former attorney had, as required by his professional obligations, never said another word about it, but Gavin de Marco's withdrawal and the resultant verdict had only cemented his reputation. And she couldn't help thinking of the effect having Gavin de Marco publicly on her father's side would have.

When he spoke again his tone was sharper, not accusatory, but not friendly, either. The questions came rapid-fire, as she imagined they would in a courtroom, except he gave her no time to answer. And he was leaning in, into her space.

"What proof is there that he didn't obtain said knife just for this purpose? What makes you sure he would tell you the truth about it? Did he know Laurel? What was his relationship with her? What is his alibi for the time of the murder?"

Her mind was racing as he fired the words at her, trying to decide what he was doing.

"Are you trying to pressure me into saying something I didn't intend to, or just showing me what it would be like dealing with you?"

He leaned back then. Kept his gaze on her. "Yes."

She straightened up, giving Cutter a final stroke between his silky ears. She met that gaze head-on. Her certainty gave her strength.

"I've told you the truth and nothing but. My father is innocent. He would never lie to me. Bring it."

For a brief moment, barely an instant, she thought Gavin de Marco smiled.

And the little jump in her pulse was ridiculous, for just a smile.

Chapter 5

Gavin looked up from the computer he'd been working on as Quinn ended his call. His boss slipped his phone back into his pocket. It was a special piece of equipment modified by Foxworth IT expert Tyler Hewitt back home in St. Louis; he had one just like it, as did everyone at Foxworth.

While Hayley continued to talk with Katie in the living room, they had adjourned to the den that had become an office.

"Brett said he'll make a call. He knows someone down in Tacoma," Quinn said.

"Is there anywhere your sheriff's investigator doesn't know someone?"

Quinn grinned. "If there is, we haven't found it yet. He confirmed that Steven Moore is the main suspect, judging by the bulletins that came out to all local agencies last week."

"That must be when they decided to let it go public,"

Gavin said, leaning back in the office chair. "A knife and that kind of carnage—that screams personal. Rage."

Quinn nodded. "Find anything?" he asked, gesturing toward the computer's wide monitor.

"Nothing that jumped out in a cursory search, no contradictions. Once I eliminated the spate of reports that hit in the last twenty-four hours, he's pretty low profile. Haven't dug into the reporting on the actual murder yet."

"Ty can do that, and send us the report."

Gavin nodded. Ty was an expert at finding things buried deep. Gavin didn't mention that the main reason he hadn't gotten to that search was that he'd also searched on Katie, and found several entries on her taking over the new library and turning it into a welcoming place for all.

Quinn glanced toward the living room. "What's your assessment, Counselor? Is she for real?"

Gavin remembered Katie's response to his string of questions, coming nearly as rapid-fire as his own words had, and, he noted, in the same order and complete. There was nothing slow about Katie Moore, for all her thoughtful consideration of things, but he'd already guessed that.

My only proof is knowing he can barely use a kitchen knife without cutting himself. He has never lied to me in my life, even when it would have been easier, and I have no reason to believe he would start now. Of course he knew Laurel; she'd been my best friend since I was nine. He liked her the most of all my friends, for my sake if nothing else. And obviously he doesn't have a provable alibi or he wouldn't be a suspect, would he?

He'd probed a little further and learned her father's story was that he'd been home, alone, watching an old movie on cable. They'd verified the movie had indeed played when he'd said, but obviously that wasn't proof that he'd watched it. A bit more pushing and he'd learned how close she and her father were, especially since her mother had died when Katie was nine. He got the picture of a loving dad who had focused on his only child during a very difficult time, and that they had gotten through it together.

"I think," he began in answer to Quinn's question, "that she believes every word she said. It's whether it's all really true that's in question."

"Agreed."

Gavin raised a brow at his friend. "Are we taking this on? Not exactly our usual. A straightforward, if ugly, murder case. The police are pursuing it, even months later, so it hasn't been forgotten."

"But they might be pursuing the wrong man."

"True." Gavin looked at Quinn quizzically. "But that alone is still not usually enough to fire your jets. So what is?"

Quinn returned his look. "That she's a beautiful woman with a problem isn't enough for you? And if you say you didn't notice, then I'll know you're lying. I saw your face when you opened the door."

"She was soaking wet. I knew you'd feel guilty if she caught pneumonia."

He wasn't sure why he was deflecting. Katie Moore was beautiful, in that quiet way that had always moved him more than the flash and glitter that had seemed to surround him back in the days when his name could get him entrée into just about anywhere. But that had nothing to do with it. He was moved by her plight, not the woman herself. The kick of his pulse when he looked at her notwithstanding.

"Nice of you to be so concerned about her health," Quinn said drily.

"And you're dodging the question."

Quinn sighed. Then he shrugged. "Cutter."

Gavin drew back slightly. "Seriously?"

"Do you need another rundown of all the cases he's found?"

"No. But hearing about it is different than seeing it."

The image of the dog wiggling through his private door, purloined cell phone in his mouth, played back in Gavin's head. *He knows a Foxworthy case when he sees one*, Liam, a fellow operative, had joked the last time he'd been here.

Gavin had laughed, but he couldn't deny the facts. The cases the dog had brought them, directly or indirectly, had all turned out to be their kind of case. He just didn't see how this one was. But he had meant what he'd told Quinn; he believed that Katie Moore believed every word she'd said. She might have been lied to, but she wasn't lying herself.

Right. And you're sure of this because your judgment is infallible, right?

But in the end, the bottom line was simple. If Quinn— or apparently Cutter—said they were taking the case, they were taking the case.

When they left the office, they could hear that Hayley and Katie were actually laughing. Cutter was at their feet, his tongue lolling happily as Hayley reached out to scratch behind his right ear.

Both women and the dog looked up as they came into the room. Quinn didn't waste any time. "Can you meet us at our headquarters tomorrow, and we'll get started?"

Katie blinked. "You're doing this?" Her gaze flicked to Gavin. "Including you?"

"I'm Foxworth," he said simply. And meant it. In the Foxworth Foundation he had found both something he hadn't been fully aware of missing, and something he hadn't thought existed anymore—good people fighting for good people and good causes. People he was proud to work with, who had given him back a pride in his own work, in what he could do. "I don't do criminal defense any longer, so if it comes to that, we'll find you someone. But I can still prepare a case."

Cutter stood up and gave a woof that Gavin couldn't deny sounded satisfied. Then Katie stood up, her eyes wide and full of hope.

"I don't know how to thank you," she began.

"Don't thank us yet," Quinn warned. "We go after the truth, and there's always a chance you won't like it."

"I know what the truth is," she said confidently. Gavin winced inwardly; he'd heard that before, and seen it explode.

In fact, he'd believed it before and seen it explode, nearly taking him with it.

"We will ask you questions you probably won't like answering," he said, adding to Quinn's warning. "About things you may not see the reason for."

She met his gaze. "They might be new, but they can't be any worse than the ones I've already asked myself."

Self-blame, Gavin guessed. It was common. People always thought there was something they could have or should have done to prevent the tragedy that in fact had nothing to do with them.

"Let's get you a ride home, then, and we'll start fresh tomorrow," Quinn said as he handed her the business card he'd picked up in the office. "Since it's Sunday, maybe a later start? Ten or so?"

"Fine," Katie said, although Gavin had the feeling if Quinn had said 5:00 a.m. she would have been there.

Cutter trotted past them toward the door, as if he'd understood that Katie was leaving and he was a well-trained doorman. Gavin found himself smiling. The smile widened when the dog raised up and grabbed a set of keys from the table just inside the door and trotted back.

"Now he's your parking valet?" he said, half joking and half astonished that the dog had understood.

"I'd say he's more *your* valet at the moment." Quinn laughed as Cutter came to a halt directly in front of Gavin and sat. Only then did he see that the keys the dog had brought were indeed the ones to his rental car. The animal stared at him intently, clearly waiting for him to do the obvious. He reached for the keys rather gingerly, but Cutter released them without protest.

"I guess you're doing the honors, then," Hayley said, and Gavin didn't quite understand the undertone in her voice. Not quite amusement, but he couldn't put a finger on what it was.

"You don't need to," Katie said. "It's only a block and a half, I can walk."

Hayley shook her head. "It's dark, and it's pouring rain. You'll end up twice as wet as you were when you got here." Cutter barked, short and sharp this time, as if to hurry them up. "You might as well give in now, save the energy," Hayley said cheerfully. "He's obviously decided."

As silly as it seemed to acquiesce to their dog, there didn't seem to be anything to do but give in. Hayley handed him an umbrella—with the standard joke about it marking him as a tourist, since practically nobody who lived here used one. But at least it would save Katie from being drenched anew even on the short walk to his rental car parked in the driveway. He would have preferred to give it to her and just take his chances, but when he realized that was because he didn't want to be as close to her, he mentally rolled his eyes at his own childishness and ordered himself to snap out of it.

"That dog," he muttered when they were inside the car and he had the umbrella tossed in the back. "Apparently his word is law around here."

"I didn't come looking for help, just my phone," she said, and he realized she had taken his words as complaint.

"That statement had nothing to do with you," he said as he started the car. "I'm just a bit…bemused at Quinn, who's one of the most grounded, practical guys I know, taking his lead from a dog. An amazing dog, I'll grant you, but a dog."

"I think it's sweet."

Gavin doubted the word *sweet* had ever been applied to the adult Quinn, at least not before he'd met Hayley.

He followed her directions and made a turn into a narrow driveway. In the dark and the deluge he couldn't see much of the yard, other than what appeared to be lots of trees and smaller plants. He grabbed the umbrella and walked around to her side of the car, then sheltered her under it up to her front door. She thanked him rather more than he thought necessary, and ended it with a smile on her upturned face that made his pulse jump oddly. For a moment they just stood there, uncomfortably and deliciously close. The sound of the rain falling on her porch roof seemed to amplify both the chill around them and the body heat between them.

If she hadn't moved first he wasn't sure what would have happened. But she did, hastily, thanking him once more, opening her front door and escaping inside.

Escaping. What a word to come to mind, he thought as the door closed. He shut the umbrella despite the good fifteen feet between him and the car. And when he got back inside it, already good and wet, he turned off the heater. As he drove the short distance back, he had to admit none of it helped, the chill of the rain or the lack of the heater's output. He was still a hell of a lot warmer than he should be, and had been ever since she'd looked up at him with that smile.

And he'd wanted to kiss her.

Chapter 6

Katie closed her door and leaned back against it, all her focus inward, on the odd hammering of her heart and the strange way her house, even at its normal temperature, felt chilly compared to standing outside in the rain.

With Gavin de Marco.

Even thinking the name seemed absurd. As did her reaction to him. She felt foolish; she should have known that that man would have "it," that elusive quality that drew attention even from those who didn't know who he was. Charisma, appeal, magnetism, whatever name you gave it, that man had it in abundance.

And apparently it worked on her just fine. She'd been hyperaware of him from the moment he'd opened the door.

She fought for calm. She began to move, busied herself with mundane things, like locking the back door she'd left unsecured when Cutter had so unexpectedly grabbed her phone and she'd given chase. She put away the bowl she'd gotten out, planning to reheat the leftover chili from last night; she had no appetite for it now, not after reliving her worst and persistent nightmare yet again.

But at least it had been for good reason this time, and intentional. Not like the way it so often snuck up on her and left her paralyzed with grief and horror. She'd reached an equilibrium here, but she knew it didn't take much to upset it. Like pouring out the ugly story to strangers, one of them Gavin de Marco…

Gavin de Marco. How impossible was that?

She went back to the living room and grabbed her phone. And once more she hit the speed dial for her father. She hadn't spoken to him since this morning, when he'd reassured her everything would be all right because he was innocent. He was cooperating with the police, of course, he'd told her. She'd suggested a lawyer then, but he'd said that he didn't need one and that he couldn't afford one anyway.

So how would you like the most famous defense lawyer in the country for nothing, Dad?

When he answered, he sounded different than he had this morning. Not quite so unruffled, but still confident.

"It will be fine, honey. I think they're grasping at straws because they have nothing else." He laughed, and there was only the slightest touch of strain in it. "They even gave me the 'don't leave town' speech. As if I would."

She cut to the chase. "You need a lawyer, Dad."

"We've talked about that, Katie."

She hesitated, but there was no way she would do this behind his back, so she plunged ahead. "I found you one. Or rather he found me. Sort of. Actually it was the dog, I think."

There was a moment's silence before he asked, "Dog? Katie, you're sounding a bit confused."

She laughed then, and it eased the tightness in her chest

a little. Then as concisely as she could she told him the story. She was honest enough to admit that she savored the moment when she dropped the name Gavin de Marco.

"Wow. He was big-league. But I thought he quit?"

"He did, but he's working for them now."

"Doesn't matter. No way on earth I can afford Gavin de Marco."

"That's just it, Dad. You don't have to." She explained about the Foxworth Foundation, and how Quinn and Hayley said it worked. And she pointed out that just having Gavin's name attached to the case could change things, and would certainly assure that the police moved carefully. "It's for your own protection. You have the right."

"I don't need—"

"At least talk to him, Dad. What can that hurt?"

By the time they ended the call, her father had—so reluctantly it surprised her—agreed to at least talk to the man if, after meeting with him tomorrow, Katie still wanted him to.

It was odd. She'd thought he would be pleased. She knew he trusted that the truth would come out, but she couldn't see why he didn't want the insurance that an attorney could provide. Especially one on the level of this one.

She walked to the small den in her house that served as an office of sorts. She opened her laptop and when the familiar screen appeared, she opened a search engine. It was time to do some homework. Research, after all, was a big part of what she did.

She began with the Foxworth Foundation. Their website was clean, simple and gave little clue as to exactly what they did. It was mainly contact numbers for the various regional headquarters. Five, she saw with some surprise, covering every region of the country; she hadn't realized just how big they were. She remembered what Hayley had said about working mainly by word of mouth, and wondered how an organization grew to this size that way. Even if they had the willing help of hundreds of previous clients, it took funding to keep something this size going.

She found a bit more on Quinn's history, including his rather stellar military career. The mentions of the foundation here and there in news articles were always scant, as if they were trying to keep a low profile. As if they didn't want public credit for what they did.

But it was the other entries in various places that told her the most. The almost tearfully thankful blog posts and public letters all made clear that what the Foxworths had said was true, that they really did take on anything that met their own, personal criteria.

This made her feel a new, bubbling kind of hope, to have this kind of organization helping her. She felt something else, a lightening of a burden now that it had been shared. And she wondered if the time of holding herself apart while she tried to rebuild a life with a huge piece missing had passed, if perhaps she should open up, let some people in. New friends, who wouldn't be always aware, who wouldn't assume that any time she grew quiet or thoughtful she was mired in grief. Not that it wasn't true much of the time, but it was easier to get through if everybody around her didn't know it. Social pressure was an effective tool.

She opened a fresh search window. She hesitated for a moment, feeling a tiny bit stalkerish. But she chided herself out of it. If she was going to go through with this she needed to know as much as possible, didn't she? The sensational headlines didn't tell the whole story, they never did. And it wasn't like she was checking out a potential date. Surely he would expect her to gather data. She was

sure he did all possible research himself. Settled now, she
reached for the keyboard.

And typed in Gavin de Marco.

Gavin traveled enough to be used to waking up in different places. When he slept at all, anyway. This time, re-
alizations tumbled through his mind one after the other.
He was in Quinn and Hayley's place. His head was pointing south, the opposite of at home. Weird quirk, but he'd
always had it. The rain had stopped.

He wasn't alone.

That was enough of a jolt to bring him fully awake. As
if his movement had been the trigger, he heard a soft woof.
Cutter. A cool, damp nose nudged his hand. Instinctively he
reached out and stroked the dog's head. Odd that he hadn't
heard him come in; he slept lightly, and usually the slightest sound woke him. On that thought he sensed more than
saw the dog hop up on the bed. Felt the slight give of the
mattress as he landed, felt the brush as he went over him
and plopped down on the other side. He nearly laughed
as he felt the swipe of the dog's tongue over his ear, then
smiled into the dark as Cutter curled up and put his head
down, his side pressed up against Gavin's back. He'd never
been allowed a dog as a kid, so this was a new experience.

It seemed rude to toss and turn as was his wont most
nights, not when the dog had just gotten comfortable, so
he tried to lie still. It was more difficult than he would
have expected.

Maybe he'd been sleeping alone too long, he thought. He
rarely considered his dearth of a sex life; years of dealing
with women who just wanted a Gavin de Marco feather in
their sexual cap had soured him. It seemed to come with
that heady territory, but that didn't mean he had to like it.

That thought, rather uncomfortably, brought him around

to Katie Moore. He didn't want to dwell on her spirited personality or her open, lovely face, because that had nothing to do with the business at hand. And his reaction to her was downright irritating.

He'd wanted to dive right into research last night, but Hayley wouldn't have it. Ty, on St. Louis time, would be up well before them and have it ready before they headed to the office for their meeting. And, she'd pointed out, since he was still on St. Louis time himself, it was two hours later according to his body clock. So she'd fed him and hustled him off to bed at what would have been midnight at home.

Usually, especially when traveling, once he woke up that was it. The brain kicked into gear and there was no turning it off. But now, Cutter seemed to have short-circuited that pattern as the warmth of the dog's presence seeped into him. And much to his own surprise, he went back to sleep.

When he woke the rain had begun again, and Cutter had his chin propped on his leg. He could feel the dog staring at him. Willing him awake? It wouldn't surprise him at this point. He ruffled the dog's fur as he turned his head for a glance at the clock. Still early, barely six, but even though it was still dark here at that hour, he knew he was done sleeping. And he wasn't complaining. He'd gotten more than he usually did by at least an hour.

"Five hours," he said aloud to the dog as he flipped on the light. "Wow. If you brought that with you, thanks."

The dog grinned at him.

Gavin blinked, staring. That was a ridiculous thought. But what else would you call that silly, tongue-lolling, mouth up at the corners expression?

He heard a sound from the other room. Somebody else was up, he thought. Cutter clearly heard it as well and jumped down from the bed. Gavin grabbed the jeans he'd had on last night and tugged them back on; he'd sort out unpacking later. He stepped out into the hallway. He followed the dog out into the great room, where he saw not Quinn—another early riser—as he'd expected, but Hayley. She was in the kitchen, laying out a rather large array of eggs, bacon, ham, peppers, onions, potatoes, cheese and spices. When she heard them she looked up and smiled.

"I thought maybe that was where he disappeared to," she said, nodding at the dog. "He seems to have decided you need his attention."

Cutter trotted over to her and she gave him a quick pat.

"I'm still trying to figure out how he got in without me hearing," Gavin said, not commenting on what she'd said about the dog's decision process; he didn't want that door opened.

"He has his ways." She glanced over at the dog's set of bowls as if to make sure he had food and water. As if on cue the animal walked over and began to lap. "Did you sleep? He didn't keep you awake?"

"Some. Enough. And no. It actually was…" He wasn't sure what to call it.

"He's very comforting. And you," Hayley added, eyeing his bare torso assessingly, "are too thin. You're going to eat while you're here."

"Hey," he protested, "not everybody can be built like Quinn."

She laughed. "He always said you run on nerves and coffee."

"Fuel of the gods," he said. Cutter, finished with his drink and a few pieces of kibble, came back and sat at his feet. He scratched the spot behind the dog's right ear that he knew he liked.

He couldn't help but notice that through breakfast— Quinn's famous scramble that was never the same twice, and which he ate enough of to satisfy even Hayley—and the rest of the early morning, Cutter was never far away. In fact, he seemed to have attached himself nearly at the hip, even following him when he took a shower and dressed.

Before, for a meeting with a client, he would have worn a suit. But Foxworth was a different place, and he was a different man, no longer worried about impressions and the look of success. Yet when he stood in front of the bathroom mirror with his razor in hand, debating whether to bother, it was Katie's image that floated into his mind. Did the local librarian like or dislike stubble? The moment he realized where his mind had drifted, he slapped the razor down on the counter, rather sharply.

When he'd packed he hadn't included one of those suits, telling Charlie that if they needed him in such a rush they had to take what they got. Of course, that had been when he'd thought they'd needed him up here for a case. A case that at the time hadn't existed. Which gave him another thought. When she'd sent him, Charlie had to have known there was no case.

Back in the guest room he picked up his phone and hit the speed dial. As he'd half expected, it went to voice mail. *Probably thinks I'm ticked. As I would be, except—*

The tone cut off his thought. "Okay, Charlie, I get it," he said for the recording. "I'm a bit restless. But now there really is a case, so you're safe for a while. See you when I get back."

He ended the call and put the phone in his pocket.

Then he started to mentally prepare for the meeting with Katie Moore, who was also the reason he wasn't really angry with his boss.

And that realization made him even more restless.

Chapter 7

Gavin gave Cutter, with whom he was sharing the back seat, another head scratch. The dog shifted in the seat, giving up his intent looking-out-the-window to lie down beside him and plop his chin on his knee. Automatically Gavin stroked the dog's head, and was once more struck at how soothing that simple action was.

He seems to have decided you need his attention...

Hayley's words played back in his head. The dog certainly seemed to sense things. Although that didn't explain the stunt he'd pulled last night with the phone. He wasn't sure anything could.

Keep it up, de Marco. Pretty soon you'll be buying everything else they say about this critter.

With an inward laugh at himself, he gave the dog a final pat as they turned off the paved road onto a gravel drive.

He'd forgotten how truly peaceful the surroundings were here at the northwest headquarters. Set back from the road at the end of the drive that curved through thick trees, the dark green, three-story structure sat in a clearing that seemed a world away from city chaos. It was unmarked; as with most of Foxworth, they didn't advertise their presence.

He noticed that the double sliding doors of the warehouse-like building set to one side were open.

"Rafe must be here," Hayley said, clearly having seen the same thing.

Despite the good working relationship they'd developed, Rafer Crawford still unnerved Gavin like no judge or opposing lawyer ever had. He also knew that building was mostly Rafe's bailiwick; the former marine sniper with the deadly eye had a knack for mechanics. He said the two went hand in hand, that the calculation on a long shot was brother to the logic of machinery.

Cutter seemed to know the man was back as well, although he seemed a bit reluctant to leave his self-selected spot at Gavin's side. Bemused anew, Gavin told him to go and shook his head when the dog gave him a final nudge before taking off for the open doors at a dead run, head and tail and ears up, letting out an odd series of barks, a staccato combination of short and long.

Rafe came out through the open doors to greet the dog, who danced around him delightedly. Gavin knew the tall, lean man was a favorite of the dog, as evidenced by the specific bark he used only for him. After a minute or two the animal left his beloved Rafe and came trotting back to attach himself at Gavin's knee. An act they all seemed to notice, including Rafe as he headed toward them.

Gavin was struck by how different the man seemed here. He, as all of Foxworth did, occasionally visited the St. Louis headquarters. Rafe always seemed more guarded there, although dressed like any other person who worked in one of the towering buildings, drawing no notice from people too busy with the bustle of their own lives to see the leashed predator among them. That he was able to go unnoticed at all was testament to his skill, Gavin supposed.

But here he was more relaxed, at ease, as if here he didn't have to hide behind a mask of bland civilization.

"Who's in trouble?" Rafe asked with one brow lifted when he reached them.

"Apparently I was," Gavin answered, not taking offense.

Rafe glanced at Cutter, who was leaning against Gavin's leg. "I see." He shifted his gaze back to Gavin and considered that for a moment. "Getting on Charlie's nerves again?"

"Interesting that that's your first guess," Gavin said drily.

Rafe's mouth quirked at one corner. "You two remind me of a pair of siblings I knew once. So alike they had to pick fights with each other now and then, just to keep life interesting."

Gavin glanced at Quinn; he was, after all, Charlie's brother.

"Don't look at me," Quinn said instantly. "I gave up trying to fight with Charlie long ago, when I realized that in the end I always lost."

"Wise man," Rafe said, without inflection. Then he looked back at Cutter. "Interesting," he said again.

"So it seems," Hayley agreed—although Gavin had no idea with what—and she didn't even bother to try to hide her smile.

"We've got a case?" Rafe asked.

"Just arrived last night," Quinn said, and gave Rafe a condensed version of Cutter's antics and Katie Moore's arrival as a Foxworth case. "She's due here in about an hour, and we'll make the final determination."

"Need me?"

"Not yet, but come on in, so you'll be up to speed."

The dog stayed close to Gavin as they went inside and up the stairs to the big meeting room. He was drawn to the wall of windows looking out over the meadow behind the building. Beyond the clearing the forest stood, the evergreens a backdrop to the brilliant fall color of the deciduous trees as their foliage flamed out before surrendering to winter. Somewhere up there, he knew, a pair of bald eagles had their nest. As a man who had lived his life in cities, he could see the appeal, even as he felt a little out of place. More than eagles roamed the forests in the northwest.

Still, he knew there were those who'd consider the city more dangerous than this place, no matter what kind of wild creatures were out there.

Doesn't take trees to make a jungle.

He smiled inwardly as one of Rafe's observations echoed in his mind. He couldn't argue that. In fact, he could attest that some of the most lethal jungles in the world were those consisting of concrete and steel and people more ruthless than animals driven only by instinct. Win at Any Cost was the motto of too many in those places, as if they'd completely lost the ability to see any view but their own. It wasn't a sense of right or wrong, just win or lose, and the latter was to be avoided no matter what, no matter if the person in the right was forever damaged.

Which was another of the reasons he'd walked away.

He turned from the expansive view and moved to the back corner of the room where Quinn and Hayley were hunched over the bank of computers.

"Ty's research," Quinn explained as the file downloaded. "He had an appointment so he recorded a video for us."

"Where is Liam, by the way?" he asked, referring to the operative who usually handled their computer work. He and Ty had a friendly competition over who could dig deepest fastest, and it made for some amazing—and sometimes frightening—results.

"Texas," Quinn said. "Checking on the kids from our last case."

Gavin nodded. He'd done a bit of work on that case, helping smooth the way for the two young brothers who had been struck yet again by tragedy to leave the state for a temporary stay with a well-qualified foster family who also happened to be Liam's parents.

"How are they?" he asked. "Those kids have had a rough time."

"Liam says they're doing great. That's about all I could get," Hayley added with a pleased smile, "because he's a bit distracted. He took his girl with him to meet the family."

Gavin blinked. "That was fast."

"When it's right, it's right," Quinn said, looking at his wife.

As he watched Hayley's smile, Gavin felt a twinge that he hated himself for. He thought he'd long ago accepted that such a connection was not in the cards for him, but being around these two seemed to shake that acceptance.

Cutter's head came up and he gave a rather emphatic bark.

"Katie must be here," Hayley said.

Gavin knew the gravel drive announced a car's arrival to the dog's sensitive ears long before they would hear it. As he listened, Cutter bumped up against him as if trying to nudge him toward the door, and the stairs.

"What?" he asked the animal, who merely looked at him steadily and continued to nudge. He glanced at Quinn and Hayley, who were smothering smiles; apparently they found their dog's odd behavior amusing.

"Go on down and get the door, would you?" Hayley said, a bit too breezily.

"We'll be down as soon as we glance through what Ty turned up," Quinn said. "I'd like to have an idea before we talk to her."

And so Gavin ended up following the dog's urgings and headed for the stairs.

"Coffee's on, and there's some fresh-baked cookies on the counter next to the fridge," Hayley called out, sounding too chipper for the circumstances.

With the feeling he was definitely missing something, he headed down the stairs to play greeter. He'd had enough sleep—barely—to alleviate the jet lag a bit, so he'd be fine. He'd handle this like any Foxworth case, if they indeed decided to take it on. His odd reaction to Katie Moore last night had only been because he'd been tired and jet-lagged.

When they got downstairs Cutter ran to the door and sat expectantly.

"Why don't you just open it?" he muttered at the dog. "That automatic door opener is for you."

Cutter tilted his head back so far he was practically looking at Gavin upside down. He wondered if that was the dog equivalent of rolling his eyes. With a sigh he reached out and pulled the door open. As he'd expected, it was Katie.

What he hadn't expected was the difference from the rain-dampened woman he'd met last night. He took it all in rapidly, noticing details as he had all his life.

This woman was pulled together, leaving little sign of her distress from last night. She wore a bit of makeup—not much, and he'd dealt with enough overdone paint to know—that accentuated her delicate features and made those incredible eyes look even bluer. Her hair fell in loose waves to her shoulders, and the streaks of golden blond seemed warm on this chilly morning.

She was dressed for the temperature in a sweater the same blue as her eyes, with a loose sort of collar that fell softly around her neck and shoulders, worn over a pair of trim black leggings and midcalf boots. No high heels for her, but a solid, block heel and leather that would withstand a northwest winter. But those legs…

His breath jammed up in his throat, his pulse skipped and then picked up speed.

"Hello," she said, and he realized that low, husky note in her voice hadn't just been from her emotional state last night. It sent a tickling sensation up his spine.

So much for being tired and jet-lagged.

Chapter 8

Katie's first thought was that he didn't remember her. She had no such problem. The image of Gavin de Marco—tousled dark hair, dark eyes that seemed to see everything, that air of crackling intelligence—was all etched into her memory. Far too deeply for a man she'd met only once.

But she doubted he forgot much, so her second thought was that he didn't recognize her because she looked so different. Which made her think of how bedraggled she'd looked when she'd gotten home last night. Her first look in a mirror had made her groan at her appearance, hair lank and flat, what makeup she'd had on washed away, eyes still reddened from her earlier crying jag.

She told herself she was embarrassed that any of them—except maybe Cutter, whom she now gave a stroke between the ears—had seen her like that, not just this man. She knew she looked more presentable now, even if her eyes were still red, although this morning it was from lack of sleep, not crying. Gavin, she noticed, had skipped the razor this morning, and to her surprise, since she usually didn't care for stubble, decided on him it looked good.

Of course, what wouldn't?

"Mr. de Marco?" she finally said.

"Yes. Sorry. I didn't mean to... Come in."

The dog was effusive in his greeting as she stepped inside, making her smile, but inwardly she was puzzled. Because Gavin seemed...almost rattled. Not that she could judge, of course, but from everything she'd read last night—and she'd been up until the wee hours, so fascinating was the subject—this man was never rattled.

One report had spoken of how on cross-examination he'd made a witness practically confess to the crime his high-profile client was on trial for. The man had come at him right over the courtroom railing. Even those who had been there weren't sure how he had managed to send the man tumbling to the floor, because he'd barely seemed to move. Through it all he'd never lost his cool. After the bailiffs secured the man, he hadn't even had to straighten his tie.

She'd also read a lot of the speculation. He'd had a career most law students could only dream of. He was, as they said, a rainmaker of the highest order...and yet he simply walked away. Some said it was because he'd made so much money he would never have to work again. Others said it was because he had nothing left to prove. While that was certainly true, Katie didn't quite believe it was that simple. And now that she'd met him in person, she was certain of it. This was a complex kind of man.

He gestured her into the large downstairs space. To her surprise, it looked more like the living room of a comfortable home than the plain, businesslike exterior had suggested. There was a gas fireplace on the long wall, and before it an inviting grouping of sofa, chairs and a large square coffee table. On the opposite wall was a stairway, rather more utilitarian. To the right were a couple of door-ways, one of them partially open and revealing a vanity and sink, so she guessed it was a bathroom. Next to it was another door, closed. Bedroom? she wondered. Did they get so involved in their work that sometimes they didn't go home?

In the back corner was a compact but efficient-looking kitchen, from which she could smell coffee brewing, making the space even smell like a home.

Even as she thought it, he spoke again. "Coffee?"

"Thank you." She meant it; she would need the caffeine after last night.

"Sit down," he said as he went to a control on the wall, flipped a switch, and the gas fireplace leaped to life.

When he had gone into the small kitchen she sank down on the couch and drew in a deep breath, only then realizing she'd barely been breathing at all since he'd opened the door. She'd expected him to be there, obviously, but not to be the one who greeted her.

"Good morning to you, too," she whispered to Cutter as he nudged her hand. She patted the dog's head again, then gave him a long stroke over the silky, soft fur. He gave a happy little whine, then turned as another door at the back of the building opened. A tall, lean, dark-haired man dressed in black walked in. Cutter was there before he shrugged off his jacket, and Katie noticed he paused to greet the dog before he finished. She liked that.

And then the dog darted into the kitchen, just as Gavin was picking up two steaming mugs, and appeared to be try-ing to figure out how to carry a small basket at the same time. Cutter solved the problem. He rose up on his hind legs and took the edge of the basket carefully in his teeth and walked back toward her. She couldn't help it, she was grinning when the animal came over and with exquisite care put the basket down on the table in front of her. It held, she saw, various packets of sugar and sweeteners, and small containers of milk and cream.

"Why, thank you, kind sir," she crooned to the dog, who gave her a tongue-lolling grin.

Then Gavin arrived with the mugs. He handed her one, then turned, obviously intending to sit in the chair at a right angle to her. But somehow Cutter was there, and they got tangled up as the dog practically pushed him the opposite way, although she was sure it was unintentional. The dog looked rather satisfied, however, as Gavin ended up sitting beside her on the couch. Not too close, but close enough that she was aware of him in a humming sort of way.

The other man, his own mug of coffee in one hand and a plate of cookies in the other, had stood for a moment watching the odd little dance with what seemed rather intent interest. But he said nothing to Gavin, just walked over to them, set the plate down and turned to her.

"You must be Katie Moore. Rafe Crawford," he said, holding out a hand. She took it, noticing a scar here and a nick there, and long, lean fingers. He didn't try to crush her hand, but didn't handle it as if she were fragile, either.

But then she looked at his eyes, eyes that were the color the stormy sky had been yesterday. She'd never seen really haunted eyes before, but she knew she had now. Reacting instinctively, she gave his hand an extra squeeze. "Mr. Crawford."

There was a split second's pause, just enough to tell her he'd noticed, before he said, "Rafe, please."

He sat in the chair Gavin had intended to use, all the while looking at Gavin on the couch. And Katie thought she saw the faintest trace of a smile curve one corner of his mouth for a brief moment.

She straightened. "I hope this isn't a waste of your time."

"We wouldn't be here if Quinn didn't think we might be able to help," Gavin said.

"I hear Cutter brought you in," Rafe said. "That's the seal on it." She blinked. The man looked utterly serious. And his eyes, those haunted eyes, did not speak of a man with a fanciful nature. At her expression, Rafe shrugged. "All I can say is he's never been wrong."

Before Gavin could respond to that—although Katie wasn't sure what he could possibly say—there was the sound of footsteps on the stairway behind them. And then Hayley and Quinn were there. After greeting her they sat in the other two chairs, leaving her and Gavin as the sole occupants of the couch.

Hayley smiled. "Shall we get started?"

At Katie's nod, Quinn picked up a remote and aimed it at the flat screen on the wall. "This is from Tyler Hewitt, from our headquarters in St. Louis. He did some digging first thing his time. Usually we're live with him, but this is recorded because he had an appointment this morning."

"Okay," she said. "What do you need me to do?"

"Just listen, watch. If anything you see or hear doesn't jibe with your perception of things, say so and we'll stop and make a note. Then, when we're all on the same page, we'll proceed."

Katie nodded again. She didn't think anything showed in her face, but Hayley said quietly, "I know this won't be pleasant for you. If you need to stop at any time, just say so."

"Thank you." She'd known she'd have to go through it all yet again, probably in more detail than she had since it had happened and she'd spent hours with the police. She'd been shoring up her mental armor all morning. But the woman's understanding made the ache of anticipation ease a bit, and she realized she really quite liked Hayley Foxworth.

"And fair warning," Quinn said, "when it gets out that Gavin's involved, and it will, there's going to be buzz."

"I'm sure there will be," she said with a glance at the man who seemed absorbed in contemplating his mug of coffee.

"All right, then," Quinn said, and pressed a button on the remote he held.

The young man in the video was a thin, wiry sort, with short, blondish hair that looked perpetually on end. He had a small patch of beard below his lower lip, and alert green eyes.

"Hi, guys," issued from the speaker. "I'll get right to it. Here's what I have on the basics of the crime itself. I'm still digging into the principals. I'll get that to you later today."

And as she had with Gavin, Katie found it easier to listen to Tyler Hewitt's matter-of-fact reciting of the facts of the case than she'd expected. Something about his tone enabled her to take a half step back and listen rationally. It began with images of everyone involved and Ty's voice calmly introducing them. Although she'd been steeled for seeing Laurel's picture and didn't react, Katie winced at the particularly stern photo of herself that flashed on the screen, pulled from her county employment file. There was a shot of Ross on a ferry crossing, grinning at the camera, his hair tossed by the wind. Laurel had taken that one, she knew, and posted it on one of her social media accounts, which she guessed was where they got it.

She smiled at the image of her father, an attractive professional portrait that was one of her favorite pictures of him. She'd spent her whole life with all her girlfriends commenting on how handsome he was, always with a note of surprise she found faintly insulting until Laurel had laughingly explained that no one ever expected a friend's parent to be gorgeous, no matter what the friend looked like.

The video went on to show shots of the neighborhood. It was all painfully familiar, their apartment building, even a close-up of their front door with the apartment number. Over it all came Ty's businesslike recital of what the police investigation had shown. How Laurel had been last seen alive at the market around the corner from the apartment. She'd purchased milk, eggs and some other staples. She'd paid with a debit card, as she usually did, at 8:20 p.m. She'd walked out with two bags and turned left, heading for the apartment. No sign of a car, which roommate Katie had confirmed; she usually walked since it was so close.

The reports indicated there had been no sign of forced entry at the door or any of the windows, leading them to assume that her attacker had a key or she had let them in. Or that Laurel had come home with hands full of groceries, had stepped inside to set them down, and the killer had followed her in. Katie had stated she and the victim had the only keys except the building management. And since the management was a middle-aged couple who were on a late dinner cruise at the time of the murder, they had been cleared.

Then, abruptly, the image changed to a black-and-white video of the front of the market. And into that image walked Laurel.

Katie's calm shattered. She closed her eyes and turned away, trying to suppress a shudder.

Then Katie felt a wonderful warmth, a strong arm coming around her shoulders. Gavin, giving support. She assumed it was just something he did, something he'd had to do before with distraught clients. But she welcomed it nevertheless.

What had she let herself in for?

Chapter 9

Gavin felt Katie suppress a shudder, and knowing she had found her friend's mangled body he could only imagine the images breaking through her calm.

"Katie—" Hayley began.

"It's all right. Just give me a moment." She drew in a deep breath, clearly trying to steady herself. "It's just... seeing her like that, alive and well... I have dreams about it, and I just had a bad one night before last and..."

"And Cutter brought you to us the next day," Hayley said. "That may be what he sensed, your distress."

Distracted for a moment, she looked at the dog and seemed to ponder that. She nodded slowly, as if it made sense. And Gavin realized she was back in control. A quick glance at Hayley and he also realized that had been exactly her intent. Distract Katie until she could regain her composure.

Well done, he thought, and gave Hayley an approving

nod. He fought down the fleeting thought that he was glad she'd done it so he didn't have to. He wasn't doing too well keeping his unexpected reaction to this woman under wraps.

Katie indicated they should go on. Hayley hit a button on the remote, backed up the recording a bit, then let it run. Since he was seeing this for the first time, Gavin continued to pay close attention. It seemed fairly straightforward, as such things go, and he was long used to reading police investigation reports—and reading between the lines.

At some point he realized he still had his arm around Katie. It startled him; that was part of a lawyer's repertoire that he had left to his assistants. She was calm now, so it was no longer necessary. Yet he found himself loath to surrender the contact. Which in turn made him barely manage not to blatantly jerk away, and, when the video ended, perhaps made him a bit harsher than usual. He stood up and turned to look down at her. Intentionally. And his voice was cold when he spoke.

"This will not be easy, or pleasant, Ms. Moore. You will have to go through it all time and again. All the bloody, ugly details. I will ask you questions you won't want to answer but you will have to, and with the truth. I will ask you things that may not seem relevant to you, but you'll answer anyway. I will dig into things you'd rather not share, things you'd rather stayed hidden. You may not look at your friend, your father, or even yourself in the same way when this is over."

She'd grown slightly pale as he hammered his point home, but to her credit she didn't buckle. Instead he saw her jaw set under the onslaught, and his instincts told him she could and would withstand the long haul.

He wasn't totally convinced he would.

A sea of mental red flags surged in his head. He wasn't

even sure what some of them were about, but he suddenly wanted out of here. Away from this, away from her.

On the thought, Cutter lifted his head from her knee and looked at him with a steady, unblinking gaze, a stare really. If he had to put a label on it, it would be *Don't even think about it*.

He shook off the crazy feeling and asked the question he had to ask.

"That said, are you sure you want to do this?"

"Of course I don't want to," she said, only the faintest trace of strain in her voice. "But I will. I have to."

"We go after the truth. Is that what you want, or do you want them to believe your father is innocent?"

She stood up and faced him head-on. Determination came off her in waves. "They are one and the same," she said, holding his gaze without flinching, something supposedly tough criminals had had trouble doing.

In that moment he believed her. He'd withhold final judgment until he met and questioned her father, but for now, they would begin.

"All right," he said. His tone revealed nothing of his own tangled feelings. He'd walked away from the criminal defense arena, intending to never go back. He hadn't been down in those trenches for a long time. This, even if it never ended up in a trial, was as close as he'd gotten, and a lot closer than he'd wanted to get. If it did come down to a trial, her father would have to hire his own attorney.

But he couldn't deny that he liked Katie Moore's spirited defense of her father. And he was here anyway, so why not help? He wasn't really stepping back into the ring, just helping to find the facts of the case. That's what he did at Foxworth.

And, he told himself, the unexpected fact that he found

this woman both quietly attractive and sharply intelligent had nothing to do with his decision.

Nothing at all.

"I'm assuming you don't need me, so I'll go back to earning my keep."

Gavin gave Rafe a glance as they stood alone in the kitchen where he refilled his mug with Hayley's coffee blend of the day. "You earn your keep just by being available to call on."

Rafe gave a half shrug. "Until then, I keep busy. Keeps me from getting bored."

Gavin wondered for a moment what a bored expert sniper might do for entertainment if he didn't have the mechanics he loved to keep him distracted. It was an interesting thought.

"And I," Rafe said as he rinsed his own mug out and put it in the compact dishwasher, "would not want to face you in court. As an attorney, a defendant, a witness or a judge."

Gavin shrugged. "It's a rough game."

"I think she's up for it."

He met Rafe's speculative gaze then, and kept his tone carefully neutral. "Agreed. She's tougher than she looks."

"Cutter thinks so, too," Rafe said. "And his track record's impossible to ignore. In more than just bringing us cases."

Gavin's eyes narrowed, yet Rafe met his gaze easily. It would take a lot more than an accomplished and notorious lawyer to intimidate this man, if it could be done at all.

"Just saying that he's good at more than matching us up with cases," Rafe drawled. "And I think you're next on his radar."

Gavin blinked. "What?"

"That little seating dance that ended up with you sitting next to our client? Not an accident."

"Come on," Gavin said incredulously. He knew the credit this branch of Foxworth gave to the dog for...changes in their personal lives. But him ending up next to Katie had been an accident. Of course it had. It was a *dog*.

"Track record," Rafe repeated. "And a familiar tactic by now."

The idea that he had been maneuvered by a dog who had some idea in his canine brain that they belonged together was the craziest thing he'd ever heard. And in his career he'd heard some very crazy things.

And some of them were true.

"She's a client," Gavin pointed out, his tone resolute. "Nothing more."

"Sure," Rafe said, but Gavin thought he was laughing inside. As much as the man ever did, anyway.

Gavin couldn't deny people had ended up together—quite happily—thanks in part to Cutter's intervention. Apparently anyway, he thought, adding the qualifier because he doubted happy endings a bit more than just about anything in life.

Except the truthfulness of people in general.

Fresh coffee in hand, he headed back to begin what could be a very nasty process.

Chapter 10

Cutter was still by Katie's side, but Quinn and Hayley had left to meet with their friend, sheriff's detective Brett Dunbar, who had apparently picked up some scuttlebutt through his extensive grapevine.

Gavin walked toward her, took a swallow of coffee, set the mug down, then looked at her.

"I think better on my feet," he said by way of explaining why he would be standing while she sat.

"So you're not standing just to try to intimidate me?"

She said it with just a shade too much innocence, enough so that he understood she was letting him know she hadn't missed the tactic earlier. He didn't apologize, but noted her perceptiveness.

"I needed to know if you were up to this."

"Then I'll take the fact that we're proceeding as a compliment."

He barely managed not to smile. He hadn't been wrong

about her spirit. *And I could think of a lot more compliments to add to that.* He quashed the unexpected thought. It had nothing to do with the case, after all.

He was true to his word and made her go through it all again, asking her questions as things came up, and often made them non sequiturs, jumping around in the story, which he'd found sometimes gave him answers that he wouldn't have gotten otherwise.

"When did you last see her?"

"That morning at 7:30. Right before I left for work."

"Why that market?"

"It's close, and she doesn't—didn't—have a car. Hers had quit on her, and she'd been using Ross's."

He noticed the stumble of someone who hadn't managed to completely change a lifetime of thinking yet, but said nothing.

"You believe Carr's alibi?"

"Hard not to. And the police did. There were at least a dozen people who said he was at that party all evening."

"How long had they been together?"

"Off and on, a couple of years."

"He ever hit on you?"

She blinked. "I… He asked me out once, yes. Before he started seeing Laurel."

"Didn't go well?"

"Didn't go at all. I said no."

"Why?"

"He's not my type."

And what is your type? "So there was no chemistry, or you sensed something…off about him?"

"Yes to the former, but I doubt I could give you an honest answer about the latter."

"Why?"

"It would be too colored by what happened. Too easy

to believe I'd seen…something, because of what happened later, when it's clear he didn't do it."

Points for that, he thought. "Let me sort that part out. I need you to give me everything you thought or felt or suspected, whether you have proof or not."

Her brow furrowed. "But if there's no proof—"

"Right now I'm looking for paths, not proof. Directions to go, places to look. Possibilities, not conclusions."

After a moment she nodded. "Then I guess…we had nothing in common. Didn't like the same things at all."

"Books?" he suggested.

She laughed. "I think for him an evening at home in front of a fire with a book would be akin to torture."

"And what is it to you?" he asked softly.

"Heaven," she said simply.

A sudden image of just that, shot into his mind. Katie curled up before a fire, light dancing over her, maybe cuddled in a soft blanket, reading with that intensity only a true lover of books could have. His reaction to the quiet, peaceful image startled him. His mind careened into crazy places, imagining the scene in such detail it seemed almost real. He projected himself into the silly imaginings, walking into that room, stopping and just savoring the tableau.

He yanked himself back to reality. He wasn't prone to mental wanderings like that, and he was a little disconcerted not only that he'd done it, but that it had caused a strange sort of ache inside him.

"What else about him?" He hoped his tone wasn't too sharp, but he needed to get back on track. She didn't seem to notice, or more likely she assumed it was his way, which was just as well.

"He was a little too smooth for my taste." She smiled then, and it held a wealth of emotions, sadness, ruefulness, pain and loss. "And then he saw Laurel and that was that anyway."

"She was an attractive woman," he said neutrally.

"She was more than attractive. Funny, vivid, gregarious, always ready to go and do. She was beautiful, and so, so alive. She was everything I wasn't, so it was no wonder…" Her voice trailed away and she turned back to Cutter as if for comfort.

"That is the first stupid thing you've said."

The words were out before he could stop them, and once they were, he didn't regret them. She was staring at him, but this time he couldn't read anything in that look.

"Some people would much prefer that book before the fire to a merry-go-round of going and doing," he said.

Wasn't he proof of that? No one had gone and done more than Gavin de Marco at his peak, after all. He'd been at the apex of the glittering world so many lusted after. He'd been amid the movers and shakers, the household names from government, business and the entertainment world. There were few of them who, even if they'd never met, wouldn't take a call from him back then. And if they ever found themselves in need of a criminal defense attorney, he would have been at the top of their short lists.

And yet he had never felt more relieved than when he had walked away and left it all behind.

"Do you think," she said slowly, still looking at him, "that it's possible to change from one to the other?"

"I did."

He wasn't sure why he'd admitted that, but it was nothing less than the truth. And no one had been more surprised than he himself. When he wondered if she was wishing she could change in the other direction, he felt a twinge of sadness and had to stifle the urge to tell her she was fine as she was.

But this was not about her, and she likely wouldn't appreciate him making it about her, so this time he stopped himself.

"Tell me about your father."

Her chin came up then. "My father is a good man. He's kind, loving and strong. He's successful now, but he wasn't always. There were tough times, some when I was a kid, especially after my mom died, but he never gave up. And he often did without, so that I didn't have to."

"Textbook-perfect parent?"

Her gaze narrowed again, as if she suspected there was sarcasm behind the words.

"As perfect at it as any human being can get," she answered. "He had his flaws elsewhere, but as a father he was the best."

"What flaws?" For a moment she didn't answer. "I warned you," he said.

"I was thinking, not avoiding," she said, her tone a little sharp. Then, more evenly, she said, "He has a tendency to bite off more than he can chew, and then has to scramble, or put in impossibly long hours to get it done. Or leave half-finished projects all over. His shop—he makes metal sculptures as a hobby—is full of them. And sometimes he's too generous for his own good."

"Meaning?"

"I'm guessing you already know he owns a mailboxes franchise." At his nod, she went on. "What you don't know is that some of the box renters are transient or homeless, so he'll carry longtime customers if they come up short. He has a few disabled or elderly customers, and if they can't get in to pick up their mail, or there's a package too big or heavy for them, he'll hand deliver it on his way home."

"Admirable," he said, meaning it.

"He is an admirable man. One of those who just quietly keeps the world turning."

"And you love him."

"I adore him. But I'm not blind. He floundered a bit—well, a lot—after my mother died. We both did. He loved her so much he changed his whole life because he couldn't bear going on as if nothing had happened. He changed his job, his car, his friends, we moved... He changed everything but me."

He studied her for a moment. "But weren't you the biggest reminder of all?"

She didn't flinch. "Yes. And that's what finally made him realize that he couldn't run from it. That grief was going to happen no matter what he did."

"Were you ever afraid he'd want to change you, too?"

"Never," she said firmly, instantly. Before he even had the chance to wonder why on earth he'd asked that one. "We were a team, the two of us."

"Maybe he wanted it to stay that way. Didn't want a third team member."

Her brow furrowed. "He's always the one encouraging me to get out more, meet people, date, all that."

He hadn't meant that, he'd meant Laurel, but he found it interesting that it apparently didn't occur to her. And he found himself interested in the answer to this, on more than one level. "You don't?"

"I haven't had time, with the new job and moving." She sounded a tiny bit defensive.

"So no boyfriend in the picture, who might get jealous of the time you spent with Laurel?"

"No," she said, sounding relieved now, as if she'd thought he was going to chide her about her social life. Which would be rich, coming from him. He steered her back to the question.

"And your father?"

She blinked. "What?"

"Was he jealous of the time you spent with her? You and he being a team of two all those years?"

She drew back sharply. Her lips parted to speak, and then she stopped. Looked thoughtful. He guessed she had been going to answer angrily, then had reconsidered. Perhaps she remembered what he'd said about asking questions she wouldn't like.

"No," she said, calmly enough. "He was not. Laurel had always been my best friend. Growing up, he included her as if we were sisters. They even threw a surprise birthday party for me together, in April, right before…"

Another layer of pain for her, he thought; for the rest of her life her birthday would be connected to the loss of her best friend. He changed direction again, wondering on some level if he was doing it to protect her. He was usually more ruthless than that, but she wasn't the suspect here, her father was.

"What about your father's social life?"

"He's only now starting to live again himself."

"So he's going out, seeing people?"

"A little, yes. He was too grief-stricken for a very long time. It was nearly fifteen years before he would even think about it. I'm glad for him."

"But he wasn't out that night."

She stiffened visibly. "I told you—"

"I know. The old movie."

"*Casablanca.* Mom's favorite classic film. He always watched it, if it was on. Even though it hurt."

"You don't?" That really had nothing to do with anything, but he was curious. He was curious about too damned much with this woman.

"I'll watch it," she said with a half shrug. "But I don't make an appointment for it, like Dad will."

"Is that—"

The ring of his cell cut him off. He glanced at it, saw that it was Quinn, excused himself and walked toward the kitchen as he answered.

"News?" he asked without preamble.

He listened to Quinn's rapid report with his back to Katie. He was glad of it when an old, familiar coldness began to spread through him.

"Got it," he said when Quinn finished, saying they were on their way back. Just as well, Gavin thought. This could get ugly.

He ended the call with a swipe and shoved the phone back in his pocket. After a moment he realized his teeth were clenched, and purposely relaxed his jaw. Then he turned and walked back, looking down at her.

"I thought we had an understanding," he said, the coldness seeping into his voice.

Her brow furrowed. Even Cutter lifted his head to stare at him, as if he sensed the change in him.

"What do you mean?" she asked, sounding so honestly confused it made the cold bite even deeper. "Which understanding?"

"That you wouldn't lie to me."

Chapter 11

Katie stared up at him. It really was intimidating, having him tower over her, whether that was his intent or not. She stood, but it didn't help much; he was still much taller than her own five-four.

But that was nothing compared to the ice in his voice. Even Cutter was on his feet, as if he sensed the sudden change in mood in the room.

"I didn't lie to you," she said, with as much calm as she could muster considering the accusation. "About anything."

"Lies of omission are still lies," he said, his voice even colder, "and I will not tolerate either. From anyone."

Some part of her mind that wasn't shrinking away from that iciness was telling her there was more than just this case prodding at him, and she wondered why he'd felt compelled to add those last two words. But right now she couldn't spare brainpower to figure it out. This was the Gavin de Marco they wrote about, and she needed all her wits to even begin to deal with him.

She suddenly remembered, in her research last night, watching a video from one of his old cases that had been broadcast across the country. The prosecutor had given his opening statement, sounding convincing if a bit strident. And then Gavin de Marco had risen, slowly, all the while shaking his head in confident amusement as he glanced at the opposing attorney, then the jury. Letting his reputation make the first statement without saying a word.

She was getting her first inkling of what it must have been like to go up against this man.

"What is it you think I lied about? Or since you said omission, what do you think I left out that makes a difference?"

"You neglected to mention your father's history."

She drew back, more puzzled than ever. "What?"

"You didn't think the fact that he used to be a locksmith was relevant?"

Her brow furrowed. "That was nearly twenty years ago. I barely remember it. Why would it matter now?"

"Can you still ride a bike?"

"What's that got to—" It hit her suddenly, belatedly. *No evidence of forced entry...*

"You think he picked the lock."

"A pro can get in without leaving any obvious signs. He was a pro, for over a decade according to Detective Dunbar's source."

Katie sank back onto the couch. Cutter made a low sound, between a whine and a growl; he clearly wasn't happy with things at the moment. And neither was she. It had been difficult enough keeping up with his seemingly random questions; she'd never expected him to jump around from subject to subject like that. Then she'd realized that was probably why he did it, to keep the person he was quizzing off balance and more likely to make a mistake or get caught in a lie.

Lies of omission are still lies, and I will not tolerate either. From anyone.

"Nothing to say?"

She drew in a deep breath. Did he really correlate a simple missed connection to lying? She'd been prepared for him to be suspicious of her father, given the police were, but she hadn't been prepared for him to doubt she was telling him the truth.

"I…it never occurred to me," she said, her voice a bit shaky. "It's been so long, and once he left it, he never went back. I don't think he even still has his tools. It was all part of his life with Mom, and he couldn't bear it."

For a long moment he just stared down at her, saying nothing. Finally, as she was sure he intended, it got to be too much.

"Perhaps I should have held out for a say in this understanding," she said with a grimace.

"Such as?" *God, the man could freeze fire with that voice.*

"Oh, something simple. Basic. Like presumed honest until proven a liar."

He let out a short, compressed breath that managed to sound amused and sarcastic at the same time. "I've found it more accurate to assume the opposite."

"Then I don't envy you your life."

"If you'd lived that life, you'd understand."

"And if you'd lived my last six months, you'd understand I would never lie about this."

For a moment he just continued to stare at her, steady, assessing, but not quite as cold. Or maybe that was her imagination. Or wishful thinking. She'd known this would be uncomfortable, even painful at times, but she hadn't expected this sense of...almost sadness, that he thought so little of her so soon. Quickly she caught herself. What Gavin de Marco thought of her meant nothing, as long as he believed her father innocent.

Which he now clearly had doubts about. Thanks to a job her dad had once done, and admittedly done well, but had left behind long ago. The unfairness of it stiffened her spine and she held his gaze steadily and, with an effort, kept her voice calm and even.

"You need to talk to my father. Once you do, even if you go in with this attitude, I'm sure you'll see that he could never have done this." She let a bit of accusation into her voice. "Unless you've already jumped to your conclusion."

For an instant she thought she saw a corner of his mouth twitch, as if he were fighting a smile. That seemed unlikely, so perhaps he was trying not to laugh at her.

"I intend to talk to him," he said, ignoring her jab.

Maybe she shouldn't have done this at all, she thought. The police couldn't possibly have any evidence, not really, because her father was innocent. They might have been better off leaving it all alone. Especially if de Marco already agreed with the police that her father was the most likely—and she feared the only—suspect.

"If that," she said rather defiantly, rising to her feet again, "is all the police have to go on, then I'd say Dad has nothing to worry about."

"I told you, you weren't going to like this."

"And you were right." She was aware that Cutter had also stood again, now directly in front of her. She kept her eyes on the man who was watching her so intently it made her skin heat.

"Sit down, Ms. Moore. We've only just begun."

What she wanted to do was storm out in some kind of high dudgeon, but he'd probably only laugh at her. And that would really sting. She was calm, even serene by nature, and she didn't like the way this man rattled her. Although she also knew she should have expected it; this was Gavin de Marco, after all.

Cutter whined, then moved, nudging the front of her legs gently but insistently. The dog was urging her to sit back down, she realized when she had to shift to keep from doing just that.

"What if I say we're done?" she asked, her tone even sharper than she'd intended. She was way out of her league with this man, and that irked her.

He shrugged. "Then we're done. Barring misrepresentation, the client decides when Foxworth quits."

She wanted to exclaim she hadn't misrepresented anything, but was afraid that might make him think she was protesting too much. So she went instead with the question his words had planted in her mind.

"And if the client never does?"

His answer was simple, concise. "Then we never quit." He smiled then. "Quinn's got a couple of things he's been chewing on since before I signed on."

"And have they ever solved any of those?"

He nodded. "Several. Eventually. Are you firing us?"

For a moment she just looked at him. Calmer now, she realized the absurdity of it, giving up the chance to have a defense attorney of his stature working to defend her father, just because she didn't like the way he went about it.

And because he hurt your precious feelings.

She chided herself rather fiercely, and pointed out to her roiled emotions that she had no right to feel hurt when he'd warned her she wasn't going to like his tactics. And firmly denying those emotions had nothing to do with how attractive he was. Even if he wasn't way out of her league, this was hardly the time.

Slowly, feeling a bit more in control of herself now, she sat back down. For just a moment she saw an odd expression flit across his face. The kind you wore when you'd just checked something off on a list.

Now you're trying to read his mind? A man renowned for never betraying what he's thinking or where he's really going?

She nearly smiled then. But she managed to rein it in and sat rather primly, waiting for him to start again.

Chapter 12

Katie Moore was definitely tougher than she looked, Gavin thought. He almost hated to start in again, but he wanted everything he could get before he started on her father. And so he would begin with the ugliest parts, because after that, talking about her father again should be a relief.

"Tell me about that day. Step by step from when you got out of your car at your apartment. Every detail, whether you think it matters or not. Can you do that?"

"I could bury you in details," she said. Too sweetly? He nearly smiled again. No, there was nothing mousy about this librarian. He wondered if there was another occupation outside of the police or military—or lawyers—that came with so many erroneous assumptions.

"Try," he suggested.

And she almost did. She gave him every step of the way, from the moment of her late arrival home after a study night at the library, from the smell of the roses, to which lights were on in the building. Her voice trembled slightly when she reached the crime scene on her mental journey.

"I thought something had fallen, spilled somehow on the entry floor, that I'd tracked it into the living room without realizing. Then…" She swallowed and went on. "I realized it was blood."

From there her account matched the reports, and he was amazed at how steady she was as she recounted finding the bloodied, hacked body of her best friend in front of the couch. The only sign she gave of how distressed she had to be was the waver in her voice and the way she wrapped her arms around herself as if she was afraid she was going to fly apart. Not unexpected.

What was unexpected was the urge he felt to sit beside her and put his arm around her again. And how he was having to work harder than usual to keep his brain on track and catalog the details she was giving him. Because that stupid brain kept wandering off into other places that had nothing to do with the case and everything to do with those blue eyes of hers.

When he had finally finished making Katie go through it time and again he felt a bit too much like a mean kid torturing a helpless animal.

Although, there was nothing helpless about Katie Moore, he noted as she simply looked at him, waiting to see if they were going to start all over again.

"Enough," he said, rather gruffly. "We can't go any further until I talk to your father in person."

"That will be the deciding factor? If you believe him?"

"Yes." He left it at that. He knew Quinn would go with his instincts on the case; it was, after all, the big reason he'd taken him on at Foxworth.

"He is innocent," she said yet again. "He was nearly as upset as I was over Laurel. He still is, in fact, just as I am.

She'd been part of my life almost forever. He would never have hurt her. He would never hurt anyone."

Gavin felt the strangest urge to reassure her, even though he had long ago lost count of how many times he'd heard that phrase and it had turned out to be wrong.

He was startled—and unsettled—by how strongly he wanted it not to be wrong for Katie.

Cutter's string of oddly rhythmic and definitely happy barks interrupted Katie's roiling thoughts. The dog leaped from where he'd been close at her feet, as he had been most of this disturbing session. He trotted quickly over to the door, tail up and wagging furiously.

She found herself amused—and thus relieved—as she watched him rise up and bat at the large, square button beside the front door. The door swung open and he squeezed through the moment the gap was wide enough.

"Quinn and Hayley," Gavin said. "That's their bark." At her look, he shrugged. "Don't ask, I don't know. All I know is I doubt they're paying him enough."

To her surprise, she found herself laughing at that, and a bit more of the tension of the past couple of hours eased. She liked his sense of humor, when it snuck out. That a sense of humor was high on her list of desirable traits in a relationship in all those silly quizzes Laurel used to make her take was incidental.

She stood up as the door swung open again. Hayley was the first in, Cutter dancing around her feet.

"And have you kept things under control here, my fine boy?"

Quinn glanced at Katie and Gavin. "Everybody looks intact and unbattered, so I'd say yes."

The greetings complete, the dog promptly returned to his selected place at Katie's feet and sat, leaning against her leg. But he kept looking at Quinn and Hayley. He seemed to wait until he was sure he had their full attention before letting out a distinctive sound that sounded half whine, half growl.

"Oh?" Quinn said, as if the dog had spoken. He looked at Gavin then. "What's the problem?"

Katie was sure she was gaping at this canine communication. Gavin only shrugged, so although she felt a bit silly being directed by a dog, Katie answered. "Your attorney thinks I purposely kept a big secret from him."

Quinn's gaze narrowed, as if he knew quite well what that would mean. "Did you?"

"I didn't tell him something from twenty years ago because I haven't even thought about it in that twenty years."

"The locksmithing?" Quinn asked. Katie nodded.

"That's a bit over-the-top even for you, Gav," Hayley said. She glanced at Katie. "You were what, nine years old when he changed professions?"

"Ten," Katie answered. "I thought he just helped people who locked themselves out of their cars. But then he quit and bought the mailbox place, and I never really thought about it again."

"What ten-year-old would? Especially with everything else you were dealing with." Hayley looked at her dog, who was leaning into Katie's leg even more. Then she looked at Gavin. "Cutter's giving you his opinion. He trusts her. And we've never gone wrong trusting his judgment."

Quinn looked once more at Gavin, who hadn't said a word since they'd come in. "Where do we stand?"

"I'm done with her for now," he said, not quite dismissively. "Next I need to interview her father."

Katie felt a stab of irritation at the way he said it, but quashed it. This wasn't personal. He was a lawyer approaching a case, and she was just an aspect of that case.

She'd best remember that and rein in her own silly reactions to this man. Even if he was exasperating.

"In case you forgot," Hayley said, giving Gavin a pointed look, "she's standing right here. Talking about her in the third person is rude."

Katie's gaze shifted to Hayley, and the other woman winked broadly at her.

"Sorry," Gavin muttered, but he didn't look at her, or Hayley.

Something sparked in Katie, and her chin went up. "That's okay," she said blandly. "I'd rather he save his energy for helping my father than waste it on being polite to me."

His gaze shot to her then. She thought she saw a sort of startled amusement in his eyes. "Touché," he said with a small nod.

"I'd suggest you not underestimate this one," Quinn said, and there was no doubting his amusement.

"Point taken," Gavin said.

"Before you leave to talk to Katie's father, there's more you should know," Quinn told him. "Brett talked to a guy who's got a brother on the PD down there. He said they're pretty set on Steven Moore as their suspect, but he thinks it's in part because every other lead has been a dead end. Moore's got the weakest alibi, but the rest is all circumstantial, and flimsy at that."

Katie didn't know whether to feel more concerned or relieved. She had faith in the system, generally, but it had miscarried justice often enough that she didn't trust it when it came to someone she loved as much as she loved her father. When it came to her father, she wanted the best help she could get.

And that meant Gavin de Marco.

Quinn went on. "The only solid thing they have is his

phone records. Regular calls to Laurel's number and vice versa for several weeks before she was killed."

Katie looked at Gavin. "My birthday party," she said. "I told you about that."

"You did," he acknowledged with barely a glance at her. Quinn looked curious, but let it go. "And what are they chewing on as motive?"

Quinn shook his head. "They're really short on that, too, Brett said. I told him to call you direct with anything else, now that he's read in on it."

Gavin nodded. Katie supposed he and their detective friend had worked together before, on the big, statewide political scandal if nothing else.

"And," Hayley added with a smile at Gavin, "Brett seems to think that just dropping your name into the mix, if you decide we're taking this on, could shift the direction a bit."

Gavin's jaw tightened. It seemed that he wasn't particularly happy with that. She would have thought he'd be delighted to still have such influence, even years after he'd walked away. She was certainly delighted; anything that turned police attention away from her father was a good thing in her book.

"I'll call my father, let him know we're coming," she said, reaching for her phone.

"You will not," Gavin said, not quite sharply but with a definite edge. "I don't want him warned."

She frowned. "You think…what, you're going to trick something out of him with some kind of sneak attack?"

His mouth quirked. "I hope I have more finesse than that, but essentially yes. Which," he added, "I could only do if it's there to come out in the first place."

She steadied herself, held his gaze, then echoed his words. "Point taken."

"And I need to talk to him alone."

If he'd meant that to rattle her, it didn't. At all. "All right."

She could almost see him register her lack of concern. Good, she thought. That should prove how utterly certain she was of her father's innocence. And Gavin would be, too, once he talked to him. And maybe that weighty name really would make the police rethink. Despite all her worry, she dared to hope.

He glanced at his watch. "Will he be home now?"

"Should be. Sunday's his workshop day. Or football. Shall I drive, since I know where we're going? It's not far."

He hesitated for a moment, then said, "I'll follow you."

She arched a brow at him. "Aren't you afraid I'll call to warn him?"

Something flashed in those dark eyes again. "Maybe I'm more worried you'll want to drive me into a pole when we're done."

Her mouth quirked upward at one corner. "Sorry, can't afford the damage that would do."

"To your car or your driving record?" he asked wryly.

"Yes." She smiled, with a little too much cheer. "I know a lawyer, though. Whether he's good enough remains to be seen. Shall we go?"

He drew back at that. Quinn laughed out loud.

"Nicely done," Hayley said. "He needs taking down a peg now and then."

"Thanks," Gavin said with a glance at his friends.

Katie was still smiling when she got to her feet. The sooner this was over with, the better. Then Gavin would be convinced her father was innocent, and he could put that prodigious brain and reputation to work proving it.

Chapter 13

I'd suggest you not underestimate this one.

Gavin recalled Quinn's statement. Truer words had never been spoken, Gavin thought as he followed Katie's car. As if he'd heard the thought, Cutter woofed softly. Gavin let out a slight sound of disbelief, shaking his head, wondering how he'd let himself get roped into taking the dog with him.

"Take Cutter," Quinn had said cheerfully. "He'll assess things for you."

"Do bring him," Katie had agreed, sounding happy about it. "Dogs love my dad. They have good judgment about people."

"Right," he'd muttered, trying not to notice that Cutter had gotten to his feet and was already headed for the door, as if he'd understood every word.

"Trust him," Hayley had said softly as he stood up.

So now here he was, with the too clever dog opining

from the back seat, wondering how it had happened. But the farther they went, the more he began to think perhaps it was a good thing. The dog would be a distraction, perhaps make Moore feel this was more of a social visit, friendly, so his guard wouldn't be up.

Katie was driving rather sedately, not speeding or rolling through any stop signs despite the lack of traffic. After a final turn onto a small cul-de-sac, she pulled into the driveway of a tidy, bungalow-style house. The driveway was delineated by a row of metal sculptures, birds, fish and some more whimsical, like a curious-looking dragon. The hobby Katie had mentioned, he guessed. Next to the house was a wide carport, extended to provide shelter up to a side door of the house. A silver coupe sat in one spot. Katie pulled in next to it.

He stopped behind her bright blue sedan. A practical four-door, but a flashy color, he'd thought when he'd first seen it. He wondered how much of herself was reflected in the choice.

He watched her through the back window of the car. Katie Moore had proven more than once she could and would stand up to him. If she'd been an attorney, he would have relished taking her on in a courtroom. As it was, he was relishing the thought of taking her on in very different ways. And that rattled him. He hadn't had a response like this to a woman in…forever? Or had it just been so long it seemed like forever?

He'd written off having any kind of permanent relationship. The kind of women he would want for that couldn't— and wouldn't—tolerate him for long. He didn't blame them. His last attempt had been Jessica, who had left him after a mere three months, expressing the rueful hope that he one day find someone who could take his skeptical nature and hell-on-wheels, 24/7 brain.

At this point he doubted such a woman existed. He hadn't been drawn enough to anyone to test the supposition.

Until now.

If thoughts really did come with hazard flags, this one would be big, bright and with a siren attached. It came from a different place than his instincts about people and liars, a place he hadn't heard from any time in recent memory. And it was swift and personal, warning of a steep drop off a cliff and churning water below.

Cutter gave him a nudge with his nose, startling him out of his strange reverie. He put the rental car in Park, but didn't immediately get out. Nor did Katie, and he wondered if she was having to gear herself up for this. He reminded himself that she and her father had been all each other had had for over two decades, so they were very likely to provide a united front. United in a kind of grief he'd never experienced.

Because you never let yourself get that close to anyone.

That little voice that often guided him in an interrogation or in a courtroom had recently taken to personal jibes he could do without. Besides, could he be blamed for finding it hard to trust when he'd spent years around people who lied without a thought?

Of course, all that had been before he'd learned his entire life was built on a lie.

A side door on the house opened. He stayed put, watching, wanting the chance to observe. Katie quickly got out of her car the moment a man stepped out onto the small landing two steps up from the driveway.

The man was smiling widely. No nerves there at an unexpected visit from his daughter. Assuming it was unexpected, of course, that she hadn't called him while en route despite her promise.

A promise he'd believed.

...presumed honest until proven a liar.

He shook his head again, keeping his gaze focused on the pair, assessing as Steven Moore gave his daughter a hug. Her father was, likely by any standard, a handsome man. Tall, broad-shouldered, with the same sandy-blond hair as Katie's, only his was just touched at the temples with gray. His good looks were more dramatic than Katie's quiet attractiveness, and Gavin guessed he could have had more than his share of feminine attention if he'd wanted it.

Was it really possible to grieve so much and so hard that a man who could probably have his pick of attentive ladies would forego all that for so long? Was it even possible to love someone that much?

There was no doubt about the love between father and daughter; it fairly radiated from them. He knew that kind of parental love existed, had observed it often enough. And it put a furrow in his brow as he wondered if that kind of love could run to lying to that daughter's face.

To protect her? Absolutely. To protect himself? To ensure her love for her father stayed unchanging? Because if he'd murdered her best friend, that would surely destroy what they had.

But he was, as were the police, hard aground on the lack of motive. And the man certainly did not look like a killer, but then they often didn't. Who knew that better than he? But he also knew that when desperate to solve a case, it was human nature to start searching for evidence to prove your suspicions instead of continuing to search for an elusive truth. Cops had gut instincts they trusted just as he did. Only, theirs were aimed at a different goal—a conviction in court. Most of the time their two goals coincided, but sometimes...

Katie gestured toward him, and her father looked his way. Something wary came into his expression. Gavin noted it, but didn't chalk it down in a column yet, because people were often wary upon meeting him, simply because his reputation so often preceded him.

And yet there was a touch of the excitement he also sometimes saw. Again human nature, meeting someone they'd read about or seen on TV was somehow different than meeting any other stranger.

He opened the car door and got out. He realized, far too belatedly, that he hadn't really considered what approach to take. He'd been too busy dwelling on the man's daughter and the weird effect she had on him.

And then Cutter was out of the car and trotting ahead, leaving him no time to ponder the matter. He was truly out of it, Gavin thought. To be honest, he'd been off stride ever since he'd opened the door to see a wet, bedraggled Katie Moore standing there. It was time he got over it and got back in the game.

The dog came to a halt in front of Steven Moore, and sat. He looked up at the man, head cocked at a quizzical angle, as if he couldn't quite figure him out.

"Well, hello there," Moore said, bending to pet the dog's dark head.

Cutter allowed it, but he didn't react with the instant warmth and affection he'd given Katie. Of course, he knew Katie from the neighborhood.

"This is Cutter," Katie was explaining. "He belongs to the Foxworths. He's quite the judge of character, so he's here to show Mr. de Marco that you're honest."

She said it with obvious amusement. But watching her father's face, Gavin was certain he'd seen a flicker of… something in his eyes. Worry? Nervousness?

Guilt?

Cutter had remained in place, sitting in front of the man. But now he was looking back over his shoulder at Gavin with the oddest expression. In a person he would have said it was a maybe, or a tentative yes, with reservations.

Trust him.

Hayley's words echoed in his mind. And he found himself wishing the dog could explain those reservations.

Laughing at himself inwardly, he walked up to the trio.

"Mr. Moore," he said, holding out a hand.

The man took it, and they shook. Good, solid handshake, not too weak, not overdone to impress him. One small box checked off.

"Mr. de Marco," Moore said. "It's an honor to meet you. I just wish my girl didn't think it was necessary."

"You don't think it is?"

The older man—Gavin figured he had to be early to midfifties at least, although he looked much younger—let out an audible sigh.

"Since I didn't do it, I don't want to think it is," he said, "but if it will make Katie feel better, I'll go along."

The denial was issued calmly, not an insistent declaration but merely as if it were a statement of fact. And Gavin found himself believing it. Which was odd, since he usually didn't reach that stage so soon.

That had him wondering even more about what the dog's apparent reservations were.

Which in turn made him think, ruefully, that he'd completely lost his mind.

Or, he added silently with a look at Katie, something else entirely.

Chapter 14

"As I explained to the police, those calls to Laurel—" his voice changed slightly with her name; definite sadness there, Gavin thought "—were us arranging Katie's birthday party. And as I also told them, we met several times to go over the arrangements."

Gavin got no hint of a lie in the words. "Whose idea was that?"

"Laurel's. She wanted it to be ginormous, she said. She teased Katie because Katie was going to turn thirty before she would."

They'd been at this for nearly two hours, Gavin doing his usual pacing while keeping a close eye on Moore. He'd begun with small talk, casual, lulling the man a bit with ordinary things before hitting him with a sudden, unexpected question about Laurel and her death. The technique had somewhat backfired on him this time since the topic had, inevitably, veered to Katie. It had been all he could do to stay mentally here in this room when she was right outside, working in the sizable vegetable garden in the back. Doing what, he wasn't sure, as his skills didn't run to such things. Something to do with the coming winter, he supposed.

She'd pulled her hair back and secured it in that ponytail that bounced when she moved. To keep her hair out of the way as she worked, he supposed. He was supposing too much and too often, he chided himself. But it was difficult not to when Moore had spoken of her with such pride and love. There was absolutely no doubt in Gavin's mind that the man loved his daughter. Or that he had cared a lot about her best friend.

He'd been open and calm about answering questions, although he did blink a time or two when Gavin would jump to a new subject. But he always answered, sometimes with thought, but most times with the ease of someone who'd either thought about it a lot, or answered the questions before. In this case Gavin thought both probably applied.

In fact, everything Moore said felt genuine. Yet the old instincts were firing. He couldn't put a name to the rather vague misgivings he was feeling, but something was off. He was usually able to tell when someone was lying, but as with Katie, omission was something else. In her case, he now thought she'd honestly forgotten about the locksmith thing, since she'd been so young. And he shoved aside the feeling of relief it gave him to no longer think she'd been trying to hide it from him. She was clouding his judgment, and he shoved that realization aside as well, even as he noted he was doing a lot of that since last night when Cutter had practically dragged her into his life.

But in her father's case…

He just couldn't pin it down. He didn't think the man was outright lying, but something was triggering those old gut feelings. He had the sudden thought that he was agree-ing with the dog. Yes, but with reservations.

Maybe you've been out of the game too long. And while the media used to trumpet that your judgment is flawless, no one knows better than you that it's not. It's very, very flawed, and always has been.

He heard Cutter bark from outside and stopped his pac-ing and turned to look. He'd kept his gaze away from the large window that looked out on the garden, since Katie puttering around out there was apparently more of a dis-traction than his suddenly unruly mind could handle.

Right now, the dog was crouched in front of Katie in that universal, front end down, tail wagging in the air posture of canine play. She was holding up a stick about a foot and a half long. Cutter barked again, happily. He couldn't hear it, but Gavin knew she laughed; he could see her face. It sent a bolt of heat through him that was out of proportion to the simple vision of a woman playing with a dog.

She raised the hand with the stick and leaned back, that ponytail swaying. He had a sudden image of pulling away whatever held it, and watching her hair tumble back down to her shoulders, and heat jammed through him again. He sucked in a breath as he watched her throw the stick, fol-lowing through with the swing of her arm and sending it a decent distance toward the trees at the back of the lot. Cutter took off after it in clear delight.

"I should have gotten her a dog, after her mother died."

The quiet words came from barely a foot behind him. Gavin stiffened, barely managing not to jerk around. He hadn't even heard the man move, he'd been so focused on the tableau outside. So focused on the woman out there that he'd lost all sense of his immediate surroundings.

Great. You've got your head so far up your backside

you let a guy who might be a murderer completely get the drop on you.

"But I was too deep in my own pain. There are so many things I wish I'd done for her. She was so young and hurting so much. But I just wasn't thinking clearly at the time."

There was, Gavin thought, no denying those emotions were heartfelt and real. He knew that without even looking at Moore's face, because it was all there in his voice. And a sudden image of a nine-year-old Katie, maybe with that same ponytail, broken and weeping inconsolably sent an entirely different kind of jolt through him. Pain, sympathy and a sudden wish that she never again have such a horrible ache in her heart.

If her father took the fall for Laurel's murder, her pain would be unbearable.

He turned then, and stood face-to-face with the man. They were almost the same height, and he found himself looking into eyes exactly the same shade of blue as Katie's. It was disconcerting for a moment. But then he asked, his voice low and intense, the question he had yet to ask.

"Did you kill Laurel Brisbane?"

The answer came immediately, firmly. "No, sir, I did not."

Whatever Moore was lying about, Gavin couldn't convince himself it was this. His misgivings were too vague to even hang a name on. For all he knew, they could stem from something else entirely. There had been a time when he would have trusted them without hesitation, but that time had ended four years ago. December 21, to be exact.

"And if you think I did," Moore added quietly, "then you should leave. I know your reputation, Mr. de Marco. And what it can do. Don't get my girl's hopes up any further."

For the first time Gavin saw concern in the man's expression. And he realized Moore wasn't quite as casual about being a murder suspect as it had seemed. He was putting on a good front for Katie, Gavin thought. He didn't want her to worry. In a way this relieved him; he'd been afraid the man didn't understand the gravity of his situation.

And then another realization struck him. That on some level beneath conscious thought, he'd already decided.

"Sit down, Mr. Moore," he suggested. "We have a lot of work to do."

Chapter 15

"That de Marco is really something."

Katie looked across the table at her father. It was the first time he'd paused in eating the meat loaf she'd fixed for his Sunday dinner and lunches next week. The dish was his and her favorite, from her mother's recipe she'd found in a box shoved in the back of a closet where he'd put many of the painful reminders he'd moved with him from the old house but hadn't wanted on daily display.

"Yes, he is." *And isn't that the truth*, she added silently. Although now, away from him, she could think of him much more rationally. She wondered what it was that gave some people that kind of overpowering charisma. Was it something in them, some quirk of genetics or chemistry? Or was it something in the people around them, making them react that way? She'd have to research that, see if anyone had ever come up with a plausible theory.

"And that's really the story, how you met him? The dog?"

She nodded, smiling now although she hadn't been then. "Cutter's quite something, as well."

"He sounds scary smart."

"Yes." She wondered if he'd meant the dog or Gavin, but since the same answer applied in either case, she left it at that.

She hesitated before speaking again. It had been a long day, for both of them, but particularly him because he'd spent those hours getting, as he put it, "grilled." But since she'd been exiled to the garden, she was beyond curious.

"So...did he ask you anything unexpected?"

Her father shrugged. "Some questions I couldn't see the relevance of."

"He did that to me, too. I suppose it must mean something to him, or else leads to something else."

"You know, usually I can figure a man out, after a while. But I have no idea how this one's mind works."

"Maybe that's partly why he was so good at what he did."

Her father looked at her curiously now. "Do you have any idea why he quit?"

"No, other than to work for Foxworth."

"I never heard any rumors that he was in trouble or anything."

Katie was surprised at how much just the idea of that shocked her. She hadn't found anything in her research to indicate he'd left under a cloud, but she didn't think she would have believed it if she had, now that she'd met him. Gavin de Marco was intense, brilliant and charismatic, but if he was ethically challenged she'd eat the plate the last bit of her meat loaf sat on.

"I can't imagine him working for a place like Foxworth if he was that type," she said. "Quinn Foxworth appears to be the straightest of straight arrows."

"But de Marco is a lawyer."

"I think he's more of an advisor now," she said.

"Seemed like a guy in charge to me," her father said drily. He leaned back in his chair, took a sip of the small glass of wine he allowed himself in the evenings, and studied her. "You seem…quite impressed with him."

She managed not to flush, but it took a very deep breath and great effort. "I've never met a household name before."

"He's a good-looking man, wouldn't you say?"

The flush won that time. "Are you asking me or telling me?"

"Aha!" her father exclaimed. "I always know I've got you when you answer a question with a question."

"I'm just trying to figure out what that has to do with anything. And how you can tease me when…when…" She couldn't finish, and lowered her gaze to that last, lonely bite of meat.

"Baby," he said, instantly contrite, "I'm just trying to cheer you up. You're so worried, and I keep telling you there's no reason. The truth will out eventually. Or maybe sooner, now that Mr. Gavin Household Name de Marco is involved."

Her gaze shot back to his face. "Then you're not upset with me for talking to him? You seemed less than excited about it at first."

"I was," he admitted. "Maybe I just didn't want to admit that I might need a lawyer. I'm still not sure I do, mind you, but if I'm going to have one… Well, damn, Gavin de Marco!"

She laughed at both his tone and expression, feeling much better now. Because it was true. Having Gavin on your side was a very big deal.

And given her silly reaction to him, having to deal with him herself was going to be a huge task.

* * *

"Damn, that was fast."

At Quinn's words Gavin looked up from the legal pad he was holding. He was sitting beside the fireplace at the Foxworth headquarters, the flames casting a flickering light across the page. Cutter was curled up before the fire, no doubt still a bit damp from his romp in the meadow earlier.

"What?" Gavin asked, lifting the fountain pen from the page. He still took notes with pen and paper because he'd found there was something about the process that got his brain into that zone he needed. Even when he did record an interview, he made written notes, adding to them as he listened to it later, usually with his eyes closed to summon up the memory of how a person had looked or spoken, which was sometimes as important as what they'd said, or more so.

Quinn held up his phone before sliding it back into a pocket. "That was Brett. Word's out that you're involved, and already the police are rethinking. Or at least questioning their assumptions."

"Question is, are they angry?"

"Brett says they'll get over it. They knew they'd settled on Moore because every other lead washed out," Quinn said. "Brett gave me the name and number of the lead investigator, who by the way wasn't at all interested in talking to Moore's attorney until he mentioned your name."

Gavin's mouth tightened. His reputation was the biggest double-edged sword he'd ever dealt with. It sliced through protocol and often reluctance, but it also affected things in ways he wasn't comfortable with. No one should ever have been negatively impacted just because he was too busy or didn't want to handle their case. And yet he knew it had happened. It was one of the other reasons he'd walked away.

"If I haven't said so lately, thanks for taking me on," he said, not exactly sure why.

Quinn looked startled, then smiled. "I think you have that backward."

Gavin shook his head. "No. I come with a lot of history, not all of it good, and I know I'm sometimes tough to work with."

"Tough to keep up with," Quinn said. "Entirely different thing."

"Speaking of which, now that we're rolling I'm going to stay here," Gavin told him. At his announcement Quinn lifted a brow quizzically. "It'll be easier on everyone if I'm out of your place," he explained. "You know how I get."

He didn't sleep much anyway, but when he had a case he was up at all hours pacing and going over things, sometimes talking things through out loud.

"Hayley wouldn't mind, and you know I don't."

"But I do. Besides, worrying about disturbing my hosts affects my focus."

Quinn shrugged. "Well, this is now your baby, so you're the boss. How did it go with Moore?"

Gavin's mouth twisted. He stared into the fire, wishing he could let go of that tiny, nagging instinct that said Katie's father was hiding something. "I quizzed him up and down for nearly three hours. I couldn't shake him off his story, and I used every interrogation technique I know."

"Short of torture, I hope?"

His gaze shot back to Quinn's face. He was clearly joking, but it always rattled him a little to remember that this man had been one of the most elite operators in the military, one who had no doubt been trained in just that sort of technique. He was glad Quinn was on the side of the angels; he shuddered to think what the man could do if he'd gone rogue. But nothing could ever shake the core of who Quinn Foxworth was. Having Hayley in his life now had only solidified that, made him even stronger.

I envy him.

The stray thought flashed through Gavin's mind. How those in the world he'd once inhabited would laugh at the idea of Gavin de Marco envying anyone, he who had it all. But he did envy Quinn, and what he'd found in Hayley.

He quashed the thought, and the odd shiver that had gone through him when he'd acknowledged it. He was here to work, not indulge in idle musings. And certainly not to have Katie Moore pop into his head every time it happened.

"What does your gut say?" Quinn asked.

"That he's hiding something," Gavin admitted.

Quinn cocked his head to give Gavin a curious look. "But we're taking the case anyway?"

"He's hiding something," Gavin repeated, then added, "but I can't buy that the guy's a murderer. Especially not of his daughter's best friend."

"All right. Need anything from us?"

"Not yet. I'll be contacting the cops tomorrow, and the victim's family. Ty's running down data on them for me."

Quinn nodded. "Another session with Moore?"

Steven or Katie?

Damn, he needed to get this crazy reaction under control. "Probably. Go home to your wife."

"Always," Quinn said with a grin that made that envy spark again.

Quinn headed for the door, then turned to look at Cutter, who hadn't budged an inch from Gavin's side. The dog stared back, and Gavin had the craziest feeling they were communicating somehow.

"Not coming?" Quinn asked lightly.

Cutter gave a low woof. Quinn's gaze shifted to Gavin. "Well, well. It seems you have a roommate."

Gavin blinked. "What?"

"I'd say he's appointed himself your guardian."

Gavin stared at the dog, who looked up at him with eyes full of utter innocence. "Guardian?"

"He saw you in the aftermath of the whole governor thing. I'd say he knows you'll bury yourself in this and forget to eat and sleep without someone around to remind you."

He looked back at Quinn, but saw no trace of a joke in his expression this time. "Seriously?"

Quinn ignored the question. "His food's in the cupboard next to the sink. Just keep it topped off. He'll self-regulate. He'll let you know when he wants out, and he'll stay close, especially now that he's adopted you. Oh, and his carrots are in the fridge. Not too many of those, though, or you'll be sorry one way or another."

"You're really going to leave him here, to…what, baby-sit me?"

Quinn grinned. "Consider yourself a dog sitter, if it makes you feel better."

Before he could even formulate a response to that, Quinn gave him a mock salute and was gone. Cutter jumped up on the couch beside him, avoiding his loose papers with delicate care. He settled down against the back cushions, and plopped his chin on Gavin's leg. He looked utterly at home and satisfied.

Gavin looked down at the dark head, and into the amber-flecked dark eyes looking up at him. With a sigh he picked up his pad again and uncapped the fountain pen.

But when he started writing again he was smiling.

Chapter 16

Gavin awakened in the headquarters bedroom with Cutter once more curled up beside him. He couldn't deny he again had slept better than he usually did, but he was hesitant to ascribe it to the dog's presence. But then, Cutter wasn't your garden-variety dog.

Uncharacteristically, he spent a few minutes petting the dog before getting up. Cutter waited until he was upright, then went and politely sat at the back door. Gavin took the cue and let him out, stepping out himself into the crisp, predawn chill. It felt wonderful to someone used to the frequent humidity of St. Louis, and he breathed it in deeply.

The motion-sensor light came on as Cutter came trotting back. He paused at a basket beside the door, nosing at it. He came up with a grayish-yellow tennis ball and sat before Gavin hopefully. He couldn't stop the memory that shot into his mind of Katie happily and fairly efficiently throwing a stick for the dog. He shook it off.

"It's too dark to see it, isn't it?" He wasn't used to being this far north this time of year, where it was still dark at this hour. But then, he'd also usually been up and working for a couple of hours by this time, so he'd better adjust.

Cutter cocked his head at an angle, ball still in his mouth.

"I get it. No problem for you, right?"

He hesitated, but figured if it got lost they'd find it once it got light. So he took the rather grubby ball. Cutter, seeing that the human had apparently figured it out, came vibrantly alert, his gaze fastened on the hand that held the ball. Gavin threw it, somewhere between a casual flip and giving it everything he had. The dog raced into the darkness, vanishing the moment he left the circle of the motion light, and Gavin had the sour thought that if he didn't come back he was going to have some difficult explaining to do to some people he really liked.

A moment later the victorious animal came trotting back, dropped the ball at his feet and spun, clearly ready to do it again. And something about the dog's playful posture made it impossible to resist. It was thirty minutes later that he finally called a halt. The sky was just beginning to lighten when they went back inside.

He put on a pot of coffee, a little surprised at how much company an animal could be. He waited for the coffee to finish, stifling a yawn, anticipating that first hit of caffeine. And when it came it was worth the wait, and the groggy morning feeling started to slip away.

Cutter nudged his knee. He looked down. The dog started toward the patio door, pausing to look back over his shoulder. That, Gavin thought, was a dog signal anybody understood.

"Already?" he asked. Maybe the ball chasing had distracted him from the real business at hand. He followed obediently, laughing inwardly at himself as he did so.

They stepped outside, but instead of heading off into the meadow the dog stopped, then turned sideways to the building, looking toward the drive. Gavin turned to look, but saw nothing but the empty gravel approach and the thinner stand of trees between them and the road.

"Waiting for Mom and Dad?" The inner laugh was sounding in his voice now.

As if in answer Cutter sat at his feet. Gavin was wondering what to do with him when a brilliant blast of golden light burst through the trees. Cutter stayed still as Gavin stood there watching the sunrise flare, lighting up the sky and clouds in an explosion of gold, orange and pink. He could see the rays as they backlit the branches of the evergreens, and above the treetops the undersides of the clouds fairly glowed with color. It was a show to rival anything he'd seen in any of the myriad places he'd been. He could see that it would soon disappear behind the heavy, hovering cloud layer, but right now it was a glorious stripe of brilliant light and color play along the horizon. And all the more precious for being fleeting.

And when did you start getting philosophical about things like the sun coming up in the morning?

Cutter woofed softly and Gavin laughed because he was the one who'd gotten him out here to watch this amazing show. Of course, that couldn't really be why he'd done it. Dogs couldn't even see in color, could they? And did it really matter, when it had worked, had gotten him to stop and watch something he probably would have ignored or been completely unaware of?

"Maybe you should take credit," he said, and got another quiet, approving woof. "How about some carrots, dog?"

Cutter jumped to his feet eagerly. When Gavin opened the door he darted inside, raced to the kitchen and sat expectantly while Gavin retrieved the treats.

He headed for the shower. In twenty minutes, he was back at the kitchen counter pouring another mug of the strong brew he preferred and checking his phone, planning out his day. Since it was later there, he first called Ty for anything new. There wasn't much on Steven Moore, who had apparently stayed out of trouble most of his life, except for a couple of speeding tickets when he'd been a teenager. Having had a couple of those himself—one embarrassingly recently—Gavin wasn't going to hang the man over that, but he told Ty to keep digging.

"I will. Oh, and the ex-boyfriend is apparently out of town, since Friday. San Diego, some seminar for his job starts today." Gavin made note of that, since he obviously needed to talk to the guy personally, cleared by the police or not.

Then Ty added the unexpected news that the victim had an arrest record. "Minor, but I know you want everything."

"Yes. What for?"

"For driving under the influence when she was eighteen."

"Any record of an accident or anything involved with that?"

"Not yet, but I'm still looking."

"Thanks, Ty."

Well, now. Gavin thought for a while as he sipped his coffee. No one had mentioned that fact. Was it possible they didn't know? Didn't seem likely. Perhaps they thought it of no importance, being so long ago. And maybe it wasn't.

Like Katie thought her father being a locksmith unimportant?

He grimaced inwardly. He glanced at his watch, saw that it was now after eight and made another call to the number that Detective Dunbar had provided. The man he reached, a detective named Davidson, clearly recognized his name. And that of Dunbar and Foxworth, both of which were apparently worth a lot in law enforcement circles here. He was clearly wary but cooperative enough, and agreed to meet with him this afternoon, after he completed a court appearance.

Which left Gavin a bit at loose ends at the moment. He planned on speaking to Moore again, but wanted to observe him at work, so he needed to give that another hour. He pondered fixing breakfast; there were eggs and plenty of other things available. In the end he settled for a couple of pieces of buttered toast made from bread from the local bakery, something he'd had last time he was here and liked. Cutter munched on some kibble from his bowl, but as Quinn had said, stopped on his own while it was still half-full.

When he was done and had tidied up, he stood for a moment, thinking. Or rather, trying not to think about a particular person.

He could get what he needed from the police detective this afternoon. He was certain they must have looked into that old arrest; since it was a murder case they'd dig deep. Given how long ago it had been it likely had nothing to do with her murder, but he hadn't become a success leaving unturned stones.

But right now he was more curious why Katie hadn't mentioned it.

Shoving those inner warnings into a mental box, he put his phone in his pocket, gathered up his keys and jacket and headed for the door. Cutter beat him to it and slapped the button to open it. Gavin realized with chagrin he'd forgotten to lock the front door last night. Lucky for him he was here, and not at home in the city.

Lucky, too, that he had a self-appointed guard dog in Cutter.

He was a little surprised when the dog raced out to his rental car, clearly intending to come along. Gavin wondered if the dog expected to go home now, like a kid after a sleepover. Well, if he did, he was just going to have to wait. Gavin wanted to get to his own destination.

The new community center hadn't been open when he'd last been here, but it had been under construction and he knew where it was. He found it without the help of GPS and pulled into the parking lot. He spotted Katie's blue sedan parked in a far corner, out of the way of patrons, so he knew she was here.

He'd planned on leaving Cutter in the car but the dog had other ideas and was out the moment he could squeeze past Gavin. The dog trotted over to the door of the library as if he'd been there dozens of times. Maybe he had been. Gavin hesitated, fairly certain the dog wouldn't be allowed inside and wondering how he was going to convince him of that. But then Cutter plopped down beside the library sign, seemingly perfectly happy to wait there.

"So what, dog?" he asked as he caught up. "You know you're not allowed in?"

The dog glanced up, and Gavin suddenly noticed that behind the library sign—and directly over Cutter's head— was another sign advising that only service animals were allowed inside.

"If you're telling me you can read, I'm not buying it," Gavin said, but he was chuckling inwardly. The dog put his head down on his front paws as if settling in. Gavin sighed. He was trying to think of the last time he'd been in a public library as he pulled open the door. And trying not to think of the woman inside, the real reason he'd decided to come here.

* * *

Katie hung the last floaty, cloth ghost from the beam over the library information desk. It matched the one in her office window and completed the library's Halloween decorations. This had been a huge success at the prior library she'd worked at, with parents happy to have something else for their kids to do than go door-to-door. Especially given that so often the end of October meant a rainy if not downright stormy night. She had hoped it would be the same here, but hadn't expected the number who had signed up for this first ever event at the new building tomorrow. She'd planned on getting all ready earlier, but the news about her father had disrupted everything.

She leaned back on the short stepladder to see if she liked the arrangement of ghosts and jack-o-lanterns alongside orange and black streamers.

"Nice."

The deep, masculine voice startled her, both because it was so close and because she recognized it.

But when she twisted on the ladder to face Gavin de Marco, he wasn't looking at the decorations. His eyes, those dark, smoky eyes, were fastened on her. And again he hadn't shaved, the slight stubble giving him the rakish air it usually only gave celebrities who studied the effect in the mirror before stepping outside to be seen. She was certain Gavin had merely not wanted to take the time.

She was suddenly aware that her backside was about at his eye level and wished she'd worn something a bit less snug than leggings. But she'd known she'd be up and down the ladder today, and had gone for comfort. She felt her cheeks heating, and quickly scrambled down the ladder. By the time she hit the floor she'd recovered her poise.

She waved toward the line of ghosts and pumpkins. "I'm glad you like them," she said, quietly as always when she was out on the floor. She wasn't sure if she hoped he'd say he hadn't been talking about the ghosts, or not. "The kids seem to, and that's what it's all about. It's for the story night tomorrow. You probably saw the sign out front. It's the first time here, so we're going all out."

God, she was rambling like an idiot. So much for poise. *Shut up, Katie!*

She waited, half expecting him to laugh at her. Instead he said, keeping his own voice low, "What Halloween story?"

Did he really want to know, or was he politely trying to save her from her own jabbering? Odd in itself, since she didn't tend to that. At least not so mindlessly. But the thought of him whispering had somehow derailed her efforts at composure.

Fortunately she'd had to answer this before, so she had a response ready. "It's a collection of short stories I've put together over the years. Just scary enough but not too scary for kids. Then we top it off with a movie based on one of the stories. It's good fun for adults, too. If you wanted to come, I mean."

You did not *just say that.*

But one dark eyebrow lifted, and she knew she had. If he laughed at her, at the very idea or the unintentional double entendre, she would be more embarrassed than she had been in her adult life.

And if he didn't, she would be one step closer to deep, deep trouble with this man.

Chapter 17

Katie gave herself an inner shake and put on her most professional, library sound-level voice. "What can I help you with? Not looking for a book, are you?"

Gavin's dark eyebrow arched up again. "What would you recommend if I was?"

"Depends. What was the last book you read?"

"The *U.S. Patent Prosecutor's Desk Reference*."

She blinked. "Wow. Case-related, or was that for fun?"

"Not much fun in it. But some of it is more interesting than you might think."

She looked thoughtful for a moment. "The case histories, and SCOTUS decisions?" He seemed surprised at her words. Or perhaps her familiarity. Her mouth quirked. "You're the most famous, and probably the best, but you're not the only lawyer in town."

He chose to answer her original question, ignoring the rest. "It was research. We were helping a kid who had his invention stolen. No one would take him seriously because he was only fifteen."

"Good for you," she said, meaning it.

He shrugged. "Foxworth" was all he said, as if that answered it completely. As, perhaps, it did.

"I assume you didn't really come here for a book recommendation," she said.

"No. I needed to ask you about something."

"All right." She gestured past the information desk. "Let's go to my office." When the door had closed behind them, she turned to face him. He was looking around the room.

It wasn't huge, although it was bigger than her old office. There was plenty of room for her desk and the credenza behind it, a couple of chairs for visitors, and—of course—the big bookshelf on the opposite wall. It held all her very favorite books in different genres, so that she could hand one to someone and have them read the beginning to see if they'd like it. Then she could get them either a print or ebook copy to check out. The rest of the wall space held framed book covers, of everything from Mark Twain classics to the world-famous wizard series, all stories she'd read repeatedly and loved.

She watched him, guessed there wasn't much he missed in his perusal. Now that they were in the semi-sound-proofed environs of her office, she spoke in a normal voice. "What did you want to ask?"

He took her cue and spoke normally now. It wasn't much of a relief, Katie noticed with an inward grimace. "I need contact information for Laurel's family."

"Of course. They're in Arizona now," she said, reaching for her phone on the desk, and brought up the info. Then she looked at him. "Is it all right if I call them to say you'll be in touch?"

"You've talked to them recently?"

"Last week." She didn't mention that the call to Laurel's mother had ended with them both weeping inconsolably. "They're still pretty broken up."

He studied her for a moment before saying softly, "And so are you."

"Yes." She didn't bother to deny the obvious. She would never deny how much she loved and missed her friend. "Laurel was the closest thing I ever had to a sister. I will never get over losing her. It would belittle our relationship if I did."

"Then you knew about her arrest record."

The unexpectedness of the words, which she was sure was planned, put her on edge, as did his tone. Something in his voice reminded her of how he'd sounded about her father having been a locksmith two decades ago.

"Of course I knew."

"Why didn't you mention it?"

"I'd completely forgotten. And," she said before he could speak, her voice rising a notch, "if you're thinking about saying something about me forgetting something important again, like it's a pattern, don't."

He said nothing, just looked at her the way she imagined he stared down a hostile witness in a courtroom. Or an opposing attorney. So what chance did she have to withstand him?

She was sliding beyond edgy into angry. "I probably wouldn't have mentioned it even if I had remembered."

"Because?"

She ticked reasons off on her fingers. She needed both hands. "It was twelve years ago. She was eighteen. In fact it was her eighteenth birthday, and her first time to drink alcohol. First and only time she ever broke a law. She didn't have another drink until she was twenty-one, and never more than two. She didn't have an accident. No one was hurt. She never got in trouble again. She was the textbook case of being scared straight."

Again he said nothing, didn't even acknowledge her list. He just looked at her in that same unsettling way, as if she were that witness on the stand, and that irked her even more.

"But mostly," she added, her voice tight now, "I wouldn't think to mention it because I don't think that way. I don't waste my time dwelling on old, meaningless mistakes. She's my—she was—my best friend."

"Even friends can betray you," he said, and she had the oddest feeling that mind of his had gone somewhere else for a moment. Something about the suddenly distant look in those smoky eyes. But the words themselves sent her mind racing down an ugly path, as if he were accusing Laurel of something. And that, when she wasn't here to defend herself, made Katie snap.

"If all you do is look for lies, I'm not surprised you find them. Or what you think are lies, but are in truth honest mistakes or omissions. What an awful way to live."

For a moment his eyes closed. "Yes." His eyes opened again, and she knew she wasn't wrong about the pain there. As he went on, his voice was whispery, ragged. "It is."

Her anger evaporated as she stared at him. It was replaced by an aching empathy, because in that moment he reminded her of some trapped creature, helpless. She didn't know what to say. Instinctively she knew this was a side of him he rarely let show. It would never do for the stellar defense attorney to show such weakness.

Unless it was intentional, to lure someone in, so he could get what he wanted.

And now he's got you thinking like that, suspecting ulterior motives in everything.

She heard the sound of rain hitting the window to her right. The promised storm had arrived. And just in time, she thought. Gavin must have heard it, too, because he turned toward the window. And the pain she'd seen vanished, disappearing behind what had to be a formidable wall.

"Cutter," he said suddenly, rising.

"What about him?" she asked, also getting up.

"He's outside."

She blinked. "You mean outside here?"

He was already headed for the door. Katie followed, pausing only to grab one of the towels she kept in the cupboard behind the information desk, in case of spills or damp kids dripping water on the floor.

"Why is he with you?" she asked as they walked past the nonfiction section toward the door.

"He seems to have...attached himself to me. I don't know why."

He seems to know, somehow, who needs him most...

Hayley's words, when she'd been speaking of the dog's visits to hospitals and nursing homes and a children's shelter, came back to her now. Ordinarily she'd laugh at the idea of a man like this needing the help of a therapy dog.

But she'd seen him just now, seen that look in his eyes. Maybe that was what the dog sensed, whatever had caused that pain.

Cutter was tucked up neatly near the front door, patiently waiting in the shelter of the eave, and wasn't wet yet. He jumped to his feet to greet her effusively, making her smile.

"Did you move back there because you knew it was going to rain?" she said to the dog as she bent to stroke his head. Cutter nuzzled her hand, his tongue swiping over her fingers in a doggy kiss.

"Wouldn't surprise me," Gavin muttered. He looked at his car, as if measuring the distance to it in the downpour.

Katie straightened, looked at the steady rain hitting the walkway inches away. She held out the towel, but Gavin shook his head.

"You'll both be wet by the time you get to your car," she pointed out.

"We'll dry."

"You might not like how he dries himself," she said, picturing a hearty shake with water spewing everywhere once the dog was in the car. "You can bring it back later. Or I'll pick it up from Hayley."

There was a second's hesitation, but then he reached out and took the towel. Then he said, "I'm not staying there."

"Oh? Who got tired of whom so fast?" she asked, teasingly.

"Nobody." Then, with a wry smile, he added, "But they would have. I'm…kind of a pain when I'm on something."

"I hadn't noticed. Tell me," she asked conversationally, "does that brain of yours ever shut down, or even slow down?"

He grimaced. "Not really."

"How do you sleep?"

"Not well."

"I'm not surprised."

A man with two young children approached the library.

"Hi, Miss Moore!" one of the kids called out, and she recognized him as the boy she'd steered onto a series of adventure stories about a boy around his age. He'd loved them, which to her was her job well-done. The town was too small to have a dedicated children's librarian, so she worked to keep her hand in there with current stories along with the classics.

"The new one's here," she said to him, and he lit up. "I set it aside for you."

The trio went inside. Katie hung back for a moment, giving Cutter a final pat.

"Nice," Gavin said. In an entirely different tone than he'd said it earlier.

"It's my job, and I love it."

"It shows." He gestured with the towel before tucking it inside his jacket; the rain was getting heavier now, and they were getting splashed with the bounce. "I'll likely be grateful for this. I'll get it back to you."

"When you can," she said, and watched the man and dog bolt for the parking lot through the downpour. Water was flowing over the concrete walkway in sheets now, headed for the drain just outside the doors.

And speaking of drains, she thought as she turned to go back inside, just being around that man was draining.

But he'd be gone soon, hopefully after helping to re-move that cloud of suspicion from over her father's head.

She wasn't sure if she'd be relieved, or sad.

Chapter 18

Gavin fingered the damp towel as he sat and watched the man inside the business. He'd parked far enough back to be inconspicuous, and used the small pair of folding binoculars he'd brought from Foxworth. He'd wanted to see him in this environment, watch him interact without being aware of observation, which in itself tended to change people's actions.

He'd already noticed several things. One, Steven Moore had a comfortable smile and manner that appeared to put people at ease. Many of his customers—and there were several this Monday morning—smiled and greeted him like a friend. And those who came in looking around, obviously unfamiliar with the place, he called out to but didn't swoop down on, letting them look at their leisure.

He wondered if any of them had heard that he was a murder suspect. Perhaps they had, and didn't believe it. Or maybe they thought it was a different Steven Moore; it was hardly an unusual name.

Gavin especially paid attention when there were no customers inside, but Moore seemed to busy himself, sorting mail and checking the various machines. When he disappeared into the back, he always emerged with something, be it copy paper or a stack of mail. A few times he answered a phone on the counter, beside a large scale for weighing packages, and smiled then as if the person speaking was in the room with him.

All in all, it was a fairly busy place on this Monday. If being a murder suspect was weighing on him, it didn't show.

For a while Gavin sat chewing on that largest piece of the puzzle—motive. Hopefully he would get an idea at his meeting with the detective this afternoon. They must have something. Or maybe it really was just a Sherlock sort of stab, that they'd eliminated everything else as impossible and so were left with Moore.

At a little before one, Moore walked to the front and reached for the open sign on the door. Gavin guessed it was one with a clock on the other side that would show a "back at" time, and that he was going to set it for a lunch break.

He had time, he calculated quickly. His appointment with the detective wasn't until two, and his GPS had said it would be a half-hour drive at most. He slid out of the car, tossed a "Wait here" back at Cutter, who this time seemed content to stay in the car. He reached the door just as Moore was ready to drop the sign back down with the indication he'd be open again at one thirty. Moore pulled the door open despite the sign and, Gavin noted, before he even looked at him.

"Come on in, we'll get you handled—" He'd looked at him now, recognized him. "Mr. de Marco."

Gavin nodded toward the sign. "Short lunch break."

"I'm eating here. Katie made me lunch for today. I usually just go next door."

Gavin had noticed the pizza place earlier.

Moore backed up and held the door open. There was a tiny bit of tightness in his smile, but Gavin had expected at least that; no one liked getting grilled, even if innocent. Or maybe he didn't like the lunchtime interruption.

"I'll leave the sign down, shall I?" Moore said as Gavin stepped inside.

"Nice place." He didn't comment on the subtle question of how long this would take, but noted the man had the presence of mind to not ask outright.

"I like it."

"Profitable?"

"Some months better than others. I'm not getting rich, but I don't hate coming to work every day, and that's worth a lot."

He could not, Gavin thought, agree more. Foxworth had given him that, and he valued it above any amount of fame or fortune.

"Your daughter told me about it. That you're very kind to people, carrying them sometimes, and making personal deliveries if there are special circumstances."

The man shrugged, but looked pleased. "I just try to be a good guy," he said. Then, meeting Gavin's gaze steadily, he added, "And of course, Katie wants to paint me in the best light, given why you're here."

Gavin smiled. He liked the guy. And that made things a bit difficult, because even though he wanted to take him at face value, his job here was to find the truth. And the truth might not be on the surface. When he got involved, it rarely was.

"Go ahead and have your lunch," he said. "You can eat while we talk."

He wanted the man at ease. And it was only a slight, passing thought to wonder what kind of lunch Katie had fixed for her father.

They went into the back room that took up the entire width of the shop. Full of metal shelving, boxes and stock items and bins that Gavin guessed were for mail on three walls, and the back door. Along the side wall was a tiny kitchenette, and in the center of the room was a large, high table with stools.

Moore went to the fridge and got out a reusable type of grocery bag.

"Are you hungry?" he asked as he took out several plastic storage containers and a round, foil-wrapped bundle about three inches high. "There's way too much, as always. One of Katie's lunches usually lasts me two days."

"No, thank you." So Moore had self-control, Gavin thought. He wasn't one to eat just because it was there. It wasn't always a sign of control in other areas, but he noted it just the same. You never knew in the beginning what might be useful by the end.

He waited until the man had taken a bite of a meat loaf sandwich that had been in the foil.

"She makes a mean sandwich," Moore said, wiping a trace of grainy mustard from the corner of his mouth with the napkin from the bag.

"Have the police told you what they think your motive for killing Laurel is?"

The man reacted visibly to the abrupt question, his mouth and the muscles around his eyes tightening. He set the sandwich down. "No. Because there isn't one. There's nothing on this earth that could have made me hurt that girl, let alone do…what was done to her."

He wondered if the police had identified a motive after

all, and maybe they just weren't tipping their hand yet. He took a stab at some possibilities.

"She didn't make you angry? Or jealous of the time Katie spent with her?"

The incredulous look Moore gave him seemed genuine. "The only thing in my life I've been that angry about is that Katie's mother didn't get to live to see the amazing woman she's become."

"And Laurel? What did you think of her?"

No tightening of his mouth this time. But something flickered in those eyes so like Katie's. Pain? Regret? Or was it simply a tell, that he was about to lie?

"I think that losing her hurt my girl more than anything has since her mother died. And anyone who thinks I would do that to her is vastly, vastly mistaken."

Gavin let the answer hang in the air before saying, "That's not what I asked."

Moore grimaced then. He lowered his gaze to the sandwich with one bite missing. He swallowed as if he'd taken a second bite before speaking.

"Laurel was sweet, kind and incredibly generous. I was glad she was Katie's best friend. She chose well."

He meant it, Gavin thought. But he didn't—or couldn't—look at him when he said it.

A few minutes later he left the man to his food and returned to his car, knowing he needed to leave to make his meeting with the police detective. Cutter's greeting was somewhat restrained, as if he sensed Gavin's mood. It seemed likely, given what else the dog had done so far.

For a moment he sat, pondering what he'd learned. By all appearances Steven Moore was what his daughter thought he was. Kind, gentlemanly, hardworking, all of it. And he loved his daughter deeply; it fairly echoed in his voice every time he spoke of her. Gavin couldn't quite make himself believe, at least not without a lot more evidence, that a man capable of such a brutal murder could have raised a daughter like his.

But he'd lied.

Moore had meant what he'd said, but he was hiding something. Something about Laurel. Not necessarily in so many words, but as he'd told Katie, lies of omission were still lies.

If all you do is look for lies, I'm not surprised you find them.

Oh, she had some fire, did Katie Moore. He'd already been singed by it. In more ways than one.

Was that it? Was his unexpected and unwanted attraction to her clouding his judgment? Was the fact that he was reacting to her as he hadn't reacted to a woman in a very long time messing with his perception, stifling his instincts about people who lied to him, because he wanted to believe for her sake?

He wanted to dismiss the idea as ridiculous, as it always would have been. Gavin de Marco never let the personal interfere with a case.

But he'd also never met a woman quite like Katie Moore, either.

Chapter 19

"So who *was* that this morning?"

Katie turned to see Heather Burns, the assistant library branch manager and bookkeeper, looking at her with both eyebrows raised. Gavin hadn't said anything about keeping his presence and involvement a secret. Not, she thought wryly, that that would be possible. He was bound to be recognized. And he certainly was the kind of man people noticed.

"He's an attorney," she said. "He's helping with the murder case."

She was almost proud of how even her voice was; she'd gotten to where she could say the words without her throat tightening or her eyes pooling with tears. But it was an effort, a battle every single time, and she wondered if that would ever change.

"I heard about them suspecting your dad," Heather said, making Katie's chest tighten. "That's silly."

"Yes," she said. What else was there to say?

"I was kind of hoping he was somebody you'd met. You know. You need somebody in your life."

Katie managed a credible scoff. "Does he look like my type?"

"Honey," Heather said in a tone that matched her arched eyebrow, "*that* was any woman's type. Makes you think of long, slow nights and lingering looks over morning coffee."

Katie felt the heat rising to her cheeks at the images that tumbled through her head. "He is way out of my league."

"Uh-huh. I saw the way he was looking at your cute butt on that ladder. That was not an uninterested man."

"Heather!"

"And speaking of cute butts," Heather began, undaunted. "His is—"

"Let's not," Katie said. "I need to order cupcakes for tomorrow night."

She headed for her office to do just that, but nothing could keep her from hearing Heather's laughing voice. "You not talking about it doesn't change it!"

She closed the door behind her and only realized when she got to her desk and sat down that she was actually trembling slightly. She shouldn't have skipped lunch today; she was just wobbly, that's all.

But that didn't explain the images racing through her mind.

Makes you think of long, slow nights and lingering looks over morning coffee.

Oh, yes. And cute butts.

"He's only here for the case. Then he'll leave, go back home."

She said it aloud, with more fervor than she was feeling. She didn't stop to assess whether she'd convinced herself. Instead, she picked up her phone and pulled up the number for the local bakery. She'd spoken to them before, so now it was only a matter of confirming the numbers. Ordering three dozen cupcakes got her mind back to business, where it belonged.

Detective Greg Davidson was an old hand. Gavin had suspected that from the moment the man had suggested they meet at one of the more expensive coffee outlets in his town. After all, he was doing Gavin a favor by meeting with him, so obviously Gavin could pick up the tab. Sitting across the small, round table from him now, Gavin sensed he was more than an old hand, he was good. He looked to be midforties, had a lean, wiry build, and a manner that put Gavin in mind of a hunting dog, never to be diverted once he was on the track.

"So," the man said, leaning back in the chair and looking at Gavin assessingly, "it really is you. The famous Gavin de Marco."

"Guilty," Gavin said with a shrug.

"Nothing less would get me to meet with a prime suspect's defense attorney."

Gavin shook his head. "I'm not. I work for Foxworth, who was approached by his daughter."

"Heard good things about them."

"All true. And then some."

"You're making my life harder just by being connected to this," Davidson said. "Your reputation is making everybody second-guess every step we take. Dunbar's rock solid, or I wouldn't even be here."

Gavin knew the sheriff investigator's stellar reputation was well earned, after working with him on the governor's mess. "He is."

"If you're not Moore's lawyer, what are you doing here?"

"What Foxworth does. Looking for the truth."

Davidson studied him for a long moment over the rim of his cup of double espresso, which the barista had turned to get the moment she saw him; obviously the man frequented the place. The potent brew was the fuel of many cops, he thought, to cope with long hours, ugly memories and the high risk of carrying the badge.

"Funny," Davidson said, "I didn't think defense attorneys cared all that much for truth, only getting their guy off."

"Some don't," Gavin agreed, his tone neutral. *One reason why I quit.*

"Well, you've sure got things hopping," Davidson said, and he didn't sound happy about it. "We're averaging a couple dozen media calls a day since it leaked you were involved."

"Not my intent." He looked at the detective, whose weary eyes looked like he could use every bit of the caffeine in that espresso. "And probably the less time we're seen together, the easier it will be on you."

"Thought about that. About suggesting we meet somewhere more…discreet."

Gavin glanced pointedly around at the very public, busy place in which they were sitting. He'd been aware since shortly after he'd walked in that the buzz of conversation in the room had picked up, and soon after that a few phones had appeared, no doubt with cameras activated.

Davidson grinned suddenly. "Why have a meeting with the famous Gavin de Marco and not get the perks?" Then he turned serious. "What is it you want?"

"Knowing you can't discuss details of an open investigation, just some answers. Starting with these. Is there a reason, beyond the fact that there's no one else, that made you settle on Moore? And what's the theory on his motive?"

Gavin watched the detective consider his words. Carefully, likely deciding what he could and couldn't say, and filtering what he wanted to say to a man on the other side.

"What," Davidson asked after a moment, "are the odds you're going to end up representing Moore down the road?"

"Zero," Gavin said flatly.

Davidson drew back slightly. "That was pretty definite. Don't like the guy?"

Gavin wasn't out of practice enough to miss the sudden interest. "In fact, I do. But it has nothing to do with him. The only way I'll be in a criminal court again is as an observer or a witness."

"I wouldn't like it much if you ended up testifying to what I tell you," Davidson said. "Assuming I do tell you anything."

Gavin understood that. "How about I provide the information, and you just say yes or no. That way you haven't told me anything."

"Spoken like a true lawyer," Davidson said with a wry smile. "Go ahead. But I reserve the right not to answer."

"A given," Gavin agreed. "First, are you working on the assumption that the victim's one brush with the law when she was eighteen has no connection?"

"Yes."

He had to take a moment to fight back the image of Katie's face when she'd lit into him about that subject before he moved to his next question.

"The boyfriend's alibi is truly solid?"

Davidson apparently felt confident enough to go beyond yes or no on this. "As solid as multiple witnesses can make it. They all saw him at a party, a good ten miles away from the scene, and the host swore his car never moved. It was blocked in by a couple of others."

Gavin nodded before proceeding. While he knew better than most the unreliability of the fabled "eyewitness," this seemed fairly straightforward. "Do you have anything on Moore beyond his regular and frequent contacts with the victim for several weeks before her death, and that his alibi is unprovable?"

"Yes."

Gavin knew there was no point in asking what; Davidson wouldn't tell him, nor should he.

"Anything that's not circumstantial?"

Davidson studied him for a moment before saying, "Not answering that."

Which was, Gavin thought, an answer in itself.

Davidson was getting restless. Gavin could see it in his tapping of his finger on the rim of his cup, and the way he slid the insulating ring up and down repeatedly.

"Do you have a motive?"

There was a moment's hesitation before Davidson said, "Yes," but it was enough to tell Gavin what they had was questionable. At least in Davidson's mind.

"Do you believe it?"

Davidson gave him a sideways look. "Not answering that."

Also telling.

"So how about a little quid pro quo, de Marco?" the detective asked. "What do you think? You're famous for your instincts. What are they telling you about Moore?"

Now he was the one in the tough spot. Were he representing Moore, he would have answered one way. But he was not. But in this case, the truth would do nicely.

"I'm not sure yet. But something."

And that, he supposed, was as much an answer to the obviously sharp detective as the man's responses had been to him. He sensed Davidson was on the verge of calling a halt to this meeting, and he had one more question to ask. And it had nothing to do with Steven Moore's guilt or innocence.

"How certain are you that Laurel Brisbane was the intended victim?"

Davidson studied him for a moment before asking, "Wondering if your...client, the daughter, might have been the target?"

"It occurred to me," Gavin said, his voice even, despite the roiling in his gut at the idea, which should have been another kind of warning in itself.

"We considered it, since it was her apartment. The multiple stab wounds could have been frustration at not being able to get to his real target."

Gavin had read Ty's thorough research, and with Dunbar's help the public copy of the reports, but the cold recounting still made him wince inwardly. In his previous life he'd learned to dissociate himself enough to avoid that reaction, but since coming to Foxworth he'd lost both the need and the knack.

"But you decided not to pursue it," he said.

"We dropped it," Davidson said. "Because there were indications in the locations of the wounds that it was personal. Angry. Enough to strongly suggest the killer knew the victim, or at least his target. And Ms. Moore had a routine. She worked every day, the same hours, including those study nights. There was no reason for anyone who knew her to assume she would be home at that time on a Thursday because she never was."

Gavin nodded. It made sense. So why wouldn't that knot in his gut loosen up?

"And that also," Davidson added, "points more toward Moore. He knew his daughter wouldn't be there."

"But it still doesn't tell you why."

"Right now I'm more worried about who," Davidson said, and stood up. "Thanks for the coffee."

They'd reached the end of the interview, Gavin thought. He got up more slowly, accepting that he would gain nothing by trying to extend this except to put the detective in a more uncomfortable position, and he didn't want to do that. There had been a time when he wouldn't have hesitated to hold the detective's feet to the fire, but that had been when he was a practicing attorney representing a client and had standing in a case.

His outlook had been different then.

"My pleasure," he answered. Davidson looked a little surprised, and Gavin supposed that he'd given in easily. "I'm not the enemy anymore, Detective. Unless you're hiding the truth."

Davidson's mouth twisted upward. "Can't hide what you don't know."

The man tilted his cup in a mock salute, then left the shop. Gavin sat back down, taking a minute to process what he'd learned. Which was more than he'd expected. Most important, that while the police were focused on Moore because they had little else, the lead detective wasn't convinced.

So at least he could tell Katie her father wasn't, at the moment, being railroaded.

He tossed his empty cup in the bin and walked back out to the car, telling himself he wasn't feeling that kick of anticipation at that thought of talking to her again. A text would do, he told himself firmly.

When Cutter greeted him with a soft woof, he had the crazy thought that had it been allowed, he would have liked to take the dog in with him, and get his assessment of Detective Davidson.

He nearly laughed aloud at himself. Gavin de Marco consulting his partner, who happened to be a dog. Now that would be a headline, most likely coupled with speculation that he'd gone completely off the rails.

At the moment, he wasn't certain they wouldn't be right.

Chapter 20

"Well, at least it's not midnight yet," Katie muttered to herself as she got in her car to leave the library. She couldn't blame the late hour entirely on finishing the Halloween decorations in the meeting room, after the library had closed.

No, a good half of that time she could blame entirely on Gavin de Marco. Well, and her own need to know. She'd set up an internet alert on him after he'd left this morning, setting the date parameter at when he'd arrived here to weed out the countless references and stories from his headline career. It had surprised her to see how much had popped up. Even now, Gavin de Marco being in town was apparently a big deal.

That he was looking into a local murder case was a huge deal.

Quinn and Hayley hadn't understood what would happen, that his presence here would somehow leak and that when it did the speculation would run wild. But Katie hadn't expected it to happen this fast. He'd only arrived Saturday evening, and now, by Monday night, news sites and blogs were abuzz with possibilities. Not to mention the photos that had turned up on social media, of him sitting in a coffee place, across from Detective Davidson, a man she remembered all too well from the ugly chaos of that night and the days after.

Her heart had jumped in her chest when she'd come across the first report, suggesting this meant a turn in the case, that if de Marco was here on the side of Steven Moore perhaps the police were on the wrong track. Exactly what she had dared to hope for.

We go after the truth, and there's always a chance you won't like it.

Quinn's words, which she knew had been a warning, ran through her mind. It didn't matter, she thought, because she already knew the truth. There was no conceivable way that her father could have had anything to do with Laurel's murder. Her heart was still buoyed because Gavin's presence had already accomplished her main goal—to get the police to question their assumptions and look in more than her father's direction.

The traffic signal up ahead—one of only three in town—turned red and she began to slow the car. She realized with a little jolt where she was; she'd been so lost in thought that she'd apparently been driving on autopilot.

But some part of her had already decided something, because without even thinking about it she found herself sliding into the left turn lane. The turn that would take her right by the Foxworth building.

He'd told her he was staying there, and though she didn't understand why he would forego the chance to stay with the Foxworths, given they were obviously friends, she took him at his word that it would be easier on everyone.

Does that brain of yours ever shut down, or even slow down?
Not really.
How do you sleep?
Not well.

He might be up now. It couldn't hurt to just drive by, could it? He'd texted her, rather tersely, about his meeting with the detective, saying only, He's not locked in. It was good news, but her worried mind needed more than just that.

She couldn't see the building from the road so she turned onto the gravel drive. The crunch of her tires seemed way too loud and she cringed a bit; if he was asleep, this would likely wake him up. She thought about turning back, but there was no room on the narrow, tree-hemmed drive. Then she saw the building. And a light glowing through the glass in the front door.

The front door swung open before she'd even come to a halt in the parking area adjacent to the building. At first glance she thought no one had come out, but then movement caught her gaze and she saw Cutter racing toward her. He could, she remembered now, open the door himself. She hoped he recognized her and wasn't coming at her in full guard dog mode. She was feeling a bit easier about stopping by at this late hour if the Foxworths were here. Hayley, she was sure, would understand her need to know the details of what had happened in Gavin's meeting with the police.

Cutter had reached her, and she judged it safe by his body language, a dancing sort of step with his front paws, accompanied by an almost musical whine that sounded like he was happy to see her. She opened the door, glad the rain had at least paused, although the respite was likely only temporary. She bent to greet the animal, marveling at the way her anxiety seemed to ease as she stroked the soft fur.

"You're so good at this," she crooned to the dog, who lifted his head and gave her a doggy kiss on the cheek. She laughed, and when she heard footsteps approaching she was able to straighten and smile at Gavin as he came to a halt next to her open car door. He was looking her up and down almost apprehensively.

"Why are you here? Are you hurt?"

That was very specific. He wasn't just asking if she was all right. And there had been an edge in his voice. Her brow furrowed. "No. Why would I be?" He didn't answer. After a moment she felt compelled to explain her presence. "I was late leaving the library, then I was going by and took a chance you'd be awake. I would have kept going and not bothered you if there hadn't been a light on."

"I told you, I don't sleep much."

"I know. That's why—" She stopped, not liking this need to overexplain such a simple thing. Cutter nudged her hand, and she automatically moved to pet him again. "So the Foxworths are up late, too?" She gestured at the dog. "They're here, right?"

"Sorry. No."

She looked down at Cutter, then back at him. "Wait, when you said he'd attached himself to you, you meant he's staying with you? All the time?"

"So it appears." His mouth quirked, as if he were bemused. "Hayley seems to think he's here to remind me to do things like eat and sleep."

"So he's your...keeper?"

"Implying I need one?" he asked, lifting an eyebrow at her.

"I'm sure the Foxworths know better than me," she said, rather primly.

He almost smiled, so she knew he'd noticed the tone. But then, she didn't think there was much he didn't notice.

"You'd better go or come in," he said, and only then did she realize it had begun to rain again, softly. Which told her where she was on the noticing things scale, she thought wryly. What was it about this man that distracted her so? Besides that he was dynamic, charismatic and sometimes downright dramatic.

"I did want to ask about your meeting this afternoon," she said.

"Come in, then," he said.

It was raining harder by the time they got to the door, which Cutter had raced ahead to open again.

"He really is remarkably clever, isn't he?" she said as she stepped inside, into the warmth. She could see the fire was going, and the room was quite pleasant. She began to shrug off her jacket.

"I think the word you want might be *frighteningly*," he said, his tone dry.

"Or *extraordinarily*."

He helped her with a recalcitrant sleeve. "Or *uncannily*?"

"*Amazingly*."

"*Eerily?*"

She grinned as he took her jacket and hung it on a rack just inside the door. "Thank you. I'll grant you *astonishingly*."

"And I'll see you an *unsettling...ly*." She laughed, and he chuckled himself as he shook his head. "Never get in a word fight with a librarian."

"Especially an adverb fight."

"Agreed."

He led the way into the living area, where Cutter was already drying before the fire. On the rug were spread out papers of various sizes, both printed and handwritten, and a pad that held the same kind of yellow lined paper the hand-writing was on. A legal pad, of course, she thought. He'd clearly been sitting on the floor, because even the large coffee table didn't have enough space for all of it.

He said nothing about her looking at the papers, so clearly he didn't mind. She focused on the bold, sharp writing on those handwritten pages. She noticed the pen lying on the pad, a substantial, heavy-looking fountain pen. She'd always loved them herself, but had never quite mastered the knack of not ending up with ink-stained fingers. She bet no ink would dare misbehave with him.

He gestured for her to sit down. Cutter whined faintly, so she sat on the floor next to the dog, who gave her another swipe of his tongue in apparent approval. She dug her fingers into the thick fur of his ruff and scratched. The animal leaned into her hand, clearly enjoying it.

For a moment Gavin didn't move, and when she looked up at him he was staring at her rather oddly. But after a moment he sat next to the writing pad, where she assumed he'd been before.

"What did you want to know?" he asked without pre-amble.

Everything.

The word slammed through her brain, and she bit her lip to keep it from escaping, afraid of how it would sound. She seized on something else, the only other thing that came to mind.

"Why did you ask if I was hurt?"

He drew back slightly. "I'm not sure you want the an-swer to that."

"I told you, I want the truth."

His jaw tightened slightly, as if he weren't sure this was the right thing to do. But in the end, he answered her.

"The killer is still out there. Until we know why Laurel was murdered, we don't know that you're not in danger, too."

He was right. She didn't like it.

Chapter 21

"Why would I be in danger? I know it was my place, but the police said Laurel's murder was personal—"

"I know what they said," Gavin answered. "I'm not saying you are, just that we don't know for sure you're not."

"But…after all this time?"

"You moved, almost immediately after."

"I had to. I couldn't live in that place anymore." She suppressed a shudder, fought the images that wanted to roll through her mind like some horror film trailer.

"Of course not."

She studied him for a moment, trying to gauge the level of—and the reason for—his concern. Some part of her wanted to think there was a very personal reason, but her common sense screamed otherwise. "You think he just hasn't found me yet?"

He gentled his tone; he clearly hadn't meant to upset her. "Katie, the police are probably right, but until they break the case, you can't be positive. I'm just saying be a little aware of that."

In other words, don't assume you're safe. Now that was unsettling. And it was an effort for her to steady herself.

"Was Detective Davidson chatty?" When he lifted an eyebrow at her she added, "Gavin de Marco having a cup of coffee with a local cop is worth several posts, with photos." He grimaced. She persevered. "Did you learn anything new?"

"Nothing he would say officially, no."

"And unofficially?"

He seemed to hesitate. "They have something. But Davidson's not completely convinced. Are you sure nobody else knew that Laurel had moved in with you?"

"No," she said, earning a look. "I mean, Ross knew, because she told him. And my dad knew, because I needed his key for her. And my landlords knew, because they needed to. They could have mentioned it to someone. All I know for sure is that I didn't go around telling anyone else."

"What about Laurel?"

"I can't be positive, of course, but I doubt it. She wasn't happy about the breakup, didn't want to talk about it, so I don't think she would have advertised that she'd moved out."

"But as you just pointed out, she wouldn't have had to advertise. One mention to an oversharer and it's all over the internet."

She couldn't argue that, not when his photograph—in which he had looked darkly handsome and very, very intense—had shown up while he was still sitting in the place with Detective Davidson.

She shifted her gaze back to the papers spread around the floor. The pages of bold handwriting drew her eye first, and she noticed the flair of the question marks after several entries, and the intensity of the underlining in other places. She wondered what a graphologist would make of it, and guessed it would be what hundreds of articles had already said: Gavin de Marco was exactly like his writing—bold, confident and intense.

She scanned the other papers, copies of reports, lists, some other kind of official file that looked like a short list of offenses, a map printout, a stack of photos with Ross Carr's image on top, a copy of the picture that Laurel had always had in a frame on her nightstand. She had taken it, Katie knew, and Ross had been smiling widely at her.

Instinctively she reached for it, wondering how a man could smile at a woman like that and then cheat on her.

Gavin grabbed her wrist, stopping her. She was startled by the act, but more startled at how her pulse leaped under his touch, so fiercely that if his fingers had been another inch closer to her wrist she didn't think he could have helped but feel it. Her gaze shot to his face.

"Don't," he said. "There are photos in that stack you don't need to see."

She frowned. Then, belatedly, she realized what he meant.

"Crime scene photos," she whispered. He nodded, and a different kind of shudder went through her.

"You saw the reality," he said, his voice so gentle it made her throat tight. "It's hard enough to get that out of your mind without reliving it in pictures."

"It's impossible," she whispered.

"I know."

Something about the softness of his tone, the sense that he really did know, blasted away her last barrier. If he'd been brisk, businesslike as he had been before, she could have withstood it, but this gentle understanding was too much. She shuddered again, tried to pull back. But then he was pulling her toward him, and she could not find the strength—or desire—to resist.

She was leaning against him, his arms coming around her to hold her against his chest, when the storm broke. She couldn't hold it back, not even with thoughts of how much she didn't want to do this in front of him, let alone in his arms. It had been a while since she'd had a meltdown, and she'd dared to hope she was over the worst of it. But this was as powerful, as overwhelming, as soul-killing as that first day of realization, and she wondered at that even as it reduced her to a sobbing mass of pain.

"I miss her so much," she gulped out.

"I know." He hugged her tighter.

For a long time he just held her, and his warmth, his steadiness, his strength helped her recover more easily than she'd expected. Her eyes burning, her cheeks wet with tears, she drew in a deep breath, enough to say, "I thought I was past this."

"Grief isn't linear, Katie. It's more like a cloverleaf you can get stuck on, going in circles and then back the way you came, and then around all over again."

She turned the analogy over in her mind, and it made perfect sense to her. That was exactly how she felt. She didn't question how he knew, but asked, "Does it ever end?"

He went still. She looked up at him, not even caring what her tearstained face must look like; this was too important. He closed his eyes for a moment, then opened them and met her gaze.

"No," he said simply.

She'd known that, deep down. She acknowledged his honesty, even when it would have been easier to lie, to give her some banal reassurance that of course she'd get over it, that this horrid pain would someday end.

"There will always be more of those cloverleafs," he

said, still holding her close, "and they'll be just as intense, but they'll be smaller, easier to get out of and come less often."

It rang true to her, just as the rest had. "You're very wise, Mr. de Marco."

He let out a breath, his mouth quirking upward at one corner. "I've just been taught well."

For the first time she thought, really thought about what he must have seen and heard in that stellar career. "You've seen the ugliest things, haven't you?"

"I've seen people at their worst, and best. Not enough of the latter to erase the former, unfortunately."

"Is that why you quit?"

"Partly."

"And the rest?"

"Is for another day," he said. "Are you all right?"

She realized abruptly that she was clinging to him, and draped over him in a rather suggestive manner. And that he probably wanted her off of him, but was too well mannered to say so to a clearly distraught woman. Still, it was a struggle to sit up, to pull away from the comforting heat and strength. She spent a moment wiping her cheeks and trying not to think what her mascara must look like, and not really caring anyway. Not now.

"I suppose you've been confronted with more than one weeping woman in your work," she finally said, pleased her voice sounded almost normal.

"A few."

"Practice makes perfect, even in offering comfort, I guess," she said, lowering her eyes and wincing inwardly at the inanity of it.

"I wouldn't know. I've never offered it before. I left that to my assistants."

Her gaze shot back to his face. He looked slightly bemused. It was that expression that made her ask, "Why now?"

Bemusement vanished. His gaze locked on her. "I think," he said slowly, "the question is, why you?"

She couldn't look away. She wanted to, the full intensity of his gaze, of those smoky eyes, was too much. Moments ago she'd been gulping in air as she sobbed; now she could barely take a breath.

It was he who broke the contact that was almost physical. And it was a good thing, because she doubted she could have looked away. It wasn't that she'd felt trapped or pinned, just that her brain had locked on to the crazy idea that if she looked away from him even those shallow breaths would stop.

Cutter made a low, soft sound. Glad of the distraction, she reached to pet him. The action allowed her to regain a little control, and as always, stroking the dog calmed her. Odd knack he had.

And apparently Gavin had it, too, even if he hadn't used it before.

So why now, or as he'd asked, why her?

Maybe it was the setting. It was personal, here on the floor before a fire, in a place that was more like a home than an office. Or maybe it was simply Foxworth, and their philosophy, that had changed him. Maybe they had a "comfort where needed" clause or something. That would fit. It was Foxworth, and he was doing what he was supposed to do.

And she'd be a fool, worse than a fool, to read anything more into it than that.

Chapter 22

Gavin stood beside the fire, staring into the flames. Then he moved his head to glare down at Cutter. "So what's with you, dog? Isn't the comforting and soothing thing your shtick?"

The animal, who had been watching as Katie retreated to the bathroom—no doubt to be embarrassed to see her mascara had succumbed to the torrent of tears—lifted his head to give Gavin a look he could only describe as smug. To make it worse, the dog's shoulders twitched, almost like he was shrugging.

You didn't need me.

Gavin grimaced as the words formed in his mind, the verbal equivalent of what the dog's expression and action would mean in a human. He was beginning to understand why Quinn and Hayley and even Rafe had taken to anthropomorphizing this animal.

He supposed he was getting used to the presence of his

self-appointed shadow. He even found himself conversing with the dog as if it were a two-way conversation. And sometimes he would swear it was; Cutter was a very expressive animal. He wondered, as he tried to refocus on the job at hand, how many people had pets because they felt awkward talking to themselves.

Then he wondered if he was focusing so much on the dog to avoid thinking about the woman in the other room, and his own question.

Why her?

He'd meant what he'd said. In all the years he'd been a practicing attorney, he had been confronted more than once with a weeping female. More than one weeping male, too, for that matter. He had always left it to his assistants to deal with, to do whatever it took to get the person, be it client or witness, back in hand so he could proceed with the job. It had been necessary then. If he'd gotten too emotionally invested in a case, it might affect his judgment, cloud his thinking when it was crucial that it be clear and sharp.

But Foxworth existed for entirely different reasons, and his function with them was entirely different, as well. But until now, it hadn't run to this.

He supposed it was in part because of the jolt of fear he'd felt when he'd first realized who his late night visitor was. He'd just been going over his conversation with Detective Davidson, and in fact had been somewhat stuck on that one part, about the possibility Laurel hadn't been the target at all.

Unlikely didn't mean impossible. He couldn't be one hundred percent certain that Katie hadn't been the target, or that she might not be now. What if this had been some vendetta against Laurel that could yet spread to Katie?

He'd seen too many crazy cases to pretend it didn't happen. He was mulling those over when Katie had unexpectedly arrived, so the first reason that shot into his mind for her to come here was that something had happened. And in that mindset his imagination had made the leap to her being hurt.

Cutter's head came up, and a moment later the bathroom door opened and Katie came out. She'd cleaned up the streaks of mascara, and looked fairly composed as she came back.

"Sorry for the meltdown," she said calmly.

"Don't apologize for caring. She was your friend."

"I wasn't," Katie said. "Just sorry you had to deal with it." She looked at him steadily. "But thank you for doing so."

Gavin almost brushed it off with something light. *Just part of the Foxworth service.* But looking at her, at those blue eyes of hers, slightly reddened from tears, he couldn't bring himself to do it.

In the end, all he said was, "You're welcome." Because *my pleasure* would send him down a mental path he didn't dare to tread just now. This woman did crazy things to him, and he didn't know what to do about it. And Gavin de Marco didn't like not knowing what to do.

She sat in her old spot, gave Cutter a quick pat and turned her attention back to the papers. He'd thought she might leave after that emotional episode, but she again proved herself tougher than that. Katie Moore would do what had to be done, whatever it might be.

He sat back down himself, and they went over the rest of his discussion with Davidson. She seemed worried that the detective had said they did have a motive, but heartened by his assessment that he wasn't completely sold on her father's guilt.

"I think he's a good cop," Gavin said. "He's not convinced yet, so he'll keep going after the truth."

"Good," she said. "If he does that, then he'll see my father is innocent."

He wanted to warn her not to be so certain, but given she'd already been through enough distress tonight, he held it back. Besides, that outlook was his, not hers. It wasn't her fault that he could count on two hands the number of people he totally trusted.

He settled for saying, "It's going to take more than his uncertainty to get him completely off your father."

She nodded. "I know. And I don't just want the police not suspecting him any longer. I want him proven innocent."

He knew she passionately believed finding the truth would do that, and he hoped, so fervently it surprised him, that she was right.

He also knew he'd better keep his mind on the task at hand, because after holding her in his arms, the thought that she was passionate about anything stirred feelings he didn't want to deal with right now.

Or maybe ever.

She was looking at the page he'd labeled "Possibilities," where he listed some of the most frequent reasons for murder under these circumstances. He watched as her eyes widened, and guessed she would never have thought some of them viable reasons to kill someone. Her gaze then skipped to the next page, which he'd labeled "Probabilities." Those he'd culled from the possibilities list as most likely to apply here.

Then she moved to the one labeled "Suspects," with a column for "Motive." Ross Carr was at the top, with the obvious motives listed, but next to that in caps he'd written "Solid alibi." Under that was "Other Acquaintances." As she scanned the names, her expressive face shifted from grimace to frown. She lingered the longest over the last name, her father's, next to which he'd written "Jealousy of time spent with K? Disapproval? She saw something? He saw something?" And next to that speculation, he'd written in caps, "Weak," for that's what he felt those motives were.

Underneath that was the most problematic of all, for there was nowhere to even begin: "Random."

When at last she looked back at his face, her expression troubled, he felt a pang of regret that he was going to have to make her go through it all again.

"What is it you're looking for, beyond the obvious?" she asked.

He shrugged. "Connections. Patterns. It helps me if I run the data through my brain first."

"By reading, distilling, then writing it," she said with a nod of understanding. "It's a different process than just reading it alone."

"Exactly." He wasn't surprised she understood. "I'll need to talk to you again, in detail, but it can wait until—"

"Now."

He stopped, studied her for a moment. "It's already late."

"I know you're probably still jet-lagged, and you've been working hard on this, so if you need to get some sleep I'll go. But if you're going to be awake anyway, let's get it over with."

"What about your sleep? Don't you have a big deal to prep for, tomorrow night?"

Her gaze flicked from him to Cutter, then back. "Appointing yourself my keeper?"

He couldn't stop his smile then. "Touché."

And so they began again. To her credit, she gave him no protest when he queried her on the smallest things, just marveled at the depth of Ty's work.

"I'd completely forgotten about that meter reader," she said, indicating the name of the man Laurel had filed a complaint with the city about when she caught him peering in her bedroom window at her as she dressed.

"He's unlikely. He apparently pulled that on several women, and they're all fine, plus it appears he's left the area."

"And the woman from that chain reaction traffic accident? That was years ago, and Laurel was just in the middle of the string of cars."

"But Laurel was the one who said she'd seen the woman at the stoplight moments before, on her phone."

"True," she admitted. "But a woman? Really?"

"'Deadlier than the male,' I believe is how the old phrase goes." He saw a slight shiver go through her and added, "I agree it's unlikely, but it's a base that needs to be covered."

She looked up from the page she was holding. "Is this how you did it? Before, I mean?"

"Same general approach, yes."

"Fascinating," she said, and from her expression as she looked back at the various stacks, he thought she meant it.

"Anything to add?" he asked when they'd finished discussing the list he'd made.

She looked doubtful but said, "Now that you have me thinking that way, there was a delivery driver that used to flirt with her all the time, asking her out, and she always said no. I always thought it was just sort of a game with them, but maybe he wasn't as accepting of her rejection as he seemed."

"Good," he said, adding to the list the name of the company she gave him. "Anyone else?"

Slowly, she shook her head. "I couldn't tell you the number of guys who asked me about her, if she was married or seeing anyone. And a couple of women who asked me if she was straight. No one stands out, though."

"Why did they all ask you?"

Katie shrugged. "I guess I was easier to approach. Laurel had that glam thing going on."

"And you?" he asked softly, even though it had nothing to do with the case.

"Me? I was just the sidekick. The bestie. Or in their case, information central."

She smiled, and it wasn't the least bit wry or rueful. She'd apparently been content to be just that for her flashier friend. He, on the other hand, had had enough flash and glamour—female and male—to last him a lifetime. And now he found it hard to even hold a conversation with one of those kinds of people if there were still waters like Katie Moore in the room.

He shook off the realization and pressed on, making her dig deep. It was an awful exercise, going through everyone you'd ever had contact with, searching for a possible murderer, but it had to be done and no one could have quite the perspective and range of knowledge as the victim's best friend. He knew that women shared things a guy would never even think to talk about, even to his best friend. He wanted it all, because you never knew which small piece might solve the puzzle.

A detailed picture began to emerge in his mind, of a vivacious, lively, and slightly "short of good judgment" woman, and the quieter, more solemn, levelheaded—and probably smarter—best friend.

Yes, these days it was the calm, the quiet—and the brain—that drew him.

Like Katie Moore did.

Damn. You're losing—

Her quiet gasp cut off his thoughts and he looked at her. Her eyes widened, and she was staring at him in shock. Had she remembered something, thought of someone, some possible suspect who could shift the whole case?

"You..." she began, then faltered.

"What?"

"Tell me you don't think I should be on that list? That I was jealous of her, tired of being her...what do they call it, her wingman?"

She was shivering again, her expression horrified. He reached out, grasped her shoulders.

"Katie, no. That never, ever occurred to me. You couldn't. You wouldn't."

He meant it, more than he'd meant anything in recent memory, except his gratitude for working at Foxworth. And that alone told him volumes.

She leaned into his arms again, and he felt the shivering ease, then stop. He was seized with the crazy urge to stay like this forever, make sure she was never hurt or scared or distressed again.

She looked up at him then, those wide, clear blue eyes still slightly reddened. He wanted her never to cry again, either. He could think of a lot worse things to spend his time on than seeing that never happened.

And then he did the only thing he could think of to do next.

He kissed her.

Chapter 23

For an instant, the barest split second, Katie thought she was imagining it. Her overactive subconscious had merely fed on emotions she'd been fighting and had somehow manufactured this moment.

But the feel of his mouth on hers was fiery, breath-stealing and very, very real.

Sensation rocketed through her in a way she'd never experienced. She had, on occasion, pondered the strange way that a pinch here could make you feel a twinge somewhere else. But she'd never understood how thoroughly some things were connected in the body. Never understood how a touch of lips could ignite fire in so many places at once.

Until now.

Hungry to understand more, she parted her lips, wanting to taste, to explore. And when suddenly the kiss was over, when the taste of him was suddenly out of reach, she felt bereft.

Through the echoing waves of surging heat she fought the urge to follow him in his retreat, to stay close. She wasn't even sure why she was resisting. She wanted more, didn't she?

A chill swept her as the obvious answer hit her.

She wanted more, but clearly he didn't.

The fog cleared, just in time for her to hear him speak.

"My apologies. That was…inappropriate."

Katie fought to find words. Thought of the papers that were now scattered around them. Lists. "I could give you a long list of things that kiss was. *Inappropriate* wouldn't be on it."

He stared at her as her mind raced. Did he want more of the luscious heat and sensation, after all? How could he not? Unless…it wasn't like that for him.

A new emotion began to well up inside her as she remembered exactly who she was looking at. Gavin freaking de Marco. Why would he be interested in a small-town girl with a quiet life and a quieter job?

It was much more likely that he'd tried to comfort, or distract, and she'd misread his intentions.

"Katie," he finally said, and the regret in his tone seemed to confirm her guess.

"Sorry," she said. "I think I misinterpreted that."

She saw something flash in those dark eyes, something bright and hungry. It was gone in an instant, but it had been there and real. And it blasted all her rationalizations to bits. She couldn't help the relief that flooded her; it hadn't been one-way. That glorious, surging tide hadn't been only in her.

"Attorney. Client." His voice sounded tight, as if he were finding it hard to speak.

Katie's brow furrowed. "Are you saying you meant… ethically inappropriate? I'm not your client, not like that."

"Fine line."

"But a line, nevertheless."

She saw him take a breath, and when he spoke his voice was steadier, and that look in his eyes had faded. "Mixing business and personal when it comes to legal matters— especially involving murder—is never wise."

Katie gave herself an inward shake. However dreary her social life had been lately, she hadn't yet been reduced to trying to talk someone into wanting her. And if he really did have professional scruples about it, she had no right to try and talk him out of them.

"Fine," she said briskly. "Let's get back to those legal matters, then."

When she picked up another of the pages, she heard a low, sour-sounding huff from Cutter and looked over at him.

The dog was looking at Gavin, and something about the angle of his head and the lowering of one brow made his expression seem like one of pure disgust.

It almost made her laugh, but she stopped herself.

Because it would be inappropriate.

Gavin first drove by the library early the next evening. Her car was there, and he knew she would be there for the duration. The library would close at its normal time, she'd told him, but reopen an hour later fully decked out and ready for the children's Halloween party. Since it was a school night, the event needed to start early so it would finish in time for a reasonable bedtime, she'd told him.

He'd had the idle thought that she'd make a good mom. Which was not the kind of thought he usually had about an attractive woman, and another warning jolt went through him.

It was simply, he told himself, that he'd spent too many years among women the term *good mom* would never apply to. Katie was such a stark contrast, that was all.

He kept driving until he could make the turn at the end of the block and head over to the state highway. Here and there he spotted costumes, on both kids and adults, as the evening's festivities began, apparently undaunted by the light but steady rain. He drove past what appeared to have once been some kind of buoy next to someone's mailbox, large and round, and now wearing a rather startling jack-o'-lantern face. Clever, he thought, but it was forgotten as he made the last turn and slowed in front of Steven Moore's house.

Gavin pulled into the driveway, effectively blocking the carport. He didn't really think it would be necessary, but he did it anyway. He wanted to talk to the man without Katie present; even when not in the room the presence of a loved one could affect what was said. He wanted to be sure Moore wasn't putting up a front. He couldn't quite bury the feeling that the man was hiding something. At the same time, he couldn't make himself believe Moore was a brutal murderer.

And deep down his gut was churning, afraid he was denying the obvious because of Katie. Because of how he was beginning to feel about her.

How you already feel about her, idiot.

He got out of the car, barely managing not to slam the door in his self-directed irritation. Cutter would probably yap at him if he did. Moore answered the door promptly, a bowl of candy in his hand, clearly expecting a trick-or-treater.

"Mr. de Marco," he said, startled.

"Happy Halloween," Gavin said, eyeing the bowl of treats. "Been busy?"

"Not yet, not like it usually is. Must be the weather."

Interesting, Gavin thought. Unless he was bluffing, it hadn't occurred to the man that the lack of kids coming to his house might be because word was out he was a murder suspect. He couldn't possibly be that naive, could he?

Then again, he'd raised Katie pretty much by himself, and she had that same sort of innocence, the kind that was appalled by evil and the last to see it or believe it when it arrived.

"I need to talk to you again."

He kept his gaze on the man's face, but saw no trace of hesitation or worry. "Of course. Come in. I have coffee on."

Gavin followed him into the kitchen in the back of the house. He waited purposely until Moore was pouring coffee into two mugs before saying, "Tell me about your wife."

The stream of coffee didn't waver, but there was surprise in Moore's voice when he said, "Kathryn? She was the love of my live. She made me a better man. Not a day goes by that I don't think about her." He turned and handed Gavin a mug. "Kind of hard not to, since Katie's the image of her mother."

"Is she?"

Moore didn't answer, but walked over to a desk in the corner, pulled something out and brought it back. "Back in the days before digital, when Katie was small."

It was a photo album. Gavin found himself strangely reluctant to open it, though he couldn't explain exactly why. He'd dealt with families struck by tragedy countless times. This should be no different.

Except it was.

He made himself open the leather cover. Moore hadn't exaggerated. The woman in the pictures was indeed the spitting image of Katie. Or vice versa, he supposed. It tugged at him in a way he didn't understand, the image of this woman dead and gone for years now. It wasn't just the resemblance, it was the pure happiness in her eyes, those eyes so like Katie's.

A bit belatedly he realized the little girl she was hugging so tightly was Katie herself. A sunny, bright-eyed child with blond pigtails that reminded him of the jaunty ponytail she wore much of the time now. Both of them were looking at the holder of the camera with such love it made it hard to breathe for a moment.

He glanced up at Katie's father and caught the shadow in his expression. It wasn't the powerfulness of recent grief, but the sadness of long-ago loss and a life never put quite right again. Gavin was certain that whoever and whatever Steven Moore was now, he had once loved Katie's mother completely. And they had loved him in the same way.

Could a man who had inspired such love truly have turned into a vicious, cold-blooded killer? Had the loss of that love triggered something that had lain dormant in him, something dark and evil?

But he'd still had Katie, and had by all appearances raised her to be a caring, loving young woman. Was that it? Was Gavin refusing to see the truth because of Katie? Was his judgment once more impaired because of his attachment to someone?

It was all he could do to focus on what he'd come here for. He spent the next two hours trying every tactic he knew to shake the man's story. He got him talking about random things and then zeroed in with a question that arrowed to the heart of the case. He acted as if he had total belief in Moore's innocence, but then turned on him as a prosecutor would, slamming him with ruthless questions.

When he was done, he was left in much the same place

he'd been before. He had no more indication the man was a killer, but he also was more certain than ever that he was hiding something.

Chapter 24

Katie was glad of the chaos of wrangling nearly three dozen children. It kept her from thinking about last night.

"That's not a real hatchet." A boy dressed as a zombie spoke to a smaller boy dressed as a lumberjack.

"Spider-Man's better than Iron Man!" Obvious who the combatants were there.

"Well, if Spider-Man was honest, that string would be coming out of his butt!"

Score one for Iron Man, Katie thought as she shepherded her flock of characters into the meeting room. She was gratified when all chatter stopped as they looked around the room. She, Heather and Roger, the maintenance man whose son was coming, had put on the finishing touches barely ten minutes ago. Gauzy, webby-looking drapes had been set in motion by a hidden fan. Spooky lighting, more ghosts, jack-o'-lanterns and a raven or two decorated the room, while haunting sounds played softly over the PA. The best part was Heather's brilliant contribution—slipcovers that made the plastic library seats look like old, crumbling tombstones. The kids were awed.

She glanced at Heather attired in Wonder Woman's very recognizable costume. She had been so sweet, coming to her with the idea, but very hesitantly.

"I don't want to do anything that would upset you," she'd said earnestly.

Katie had given her a heartfelt hug. "I love you for asking, Heather, but I don't expect the rest of the world to tiptoe around me. And it's too clever an idea not to use. The kids will love it, and now I'm prepared for it so I'll be fine."

Heather came over to her now, grabbed her arm and drew her off into a corner as the kids inspected the room and pronounced it a sufficiently spooky place to spend their Halloween night.

"Gavin de Marco?" Heather stage-whispered. "Your lawyer, the hunk that was here, is Gavin de Marco? And you didn't tell me?" When Katie's eyebrows rose, Heather rolled her eyes. "Please. It's all over the place. Half the posts in my feed last night were about him. With photos from the Coffee Hut."

Katie sighed. While the kids picked out their tombstones, she told the story of how Gavin de Marco had dropped into her life, all because Cutter had run off with her cell phone.

Heather was surprisingly accepting of the idea that the dog had planned it all. "I've seen some pretty darn smart dogs. I mean, just watch those dogs that herd sheep and cows. Those guys are amazing. Can't be that far from herding sheep to herding people. We're just more stubborn."

Katie laughed, inwardly relieved she'd successfully gotten Heather off the subject of Gavin. She wondered what her friend would say if she casually mentioned he had kissed her.

Would she even believe her? Katie barely believed it herself.

"You make a great Elsa, by the way," Heather said, tugging playfully at her braid.

Katie smiled. "And you're truly our Wonder Woman."

Once the children appeared to be settling, she headed up front to where one of her own dining room chairs had been placed, padded and draped to look like a throne. She swirled the long skirt of her light blue costume dress theatrically, and put on her best royal voice to welcome them all. She wasn't a performer by nature, but she did enjoy this. She watched the kids gradually lose their feigned boredom and sophistication and get caught up in the story she began to tell them.

By the time she finished the second story, a classic Edgar Allen Poe, they were rapt. She handed off to Heather, who would be giving them a more modern touch with a zombie story, suitably expunged for the audience, of course. And finally Katie came back with a reading of a section from one of the boy wizard stories known around the world. Then she handed out the appropriately decorated cupcakes and put on one of the films made from that series.

By the time they were done they'd kept thirty-three kids safely engaged for nearly four hours, and counted it a job well-done. And when Heather opened the door and regular light flooded in from the hallway, Katie was surprised to see several parents already there to pick up their kids, but who had quietly stayed in the back and watched the end of the movie themselves.

The children chattered happily as they headed out. Next year, if word got around, they might draw even more kids. They could—

"I like the costume."

She whirled around, smothering a gasp. Gavin stepped

out of the darkest corner of the back of the room. He was looking her up and down with an expression that made her very aware of how the light blue gown bared her throat and nipped in at her waist before it flowed down to her feet in a waterfall of sparkly fabric.

"What are you doing here?" she finally managed to get out.

"I believe you invited me."

"Oh. Yes."

But she had never, ever expected him to actually show up. She hoped she didn't sound as flustered as she felt. And she was very, very glad she hadn't known he was there. She had the feeling it would have turned her into a bumbling fool. Kind of like she was feeling now.

I'm such a pitiful sucker for brains and dark eyes. And thick, shiny hair that has a mind of its own in that charming way. And that way of moving that speaks of grace and power. And why don't I just drool on him and get it over with?

Only then did she realize Cutter was with him. Once she did, as if he'd been waiting his turn, the dog stepped forward and politely nuzzled her hand. She scratched that spot behind his right ear she'd learned he liked. And immediately she felt calmer, or at least not so flustered.

"Roger said it was okay to bring him in because it's a public meeting room, not the library."

"Yes. Yes, it's fine. He was so quiet I didn't even know he was here." *Or you.*

"Well, well," Heather said as she came back into the room, the last of the children safely stowed with their respective adults. "Look who's here."

Gavin looked at her and smiled. "Wonder Woman lives."

"You'd better believe it," Heather said. "I may be small, but I'm tough."

"'Though she be but little, she is fierce,'" Gavin said.

Heather looked at Katie then. "A man who looks like that and quotes Shakespeare. How could any woman resist?" Thankfully, since Katie couldn't think of a thing to say to that, Heather turned back to Gavin, who looked a bit discomfited himself. "Although, strictly speaking, you should be in costume."

"I'm a lawyer," Gavin said drily. "Many would find that frightening enough."

Heather burst into laughter. "And a sense of humor, too! Snatch him up, Katie, before someone else does."

"I'm sure Mr. de Marco could do much better than a small-town librarian," she said primly. "Good night, Heather," she added.

"He'd be a lucky man," her assistant said firmly, but she took the hint and left.

"She was right."

Katie tried not to look at him. "Right?"

"I'd be a lucky man."

Katie's heart leaped, missing a beat, then hurrying to catch up. "She's just soft for a man who can quote Shakespeare."

His voice dropped to a whisper. "What poet do I have to quote to make you soft for me, Katie?"

Katie's mind tumbled into chaos.

"Inappropriate again." His voice had changed to something tight, irritated. And somehow that gave her back the power to speak.

"Didn't Quinn and Hayley meet on a case?" Hayley had told her that at some point, but right now she couldn't exactly remember when.

He didn't pretend to miss her point. "Yes."

"So *inappropriate* is your decision, not Foxworth's."

"Attorney," he reminded her.

"Not the client," she retorted.

"No, you're a queen. It suits you." He glanced down at her costume and looked her up and down again before adding softly, "Although the ice does not."

She was surprised again, this time that he recognized the animated movie character so loved by young girls. Then again, the image was hard to avoid; the story of the icy queen and her steadfast, loyal sister had quickly become a classic.

"We had a client with a little girl last year," he said, reading her expression. "She was…enamored. I heard the whole story."

The image that formed in her mind then, of the famous attorney listening to a child's version of the tale, made her chest tighten almost unbearably.

"I'd better close up," she said rather hastily.

"Then I'll walk you to your car," he said, clearly not intending to leave her there alone this late. She appreciated that, even though it seemed unnecessary in this quiet, generally peaceful place. "I spoke to your father again this evening."

"I know. He texted me. Said he'd hate to be an opposing attorney."

"I was fairly tough on him."

She considered that for a moment. "But no tougher than a prosecuting attorney would be, if it heaven forbid came to that?"

"Exactly."

She could see that it was necessary, although she hated the very idea that her father could be subjected to such a thing for real. But she wasn't sure the cloud of suspicion wasn't worse. He needed to be proven innocent, and there was nobody who could do that better than Gavin. So she couldn't be anything other than glad he was there.

Even though *quiet* and *peaceful* were not words she could apply to herself when he was around. She thought the sound of his voice when he'd asked what would make her soft for him would be with her forever.

And she feared she already was.

He'd walked her to her car and was nearly back to his rental, pondering if he should follow her home to make sure she got into her house safely, when Cutter growled. He glanced at the animal, saw the dog staring into the shadows of the community center. The parking lot itself was brighter with the faintly yellowish glow from the tall streetlights. He wondered what Halloween character was hiding in the shadows. Then he recalled the dog had taken some pretty chilling costumes in stride tonight, without reacting like this.

He turned, looking where the dog was focused. Saw a slight movement. Animal? Person? Something glinted, catching what light there was. Metal.

A knife.

A big knife. One that looked as if its job was carving up animal carcasses.

Or people.

He was still trying to convince himself it was only a prankster in a Halloween costume when the figure exploded out of the darkness. He got the barest glimpse of a black ski mask pulled down over a face. Red trim around the eyes and mouth. Male. Nearly his own height. That was all he had time to notice before the dark-clad figure lunged at him. In the same instant Cutter launched himself at the figure.

The dog caught the attacker's free arm and the man screamed, waving the knife wildly. Gavin dived at the man, hoping he could take him down while he was preoccupied with the animal who had a death grip on his left wrist.

They careened back, the three of them falling into the shrubs where he'd been hiding. Gavin felt the scrape of a branch or thorn on his shoulder as they hit earth that smelled of damp mulch. Cutter snarled, a chilling sound. The man kicked out and connected with Gavin's left knee. He ignored the sharp pain, then an echoing pain, sharper yet, from his left shoulder.

He could hear Cutter, that snarl rumbling from deep in his throat. The man twisted, trying to pull free from the dog's grip. Gavin heard the rip of fabric, then a grunt. A curse, low and harsh. If he could just get some leverage he could pin the guy, but the dirt there was too soft. And that damned knife...

Somehow the man twisted free and got his feet under him. Cutter went for an ankle as Gavin tried to grab the man. Pain shot through his shoulder again, and he couldn't quite reach. A split second later the attacker was running, Cutter after him. Gavin tried to call him back, but the dog wasn't having any of it. He got to his feet and started after them.

"Gavin!"

He stopped dead. When he turned, he saw Katie running toward him, her costume gown sweeping after her. He didn't understand. She should have been gone. He'd seen her safely to her car. He glanced in the direction Cutter had gone. There was no question, he couldn't leave Katie there alone when there was some crazy with a knife running around. Cutter was on his own, at least until he could get Katie safely back inside.

And then she was there, her eyes wide with concern. "What happened?"

"Not sure. Guy with a knife and a ski mask." He peered

into the darkness, but could see nothing beyond the circle of light from the streetlamp. The park below the building was dark and quiet.

"My God," she exclaimed. "Are you all right?"

"Fine. Except Cutter went after him." He made a decision, the only one he could make. "Get back inside the building. Relock the door. Then I can go find Cutter." *I hope.*

"As long as you don't find the guy with the knife, too," she said, and he found himself liking the note of worry in her voice.

"I just don't want to explain to Hayley why I let her beloved dog get sliced up with a hunting knife," he said as they ran back toward the building. He shook his left hand; apparently that flower bed had been muddier than he'd thought, since it was dripping off him.

"We should call the sheriff," she said as she unlocked the library door.

"You can do that inside." She stepped in, reached for a light switch. He stopped her with a hand on hers. "Don't turn that on until I leave. I need my night vision. Now lock the door behind me."

She didn't answer. She was staring at his hand. He pulled it back, thinking this was a hell of a time for her to get prickly about being touched. She spun around to face him, and he had the crazy feeling he was about to get chewed out.

"You're hurt!"

He blinked. His brow furrowed. Sure, they'd hit the ground hard but the ground itself had been soft. And whatever branch or thorn had snagged him must have scratched deeper than he'd first thought because his shoulder was hurting.

Katie grabbed his hand. "To heck with your night vision," she said and flipped the switch. Light flooded the entryway.

He stared at her red-stained hand and realized the wetness he felt wasn't mud.

It was his own blood.

Chapter 25

Gavin tried not to wince as the EMT wrapped the bandage around his shoulder tighter. Cutter, who had thankfully come trotting back from his pursuit looking none the worse for wear yet mightily displeased, gave a slight whine. The EMT repeated her recommendation that he get himself to the emergency room for a couple of stitches; he'd already declined their transport. Gavin nodded again, although he had no intention of doing so. He'd have Quinn do it before he'd subject himself to what an ER visit would bring down on him.

He would have avoided the medical response, too, if it had been up to him, but Katie had called them before he realized what she was doing, once they'd discovered it hadn't been a branch or thorn but the assailant's blade that had gotten his shoulder. When he had protested, she'd given him a look befitting the ice queen of her costume.

And that had, unexpectedly, warmed him rather than

irritated or amused him. As did the way she was hovering now, watching. If the sight of his wound disturbed her, it didn't show.

Or she's more worried about you than disturbed by all the blood.

Again red flags snapped in his mind as if ripped by a gusty wind. *Do not go there. Don't even visit that territory.*

He was surprised, but almost grateful for the distraction when a man in a dark suit and white shirt, sans tie, arrived in a unmarked vehicle that still screamed cop. A uniformed deputy had taken the basics, what little Gavin could provide, and he hadn't expected any more than that.

"Heard it was you," the tall, lean man said as Cutter greeted him effusively.

"Brett," Gavin said as he shook hands with the detective he had come to like and admire in the days after he practically single-handedly toppled a sitting governor. "Didn't expect you."

"I was out and about anyway," Brett Dunbar said. "Busy night for us, Halloween and all."

"How's Sloan?"

"Still the best thing that ever happened to me."

"You're a lucky man."

As soon as the words were out of his mouth he was remembering what Katie's coworker had said that day. And his own agreement. *I'd be a lucky man.*

"Who's the princess?" Dunbar asked, glancing over to where Katie was talking to the EMT. No doubt she was asking if there was a way to force him to go to the ER.

"Queen," he corrected. "That, my friend, is the librarian."

Dunbar blinked. Gavin thought of all the stereotypical jokes, but if the detective thought of any of them he had the grace not to voice them.

"Suits her" was all he said.

Indeed it does. "She had a party here tonight for kids, scary stories and a movie. It was a big hit, once she separated Spider-Man and Iron Man."

Dunbar chuckled. "Impressive, given what she's going through personally."

She's impressive, period. But he only nodded.

Dunbar turned back to face him. "Want to run through it again for me?"

In truth, he didn't, but the detective had come all the way out here, and Gavin knew it was only because of him. An unsuccessful mugging was hardly worth his attention.

"I don't have much," he admitted ruefully. "Guy came out of the dark, wearing a full ski mask and waving that damned knife. Cutter went for one side, I went for the other. He nicked me as we went down."

"Then he took off?"

Gavin nodded. "With Cutter after him. I would have followed, but…" He glanced over toward Katie. The thought that this had happened so close to her made him a bit queasy.

"Of course," Dunbar agreed. "You couldn't leave her alone out here. Too tempting a target."

Tempting. Oh, yeah… Especially in that outfit that seems to highlight every luscious curve.

"—description?"

Belatedly he tuned in to Dunbar's question. "Not much," he admitted. "Just under six foot, I think. Medium build, jeans, light-color shoes, and a dark hoodie with a logo on it. The ski mask was black, with red trim. Fairly strong, but he didn't handle the knife like a pro. More the slasher type. Sorry, but that's about it."

"That's more than a lot of people get," Dunbar said. "Any idea on the logo?"

"Long, horizontal, looked like the head of...something. With a point."

"Seahawks logo, I'd guess," Katie said as she came up to them. "They're practically ubiquitous around here these days. I think half the population has one. Dad and I bought them for each other last Christmas."

"Win a Super Bowl and people who never used to care start caring," Dunbar said, smiling at her.

"Katie Moore, Brett Dunbar," Gavin said by way of introduction.

"Really?" Katie sounded as surprised as he had been at the man's presence. "Thank you for your help, Detective Dunbar. With this, and my father's case."

"Haven't done much, but you're welcome."

"Do you think you could talk him—" she nodded at Gavin "—into being sensible and going to get stitches?"

Dunbar grinned. "I could try, but given that he knows my aversion to hospitals, he might doubt my sincerity."

Katie threw up her hands. "Okay, I give up. But I reserve the right to say 'I told you so' if it gets infected or doesn't heal right."

"Duly noted," Gavin said.

Cutter nudged her hand, and she stroked his head. "You've got more sense than the both of them, don't you?" she asked the dog.

"He came back on his own?" Dunbar asked.

Gavin nodded. "Maybe the guy had a car down the hill."

Dunbar looked thoughtful. "If he took off on the highway, cameras might have picked him up. Might not get much in the dark, but it's worth a look."

"I can put Ty on it and save your guys the time."

"And get it faster," Dunbar said, his mouth quirking. Then, seriously, he asked, "Connected?"

Gavin had been pondering that since it had happened. "Maybe."

"Wait," Katie said suddenly, obviously following their cryptic conversation. "I thought the guy just waited for somebody alone. Are you saying this attack wasn't random? That he was after Gavin because of the case?"

Gavin shrugged. "At the risk of committing a logical fallacy, it has a tendency to be true."

She stared at him. "Never mind the 'post hoc, ergo' stuff. This has happened to you before?"

"My presence does have a tendency to provoke things," he said carefully.

"I'd guess," Dunbar said, "it's that annoying other tendency, that around you the truth seems to come out. I'm also guessing you don't threaten easily."

"I'm stubborn that way," Gavin said with a grin.

"*That* way?" Katie said rather sourly. "I'm going to go lock up. Again."

"All right," Gavin said as she turned to go, not reacting to her tone. "Cutter?"

The dog instantly understood and was on his feet. He stuck close to Katie's side as she walked back toward the library doors.

Dunbar looked at Gavin's arm, his blood-soaked sleeve. Then he glanced at Katie, then back to Gavin.

"I assume you didn't miss that bit of information she dropped," Dunbar said.

"You mean that her father has a hoodie like that? No, I didn't. And from what I've seen of him, he's pretty fit and could still move that fast."

Dunbar nodded slowly. "I'd hate for it to be true. She seems nice."

"She is."

"And smart."

"She is."

"And worried about you."

That one stopped him for a moment before he said, "That goes back to her being nice."

"Hmm."

Gavin had noticed before that Brett Dunbar could say a great deal without speaking a word. He saw the man's eyes flick toward the building, toward Katie and Cutter. Then back to him. And he didn't like the speculation he saw in his expression. Not from a man who had experienced Cutter's machinations firsthand.

And who had ended up with the woman who was indeed the best thing that had ever happened to him.

Don't go there. Don't even think about going there.

As he watched Katie secure her domain and turn with Cutter to come back, he had the crazy thought he should be saying that to the dog instead of constantly repeating it to himself.

Chapter 26

Katie was beyond frustrated. By the time all the details had been handled it had been a very long day. She was tired, yet she couldn't fall asleep. Even the sound of the rain, which had begun again just as she arrived home, didn't help lull her.

She finally gave up for now, pulled on a pair of lounge pants and a long-sleeved T-shirt, and shoved her feet into her favorite shearling winter slippers. After what had happened at the library following the party she should be nothing but glad it was over, and that no one had been seriously hurt. That is, if you didn't count a wicked gash and copious bleeding as seriously hurt, as Gavin obviously didn't.

She kept replaying the moment when she'd realized the wetness she'd felt when he'd touched her hand was blood. Remembering the bright, unmistakable redness of it when she'd flipped on the light. Reliving her horror as it dripped from his hand to splat on the floor.

That moment should have warned her, but she'd been too swamped by the images in her head to think clearly. But now she had to admit the truth. No matter how ridiculous it was, no matter how foolish, she was getting herself in a tangle over this man.

She supposed it was only natural. How did someone who'd lived, for the most part, such a quiet, unobtrusive life, come in contact with someone like him and not get sucked into the vortex? Gavin de Marco was a force of nature, one to be reckoned with, and she obviously wasn't immune.

On the thought, her cell phone signaled an incoming text. She'd forgotten to even get it out of her purse, and if she hadn't already been awake and pacing, she probably wouldn't have heard it. She frowned, wondering who'd be texting her after midnight. As she walked to the dresser, where she'd left the purse, she tried to rein in her thoughts that it had to be more bad news.

She pulled the phone out and read the text.

From Gavin.

Hope you don't get this because you're asleep.

She let out a sigh, then tapped the screen to bring up the keyboard. I wish.

Are you all right?

She blinked. Read it again. He was asking her? I'm not the one who got carved up with a hunting knife.

It was barely a slice.

That should have had stitches right away.

Not enough to put up with what a trip to the ER would have caused.

She stared at that one for a moment. It had not occurred to her what kind of commotion Gavin de Marco showing up in an emergency room after a knife attack would create.

Never thought of that.

No reason you should. Quinn came by. He stitched it up.

She blinked. Then she remembered Quinn Foxworth's military background and realized he was probably quite capable. His work might lack a bit of finesse, though.

Ouch.

She got back a smile. A bit. Sorry it was messy. Try not to let it remind you.

She stared at the screen. It was true, she hadn't seen dripping blood even on a small scale since that awful night, so she couldn't say the memories hadn't slammed into her mind. But practical concerns, especially in those moments before she knew he wasn't horribly injured, had pushed them out again.

She tapped at the keyboard again.

Too late.

The moment she hit Send she wished she hadn't. The last thing she wanted to do was whine to him, of all people. He was the one physically hurting. She was just dealing with memories. She—

Answer the door.

What? She stared at the phone. A split second later a quiet knock came on her front door.

For an instant she thought of not answering. But she could hardly pretend she wasn't here or hadn't heard it when she'd just been texting him.

She sucked in a deep breath and walked to the door. She spared a brief thought for her no doubt tousled appearance, then decided after tonight she didn't care.

He, on the other hand, looked none the worse for wear. He'd changed, thankfully discarding the blood-soaked shirt. He wore a heavy, cable-knit sweater that looked too damned sexy on him. He certainly didn't look like he'd nearly had his throat slashed mere hours ago.

Life was damned unfair sometimes.

"You're not all right," he said without preamble.

"I'll be fine." Cutter was with him, she noticed. The dog stepped forward and automatically she patted his head.

"You should be sleeping," Gavin said.

She couldn't hold back her wry laugh. "Not likely."

"That's why I'm here. To go over what happened tonight. Get you past it."

"Again? To get past it, you want me to hash it out all over again?"

"Yes. Ignoring it doesn't work."

She couldn't deny the truth of that. She'd tried too often to ignore the emotions that those memories, those awful images, brought on. She'd only succeeded in delaying them, which in turn only seemed to intensify them when they finally broke loose.

Cutter gave a soft woof. She realized belatedly she was still standing holding her front door, and they were still out on the porch. They were under cover from the rain, but it still seemed beyond rude to keep them standing out there. Especially since Gavin clearly wasn't going to be easily persuaded that he was the one who should be resting.

With an inward sigh she stepped back and gestured them inside. If Gavin had noticed her reluctance it didn't show, but she imagined his poker face was pretty good. It had to have been, given his reputation for startling juries with unexpected turns in cases.

"Ty's pulling the video from the traffic cam near the library," he said as he stepped inside, bringing with him the scent of rain and the outdoors.

"You really think it's connected?"

"Doesn't matter. When somebody comes after me like that, I like to know why."

"You say that like it happens a lot."

"Not so much anymore," he said.

She saw him look around the living room. It wasn't perfectly tidy. The latest *Library Journal* was on the coffee table next to her tablet, and the heated throw she used when curled up in her favorite chair to read was sliding onto the floor, but she didn't care. It had taken her time to get this room just how she wanted it, and she'd been grateful for the distraction of doing so when she'd first moved in. She'd relocated to get away from the scene of tragedy, but at first the new surroundings only reminded her of why she was no longer where she'd been.

But now it was her own place, her own quiet refuge in the woods, and she loved it. She loved the blue and green tones of the outdoors brought inside, loved the textures of the furniture and the patterned rug, and the way the bright, vivid colors of the painting she'd bought at the local arts fair and hung over the couch contrasted with the cool colors of the rest.

Cutter, tail wagging gently, began to inspect the room

less surreptitiously than Gavin had. She didn't think there was anything he could get into that would hurt him, so she let him go and turned back to her human guest.

"This is nice," he said. "Comfortable."

"If that's your way of saying it's not fancy, agreed."

His gaze shifted to her face. "Something wrong with that?"

"Not for me. I would have figured you for more of a chrome-and-glass kind of guy." In fact, she knew it, having seen in her research photographs of the office he'd had at the peak of his renown.

"I had it, once," he admitted. "Doesn't mean I liked it. It was part of the image. This, I genuinely like."

She couldn't even imagine what it would be like to live like he had. But the tone of his compliment had seemed sincere, so she decided to take it at face value.

"Thank you. I'm afraid there's no coffee," she said, "but I have cocoa."

He shook his head as he sat down at one end of her small couch. "I didn't come here to make you work. At least, not at that. Besides, the last thing you need is caffeine keeping you awake."

"No caffeine seems to be required," she said wryly, walking toward her chair. At least sitting there, safely apart, had been her intention, but somehow Cutter got in the way. And he kept getting in the way, until she had little choice but to sit down on the couch, as well. Strangely, the thing had never seemed so small as when Gavin was barely two feet away.

She looked at him and noticed him glaring at the dog rather balefully. As if the animal had done this intentionally.

Or as if her sitting so close was annoying.

Tough, Mr. Famous Lawyer. It's my house, I'll sit where I want.

Of course, she hadn't intended to sit there. The dog made her. Still...

She shifted in her seat till she faced him. Mr. Famous Lawyer.

"If I asked you something," she said slowly, "would you give me the truth?"

He raised an eyebrow at her. "I don't lie."

She gave him a sideways look.

"I don't," he repeated. "Ever."

"And what about those lies of omission?"

"If I can't or won't tell you something, I'll say so."

"What's the difference?"

"The difference is honesty, admitting there is something you're not saying. Like there's a difference between something honestly slipping your mind, and withholding something the other person needs to know or should know."

Her tone was a bit frosty when she said, "And have you decided which you think I did, about my father's past career?"

He studied her for a moment. "I think," he said slowly, "that you're just not used to thinking the way I have to."

That simply he disarmed her, melting the frost and making her feel a bit of an ache for him, for she couldn't imagine living a life where you had to think that way all the time.

"How do you ever trust anyone?" she asked, more rhetorically than anything.

"Very carefully," he said. "But I don't think that was the question you wanted to ask."

He waited, silently, giving her room to ask or not. Either choice would tell him...something, she supposed. She hesitated, then admitted she wanted to know badly enough to betray…whatever this would betray to him. And she asked her question.

"Why did you really walk away?"

Chapter 27

Gavin was startled; he hadn't expected that from her now. He thought he'd headed her off when she'd asked earlier.

He'd been asked for the real reason before. Often. By acquaintances who were genuinely curious, more often by reporters who were rabid for a juicy story. For the most part they all got the same bland, noninformative, packaged response. Not that it mattered. What saw publication was all the usual speculation. He was rich enough to never have to work again—that much was true. He had nothing left to prove—he supposed that one was true, too, but still not the reason. He wanted to run for office soon—so far from truth he'd burst out laughing the first time he'd seen that one.

His true reasons were his own business, and not something he wanted to share with a gossip-hungry world.

And yet now, sitting here in this cozy room, too close to the woman who threatened to convince him there were people you could trust on sight, he felt an urge he couldn't resist. And to his own surprise, he abandoned the usual practiced response.

He had to think for a moment. He'd almost never told the whole thing except to Charlie, who asked, and Quinn, who had never asked, but Gavin had felt he deserved it before he hired him. He took a deep breath, and started.

"When I was in college my best friend, Ben Olsen, was arrested for murder. I knew there was no way he could have done it, and he swore to me he didn't. But he was convicted and sent to prison. Consensus was it was because of an incompetent, inexperienced attorney."

"I'm guessing that was your inspiration? To become a defense lawyer?"

"Yes." Nearly two decades later it still left a bitter taste in his mouth, even knowing how it had turned out in the end. "While I was in school, I spent every free hour searching for new evidence to get the case reopened. I visited Ben in prison regularly, made him go through it time and again, trying to find something, some new angle, anything that would convince a judge to take another look. And every time I worried more as Ben got worse. Being locked up was pushing him to the edge. By the time I passed the bar, I wasn't sure how long he could hold on."

"I can't imagine," she said softly.

"It went on while I was getting established. I built that reputation as much in the hope it would help Ben as anything else. I wanted the fact that I knew he was innocent to be worth something."

He stopped, swallowing against the lump forming in his throat. She was watching him intently, and something in her eyes made him able to go on.

"And then… Ben got cancer. And it became imperative to find something, fast. So I put everything else on hold. It was all I did for six months, 24/7. I was…driven."

"Understandable."

His mouth tightened. "Yeah. Until Ben took a turn for the worse. Or worst."

"He died? In prison?"

He nodded, becoming aware of how hard this next part was going to be. But he was in it now, and he was going to finish it.

"Gavin, I'm so sorry—"

He held up a hand to stop her. "Don't be." His voice had become a cold, harsh thing. "On his death bed, Ben confessed."

She drew back sharply. "What?"

"He confessed he'd done it, told them where he'd buried the body. They found it right where he said. All the forensics matched his story. He'd done it."

"He lied to you? All those years he let you go through that?"

"I was so convinced he was innocent I built my career, my entire life around saving him, and others like him. And then he destroyed it all."

"My God. No wonder you have no tolerance for liars. And that's why you walked away?"

"I walked away because I no longer had any faith in my own judgment."

Her brow furrowed. "But you were right, all those other times."

"Was I? How do I know somebody I got off, who's out walking around, wasn't another case where I was wrong? How do I know I didn't get off a vicious child molester, or worse, just because I took his case and the state pled out to a lesser charge? And that's not even counting the times when I had to withdraw for an unrelated reason and the buzz was that client must be guilty, when I knew he wasn't. My reputation was a double-edged sword, and I'd lost control of it. I didn't wield it anymore, everyone else did. Judges started refusing to let me withdraw for anything short of a blatant conflict of interest because it would prejudice the case."

For a long moment she was silent. And he felt scoured out, with nothing left to say. He felt like he was teetering on the edge. When she finally spoke, her voice was so gentle it brought him even closer to that edge.

"You must have felt like your entire life was based on a lie."

"It was." His voice sounded as bleak as he felt. "And I was so damned tired of being a step back. Dispassionate, detached. I'd started not to feel anything at all anymore. If I hadn't met Quinn when I did, I'd be digging ditches somewhere, and glad of it."

And then Katie changed course completely, and caught him by surprise.

"I did my homework on you, you know."

"I would expect no less." She was a librarian, after all.

"And nowhere," she went on, "did I see even a hint at what you told me, about why you quit."

"Not something I advertise," he said drily.

"Who else knows?"

"Charlie. Quinn."

"Your family?"

"My mother did. I suspect she told my father. Moot point. They're both gone now."

"I'm sorry." Her words resonated. From her it wasn't some routine, meaningless expression of sympathy. She'd lived it; she knew. But thankfully she left it at that. Perhaps also from experience. "Who else knows?" she asked.

He shrugged. "No one. Not from me, anyway."

"Why did you tell me?"

And there it was, the question he couldn't answer because he wasn't sure himself. And that was because the only answer he could think of would be foolish beyond belief.

Something must have shown in his face, because the next thing he heard, in that low, gentle voice that felt like brushing his skin with soft velvet, was, "When you figure that out, come tell me."

"You say that like you already know the answer."

"I do."

He went still. He couldn't deny he wanted her. And she had to know it, after he'd slipped and kissed her, an action he still didn't quite understand. He shoved that aside to confront the matter at hand. Did she think this...oversharing was part of that? That he was the kind of man who would bare his soul, as it were, just to get her into bed with him?

He'd never put it in so many words before, not even in his head. And now that he had, his imagination fired up as if it had only been waiting for that. Images poured through his mind. Katie coming to him, naked and wanting. What her skin would feel like in the soft, hidden places. What her eyes would look like hot with desire, and aimed at him...

"Gavin? Are you all right?"

Hell, no. "Just what is it," he said with an effort, "that you think you know?"

She gave a light, simple shrug that was completely at odds with where his mind had just gone. "You're starting to trust me."

He stared at her. After that flood of racy, lascivious visions he was having a little trouble with her take on it.

"I know you thought I purposely didn't tell you about my father's past work, but I think you see now I didn't really lie. I just didn't see the connection you were making, because, as you said, I'm not used to thinking the way you do. The way you have to think to do what you do."

"I see." It was all he could manage.

"And as I said, it's no wonder you can't tolerate liars. Why that above all things is what you can't forgive. But I don't lie, any more than you do, and I think you see that now."

"Got me all figured out, do you?" He hadn't meant to sound mocking, but it came out that way anyway. On some level he knew he was flailing out because Katie Moore was digging into places he ever and always kept hidden.

And who opened the door for her?

"I would never presume to think I had you all figured out," she said. "That would be a lifelong challenge."

Lifelong.

Gavin sucked in a breath, wondering why it was suddenly so hard to get enough air. Maybe that was it. His brain was starved for air—that's why he'd told her that pitiful tale. Hypoxia might explain it.

Even as he thought it he nearly laughed. He could almost feel his mind squirming, looking for a way out of the simple truth of what she'd said. He was beginning to trust her. In fact, he'd gone well beyond just beginning. But it wasn't his usual conscious, carefully considered process. It had happened on some level he hadn't even been aware of. Some level he hadn't even realized existed before.

A level that heard the word *lifelong* and yearned instead of recoiling.

Chapter 28

Katie didn't know what she'd said that hit him so hard, but she hadn't been giving it her full attention. She was still too thankful that this was likely the source of his doubts about her father, why he suspected everyone of lying at some point.

She didn't care for the "guilty until proven innocent" aspect of this trait of his, but now she understood it. Given his history, it would be amazing if he didn't feel that way. For her, it would be like finding out her father was in fact guilty; it would shatter the very foundation of her life, her entire concept of who she was.

But now she was staring at him, and the way he was looking back was sending shivers through her. And making her think of that kiss. That inappropriate, heart-stealing, pulse-pounding kiss. That kiss that had been so quick, over so fast, that there was no way the memory of it should be able to do this to her.

And yet here she was, her heartbeat quickening, her skin flushing, long-dormant parts of her awakening. And no amount of telling herself she was a fool seemed to help her get herself back in control.

Not when he was looking at her like that, as if he was thinking the same thing.

"I'd better get out of here." He said it sharply, almost harshly.

"I didn't mean to make you angry." She still wondered what had set him off.

His eyebrows rose. "Angry? When you were looking at me as if—"

He cut off his own words, and she couldn't help herself, she couldn't just let it go. "As if what?"

The answer came in a low tone that practically vibrated up her spine. "As if you wanted me to kiss you again."

Her breath caught. One part of her, the part that he brought voraciously to life just by looking at her like that, wanted to say simply, "Yes."

"There are so many reasons that would be a mistake," he said, his voice even lower, rougher.

"And only one reason it wouldn't?"

"I can think of several, but they're all just different words for the same thing."

She could think of several, too. *Want. Need. Desire. Crave. Yearn.* She'd never felt anything quite like this. The intensity of it was nearly overwhelming.

He turned to go, clearly determined not to make that mistake, as he called it. She stiffened her spine, reeled in her uncooperative senses.

Fine. I'm certainly not going to beg the man to kiss me. She thought it with solid determination. At least, she thought it was solid until her sneaky mind added in almost a whimper, *Even if that's what I feel like doing.*

She hadn't made that whimpering sound. She knew she hadn't. And yet Gavin turned back suddenly. Crossed the three feet between them in one stride. She felt his hands cup her face in the moment before he lowered his mouth to hers. The unexpectedness of it didn't lessen the jolt, or slow the fire that leaped to life in her anew, as if it had only been banked, not extinguished. The feel of his mouth on hers rekindled it thoroughly, sending heat and sensation racing along every nerve. She forgot to breathe, and when he finally pulled back she sucked in air in a gasp.

She stared at him, seeing an echoing heat in his eyes, but unable to tell if he was glad or regretted that his determination had crumbled.

And then he was gone, without another word, leaving her with senses clamoring for more, need caroming around inside her, and a wry—and tardy—common sense telling her she should be thankful he hadn't pushed for what she would have apparently given him without another thought.

She should be thankful.

But she wasn't.

Gavin didn't make a habit of calling himself names, but he was still rattling them off the next morning. Especially when he looked in the mirror to shave, after a night of restless sleep that had him thinking he'd have been better off if he'd just stayed awake all night. As it was, he had a dull, thudding headache and his eyes looked as if he'd been on a three-day bender. Even Cutter had stayed clear, as if sensing not even his calming presence was going to help.

But at least he had a plan. A plan that would keep him safely out of Katie's orbit for a couple of days, at least. Which wasn't the goal, he assured himself. He'd just moved something up on his mental schedule, something he'd planned to do in the next few days anyway.

He had the names and details on the witnesses who had backed up Laurel's ex-boyfriend's story, had copies of their sworn statements, but for him nothing took the place of an in-person interview. That after this much time they might be less certain of their stories could be both a curse, in that the details might be fuzzy, and a blessing, in that they might not feel the same urgency to stick to the narrative.

If there was one, he thought as he got dressed. The police had been satisfied the dozen or so witnesses from the party Ross had been at during the time of the murder had been truthful. And given some of the rather embarrassing details of that night they had confessed to, he tended to agree. It had taken a promise from the police not to pursue the details of some of the more illicit party favors to get anything at all out of a couple of them.

"You look like you've been rode hard and put away wet, as my gramps used to say."

Gavin whirled to face the man who had seemingly appeared out of thin air in the doorway of the bedroom. Rafe Crawford looked at him steadily over a mug of coffee Gavin could smell and suddenly craved.

He fought down the images the old saying had blasted into his mind, images that had nothing to do with horses and everything to do with a naked Katie Moore riding him. Hard.

He swore under his breath, glared at the dog beside Rafe for the lack of warning, and headed for the kitchen, thinking if the man hadn't left enough coffee for another mug, he was going to take his head off. Then he remembered who exactly he was dealing with and realized taking on one of the best snipers in the world was hardly within his skill set.

"And they call me grouchy before my coffee," Rafe observed, his tone almost amused as he watched Gavin fill a mug and get to the caffeine infusion. "But then, you sleep even less than I do."

Gavin grimaced. "You here for the day?"

Rafe nodded. "Generator wobbled a little on the last exercise cycle, and the chopper needs service."

Gavin nodded. Idleness did not suit the man. In that they were alike.

"I'm going down to Tacoma," he said. "Witness interviews."

Rafe lifted an eyebrow at him. "Any reason you're telling me, not Quinn?"

"Quinn knows. But I'm leaving him here," he said, gesturing at Cutter. "Might take a couple of days for me to track down everyone I want to talk to, so I'll probably be staying over. If you're going to be here, saves me dropping him off at their place."

"Fine with me," Rafe said with a shrug. "He can supervise." He gave Gavin a considering look before adding, "Does he know you're leaving him behind?"

"Quinn?"

"Cutter."

Gavin blinked. Then his mouth quirked. "I haven't discussed it with him, no."

"Better. Or you'll find him in your car and not so easy to get out."

Gavin had the sudden feeling that he was far from knowing all the ins and outs of dealing with this dog. "And just how do I do that?"

Rafe shrugged. "Just tell him 'Not this time.' Now, that doesn't mean he'll accept it. He may have his own reasons for insisting he go along, in which case you might as well give in and save the energy."

"I'm beginning to see who really runs this place," he said drily.

"Hard to argue with his track record," Rafe said blandly.

Gavin wondered exactly which track record he was talking about, but didn't ask because he was afraid he knew. Which brought him right back to the subject he'd been trying to avoid. Katie.

He gave himself an inward shake. Wondered if there was something about the surroundings or the atmosphere here that screwed up his focus. He looked at Cutter and said firmly, "Not this time."

The dog angled his head as if thoughtfully considering. And then he walked over and sat at Rafe's side.

"Looks like you got permission," Rafe said, with a grin Gavin had never seen from the man before. That dog was a miracle worker in more than one way.

Gavin sat in the all-night diner, tapping his pen on the pad with his notes. The remains of his meal—a burger that he'd figured was the safest choice but had actually turned out to be pretty good—was pushed to one side but the coffee cup, due for another topping off, stayed close. There weren't a lot of other customers at this hour somewhere between late night and early morning, so he didn't feel pressured to leave. And the waiter was a good one who, when he saw Gavin was working intently, just refilled his coffee without saying a word and otherwise left him alone.

The first night here he'd tried working in his hotel room, but the bed seemed to mock him. He was seriously tired, but his brain was in overdrive, and he knew if he lay down he would be wide-awake the moment his head hit the pillow. And if he let his guard down enough to try and sleep, he knew where his unruly mind would go. So tonight he didn't even make the effort.

He stared down at his notes. Considering the months that had passed, the stories from the witnesses had stayed

quite consistent. He reread the statements of four men he'd
spoken to the last couple of days, one of them Carr's admitted best friend. The man had begun by reaffirming the
alibi and, after a drink or two provided by Gavin, ended
up cheerfully recounting some of the raunchier details of
the party.

One of those details led Gavin to add a name to his list
of people to talk to—the girl Ross had hooked up with at
said party. The men had confided they'd thought it just
a one-time thing, that Ross *might* have gotten her a little
drunk, or otherwise convinced her not to fight it. Gavin
had wondered if they were suggesting he'd used something
stronger than alcohol, but he wanted the rest of the story
more than he wanted to pursue that. Anyway, according
to the witnesses, Ross and the woman had taken over the
back room set aside for just such encounters.

It must have been good, one of them had joked, *because
Ross is still hanging with her.*

When Gavin had tracked her down, the girl had looked
to him to be not even old enough to drink, which he supposed said more about his jaded state than anything. She'd
been shy about sharing details, but finally admitted she'd
been too drunk to remember much, but was grateful Ross
had made sure she got home after the party ended in the
wee hours. And that was why she'd agreed to see him again
the next day and then the day after that, until, she said with
a genuine blush, they were apparently a thing.

He believed them. All of them. Believed they were telling the truth. At least as far as they knew. Which didn't
bode well for Steven Moore. And just how would Katie feel
if he ended up proving her father guilty instead of innocent?

He was in no way ready to face that possibility yet. He
could have headed back to Foxworth tonight—well, yesterday, really since it was after midnight now—but he had

opted to stay, telling himself he wanted to go over everything once more. It had nothing to do with staying away from Katie one more night. And asking Quinn, when he'd spoken to him this afternoon, to pass along that the alibis indeed seemed solid had nothing to do with him not wanting to talk to her.

Nothing at all.

He downed the last of his coffee in a gulp, then stood. He picked up the bill, glanced at the total, doubled it for the tip and dropped cash on the table. He paused long enough to thank the observant and efficient waiter, then headed out into the chilly night air. After the warmth of the diner it felt like a slap in the face.

Just what he needed.

Chapter 29

Katie took a last look at the public meeting room on Friday to be sure they'd gotten all the Halloween decorations. They hadn't gotten to it until this morning, but nobody had seemed to mind the decorations lingering for a couple of days. But there was a community meeting scheduled here tonight, so she made sure every last ghost had been vanquished.

Except for that one floating around in your head. The one named Gavin.

She shook her head sharply. She saw Heather approaching, and felt a twinge at what probably was showing in her face. To head off any questions from her too observant friend, she spoke first.

"Why don't you take off? I can finish up here, and you can go get your kids."

"Last patron just left, so thank you, I will." But undeterred, she added, "I was hoping you'd have a hot date to-night. Where is that gorgeous man, anyway?"

Gone. A couple of kisses and he ran like hell.

"Never mind," Heather said, her eyes lighting up as she looked past Katie toward the glass doors. "He's here."

Katie sucked in a breath she was sure was audible, and barely stopped herself from spinning around to look.

"You have fun," her friend said archly. "Lord knows I would, with that man. As much and as fast as I could get it."

And then she was gone. Katie heard her say something, no doubt to him, because it was in that light, flirty voice she could turn on like a spigot. Katie still hadn't turned to look. Instead she made a last, unnecessary circuit of the meeting room, then carefully—very, very carefully—closed the door and locked it. And then, the keys clutched so tightly in her hand her knuckles were white, she turned around.

He looked like hell. At least, as much as he could. His hair looked windblown, as if he'd driven all the way back from Tacoma with the window down. He was clean shaven, but she noticed a nick on his left jawline, as if he'd gotten too rushed or heavy-handed with the razor. His eyes were a bit bloodshot, and he looked beyond weary. As if he hadn't slept the entire time he'd been gone.

She'd intended to not say anything, to make him say the first words, because she had no idea where things stood between them. But when he just stared at her, she finally broke, with a wry acknowledgment that she'd been fool-ish to think she could outmaneuver the man who'd tricked serial killers into confessions. But the only words that she could manage were the ones she'd already thought.

"You look like hell."

His expression didn't change. "And you look incredible. As always." Only then did his mouth quirk upward at one corner, in that way he had. "Even if you do look like you want to throw those keys at me."

Since there were several keys on the ring run through a large wooden carving of an evergreen, that would definitely hurt.

"Hadn't occurred to me, but thanks for the suggestion."

Something in his gaze shifted then. "No, it wouldn't, would it." It wasn't a question. "You don't live in that kind of world."

"I don't have that kind of nature," she corrected. "And aren't you out of that kind of world now?"

"I am," he said quietly. "But sometimes I forget. Both that that's not my world anymore, and that there are people who really are what they seem. People who are good and honest and true, as Hayley says."

"Hayley is wise."

"Yes. And I—as she told me in no uncertain terms this afternoon—am an idiot."

Katie's eyebrows rose. She would have liked to have seen that exchange. "And what brought on that assessment?"

He drew in a deep breath and then let it out as he gave a rueful grimace. "You."

Katie blinked. She hadn't expected that.

"And Cutter," he added, confusing her even more. "It seems I'm trying to avoid the inevitable."

"Which is?"

"You," he repeated.

She'd been called a thing or two in her life, but never inevitable. She wasn't sure how to take that.

"He's outside, by the way. He let me go to Tacoma on my own, but apparently that's as far as my leash goes."

She couldn't help but smile at that.

"It's probably cold out there," he said. "And about to rain."

"He's got a lot of fur."

His mouth quirked again. "You're not going to make this easy, are you?"

"I'm not even sure what 'this' is."

He sucked in another breath. "This," he said, "is me apologizing."

"Wow. You need some practice."

He let out the breath audibly. "Yeah."

"Apologizing for what?"

"Kissing and running."

She hadn't expected him to admit that. "So why did you?"

"I had to...wrestle with something." He held her gaze now. "Like how you would feel if it ends up I help to prove your father guilty instead of innocent."

The words rocked her, made her wonder if he'd learned something down south that he hadn't mentioned. Something she wasn't going to like. Perhaps he'd met with the police there, and was now convinced they were on the right track.

She steadied herself before asking, "Are you speaking theoretically or specifically?"

"Theoretically." He seemed to realize where her mind had gone. "I have nothing new or more than the police do. Which is only theory."

She breathed again. And then she realized the full import of what he'd said. He'd kissed her. Twice. Had clearly wanted more. But instead he had vanished because he was worried about how she'd feel if he ended up being the one who proved the police right.

From the safety of her certainty of her father's innocence, she was thoroughly touched. She wondered if he even realized what his actions revealed.

She did realize what her reaction revealed. She'd turned

to mush inside so fast it was impossible to deny. And even knowing she was setting herself up for heartbreak—because he would leave, she knew that—she couldn't walk away from this.

She spoke words she'd never expected to say to him. "Come home with me."

The breath he sucked in was audible. She saw in his eyes, his face, that he knew exactly what she was saying.

She might regret this. Probably would.

But she would regret not doing it even more.

He still liked her place.

He followed her in, looked around once more. It felt more like a home than any place he'd ever lived, including his loft now. That was just the place he went when he wasn't working. This was a place he could see spending time not doing anything in particular. A place he could see just relaxing. Or working through a list of things to keep it in shape.

Or sleeping in, wrapped around Katie?

Oh, yeah. He could see that.

He ordered his body to calm down as he shrugged off his jacket. Now that it seemed he was going to get what he'd wanted from the moment he'd opened Quinn's door to her, it was a lot more difficult.

Besides, she could still change her mind. She'd seemed eager enough when she'd suggested her place. It was closer, she'd said, and there was a drugstore on the way for…a certain purchase. The mere mention of protection had her blushing and him fighting down a wave of renewed heat.

He wouldn't blame her if she was just avoiding Foxworth; for all the homey atmosphere it was still a workplace and only temporarily his place.

His train of thought derailed as something else hit him.

She'd chosen to let him into her home, her sanctuary, where she'd come to rebuild a life shattered by a tragedy no one should have to endure. He'd never had the feelings some people had for the place they lived, but he'd dealt with people who had, and understood it. And suddenly it seemed imperative that he let her know.

"Katie."

She turned, tossing her own jacket beside his on the back of the chair closest to the door. Somehow even that little act seemed significant.

She busied herself with Cutter for a moment, asking, with apparent seriousness, if he would prefer the couch or a blanket on the floor. His answer was to hop on the couch and curl up as if settling in.

Finally, she turned back to Gavin. As she stood there looking up at him, those blue eyes wide, her expression a combination of anticipation and nerves with a touch of wariness, he felt a jab of nerves himself.

"Are you sure about this?" he asked.

She laughed, and the nerves were in the sound of it. "Are you sure you should be giving me a chance for second thoughts?"

"I'm sure I would be sorrier if you end up regretting this."

She smiled then. It was steadier, the tension retreating. "I thought about that. I know you'll be gone soon. But I decided because I would regret passing this up even more. This…kind of feeling doesn't come along every day."

"No," he said fervently, "it doesn't."

He was past worrying about what that implied. And his body had had enough of being patient.

Tough. You're going to go slow and easy. This is Katie, and she deserves that.

"I'm a little rusty at this," he said, afraid he wouldn't be able to keep that vow.

She looked him up and down, and there was such pure appreciation in her expression he felt humbled. "Not," she said, reaching out to trace his jawline with one finger, "from lack of opportunity, I'm sure."

It was true. But he was honest enough with himself to understand why, that many of those opportunities stemmed from his reputation, status or just his looks, and were shallow, momentary things.

Katie Moore was anything but shallow.

"Lack of interest," he said.

She smiled. For a long moment he just stood there, staring at her, his blood pulsing so hard and fast he could hear it in his ears. Then he heard a rustle of movement as Cutter vacated the couch. In the next instant he felt a not insignificant shove at the back of his knees as the dog leaned into him. He had to take a step to keep his balance.

And just that easily he and Katie were pushed together. For a split second all the stories he'd heard of the dog's matchmaking shot through his mind, but then Katie was in his arms and it was gone. Everything was gone except the feel of her, the warmth of her, and this damned aching need that he realized now had been growing every moment since he'd met her.

He'd meant to kiss her softly, gently, as he'd vowed. But the moment his lips touched hers, that went out the window. She was too sweet, too hot, too entrancing to go slowly. And she was kissing him back. Hotly, fiercely, destroying the last remnant of his determination. What had come before was nothing, a mere spark: this was a conflagration.

He ran his hands down her back, pressed her closer, needing as much contact between them as he could get. She arched against him, and he felt her hands against his chest, not pushing away but stroking, as if she were tracing him. When he finally broke the kiss, only because he needed to breathe, they were in the hallway off the living room. He hadn't even been aware of moving. Which told him how far gone he was.

"Katie," he began, but stopped, with no idea left in his head of what he wanted to say beyond her name.

"Gavin," she said back at him, as if she felt the same. And he realized that it was all that mattered, that nothing more was needed but that heartfelt calling to each other.

It was the last coherent thought he had because she took his hand and led him to her bedroom. He barely noticed the room he'd never been in, because she began to unbutton the silky blouse she wore, one of those that managed to look businesslike yet incredibly sexy.

The moment the blue material separated over her breasts, revealing them nestled in a matching bra trimmed with delicate lace, he was lost. He could think of nothing but the fire inside him that had erupted into an inferno, hot, wild, demanding. And he was kissing her again, urgently, and when her lips parted beneath his he swiped over them with his tongue, amazed that a kiss could be so sweet.

He probed deeper, and the sweetness became a honeyeyed fire that threatened to consume him. He caressed her breasts through the bra, but it wasn't enough and he clawed at the straps to pull the lace out of his way. Then he cupped that soft flesh and it rounded into his hands as if made for them. She moaned softly, and it fired his blood even more. He was mad, mindless, and it was a place he'd never been before.

He didn't realize how mindless until his gasp for breath broke the kiss and he saw that not only was she naked to the waist, but his own shirt was unbuttoned and half off. And then he felt her hands moving down from his chest over his abdomen, stroking, her fingers leaving little trails of heat and fiery sensation everywhere they moved.

It was more than he could bear. He moved suddenly, picking her up and going down to the bed with her. He pulled off the rest of her clothes, felt her tugging on his and did everything he could to help, short of letting go of her. Finally they were pressed together knees to lips, skin against skin. He couldn't touch her enough, stroke her enough. He wanted to learn every precious inch of this woman who had reached him so quickly, in ways no other ever had.

When she began to caress him in turn, he nearly forgot to breathe. Every touch stoked the fire that was already beyond bearing. He rolled her beneath him, groaning aloud at the feel of her, and again at the way she seemed to welcome his weight. And when her hands slipped down to cup his backside, her name and an oath broke from him in one breath.

When he could take no more he lifted up slightly, looking into her eyes. She arched upward, pressing herself against him, and he could feel the taut points of her nipples against his chest. He couldn't ignore that readiness, could he? He bent his head and caught one with his lips, flicked it with his tongue, then suckled deeply. She cried out, her body fairly rippling in response.

He was too close, he had to pull back. But when he did, her hand slid down his body, then hesitated, almost shyly. He couldn't resist and took her hand to move it that last critical distance. Her fingers curled around his erection, stroked. His breath came out in a hiss, and her name broke from him just at her touch.

He was hanging on to his last bit of control by a thread. For a man used to ever and always being in control, this was uncharted territory, a place he never thought he would find. He fumbled for a moment, but her hand was still on him and she guided him. And then he was sliding into her body, his way eased by her own readiness, and that alone roused him even further. When he was sheathed in her, her body hot and tight around him, he shuddered at the feel of it. And then she moved, as if wanting him deeper, and that thread snapped.

He became something he didn't even recognize, voracious, starving, and she was the only thing that could slake his hunger. The man known for orchestrating a trial, for coaxing a jury with elegance and finesse, for having a mind that never lost track or focus, was beyond thinking of anything other than the woman in his arms. It wasn't simply that she fired every sense, inflamed every nerve. It was more, deeper, and if he hadn't been so consumed by the sensations she was triggering he might have been alarmed at the intensity of it.

In the end he could not think at all but only feel. When he felt her body clench around him, heard her cry out his name in a voice unlike anything he'd ever heard, he gave up trying to hold back. He groaned her name in turn and poured himself into her.

He had never believed in this kind of fierceness but now he had no choice but to believe. Because Katie Moore had not only reached places in him that had never been touched, but she had reached places he hadn't even known existed.

Chapter 30

Gavin had always figured it would be Katie who had second thoughts. That was, during those moments when he'd allowed himself to even consider giving in to the need she inspired in him.

Of course, he'd been incredibly, impossibly, a million times wrong about what that would be like, too. Heat rocketed through him at the memory of all the times they'd come together last night, making the cold outside the car now and the rain splattering on his windshield meaningless. He felt his body clench involuntarily when he thought of the last time, in the early hours of the morning, when it had been Katie who had awakened him, wanting. And in those moments, nothing could have shaken his conviction that she was the most genuine, honest woman he'd ever met.

But now he was in a quandary. The logical, common sense side of him was declaring last night a mistake. An unwise, entangling, complicated mistake. But every other part of him, body, heart and soul, was reveling in the wonder of the purest, most consuming experience of his life, both physical and emotional. All the references he'd heard about mind-blowing sex applied, but there was so much more.

So much that last night he hadn't been able to even think coherently about those reasons it was a mistake.

But now, as he drove to Foxworth in response to Quinn's call, Katie driving behind him in her own car so she could get to the library in time for Saturday hours, all those reasons hammered at him. That he was, in essence, working for her was only the smallest of them.

The largest was a looming fear that what faith he had left in his judgment was going to be destroyed. He'd sensed all along that Steven Moore was hiding something. Yet he hadn't believed it was guilt for the murder of Laurel Brisbane. But by then he was already attracted to Katie, and now he couldn't stop wondering if he'd done it again, let his attachment to someone cloud his vision.

Although, what he felt for Katie was a lot more than just attachment. It was like nothing he'd ever felt before.

...a lifelong challenge.

He knew in his gut that the words she'd said would apply both ways. It would take a lifetime to learn all the qualities of this woman. And what an amazing exploration it would be, of the Katie who could discuss deep philosophies or quote poets, then turn around and dress up as an animated character to entertain a bunch of kids.

And me, too.

He couldn't deny that seeing her in that long, silky blue dress with her hair down in a braid had been...entertaining. At least, it had had him entertaining thoughts that had only propelled him further down this path he'd tried to avoid.

He should have tried harder, he thought as he made the turn the GPS indicated, only vaguely aware of where he was in relation to Foxworth. He should have tried harder because what if his instincts had betrayed him again? What if the more he was personally connected to a case, the more likely his gut would go haywire?

For the first time in his career, both in the limelight and out, Gavin considered options he never would have thought of before. Options like not digging too deep, for fear of what he might find. Like looking for innocent explanations instead of the truth.

Like lying.

He felt the thought as if it were a physical thing, a solid blow to the gut driving all the air out of his lungs.

He had actually thought that. Thought about lying, the thing he hated most, to protect Katie's feelings. Because learning her father was guilty wouldn't just break her heart, it would shatter it irreparably.

And there'd be nothing of it left for you.

He groaned inwardly at the knowledge that a week ago he hadn't even known she existed. And now...

Memories of last night again shot through his brain like a summer lightning storm, the brilliance of them blinding him to anything else. Wouldn't hanging on to what he'd found be worth any price? Wouldn't—

Cutter yelped, sounding alarmed. Gavin's attention snapped back to his surroundings. The oncoming car he'd only been aware of on that autopilot level veered sharply, suddenly, into his lane. He hit the brakes. Rafe had told him once that in hot situations time sometimes seemed to slow down. It was really your brain kicking into overdrive, but the effect was as if everything else was going in slow motion. He'd never experienced it before, but he did now.

His mind sorted the possibilities rapid fire. Swerve right? Fairly deep ditch on that side of the road. Crash could be ugly. Swerve left? The other driver would likely try to correct, and put them back on a head-on course. Unless he was hydroplaning and had no control.

Or unless it was intentional.

The oncoming car was barely fifteen feet away now. He had no choice.

"Hang on, dog," he muttered and yanked the wheel to the right.

A gasp broke from Katie as Gavin's car swerved ahead of her. She heard an impact, and a loud scrape of metal. Something hit the street, bounced toward her. In a split second she decided to go over it with the center of her vehicle, her brain telling her it was small enough and to keep her tires away from it. She caught only a glimpse of the other car, the one that had sideswiped Gavin's rental. It sped past, clearly not intending to stop.

And then she saw nothing but Gavin's car skidding sideways. Heard nothing but the screech of tires. And then came the heart-stopping, horrendous thud that she'd swear she felt as his car ended up on its side in the ditch, facing back the way they had come. Which meant the driver's side not only took the brunt of the impact, but ended up embedded in the rain-softened dirt.

She hit her emergency flashers as she braked, hard. She left her car half in the lane, thinking it would both draw attention and act as a barrier. If it got hit, so be it.

She grabbed her phone and dialed 9-1-1 as she hurried toward the edge of the road. She tried to speak coherently as she half ran, half slid down the embankment, heedless of the mud, focused only on getting to the vehicle that was lying ominously on its side. She barely heard the dispatcher's assurances before she stuffed the phone back in her pocket and kept going. A memory flashed through her mind, of him getting into the car in her driveway just minutes ago. Of how she had been wishing she didn't have to work today, so she could stay with him, so they could have a leisurely Saturday exploring this new, wonderful thing that had sprung to life between them.

Had she seen him fasten his seat belt, or not? She couldn't remember. But surely he had.

A rush of sensation flooded her as she remembered those luscious hours in his arms last night. And in these moments now, when she was terrified of what she might find, she faced the truth. However foolish, however fast it had been, she had fallen, hard and irrevocably, for Gavin de Marco.

She heard a bark, realized that somehow Cutter had gotten out of the car. He seemed unhurt, because he was digging madly in the mud, sending up a spray behind him. Trying, she realized, to get to Gavin.

She skidded the last couple of yards. Felt the rush of cold water on her feet as she reached the bottom. The car was indeed embedded; it had hit hard. There was no point in her even trying to get to him from that side.

Cutter looked up at her, whined. She clawed her way over to the passenger door, peered through the wet, mud-spattered window. Belatedly she realized the back side window was down and noted vaguely that that must be how the dog had gotten out. Why had Gavin been driving with it down and why hadn't she noticed, she wondered inanely. Then she realized she was thinking of unimportant things to avoid the most important.

"Gavin!" It broke from her, everything she was feeling echoing in her voice.

And then Gavin moved, lifting his head. He looked at her. She saw blood streaming down the left side of his face. She bit back a scream; hysteria was the last thing he needed right now.

She reached for the passenger door. It unlatched, but seemed impossibly heavy. She got it open to where she could get her shoulder against the inside, then pushed. Since she was trying to open it almost vertically, it took her a moment. She didn't know if the latch would hold once she got it open, but as long as it let her in she didn't care.

She clambered in, heedless of the mud she was spreading from her boots. She heard a scratching noise, realized Cutter had jumped back through the window he'd escaped out of, and into the back seat. She grabbed at anything she could reach to keep from just dropping on top of Gavin.

"Pinned," he said, and she heard the sound as he tried to pull his left leg clear of the crumpled door and dash.

She had to tear her gaze away from his bloody face and order herself to calm down. She had to bend and twist awkwardly, but she got to where she could reach his leg. Urgently she ran her fingers over it, probing, looking for injury or a reaction from him.

"It's not broken," he said, sounding steadier. "Just trapped."

She reached farther, down to just above where the driver's door had crumpled inward. "I think it's your jeans, mostly," she said. "There's a piece of bent metal and it's snagged them."

"I told you I shouldn't have gotten dressed this morning."

Her head snapped around and she stared at him. He gave her a rather lopsided, wry grimace, but then he smiled, as if he were remembering what had prompted those earlier words. That he could look at her like that, despite being bloodied and trapped, sent a thrill through her that was entirely unsuited to the moment. She dared to hope she wasn't alone in this madness he'd brought out in her.

"When I get out of here," he said, his voice sounding

a little strained, "I'd like to talk about whatever you just thought."

No, you wouldn't, she thought, but she said briskly, "Let's take care of getting you out of here first. Although perhaps we should wait for the fire department."

Cutter gave a sharp bark then, and if he was expressing an opinion about waiting, it came through loud and clear.

"Agreed," Gavin said. "I want the hell out of here."

"Right," she said. "You don't happen to have a knife in the car, do you? I can go get my escape tool—"

"Glove box."

She scrambled over and opened the compartment. It only took her a moment to find a tool similar to the one she carried on her key chain only larger. In this land of water and bridges, it only made sense to have something that could both break a window and slice through a seat belt. The blade, however, was in a protected notch of the tool, and not really designed for slicing through an awkward fold of denim. And one she was having trouble keeping a grip on while sawing at it.

When Cutter wiggled his way first into the front seat, then down onto the floorboards, Katie almost shooed him away; he was only lessening what space she had to maneuver. But as she opened her mouth to speak to the dog, he caught the hem of Gavin's jeans in his teeth and pulled.

The fabric was suddenly taut, and Katie had both hands free to maneuver the blade. In a matter of seconds she had cut through the fabric and his leg was free.

Immediately he started to move.

"Are you sure you shouldn't stay still?"

"Nothing's broken," he insisted. "I'll be stiff and sore later, and probably have a hell of a headache, but right now I can move."

Cutter apparently agreed, for he scrambled back out of

the car. Katie, too, eased her way back out. Once she was standing on the muddy ground again, she held the door, making sure it didn't slam on Gavin as he worked his way up out of the car.

As Cutter nosed at him Katie looked him over anxiously, afraid there might be some serious injury—as if his bloody head wasn't enough—they hadn't noticed.

"I'm fine," he assured her as he reached down to Cutter. She thought he was just going to pet the helpful dog, but when he began to run his hands over the animal she realized he was checking for any injury. Something she should have done, she thought with no little regret. But he seemed to find nothing of concern, and gave the dog a final pat.

"Thanks for the help, buddy." He straightened, shifted his gaze back to Katie.

"I'm still trying to figure out how he got out," she said, relieved a bit at how easily he'd bent over to inspect the dog.

"Knowing him, he probably opened the window. He could have gotten to the button."

Katie managed a smile. "I wouldn't put it past him."

Gavin shook his head. Or at least started to, then stopped, quickly enough that her concern spiked again. "I know he was probably just trying to pull me out," he said, "but funny how he ended up doing exactly what you needed."

"More like amazing," Katie said, still not quite able to accept that he had escaped serious injury. What if something turned up later? It happened that way sometimes. Especially if that cut on his head was something more. She didn't want to think about that, didn't want to think of him being seriously hurt, or worse. What would she do if she lost him, now that she'd just found him? It had been bad enough when he'd been attacked outside her library, but now, after last night, she couldn't even bear the thought.

"I'm fine," he repeated. "But keep looking at me like that."

Her gaze shot back to his face. Sometimes she forgot she was dealing with a man who'd become famous in part because he could read people like few could.

Cutter let out a loud, sharp bark. It snapped her out of her emotional morass.

"Can you get up the slope?" she asked briskly, not wanting to have this conversation here and now. "I've got a first aid kit in my car. We can clean up that cut on your head."

Gavin was once more looking at Cutter, who was staring toward the road. "Might as well leave it," he said. "I'm guessing the cavalry's approaching."

Even as he said it she heard the siren. Cutter's sharper canine ears had obviously picked up the sound much sooner. Katie relaxed slightly; the professionals were there now, and if there was any hidden injury, like a concussion, they'd find it.

That was, they would once the younger EMT quit gaping at him.

"You are Gavin de Marco, aren't you?" he asked.

"Afraid so," Gavin muttered.

"We heard about your incident with the guy with the knife."

"News travels fast."

"Small department." The older partner, a man in his midthirties who was apparently training the younger, stepped in and took over. His brisk tone was a mild rebuke to the trainee's loss of professionalism. "Sheriff's traffic unit is on the way. Guy never stopped?"

"No," Katie said. "He just kept going. I didn't see which way at the intersection, because…"

She let her voice trail off and gestured at Gavin. The man nodded; she guessed he understood the priorities here because they were his, as well. He checked Gavin over quickly, then checked more thoroughly while the younger partner cleaned and bandaged the cut on his temple. He used his flashlight to do a vision test, then had Gavin watch his fingers as he moved them. Finally he nodded.

"Doesn't look like there's a concussion," he said. "And your leg will probably bruise, but I don't think there's any serious damage."

"Lucky me," Gavin muttered, but added a sincere "Thank you" to the medic.

The older man studied him for a moment. "First a guy with a knife, now a hit and run? How long have you been a trouble magnet?"

Gavin grimaced. "Normally, I'm not anymore. That seems to have changed since I got here, though."

Katie stared at him. A shiver rippled through her. She hadn't yet made the connection between the two incidents. She'd been too focused on him, and worrying if he'd been seriously injured.

But now she had to consider the very ugly possibility that neither of these events was random or accidental.

The possibility that somebody was trying to take Gavin out of the equation.

Because they were afraid he would do what he was famous for doing.

He'd find out the truth.

Chapter 31

"What the hell happened to you?"

Now there's a question. The earth moved? My world changed? I changed? Take your pick.

Gavin could only imagine what he looked like to Quinn, with his head bandaged, a bloodstained shirt, and a chunk cut out of his jeans. He gave him the condensed version, facts only. Without mentioning Katie; he wasn't quite up to explaining that. He'd sent her on to work, made one call and accepted the traffic investigator's offer of a ride to Foxworth, since it was so close.

As he expected, Quinn reached his same conclusion quickly.

"I don't believe in that much coincidence," he said grimly. Cutter barked as if to add emphasis.

"At least he's okay," Gavin said, looking at the dog.

"He's learned to take care of himself," Quinn said, "since the first time."

Gavin knew the story, of the operation where Cutter had gone down during a hail of gunfire. The dog had made a complete recovery. Quinn on the other hand, had never been the same; he had met both Hayley and Cutter, and changed his life.

And now he had met Katie, and one way or another, his life would never be the same, either. He knew that, that even if he walked away, went back to St. Louis and never saw her again, he would never be the same.

Hayley came out of the kitchen and handed him a much-needed mug of coffee. He took a big swallow, going for the effect rather than taste just then.

Hayley let him finish before saying, "So how is she?"

He froze, the mug halfway back to his mouth. "What?"

"Katie, of course."

"I…" He flicked a glance at Quinn, who was studying his wife, his head tilted as he considered her words.

"Please," Hayley said, her tone dry. "You weren't here, you weren't at our place, and where this crash happened is directly in between here and her place. Not to mention the sparks that practically ignite every time you're together."

"Look," Gavin said, "I know you think that—"

Hayley cut him off, smiling. "Cutter didn't just attach himself to you because you needed him, he also must have sensed you were ready."

"Ready?" Gavin asked warily.

"Or he knows Katie's the one," she added.

Gavin looked at the dog, who now sat beside Hayley, looking…smug. That was the only word he could think of for the animal's expression.

"You adjust to that," Quinn said, still laughing, "while I go get Ty started on digging into your nonaccident."

Glad of the distraction, Gavin said, "No traffic cams along there."

"No, but there are up on the highway, which he may have taken to get away. I'll have him look for a silver car with driver's side damage."

"And a missing mirror," Gavin said. "Katie nearly ran over it in the road."

And he had just confirmed Hayley's guess. Or maybe it wasn't a guess. Maybe it really did show. After last night, he wouldn't be surprised.

"She was behind you?" Quinn asked.

He nodded. "She had to open up this morning." His mouth twisted. "She was late, thanks to this. Oh, I borrowed Rafe."

Quinn frowned. "I was about to call him to ride shotgun with you."

"I'd rather he watched Katie. Just in case. Besides, he's a bit above watching over a guy who should be able to take care of himself."

"He wouldn't mind," Hayley said. "He admires you."

Gavin blinked, startled. Glanced at Quinn, who shrugged. "He admires anyone who's the best at what he does."

Hayley added, "Probably because he's the best, and he knows what it takes to get there."

"That's why I want him looking out for Katie," Gavin said, surrendering any pretense of detachment when it came to her.

"Your call," Quinn said.

"I told him I didn't want her to know."

"Then she never will, unless he has to act." At Gavin's nod, Quinn continued. "Meanwhile, Ty found something interesting."

"What?"

"That seminar that Ross Carr was supposed to be attending in San Diego? It was canceled. Hotel had a sewage problem. They tried to find another hotel or venue, but last minute, no luck."

Gavin frowned. "When?"

"First day."

Gavin got there instantly. "The day before the knife attack."

Quinn nodded. "Exactly. Hayley called and chatted up the receptionist at his job. She said about half the attendees just came home, but the others opted to stay and spend the week basking in the sun."

"Let me guess. Including Carr."

Quinn nodded. "But of course no one's seen or heard from him."

"Who would expect to?"

"Exactly. Perfect cover for dropping off the radar for a week."

"I presume you have Ty checking to see if there's any sign Carr headed home instead?"

Quinn nodded. "Nothing yet, but he's just started."

If it was there, Ty would find it, Gavin thought. And now he was really itching to talk to Carr. He had wanted to anyway, but this first and only blip on the screen of a solid alibi made it imperative.

Gavin found himself watching the time incessantly, telling himself it was because he needed what Ty was searching for, but knowing that in truth he was counting down the hours until he could see Katie again.

And that thought made him more edgy than anything else.

That is until an alert tone drew their attention, and seconds later Ty appeared on the screen above the fireplace. Without preamble, he sent them the photo he'd isolated of a damaged vehicle heading southbound on the state highway. The time frame fit, and the camera where it first appeared fit with the location of the crash. And the damage fit, driver's side, rearview mirror missing.

He stared at the image, at the make and model, remembered the flash of silver he'd seen in the instant before the crash. His stomach churned.

"Can you get the plate?" Quinn asked; it was nothing but a blur in the enlarged shot.

"Working on it," Ty answered. Gavin knew if it was possible at all, Ty and the Foxworth enhancement program—much of which Ty himself had written—would do it.

Instead of signing off abruptly without comment as he usually did, Ty cleared his throat and looked to the right of his own screen. Where, Gavin realized, he himself was sitting.

"Glad you're okay, sir," Ty said, sounding awkward.

Gavin knew what a rarity this was, both the comment and the "sir," so he held the young man's virtual gaze for a moment, before saying, "Thanks, Ty."

As the screen went dark, Quinn leaned back on the couch. "Now, that's a pinnacle few reach."

Gavin smiled; he liked the young tech genius Quinn had snatched off an unsavory path. "At least he's not afraid of me anymore."

"So he can focus on being afraid of Charlie," Hayley quipped, and they all laughed.

And it was a full minute or two before Gavin found himself contemplating what a meeting between Charlie and Katie would be like.

And wondering when he'd begun relating damn near everything in his life to her.

Katie tapped her finger idly on the steering wheel as she sat at the red light. There were four cars in front of her, which pretty much constituted a traffic jam for this place.

She smiled inwardly at how her attitudes had changed since she'd moved here from the city. When she realized she was smiling outwardly, too, she laughed. Happily. She wondered if everyone around her could read her expression as easily as Heather had; her colleague had guessed immediately how last night had ended up. And she'd been delighted, hooting with pure feminine appreciation for her taste.

"That man is pure *hawt*!" she'd drawled out with glee. "Good for you. About time."

And that brought Katie back to her main topic of thought all day: Gavin. Saturdays were always busy, the library full of people who couldn't get there any other day, so she hadn't been able to talk to him, but she'd texted a couple of times, just to be sure there were no unexpected after-effects from the crash. He'd assured her he was fine, and that they were working both on a possible new lead and on the hit and run.

He'd texted nothing more personal, and she told herself she shouldn't be disappointed. He was working, after all. She had hoped he might say something about tonight, about seeing each other. She felt a sudden qualm that perhaps he was having second thoughts.

"Never mind second thoughts, quit second-guessing," she muttered as the light changed.

Yet she found herself shying away from going home, and told herself it wasn't because she didn't want to be back there without Gavin, back at the scene where she'd learned more about what glory was physically possible between two people than she'd ever imagined.

Since he was wrapped up in work that was at least in part for her, she shouldn't complain that he hadn't said anything more personal. Guys didn't think that way, she reminded herself.

She would stick to her routine, she thought. She would stop by her father's place, which she did at least once a weekend. No reason to change that now. Especially now, when her father needed her support. And she hadn't even talked to him for two days. Of course, she'd been a little busy…

She felt the heat rise in her cheeks. No wonder Heather had guessed right off what she'd been up to last night. She wondered if her father would notice, and what she'd say if he asked.

Yes, Dad, as a matter of fact, I did have wild, crazy, superhot sex with the most amazing man last night. And by the way, he happens to be your lawyer.

Her fingers tightened around the steering wheel as she fought not to let the next words form, even in her mind. She failed.

And I think I love him.

She knew it was crazy. Love didn't happen that fast. Infatuation, yes. But that didn't last. He'd be heading back home soon, anyway. And he'd made no promises. In fact the most romantic thing he'd said when they'd left this morning was that he'd see her later. No specifics on when "later" was. Of course then that car had swerved out of nowhere and nearly put an end to everything. When she thought of how close he came to being seriously hurt, or worse, it sent a shiver through her. She didn't like even—

Her breath jammed into her throat, and every meandering thought vanished as she pulled into her father's driveway. And saw his car sitting in his carport. His silver car.

With driver's-side damage and a missing side mirror.

Chapter 32

Quinn ended the call on his cell, stood still for a moment, then turned to look at Gavin. Gavin took one look at his expression and quickly wound up his own call with his contact at the hotel in San Diego; he'd connected with the manager during a bar association meeting there some years ago, and had more recently steered him to Foxworth for help on a personal problem. The man had been more than willing to help, and Gavin now had confirmation that the room allotted to Ross Carr had been paid for, for the week, but according to hotel staff it had shown no sign of being used after that first day.

Normally he would have immediately relayed that information, but something in the way Quinn was looking at him stopped him. Cutter, who had been inspecting the building as if to make sure nothing had changed here after a night away—and what a night, Gavin thought—stopped and came over to sit at his feet.

I'm lucky you can't talk, dog.

"That was Brett," Quinn said after a moment. "Ty sent him what he was able to get on the license plate." Gavin stiffened, apprehension shooting through him. It intensified when Cutter plopped his chin on Gavin's knee and looked up at him worriedly. "He narrowed it down to a dozen or so registered in the county."

Gavin waited. His stomach started to churn again because he knew what was coming. Quinn let out a breath, looked back at his phone, tapped a screen and waited a moment. Then he handed it over.

Gavin scanned the list of registrations that had come attached to an email from Brett Dunbar. His gaze snagged on the fifth one on the list.

Steven Moore.

The churning became nausea. He'd been keeping the fear at bay since the moment he'd seen the photo and recognized the make, together with the fact that the car that hit him was silver—the same color as Moore's. But now it erupted in his gut.

Theories exploded in his brain. He noticed the first ones were efforts to make this innocent, to make the obvious not true. He waited, staring at that name, trying to summon up the detachment that had always enabled him to analyze coolly and dispassionately. But when he did he regretted it because the pattern he saw once he got his emotion out of the way was an ugly one.

Steven Moore, or someone using his car, had intentionally sideswiped him on that rain-slick road, sending him into that ditch. Gavin could easily have ended up hurt much worse than he had been. Or dead. Had that been the goal?

Questions caromed through his mind, rapid fire. Did Katie know? She'd been the one to suggest the route they both took; had it been for this reason? Had she set him up for her father to take out? But why would she do that when she'd asked for Foxworth's help, or at least not said no? Why would she bring him into the case, only to try and kill him when he got close to finding an answer?

Or maybe she really had thought her father innocent, but found out he was not and then quickly and easily changed course. He thought of the women he'd met over the years who would be quite capable of doing that. He would have sworn Katie wasn't like that, but who knew better than he how wrong he could be if he cared about someone.

And he cared about Katie. In fact, ten minutes ago he'd been close to facing the possibility that he was falling in love with her. Why the hell else would he be thinking about staying here longer, perhaps long term?

Fool.

The chill that crept over him now froze out the heat Katie had fired in him. Because the final possibility, the one he'd been mentally fighting off, was hammering at him now.

"You'll have to tell her," Quinn said quietly.

Gavin let out a short, harsh laugh. "What makes you think she doesn't already know?"

Bitterness flooded him. The dominoes fell in his mind. Katie had known, known all along her father was guilty, had lied and used Gavin—and his reputation—to save him. She'd lied to him about her father, the murder…and herself. It hadn't been a simple mistake that she hadn't mentioned her father's prior career as a locksmith. She probably hadn't realized how deep Foxworth would dig, had hoped they wouldn't find it. She'd lied to them from the beginning, and to him up to the end.

The finality of those last two words hit him hard.

The end. He hadn't even been sure what it was, what had sparked to life between them. And now it didn't matter.

Because this was indeed the end.

Katie stared at her father.

"That's it? That's your story?"

"It's what happened," Steven Moore said, giving her a puzzled look. "Why are you so—"

"Somebody stole your car, and you didn't know it until you came out and found it—" she gestured toward the carport "—like that?"

"I didn't hear a thing. They must have rolled it out of the driveway before starting it."

"With your keys," she said.

He grimaced at that. "That's worse than the car. That's always been a possibility with just a carport here, but I never thought anyone would actually go into the house to get my keys."

"Through the door you just happened to leave unlocked?"

"I told you I was working in the shop all day." His brow furrowed. "Why are you talking like this? Like it's my fault my car got stolen?"

"And conveniently returned."

"Obviously someone took it for a joyride this morning and brought it back after they crashed it."

"And you never heard a thing."

"I had earphones on," he said. "The ones you gave me, the wireless ones."

Katie took a deep breath to steady herself. She was trembling, she could feel it, but kept on. Because she had to. She hadn't thought through all the aspects of this, hadn't had time to, but some part of her knew the entire rest of her life would turn on this. She looked at the side of the car for a moment, and the telltale streak of paint transfer that was the exact color of Gavin's rental.

She shifted her gaze back to her father's face, where it would stay until she was sure, one way or another. "Is that what the police say?"

He looked discomfited. "I haven't actually called them yet."

Her heart, which had kept hoping for a way out of this, sank. But even knowing there was no answer she would like, she asked, "Why?"

"Well, I only just discovered it a little while before you arrived. And...I did leave the door unlocked, as you said."

Was that hesitation, him deciding to use the out she'd already provided?

"But you will call them now?"

He didn't look happy. "Maybe I'll just have it repaired."

He didn't want to call the police. And there was only one reason she could think of for that. She was shaking now.

"And if your insurance wants a police report?"

"Don't you see?" he asked, sounding oddly eager as he rapidly spoke. "That's just it. I make a report, and both my car and home insurance is likely to go up."

It did make sense. But she couldn't judge his tone. Did he sound that way because it was true, or because she'd again given him an out, a logical explanation? And how on earth had her life degenerated to where she was questioning her own father? Suspecting him of lying to her face?

Lying. The very idea made her think of Gavin. What would he think? What would he do? What would those vaunted instincts tell him?

She tried to think as she imagined he would. She knew he was an expert at reading people. She wasn't, but she knew—or thought she knew—her father better than anyone. So she set out on an exchange that she was inwardly hoping against hope would prove the awful things she was thinking wrong.

"You're missing a mirror."

"Yes. Lucky there are a ton of these cars on the road. Shouldn't be hard to find a replacement."

Another effort at covering, pointing out his car was far from unique? God, she hated this.

She stared at him as she said, "I can tell you where to find the original."

She would swear his blink was one of genuine bafflement. "What?"

"The original mirror. The one that came off when your car sideswiped Gavin de Marco's."

"How— What are you talking about?"

Her throat tightened. Had he been going to ask her how she knew about what had happened? Of course, that could be interpreted innocently, too. And he hadn't really said it. So why was she even questioning it? This was her *father*.

"The mirror I almost ran over when it was bouncing down the road in front of me."

His eyes widened. "Katie, you were in an accident? Why didn't you—"

She cut him off, her gaze fixed on his face, searching for anything that would help her believe. "Gavin was in the accident. When your car purposely drove him off the road and into a ditch."

"My God. Is he—"

"If the goal was to kill him, it failed. But he was hurt, and it could have been fatal." It was killing her, but she kept her gaze fastened on his face, that beloved face that she had loved from her earliest memories. It showed nothing but concern, and relief, that she could see.

"Thank goodness it wasn't!" If he was faking it, he was

doing a fine job. But then, if he was capable of that, then she didn't know him at all.

"Why do you suppose someone would try to kill him?"

He frowned then. "I'm sure he's made enemies...but what are the odds someone after him would steal *my* car?"

"Exactly."

"Why here, why now?" His brow was furrowed. He was rubbing at his chin in the way he always did when thinking hard. "You don't think it's connected to him helping us?"

And again, she would swear his shock was real. As was the "us."

"I think it's connected to him having a reputation for always finding the truth."

For an instant, just an instant, something flashed in the eyes she knew so well. And more telling, he looked away. She felt something inside her squirming, twisting, as if trying to get away. She made herself go on.

"Someone is worried enough to try and kill him. Or at least take him out of action." She stared at him, hating the way he now wouldn't meet her gaze. "Someone driving your car."

Finally, after more than enough time for him to get himself in hand, he looked back at her. "Katie, surely you're not saying you think it was me?"

"I don't know anymore, Dad. Something's wrong, and I—"

She stopped before she said something irrevocable. He was holding her gaze once more, and now she was doubting her doubts.

"You know I would never do such a thing."

That she would have staked her life on.

And instead you staked your love, although you didn't know it then.

"I'm a little rattled," she said after a moment. Again kept

her eyes on his face, trying to read it as she added, "If I hadn't had to work, I would have been in the car with him."

Her father's eyes widened. "What?"

"I could have been hurt, or worse, too."

He went pale. And when he reached out to hug her, he was the same beloved father who had always been there for her, who had gone through hell with her.

And yet, for the first time in her entire life, she didn't quite believe him. Not all the way. She couldn't quash the feeling that he was hiding something. She thought about the difference between lies and lies of omission. And how Gavin felt about both.

"I'll call the police right now," he promised.

"You do that. I have to go."

"Katie, wait."

She ignored him and walked back to her car. She drove home in such a numbed state she was lucky she didn't have an accident herself. Not that Gavin's crash had been an accident.

Once home she huddled in her favorite chair, in the dark, alone.

She couldn't doubt her father's concern had been genuine when he'd heard how close she'd come to being in that car. She wondered vaguely how he'd feel when he put together why she'd had reason to be with Gavin at that hour of the morning. That seemed minor compared to the fact that she was certain, on some deep level, that her father was lying to her. Or at the least keeping something from her.

Her entire lifetime perception of him had shifted in just those few minutes. Until just now, she would have sworn—in fact had sworn—that would never happen.

She had sworn to Gavin.

Who didn't tolerate liars.

Who would probably now think her one. Again.

She shivered, not even the plush throw enough to reach the chill that went bone deep. She was caught between her suspicions of her father and the knowledge that if she told Gavin, he would walk away from the case, which was practically a conviction even if he never really was his legal representative.

But if she didn't tell him and he found out, she would certainly lose him. She knew he meant what he said about people who lied to him.

She shivered again, wondering how her life had turned once more into heart-crushing chaos.

Chapter 33

Gavin realized now what he missed about the city. The thousands of people, each with their own set of problems. Each one trying to get through their lives with the minimum of upset and discomfort, sometimes succeeding, sometimes not. Somehow all that shared, communal worry seemed to make your own seem less, because you could turn any direction and find someone in worse straits than you were.

Out here, he thought as he stared out the patio door across the meadow, you were pretty much alone with your thoughts unless you made an effort. While most of the time he found that soothing after the chaos of the city, right now it was leaving him far too much time to wallow in the mire he found himself in. It had been a hellish night, and the morning, despite being sunny for a change, had brought him no relief. Because the bottom line hadn't changed.

He'd fallen like some high school kid with his first crush.

For a liar.

He'd been lied to and used in a way he'd sworn would never, ever happen again. Damn, she'd even slept with him—

He spun on his heel away from the window as his mind recoiled from the memory…the way she'd touched him and let him touch her, the sheer consuming joy of holding her, joining with her, the way it had burned through to his very soul. It had been the most amazing night of his life. If he had to believe that was all faked, that was all a lie, then he should just drive off the bridge on his way to the airport because he was obviously too stupid to live.

But if it had been real… No, it couldn't be, because she'd lied. But maybe she hadn't lied about that.

Believing in selective lying now, are we, de Marco?

He sat down on the couch before the fire; although sunny it was still November, and cold without the cloud cover to hold in what warmth there was. He was lucky he'd found out now, he kept telling himself. It didn't improve his mood any. He'd warned Quinn when they'd arrived this morning that he was in no state to either talk or be sociable, but Quinn had only raised an eyebrow and said, "Somebody ask you to do either?"

Neither Quinn nor Hayley had bothered him beyond offering coffee and ibuprofen. He took the pills; the meds they'd given him after the crash had worn off.

When he'd declined the use of one of their vehicles, Hayley, with her usual brisk efficiency, had taken on the task of dealing with his rental car company. The accident report clearly showed the other driver completely at fault, and that he'd left the scene without stopping put the seal on it. Even on Sunday she now had delivery of a replacement car promised by midday.

He turned to her as she hung up the phone.

"Maybe he'd be better off with you," he suggested, gesturing at Cutter, who was sprawled on the couch beside him, his chin now parked on Gavin's leg. He'd been watching the dog carefully—the only distraction he'd found from his thoughts—for any sign of injury that was late showing up, but the emergency vet's assessment appeared accurate and the animal seemed fine.

"I think we'd have a fight on our hands," Hayley said as she looked at the dog. "Nope, you're his chosen task, and interfering with that does no good."

"Mmm." Gavin shook his head at her words, even though he'd caught himself more than once attributing humanlike motives and intelligence to the clever canine.

Hayley shifted her gaze to Gavin. "You know, Gavin, there could well be an innocent explanation for all this," she said, obviously reading his mood. "Or Katie genuinely might not have known."

"Not likely."

"She deserves a chance to explain," Quinn put in from where he sat nearby.

Gavin had his mouth open to say he was done with this when Cutter's head came up and he let out a soft woof. Then another as he got to his feet, jumped down from the couch and headed for the door. As soon as he got there he raised up on his hind legs and batted at the automatic opener. Gavin's gut knew who was there before the door swung open. Still, it knotted up the instant Katie stepped inside.

He realized, with a little shock, she looked like he felt. The usually tidy, together woman looked a bit ragged, her hair tousled, her jeans and sweatshirt just thrown on.

And her eyes were reddened. Seriously reddened. She'd been crying. A lot. And the slight sheen on her cheeks indicated she hadn't stopped crying on the way here. Even now she wiped at her eyes with the sleeve of her shirt, as if it had become habit.

It was instinctive for him to stand, but he made himself stop. And unlike her usual considerate self, Katie ignored Quinn and Hayley, her eyes focused only on him. In his peripheral vision Gavin saw the Foxworths exchange a look. He wondered if they'd felt the sudden ice in the room.

"We'll just let you work it out," Hayley said then.

"You've got the number if you need reinforcements," Quinn added, and Gavin noticed he didn't specify which of them that was aimed at.

They murmured something he couldn't hear to Katie as they passed. But their stubborn dog stayed, escorting—hell, herding—Katie toward him. In fact, the dog shouldered and nudged and even pushed until she had little choice but to sit in the spot the dog himself had just vacated. Next to him.

Gavin stared at her but said nothing. What she said first would determine what he would do. Silence spun out. She picked at a thread on her jeans. Again she wiped at her eyes. He felt uncomfortable ignoring her obvious distress, but he made himself do it. Even if going from the incredible intimacy of the other night—God, had it just been one night ago?—to this was stomach churning. Especially when she wouldn't look at him.

"Are you all right?" she asked first.

"Obviously," he said, his voice cool.

She winced. He felt a twinge and wondered at it. When had he started feeling anything but abhorrence for liars?

"I'm sorry," she finally said.

For lying? he wondered. But still he said nothing.

"I love my father. I never would have agreed to this if I hadn't been utterly certain of him."

Gavin went very still. He hadn't missed the past tense. She lifted her head, finally met his eyes. She drew in a long, deep, audible breath. "I went to see him last night, when you—"

She stopped. He guessed she'd been about to say something about him dropping off the radar, after the night they'd had. Under normal circumstances, it would have been a piggish thing to do. But these were hardly normal circumstances.

She took another deep breath. She clasped her hands together, as if she needed the pressure, needed to do it to hold herself together. She lowered her gaze to her fingers, and he saw a shiver go through her. Again his stomach knotted; he wanted nothing more than to reach out for her, pull her into his arms, comfort her. Only a single word stopped him.

Liar.

Once more she lifted her head and met his gaze. And this time she held it. When she spoke again, her voice was steadier, businesslike, and the words unrolled rapidly.

"It was his car that hit you. I saw the damage, the dark paint, the missing mirror. His explanation is that it was stolen while he was working in his shop, and brought back after the damage was done. That someone got into the house and took the keys. That he had earphones on so he didn't hear anything. That he'd only discovered it right before I got there."

Gavin stared at her. He hadn't expected that. Hadn't expected that she'd come here to tell him what she'd learned, not when it was evidence against her father.

For a moment she just looked at him. Then her breath caught audibly. "You already knew."

"Thanks to Ty and Brett Dunbar."

She figured it out quickly. "The traffic camera on the highway. You got a license number."

"A partial. And your father was fifth on the list of matches. I don't believe in that much coincidence."

"Neither do I."

His certainty that she'd been lying all along was shaken. Why would she come here like this, tell him about the car if she was? And her reaction when she realized he already knew had been genuine surprise, he was sure of that.

"You believe his story?" He kept all trace of accusation out of his voice.

"I want to. He's never lied to me before."

Want to wasn't the same as *yes.* "But now?"

She steadied herself again, and Gavin saw in the tenseness of her posture, the tightness around her eyes, the way she clenched her hands, just how much this was costing her. And yet she was doing it. Admiration spiked through him.

"Now I'm not sure. I still can't believe he would hurt Laurel. And he seemed totally honest about the car. And why would he want to hurt the person trying to help him? But the car being stolen out from under his nose, and just happening to hit you? That's so…implausible. He's keeping something from me. I can feel it."

He couldn't put a single name to how she sounded. Bewildered. Hurt. Confused. Yet she also sounded determined, and maybe the tiniest bit angry. He analyzed his options for a moment before he quietly repeated her own question.

"Why would he want to hurt the person trying to help him?"

"There's only one reason I can think of," she said, her voice going dark, wounded. "He doesn't want the truth found."

She was no coward, Katie Moore. When it was staring her in the face, she didn't run away, no matter the pain it had to be causing her. *Admiration* wasn't a strong enough word for what he felt for her.

But the other words that fit scared him.

"And what do you want, Katie?" he asked softly.

She steadied herself once more, and her voice was level when she answered, "I want what I said I wanted in the beginning. I want the truth."

"Do you?"

She frowned. "Why else would I have wanted you to get involved in the first place?"

There was that. He leaned back on the couch, keeping his gaze fastened on her. She met his eyes unflinchingly. So unflinchingly he found himself rethinking his assumptions. All of them.

This time it was he who found he couldn't look at her. He shifted his gaze, realized Cutter was sitting at her feet and staring up at him intently. The dog held his gaze with the intensity Gavin imagined his breed used on the animals it herded. And then he put his chin on Katie's knee. What was Cutter trying to indicate? Trust? Belief? Faith? All three?

Gavin gave a shake of his head, as much at falling into the pattern of Foxworth crediting the animal with such uncanny abilities as anything.

Were she anyone else, he'd be certain he'd been played and she'd been lying all along. Yet a dog's simple gesture made him want to believe.

"So that's it," Katie said, startling him. His gaze shot back to her face. She was watching him and frowning. "You think he did it. All of it, Laurel, too. And you think I knew all along."

She'd obviously thought his shake of the head was aimed at her, not the dog. He found himself considering denying her words. Once more thinking about lying. When had he become such a hypocrite? He steeled himself; he couldn't be less strong than she was being right now.

I don't lie.

His own words to her rang in his head. He had no idea

how she would react, and a lie would be kinder, especially after— He stopped himself before a heated string of erotic images could derail him entirely.

She wanted truth. He would give her that. Even knowing what it would do, to her and to what they had found together.

One night, that's about all you're good for, de Marco. Then you blow it to bits.

"I did think that, when it first came together," he admitted.

"You thought I was lying from the beginning?"

"I don't now," he said. But that didn't change the fact that he had.

For a moment she just stared at him. He waited for some kind of eruption, a flash of anger. After all, he'd just admitted he'd suspected her of some very devious machinations. What he saw in her face was plainly readable, but it wasn't anger. It was pain, and it echoed in her voice when she spoke.

"And you thought I was the kind of person who would do something like that? Use you like that?"

Only then did he realize he'd done worse than make her angry. Even Cutter sensed the change and straightened up.

He saw it in her eyes. It was impossible to miss. He'd shattered her. He'd taken the closeness of that night and made it a travesty, a sham, at least in her eyes.

"Katie—"

She waved him off and stood up abruptly. Cutter whined, clearly displeased by what was happening. She folded her arms in front of her, and Gavin had the distinct feeling that if she'd been alone she'd have wrapped them around herself for some small amount of comfort. Something he should be doing for her.

Except now he didn't have the right.

She walked over to the patio doors, stood for a long, silent moment staring out across the meadow. He wanted to go to her, wanted to ease her pain, but since he was the one who had caused it with his lack of trust, he would likely do more damage than good.

She turned and came back. He rose slowly as she came to a halt in front of him. When she spoke, it was so controlled it made his own muscles tense up. "Are you quitting?"

"Katie—"

"Have you decided my father is guilty, Mr. de Marco?"

The formality stung, as he knew it was supposed to. What surprised him was just how much it hurt. It took him a moment to get past the unexpected, wrenching pain. He tried to match her flat tone, and it took an effort that amazed him.

"I haven't decided anything. And I won't until I speak to your father again."

"Fine." He had the feeling that single word would have sounded the same no matter what his answer had been. "Now would be a good time. He'll be home."

She turned and walked out without another word.

Cutter growled. Gavin looked down at him.

He had never realized an animal could express disgust.

Chapter 34

She was going to see this through.

Katie repeated the words in her head like a mantra, as she had all morning while waiting for the rental, because she didn't want to be suspected of sneaking ahead to warn her father. She repeated the words as if they were the only thing that could keep her together. She'd vowed to see this through and that's what she would do. Her feelings didn't matter now. Nor did the fact that her belief in her father was on the edge of obliteration. Or her belief that what she'd found with Gavin was real, and wonderful. Because she couldn't love a man who could think her capable of what Gavin had thought.

It didn't matter, she repeated to herself. Nothing mattered but the truth.

She drove rather dangerously, since she refused to look in the rearview mirror to see if Gavin's new rental was behind her. When she got to her father's house, she saw his damaged car in the same place it had been. But there were new tire tracks in the soft dirt next to the driveway, indicating someone had turned around. The sheriff?

She felt a surge of hope. Her father had called her last night, but she hadn't answered, hadn't wanted to talk to him. But the message he left said he'd reported the theft and damage. Surely if her father had actually tried to take Gavin out of the picture, he wouldn't have actually done that. He wouldn't want law enforcement involved at all, would he?

But her certainty meant nothing to Gavin. Clearly any emotion of hers meant less than nothing to him. On the bitter thought, she heard another car pull into the driveway. It came to a stop beside her. She got out, started to head for the house, then stopped. She waited for Gavin to get out, followed by Cutter. He walked toward the car, but paused to look at her questioningly.

"Wouldn't want to give him any warning," she said, her tone as chilly as the air.

He didn't respond, only nodded and walked on to look at the car. He studied it for a moment, and she was sure he was taking in the missing mirror and the long scrape that showed a streak of color that exactly matched the car he'd been driving.

"He reported it," she said, leaving out the hopes attached to that thought. He looked at her, lifting an eyebrow. "He left a message late last night that he'd done it. And," she said, gesturing toward the tire prints in the ground, "those weren't here last night."

Again he only nodded. Plainly he didn't want to talk to her. And why would he, when he thought her capable of such deviousness? A belated thought suddenly struck, with such power it took her breath away. Did he think Friday night had been a lie, too? Did he think that part of some great manipulation on her part?

She didn't think she'd made a sound, thought she'd stifled the moan of pain, but he looked at her as if he'd heard it. Something flickered in those dark eyes but she couldn't tell what it was, and allowed herself no foolish imagining that it might be caring.

When Cutter came to her and nuzzled her hand, she automatically stroked his head. She felt a slight easing of the turmoil inside her, as if the dog had somehow taken some of the ache away.

The house was locked front and back, and her father didn't answer the door. She led the way around the back, saw a distant light on in the shop.

"At least he locked the back door this time," she said, almost to herself as they started that way. It was a bit of a trek over the soft, uneven ground, past the vegetable garden and through the trees to the small building at the very back of the property. The trees and shrubbery back there were a bit overgrown, but her father liked it that way, said it gave him a sense of peace and solitude when he was there.

"This is why he didn't see or hear the thief," she said when they had passed the first stand of greenery and the house—and carport—were barely visible. Gavin looked back, but he again said nothing. She resolved to say nothing more; obviously he didn't care to hear anything from her.

Especially that you fell in love with him.

Even in her thoughts the past tense hurt, and she kept her face steadfastly forward until they reached the shop.

Her father was busy tweaking his latest project, welding something on an intentionally crooked weathervane he was making for Mrs. Collier down the street. A few more of his pieces, in various stages of completion, adorned the workbench and shelves. She didn't look at them, she'd seen them all, but she watched Gavin look at them and saw the fleeting expression of surprise on his face as he took in the room.

Good. I'm glad you're surprised. Maybe you'll see that he's not who you think he is.

With a rueful inward laugh at herself about people not being who you thought they were, she watched as her father whipped off his helmet. His face lit up as he looked at her, clearly delighted to see her. Especially after the way they'd parted.

"Katie, honey," he said and strode quickly over to envelop her in a hug. She accepted it, although with some lingering hesitation.

When he released her she nodded toward Gavin. "He needs to talk to you," she said, not even using his name.

She saw her father's expression change, take on a look that could be fear, or simply wariness at facing the fierce Gavin de Marco.

"Let's go up to the house," her father said, and such was her state of mind that she wondered if he suggested that to give himself time to think, time to decide what he was going to say. And not say.

But Gavin didn't press, merely agreed. Once inside, she went into the kitchen she knew as well as her own and put on a pot of coffee. She'd pass on it herself. The last thing she needed was a caffeine hit when her mind was already running in circles, but she was sure her father at least would welcome it. And at a second thought, she checked the vegetable bin and found a bag of carrots, broke a chunk off of one and offered it to Cutter. The dog took the treat with a wag of his tail as a thank-you.

When the coffee was done, she poured one for her father and added his usual large dollop of milk, and pondered for a moment over pouring a cup for Gavin, as well. She hadn't asked if he wanted any. In fact she hadn't spoken to him since her explanation about the shop's location had been met with no response. In the end she poured it anyway and carried the two cups out into the living room.

Oddly, they were talking about his shop projects, her father explaining how he'd gotten into the whimsical sideline when someone had stopped to ask about the Christmas decoration he'd built one year, a row of wire structures of different sizes and shapes that, when strung with lights, looked like a little village lit up for the holiday.

She handed her father his mug first, and then held the other out to Gavin.

"It's black," she assured him as he hesitated; she knew he drank it that way or not at all. No multinamed concoctions for him; he drank it for the hit, he'd told her, not the taste.

Her father was watching them, a considering expression on his face. And then he focused on Gavin. "If you hurt my little girl," he said conversationally, "I have a welding torch."

"Dad!" she exclaimed, her cheeks flushing. Between the coffee and her telling him she would have been with Gavin yesterday morning had she not needed her car, he'd obviously put it together.

"I think," Gavin said quietly, "that warning's a little late. To my anguish."

Her head snapped around. Gavin was looking at her, not her father.

"Well, you'd damned well better make it up to her, then," her father said sternly.

"I never intended to hurt her."

Katie felt as if she should say something, but she had no words. It wasn't exactly an apology, but it was close.

"That said," Gavin went on, "why are you hurting her?"

Her father drew back, clearly startled. "What?"

"You're lying to her. Or hiding something. And she knows it. Why?"

Katie's breath caught. Her mind careened between two things, that the near-apology had not been sincere but a lead-up to this, and that it seemed strange that Gavin had asked why he was lying rather than what about.

"Mr. de Marco," her father began.

"Gavin, please," he said, and his tone was as it had been, conversational, lacking even a hint of accusation. "You had the sheriff out, for the car?"

"I did," her father said, sounding relieved at the sudden switch. "They took a report. I even told them about what happened to you. I have nothing to hide. I'm sorry about your accident, by the way."

"It wasn't an accident."

"Well, yes, but you know what I mean."

"I know several things. I'll list them for you later, if you like. But right now I'd like to know why you feel the need to hide something from your daughter."

It went on and on, Gavin letting her father veer away from the subject, get to thinking he'd successfully diverted the conversation. Then, in the moment she sensed her father relaxing, he was back to it, again catching her father off guard. First from his artwork back to the question, then from the car incident back to it again, then from what he'd been working on at the time back to why he was hiding something. And again, not what he was hiding, but why. As if he thought he would get an answer to the one but not the other. Or that only this answer really mattered.

She stayed silent, watching and listening intently, trying to shore up her faith in the father she loved. She wondered if that was why Gavin had said nothing about her staying in the room, because he wanted her to see this, to learn what he learned. But that would mean he believed she hadn't known all along, wouldn't it? If her father was lying, that is.

She cut off the circuitous thoughts that got her nowhere and continued to watch and listen. She wondered if this was what he'd been like in a courtroom, pressing, luring, ensnaring until he finally got to the truth. Quietly, determinedly relentless, knowing what he wanted and digging from whatever angle would get him there. Reluctantly, since he was grilling her father, the admiration she'd felt when she'd first watched a trial video of him sparked anew.

"Why put your shop so far from the house?" Gavin asked, seemingly apropos of nothing. Unless he was insinuating her father had buried bodies back there. The thought came with the bitter memory of Gavin admitting he'd believed she'd been lying all along.

Her father's brow furrowed, but he was apparently getting more used to the rapid switching of subjects. "I do some grinding, and other work that makes some noise. I didn't want to disturb the neighbors, so I put it as far back as I could from the other houses."

"Not hiding anything back there?"

Her father looked offended. "Nothing but Katie's Christmas present, and thanks for making me give that away."

For the first time since this had begun, Katie smiled. "I promise not to snoop."

He managed a smile back. "Then it's safe. Your promise is golden."

"Is yours?" Gavin asked her father quietly. "Will you promise her you're not hiding anything from her?"

Katie nearly gaped at him. Was there nothing he couldn't turn to his goal?

"We all have secrets," her father said, looking uneasy once more.

"But why do you feel the need to hide this one from her?"

"I love my daughter," he answered, as if that explained it.

"And she loves you," Gavin said, still quietly. "Is that it? You're afraid your secret will change her love for you?"

Katie nearly gasped aloud as her father's expression changed again. And this time there was no denying what was right before her. Gavin had hit upon the truth. Or *a* truth, at the least. Her father truly was hiding something, and it was something he was not just reluctant but afraid to tell her.

"Dad," she whispered, staring at him.

Her father wouldn't meet her eyes. Gavin's voice was barely above a whisper now. "I've gotten to know your daughter a little. And once she gives her love, only something unforgivable could change it. Something indefensible. So indefensible even her great love can't get past it."

Katie's breath caught once more. *Is this aimed at me, too? Is he talking not just about Dad, but us?* She answered her own inward questions. *This is not about you, and there is no us. Didn't he make that clear enough for you?*

"I believe you about the car," Gavin said. "Have you done something else, Steven? Something so bad that even Katie's love can't withstand it? Did you kill her best friend?"

Her father drew in an audible breath. "No."

It was flat, solid, and to Katie utterly believable. He hadn't done it. And she realized she'd never really believed he had. He was hiding something, but not that.

"Then what?" Gavin persisted, still gently.

Her father glanced at Katie, and she read an apology there for what he was about to say. She wanted to encourage him, assure him nothing could change her love for him, but she was afraid to interrupt the flow Gavin had finally established.

"Get it out," Gavin said. "It's eating you up."

Her father looked at his feet. And then, in a voice she'd never heard from him before, he answered.

"Laurel and I had an affair."

Chapter 35

Gavin heard Katie's gasp, but didn't look at her. He kept his gaze fastened on the man before him. But inside he was relieved. Katie would be hurt but not destroyed. Another warning bell went off in his head, that his first thought wasn't about Moore's guilt or innocence, but Katie. And she was apparently Cutter's first thought as well, for the dog was quickly at her feet, leaning in, offering comfort in that way he had.

"I know it sounds silly," Moore said, "me more than twenty years older, but she didn't care. Her only worry was that Katie might not like it."

He gave Katie a quick, sideways glance. She was staring at her father, clearly stunned.

"It started when we were planning Katie's birthday. The breakup with Ross was already starting. So she cried on my shoulder and then one day…she kissed me. It startled both of us, I think."

"Dad," Katie began, then stopped as if she couldn't find any words.

He didn't look at her, kept his eyes on Gavin. He was clearly uncomfortable, but now that he'd started he was going to finish. Gavin stayed silent, knowing that right now, this was nothing to do with the case and everything to do with what kind of relationship Katie and her father would have from here on.

"We laughed it off, but…it wouldn't go away. It kind of…morphed from there into something else. Something special."

"So special you kept it secret?" Katie asked. Gavin tried to assess her tone, but there was so much shock there he couldn't separate out much more.

"In the beginning, we didn't even know what it was. At first we met to make plans for the party. Then we ended up talking about other things. For hours. She'd ask for advice. I thought she looked at me as a sort of surrogate father."

Katie absently stroked Cutter's fur. "She always thought you were hot," she said slowly. "When we were in elementary school she used to joke that she couldn't wait until she grew up so she could marry you."

Gavin saw Moore's eyes widen, then saw him blink rapidly as moisture pooled there. Whatever the man had felt for Laurel, it had been real.

"I was the one who wanted to keep it quiet," Moore said. "I wanted to be the one to tell you, but I was afraid to."

She was still stroking Cutter's dark head as if it helped her think. She was processing it now, Gavin thought. Getting past the shock. "I told you I would love for you to find someone. You've been alone so long. But…"

"Not your best friend."

"It would have taken time for me to get used to it." Gavin could tell by her expression she was turning it over in her mind, looking at it from all angles. "But," she added softly, her gaze seeming to turn inward, making Gavin guess she was remembering things, "maybe I should have known. Not just because she'd always had a crush on you, but looking back…she did drop some hints here and there. I just never realized it at the time."

"You two were so close, she hated not telling you. I was the coward."

Gavin could almost feel Katie leveling out. She was dealing with it now.

"Back in high school she used to joke that if she married you, she'd be my stepmother. We both laughed hysterically at that idea, so… I guess I never took it seriously."

Moore was looking at Gavin now. "So do you believe me now? I would never have hurt Laurel."

In that moment Cutter got up, crossed over to Moore, turned and sat. He looked at Gavin, in fact stared at him with that same intensity he'd seen before. Something flashed through Gavin's mind, a memory of the first day Cutter had met the man, and the odd look that Gavin had categorized as a maybe. There was no reservation in the look the dog was giving him now. He might as well have been able to talk. It was almost as if he'd had the same instinct Gavin had, that he knew the man had been lying about something, but now that it was out, the animal sensed what was left was the truth.

In fact Gavin did believe Moore, now that he knew what the man had been hiding. But he also knew now what Detective Davidson had been talking about when he'd said they had something on Moore. "Some would say there's more motive than ever. Who ended it?"

"I did. I thought it was best. She needed to find someone her own age."

It sounded like the truth, Gavin thought. But if Davidson had found out, it would explain the police looking in Moore's direction.

Katie was shaking her head, clearly still trying to wrap her mind around this. "I felt like Laurel was hiding some-thing, but… So when I thought I was helping her get over Ross, it was really you? And when she said there had been cheating involved, it was her, not Ross? With you? That's why you were so broken up about it, because—"

"When did you last see her?" Gavin asked, cutting off the flow of clearly distressed questions. He needed more answers before leaving Katie to deal with the personal fall-out.

"About a week before she…died. She wasn't happy about my decision." His expression was bleak. "She wasn't happy about anything at that point."

Katie spoke again. "But Ross was—"

"One of the things she was unhappy about," her father finished for her. "He wanted back in her life, but she was afraid he hadn't changed. She wanted to meet, to ask one last time if I was sure."

Gavin's gaze narrowed. "One last time?"

"She was considering going back to him. I told her I didn't think she should, that I—"

He stopped as Gavin's phone beeped with an incoming text. He pulled it out, swiped the screen and glanced at the message. Timing, he thought, considering where his mind had just turned, what had clicked into place with Moore's confession.

He looked at the man, who seemed relieved to have the truth out at last. At Cutter, who was still giving him that signal that Moore was now to be trusted. And finally he looked at Katie, who was looking back at him with only mild curiosity. As she might look at anyone, not someone who just one night ago had been naked in her arms, her name ripping from his throat as he drove into her body in a heat he'd never known before.

A flame of that heat singed him, and he had to steady himself to speak with a semblance of casualness. "I need to talk to someone, so I'll leave you two to work this out."

He rose, and so did Katie. "Who?" she asked.

"Someone I've been waiting to interview."

She studied him for a moment as he got up. Cutter got to his feet as well, and before Gavin had even taken a step was headed for the door. Katie was right behind them.

"I'm going with you."

"Don't you think you need to stay with your father and talk?"

"No. Right now I need to see this through. To the end."

Something in the way she said the words sent a chill through him. The end of what? The case? Or them? Had his lack of faith in her put the finish to both? He couldn't blame her. He saw so clearly now that he should have trusted her, but hindsight wasn't going to fix what he'd done. And he was shaken to the core by how the idea of losing her, what he'd found with her, nearly shoved everything else out of his mind.

She followed him outside and toward the cars.

"Katie, just—"

"No."

The finality in her tone told him he would get nowhere arguing with her, and at the moment he didn't have time to waste. If his hunch was right, he needed to get moving now. He'd just have to keep her out of it, somehow.

"I should drive," she said as he reached for the keys to the rental.

His brow furrowed. "Why?"

She pulled out her own keys. "Because I know where we're going."

That stopped him in his tracks. He turned to stare at her. "What?"

"Tacoma, right? Ross?" She hadn't seen the text. He knew she hadn't. "Please," she said scornfully at his expression. "He's the only one you haven't talked to yet, isn't he?"

His appreciation for her quick deduction warred with the sting from the tone of her voice. For one of the few times in his life he was unable to think of a word to say. Instead he gave a half shrug and walked to the passenger side of her car. Without comment, Katie unlocked the car, and even opened the back door for Cutter to jump in. The dog did so without hesitation.

She drove, as he would have expected, with calm efficiency.

And in total silence. Which he probably should have expected, given what she thought of him at the moment.

In his mind he turned over a hundred ways to try to talk to her, but none of them seemed likely to earn him anything but more scorn. He knew now—too late—that Katie Moore was exactly what she seemed to be. Smart, kind and completely honest.

Cutter gave a low sigh from the back seat. Gavin glanced back at him, and saw that look of disgust again. He was beginning to give up on trying to rationalize the dog's traits in any ordinary canine way.

Her silence began to wear on him, and since he couldn't think of a damned thing to say, he took out his phone and called up the images of the notes he'd made on Ross Carr; he might prefer to make his notes by hand, but carting around reams of paper was another matter. He read through them, this time with a fresh eye, refocused thanks to what he'd just learned.

For the sake of completeness he added Quinn's text to the file. Brett Dunbar was true to his word, as usual, and the moment he'd heard from his friend in Tacoma that a unit had reported Carr had returned home, he had sent the information on. Quinn in turn had sent word to Gavin, and added that he and Rafe would be heading that way, just in case. Gavin knew Quinn hadn't liked Carr's disappearing act, any more than he had.

As they drove, the inkling of a suspicion that had come to him during Moore's revelations grew. He turned it over and over in his mind to inspect all sides. By the time they were nearly there, he wasn't much liking the conclusions he was drawing.

When they finally got off the highway, Katie drove so confidently he belatedly realized she knew where she was going because Ross Carr's house had once been Laurel's, as well.

"I need you to stay in the car when we get there," he said. They were the first words he'd spoken in nearly an hour.

"I'm not—"

"You've seen how I work. I need to talk to him cold."

She hesitated, and he saw her forefinger tap on the steering wheel. "All right," she said after three taps.

"Thank you." God, the formality was clawing at him, but he didn't know what else to do. And for a man used to always knowing what to do, it was an unsettling feeling.

She continued on through three more turns, then slowed after the last one. "Up here on the right, by that car with the trunk open," she said.

He nodded, glanced at the house the vehicle was parked in front of. He saw someone coming down the walkway, a large box in his arms, apparently heading for that vehicle.

Cutter was suddenly on his feet in the back seat, a low growl issuing from his throat.

"Wait, that's Ross," Katie said. "Is he packing? Moving?"

Gavin glanced at Cutter, who was pawing the door madly, wanting out. He looked back as the man set the box he'd been carrying in the trunk, then turned.

His size. Build. Way of moving. The knit hat, cuff now rolled up on his head, but still black with bright red trim on the edge. Cutter's reaction.

All that made him certain.

Ross Carr was the man with the knife.

Chapter 36

Ross spotted Cutter first. Even from here Katie could see his eyes widen. Gavin had let the dog out first, snapped an order for Katie to stay and headed after the dog at a run.

Ross darted back toward the house, vanishing behind the section that jutted out toward the road, where Katie knew the living room was. Cutter raced across the yard, disappearing in turn around the building. Gavin wasn't far behind. And then…

Nothing.

She rolled down her window. Silence.

Her mind was racing. Of course Ross would run from an oncoming, growling dog. Anyone would. The question was, why was the brilliantly clever, normally very sweet Cutter bent on mayhem against Ross? He'd never met him, why would he—

It hit her then.

Maybe Cutter had met Ross. That night outside the library.

Her breath caught. And now her thoughts were tumbling. Had it been Ross who'd attacked Gavin? Had he been here all along, not in San Diego? Had he even perhaps been the one to steal her father's car and try for Gavin again after his knife attack had failed? But why? Why would—

Again it clicked into place, the reason for the way Gavin had reacted to the news that Ross was home.

What if Ross had found out about Laurel and her father? He'd always been able to lure Laurel back from her efforts to leave him, but there had never been a third party involved before.

She couldn't bear it any longer. Her thought process had taken only seconds, but it felt like she'd been sitting there, doing nothing, for an eternity. She grabbed her phone, keyed in 9-1-1 but didn't send it. Then she got out of the car and headed for the house.

When she rounded the corner, she heard a shout. In a corner near the door, she saw the two men on the ground. Gavin nearly had Ross pinned. Ross threw a wild punch that Gavin easily dodged. And then Cutter darted forward, fangs bared and growling fiercely. He went for Ross's leg, catching his ankle. Ross screamed, kicked. Cutter held on. His growl scared even her.

And then Gavin had him, his forearm locked around Ross's neck. She ran forward.

"Get him off me!" Ross screamed again.

"You're lucky it's not your throat," Gavin snapped out. He gave Katie a warning glance, and she stayed carefully out of Ross's reach.

"Just get him off!" Ross begged. She saw now why police K-9s were so effective. A determined, fierce dog could clearly be terrifying.

Gavin ignored Ross's plea. "I know you faked being in

San Diego and came back here. I know it was you with the knife. And then the car. You clearly wanted me off this."

Ross paled at each statement. He twisted harder, trying to escape both Gavin's hold and Cutter's teeth. He failed at both.

"There's only one reason I can think of to make you go through all that."

"You did it," Katie said, barely managing to speak past the tightness in her throat. "You killed her, didn't you?"

"Stop, Katie." Gavin's order was remarkably calm, considering.

"But—"

"Don't ask him anything. That's for the police. After he's been read his rights. We don't want him to wiggle out of this, do we?"

She let out her breath. She realized then that Gavin never had actually asked anything; he'd only stated what he knew. But he hadn't needed verbal answers. Ross's face said it all.

"Cutter, release," Gavin said. The dog let go, but didn't look happy about it. But Gavin's sharp command of "Guard" seemed to cheer him up. Gavin backed off Ross, but remained crouched beside him. "If you move, he will go for the throat this time."

As warnings went, it was immensely effective; Ross was staring at the dog in near terror. Gavin looked up at her then.

"Why don't you make that call?" he suggested. "And then call Quinn. Never mind. They're here."

Katie spun around and indeed saw Quinn coming around the back corner of the house. He took in the situation quickly, then called out, "Clear!" Then Hayley came out from around the other side of the house, while a second man unexpectedly appeared above her on the roof. She recognized the other Foxworth operative she'd met, Rafe

Crawford, as he slid a weapon into a holster, then tugged his jacket over it before he dropped down to the ground. Quinn was armed as well, Katie realized. And even Hayley? She saw the other woman slide something into her belt and had her answer; Foxworth had come prepared for anything. Unnecessarily, but still comforting.

Gavin stood up then. Cutter greeted his teammates with a brisk bark, but his eyes never left his assignment.

Katie felt a sudden wave of reaction, as if the ground had rippled under her feet. If not for Gavin jumping to her side, throwing an arm around her to steady her, she very probably would have ended up on the ground beside Ross.

It was over.

"So that's it?" Katie asked. "He found out about Laurel and my father and killed her for it?"

"That's his story," Quinn said. "In his mind, they hadn't split yet, so she was cheating on him."

They were gathered at Foxworth once more, the five of them plus Cutter, who, after obtaining another carrot snack for a job well-done, settled before the fire to happily crunch. Katie herself had been unable to settle; there was too much turmoil in her head and heart. So she'd been pacing the floor since they'd arrived after turning Ross and their information over to the police, who went into action quickly and efficiently. The Foxworth name garnered respect in all corners, it seemed.

"But his alibi," Katie began.

"He drugged the woman," Hayley said in disgust. "But a small dose, so she would only be out for a while. Just long enough for him to sneak out, borrow another partier's motorcycle, leaving his car unmoved, get to Laurel and get back with no one the wiser."

"So they all assumed he was with the woman the whole time?"

Quinn nodded. "And she thought she'd just gotten drunk. When she passed out he was with her, when she woke up he was with her."

"And keeping her around was insurance," Rafe said sourly from where he stood by the fireplace.

"He manufactures this alibi, and it holds," Hayley said. "So he thinks he's going to get away with it."

"Until," Quinn said with a grin, "the famous Gavin de Marco shows up and starts poking into things."

Katie stopped her pacing on those words, saw Gavin grimace, but he didn't speak. In fact, he hadn't said anything since they'd begun to lay it all out.

She looked at Quinn. "And then he decided to try and pin it on my father?"

Quinn nodded. "One final bit of revenge."

She shook her head slowly. "It could have worked." She looked back at Gavin. "If you hadn't been here, hadn't taken this on, it could have worked."

Gavin wouldn't look at her. "Thank Cutter. He brought it—and you—to Foxworth."

"Oh, I will," she said with a glance at the dog. "Carrots for life, m'boy."

The dog gave a happy bark, so far removed from the ferocious, intense working dog she'd seen, it was hard to believe it was the same animal.

The Foxworths exchanged glances, and then Hayley said brightly, "We're going to go up and finish off our reports. There's more coffee on if you need it."

Cutter did not head up with them, but stayed where he was. He was still Gavin's self-appointed guardian, it seemed. And Rafe lingered for a moment, looking at them both. She saw Gavin lift an eyebrow at him.

The dark, intimidating man shrugged. "Just thinking. You hate liars, now she hates the results of lying. So you'll probably never lie to each other."

Katie's breath caught. He'd said that like he expected she and Gavin to...what? Be together? The unlikeliness of that jabbed at her. She watched as he went out the patio door and headed toward the warehouse building.

Cutter did not follow him, either.

She was unable to keep still. She was relieved that her father had been exonerated, but a sour taste remained when she thought of how he had lied to her all this time. Her own father, the man she'd relied on her entire life and would have sworn she knew inside out.

Not to mention Laurel. Her best friend of nearly twenty years, and she had not only had an affair with her father, but had also lied about something as major as that. She found the latter much more upsetting, and that it was a lie of omission didn't ameliorate it at all. Gavin was right about that. And yes, she hated the results of lying. Rafe Crawford had been right about that.

Now it was over. And it was time to extract herself and try to put her life back together. What there was left of it.

She stopped pacing and turned to face Gavin. Slowly, he stood up. "Katie," he began, but she shook her head.

"Thank you, Gavin," she said formally. "For...everything." She saw something flicker in his eyes and kept going. "I mean not just clearing my father, but everything. You taught me about things I never knew existed."

"Katie, stop. I—"

"I understand. You were never going to stay. I don't regret it, any of it."

"What are you—"

She put up a hand to stop him. "I get it now," she said. It came out tight, with a quaver. "I understand completely why you want nothing to do with liars. And I... I seem to attract them." She didn't care that a note of bitterness had entered her voice. But this was for his sake, so she said it. "Goodbye, Gavin."

She headed for the door. She'd meant to just walk, but halfway there she broke into a run, afraid if she was in the same room with him one more second she would break down.

He didn't say a thing, and the door swung closed behind her.

Chapter 37

Gavin stared after her, feeling unable to either speak or move. He who had the reputation for always knowing what to do next, couldn't think of a thing to say or do now. All he knew was that this felt wrong, completely wrong, more wrong than anything in his life.

He'd barely acknowledged that when Cutter exploded into action. Letting out a howl the dog raced for the door, hitting the open button with a furious swipe of his paw. The moment he could squeeze through he was gone, still howling, in a way that spoke of lonely wolves in the distance. Gavin had never heard anything like it, and it raised the hair on the back of his neck.

Galvanized by the sound, he ran to the door, just in time to see Katie pause at her car, keys in hand, and look back at Cutter. Something slammed into his chest when he saw the tears streaming down her face. Not Katie, who was so strong, so tough, who had handled all this with a strength that had amazed him. She wouldn't break. Not his Katie…

And then Cutter was back, nudging at him, then flat-out pushing him toward her. When he looked at Katie again, she was looking at him. And there was no mistaking what he saw in her face. Not just sadness, not just longing, but…love. It was there, written large, and in that instant he knew.

If he let this woman go, it would be the biggest mistake of his life.

"Katie," he whispered, even knowing she couldn't possibly hear him.

He didn't need Cutter's urging. He simply ran, caught her up in his arms, the words that wouldn't come before coming in a rush now. He doubted if they made any sense at all, yet somehow she understood.

"You can't go. Don't. Please. Stay. He doesn't matter. Their lies don't matter."

"Gavin," she began to protest, but he shook his head. He felt like he was about to cry himself, and tried to put some sensible words together.

"You've given me back everything, Katie. I went too far down that path. Lost my trust, my faith in people, my willingness to believe anyone who hadn't already proven themselves to me. But you've changed that. No more guilty until proven innocent."

"But you were right. Because I'm obviously surrounded by liars. And you don't want that around you, so this is for your sake."

He drew back, stared at her. His sake? "But what I did… suspecting your father…"

She gave a sad smile. "It's what lawyers do, isn't it? You cover anything that could go wrong by thinking everything could go wrong?"

"So it wasn't…unforgivable?"

Her expression changed, and he knew somehow she was

thinking of what he'd said to her father. Only something unforgivable could ever change her love. With a sigh she said, "That's probably the most forgivable thing that's happened."

He hated that she sounded so beaten. "No. Don't let my mistrust infect you. They made mistakes, big ones, but... Please, Katie, don't lose that thing that makes you you, that sweetness, the kindness, the honesty. It's what makes you so strong."

She was staring at him, and he had the feeling she was holding her breath. Waiting. If she'd been willing to leave for his sake, he had to say this for hers.

"It's what I love," he said hoarsely.

Her eyes widened.

"I love you, Katie. I know it's too fast and too crazy, but—"

He stopped when she lifted a finger to his lips. Just the touch sent fire racing along every nerve.

"I love you, too," she whispered, and his heart jammed up into his throat. "No matter how fast or crazy. But what I said is still true. I have liars all around me."

He swallowed tightly. "But you're not one of them. And that's all that really matters. And I wouldn't blame you if you walked away, after what I thought, but don't. Please don't."

"You're sure of that?"

"Yes. Are you sure you want to take on that lifelong challenge?"

He saw her remember her own words, and a slow smile curved her lips. Those lips that drove him mad. "I think I'm up to it," she whispered. "In fact, I think I'll start right now."

It was much later, long after Quinn and Hayley had discreetly departed—Cutter with them, after a last, happy

woof that seemed to indicate he knew his job was done—
that Gavin broke a long, slow kiss and broached the subject he'd been pondering.

"You've had a rough time here the last few months."

Katie nodded, then smiled up at him from where she
lay beneath him on the couch. "But things are definitely
looking up."

He smiled back. "But maybe a change of scenery for a
while might be good."

"I kind of like the scenery here."

She ran a finger down his chest. He put a hand over
hers, knowing if she continued he was going to forget everything he wanted to say.

"I need to go back to St. Louis, for a while at least. There
are logistics I have to figure out."

She went still. "What are you saying?"

"Come with me," he said. "Away from all the reminders,
where you can think more clearly. Just for a while. While
we decide what happens next."

"Next?"

"You love your work here," he said, "and you're damned
good at it. And I can work anywhere. It's easier from St.
Louis because it's in the middle of everywhere, but I don't
have to be there."

"You'd move? Here?"

"I like it here." He wasn't sure if it was the place, or just
her, and in the end it didn't matter. "I would, if that's what
works best. For us."

She kissed him, hot and fierce. "I love you, Gavin de
Marco."

He kissed her back. This time they ended up on the
floor before the fire, and it was more explosive than ever.
He thought he might have shouted her name when they hit

the peak. And it took him a long time to work up the energy to speak again.

"Fair warning. If you come with me, you'll have to meet Charlie."

"That sounds like you're going to introduce me to royalty."

He laughed. "That's more fitting than you know."

"I'll practice my curtsy."

He laughed again, thinking he was almost getting used to doing it. "Does that mean yes?"

"I'd go anywhere with you."

He raised up on one elbow and looked down at her, smiling.

"Welcome to Foxworth," he said.

* * * * *

SWAT SECRET ADMIRER

ELIZABETH HEITER

For my critique partner, Robbie Terman. Thank you for convincing me that I could write romantic suspense, and lending your expertise.

Chapter One

"Invisibility in three...two...one...now!"

The words echoed in Maggie Delacorte's earbud as her SWAT teammate stepped back from the neat hole he'd cut in the window. Behind her, everything was quiet in the predawn darkness. But that wouldn't last for long.

The FBI had gotten the word that a wanted fugitive was hiding out in this gang-infested part of DC, armed with an AK-47 and surrounded by a pack of die-hard supporters. Maggie and her teammates were here to make sure his time on the run was finished.

She moved quickly forward, tossing a flash-bang grenade through the window. The world in front of her exploded in white light, a massive *boom* echoing as the flash bang landed. Smoke billowed, providing cover.

"Go, go, go!" Grant Larkin yelled in that deep voice that always sent goose bumps running up her arms, as he used a ram and his massive upper-body strength to break down the door.

Maggie raced around the corner to follow, just as the door flew open into the one-story hideout. Grant went in first, moving right as planned, then the two teammates behind him dodged the splintered door and went left.

Her MP-5 raised and ready, Maggie barely felt the weight of the extra fifty pounds of gear she carried as she darted through the door, clearing it fast the way she'd been trained.

A bullet whizzed by her ear, coming from her left, but she didn't turn her head. That was in a teammate's sector. He'd handle the threat. Maggie's sector was straight ahead, and she stayed focused as she forged through the swirling gray smoke.

Reports came in over her radio as she entered the hallway to the bedrooms. The fugitive's allies were dwindling fast, either from bullets, or because they threw their hands up and their weapons down at the sight of the six FBI SWAT agents converging on them. But there were at least two left, including the fugitive himself, a three-time offender, who was surely looking at a life sentence this time around.

A gangbanger popped out of a doorway ahead of her, his modified AK-47 coming up fast, and Maggie moved her weapon right, firing at center mass.

The threat down, she kept going until she was beside Grant. He outweighed her by a solid eighty pounds and in the narrow hallway, with all their gear, they barely fit side by side.

He nodded his head to acknowledge her presence, glancing briefly her way. She registered it through her peripheral vision, but kept her focus where it needed to be: on the rooms to the right side. One more for her to clear, one for Grant.

Grant went through the doorway to the left and Maggie through the one on the right, her weapon instantly sighting on the threat in the corner. The fugitive himself, all three hundred pounds of him.

His finger quivered on the trigger, and Maggie barked, "Drop it! FBI!"

She'd been on the Washington Field Office's SWAT

team for the past four years, but perps sometimes made the mistake of thinking she wouldn't fire just because she was a woman. So Maggie leveled her meanest stare at him, hoping he could see it through her goggles. She wanted this guy alive, wanted him to rot in a cell and help them bring down the rest of his crew.

He scowled back at her with a nasty grimace even as his eyes watered from the smoke. But the modified AK-47 he'd been clutching fell to the floor beside him.

From the room across the hall, she could hear Grant yelling at another suspect to get down on the ground, and Maggie demanded the same of the fugitive.

She didn't get close until he'd followed her order to lie flat on his stomach on the filthy carpet, his hands clasped behind his head. Then she switched her MP-5 to safe mode, slung it over her back and unhooked the handcuffs from her belt. She approached him and planted a heavy knee in the center of his huge back. Yanking his left hand down fast, she slapped on the cuff then grabbed his right hand.

As she shifted her balance right, he ripped his cuffed hand away, using his bulk to toss her sideways.

She landed hard on her MP-5, and pain tore through her back. That was going to bruise. Cursing loud and creatively, she was up before he could get to his feet. Wrenching his cuffed arm backward, she rammed a foot in his armpit.

He squealed as she muttered under her breath about men who thought bigger meant they had the upper hand. A decade ago, she might have agreed with that assessment. But six years in the FBI, four of them on the super-competitive SWAT team, had taught her it just wasn't true.

She didn't have to be bigger. She just had to know how to leverage her strength, and her skill set.

The fugitive was still screeching as she slapped the cuff on his other wrist and then Grant was in the room, dragging a gangbanger behind him as if the guy weighed nothing. He took a handful of the fugitive's shirt, and the two of them pulled him to his feet.

"Nice job, Delacorte," Grant said.

Her heart rate—which had stayed relatively even during the entire arrest—picked up at the sound of his voice.

Grant Larkin had moved from the New York Field Office to the Washington Field Office, WFO, and her SWAT team, nine months ago. He was just shy of six feet, but even on a team filled with muscle-bound men, he stood out. The guy was *built*, which was why he was usually the door-kicker.

He also had deep brown eyes, light brown skin and an infectious grin, even in the middle of a grueling SWAT workout. In short, exactly her type. If only he wasn't a teammate, making him off-limits. And if only she didn't have baggage from her past that weighed more than he did.

Maggie nodded at him and called in their status over her radio. She got the "all clear" from all sectors and told Grant, "We're set. Let's get out of here."

"Sounds like a plan to me," he replied, letting her go ahead of him with the fugitive as he brought up the rear with the cuffed gangbanger.

The rest of the team was waiting outside the dilapidated one-story, loading a few other prisoners into their vehicle for transport. A couple of her teammates hooted when they saw her pushing the enormous, scowling fugitive in front of her.

She grinned back, because she knew they were laughing at the furious threats the fugitive was making, and not at the fact that she, at five foot eight and a hundred and forty pounds, was bringing him out. She'd worked with most of them for four years, and they'd learned fast not to coddle or underestimate her because she was a woman.

That was why being on SWAT had been good for her. It had shown her exactly how much she was capable of, and she wouldn't trade it for anything.

After they'd loaded the last two prisoners, Grant came over to her, yanking his goggles up over his helmet, and leaving behind indents around his eyes that didn't diminish his attractiveness at all. "I think this calls for celebration."

"O'Reilley's?" Clive Dekker, the team leader, asked. It was the pub the team usually hit after a particularly good or bad day.

It didn't matter that it was almost three in the morning. O'Reilley's catered to cops. They stopped serving liquor at two, but they were open twenty-four hours. And after the adrenaline rush of a high-risk arrest, most of the team couldn't just go home and go to sleep.

"Let's do it," Grant agreed. He turned to her, looking hopeful. "Delacorte?"

She hadn't gone with them in six months. Not since she'd started getting the letters, because the stress of it made it impossible to go out and joke around, to pretend everything was okay.

A lump filled her throat, and she tried to push back the memory that always surged forward when September 1 came around. In exactly thirty days, it would be ten years since the day that had changed her life. The day that had led her to the FBI. To SWAT.

And whatever happened on that tenth anniversary, would she regret not having spent as much time with Grant Larkin as she could?

She nodded at him. "Sure. I'm going to run home first. I'll meet you all there."

He looked surprised, but then grinned in a way that made her positive she'd made the right choice.

She stared back at him, momentarily rooted in place. Maybe it was time to forget her past. Maybe it was time to forget the rules.

Maybe it was time to see what could happen between her and Grant Larkin.

MAGGIE FELT HERSELF smiling with anticipation as she unlocked the bolts on her DC row house and entered, flipping on the lights. She stepped over the mail scattered in the entryway, realizing she hadn't been home in close to twenty-four hours.

As she locked the door behind her and kicked off her boots, it occurred to her that she should be exhausted. She'd worked a full day on her regular FBI civil rights squad, then been out with her brother and best friend when she'd gotten the call to come back for the SWAT arrest. But she was full of energy. When was the last time she'd been this happy?

Six months ago, she realized. Before the first letter had arrived. Grant had been on her team for three months at the time. They'd hit it off from his first day. Besides being a solid addition to the team, he was funny and just so dang happy all the time. Being around him made *her* happy.

SWAT was an ancillary position—agents did it on top of their regular squad duties. Still, dating a teammate, even in a secondary team like SWAT, was forbidden. So she'd tried to keep her feelings hidden. But just knowing that she was capable of feeling this way, after everything...

Stop dwelling on the past, Maggie scolded herself. She knew Grant had been able to tell these past few months that something was wrong. But unlike a lot of agents at the WFO, who'd heard the rumors over the years, she was pretty sure Grant didn't know her history. And she wanted to keep it that way.

She liked the way he looked at her, no trace of pity or worry. He'd never shown any sign that he'd heard about her past. The case agents had been good about keeping her connection under wraps over the years; though inevitably agents who'd been in DC for a long time found out. But Grant had only been here nine months. In that time, the only thing she'd ever seen in his eyes was friendship and camaraderie. And lately, something else, something that went beyond the bonds of the team.

Maggie carried her gear up the narrow stairs to her bedroom, flipping lights on along the way, then stared into her closet. She didn't own date clothes. Not that this was a date.

Everything in her closet belonged to a woman who, somewhere deep inside, was still afraid. Not of being a victim, not anymore. But when was the last time she'd actually wanted a man to look at her with appreciation?

Frowning, Maggie grabbed what she'd always worn to O'Reilley's—jeans, combat-style boots way too similar to the ones she wore for SWAT and a loose-fitting T-shirt. They'd only stay an hour or so anyway, chat and play darts and let the adrenaline fade. Then, one by one, the exhaustion would inevitably hit, and they'd head home and conk out.

She needed to get over there, or she'd miss everyone. Changing quickly, she looked into the bathroom mirror, taking a minute to lift her shirt up and look at the damage to her back. A bruise was blooming fast, huge and purple, snaking its way along her spine in the general shape of a sub-machine gun.

She poked at it and flinched, then pulled her shirt back down, combing a finger through her bob. It was just long enough to cover the back of her neck, and Maggie's fingers twitched as they skimmed the puckered skin there.

The tattoo she'd gotten years ago hid the image of a hook, but nothing could fix the damaged skin underneath. The brand that had been left on her.

She threw some water on her face, then dug through the drawer under her sink until she came up with some lipstick and mascara. The guys were probably going to stare at her as though she'd grown an extra head. Or maybe they wouldn't even notice. Most of them were like brothers.

Only Grant might spot—and appreciate—her pathetic attempt to look a little more feminine, since most of the time she tried to hide it.

She stared at herself in the mirror, resisting the urge to wipe off the makeup, then laughed aloud. She was being ridiculous. Just because she didn't wear makeup to work didn't mean everyone at the bar would know why she'd put it on tonight.

Maggie took the stairs down two at a time, still grinning. It wasn't that she didn't date, but most of the time, even when she truly had feelings for a guy, it felt obligatory. An attempt to feel normal that never quite worked.

But nothing about Grant Larkin felt obligatory.

And she was ready to take a chance. She had no idea how they'd handle the FBI rules—assuming he was interested. But the heated glances he hadn't quite been able to hide over the past few weeks told her he was.

At the bottom of the stairs, Maggie picked up the pile of mail and dumped it on the table and reached for her keys. But before she'd finished turning away, dread rushed over her. The plain business envelope. The corner of a neatly printed return label sticking out from the huge pile of mail like a flashing beacon.

She looked back at the mail slowly, dreading what she was going to find. But she hadn't been dreaming. She didn't have to open it to know. Another letter.

All the excitement drained out of her, buried under a decade-old fear.

Her movements robotic, she walked into her kitchen and slipped on a pair of latex gloves before returning to the front hall, even though she knew there'd be no prints. There never were.

She shouldn't even open it. It was evidence in an ongoing case. She should call the agents from the Violent Crimes Major Offenders, VCMO, squad assigned to the case. They'd have to be called anyway, because this letter would have to go in the case file along with the others. She should just let the case agents open it.

But even knowing what would be inside, she couldn't stop herself from carefully slicing open the top of the envelope. She slid out the plain white paper and unfolded it carefully, only touching the edges. She knew it was useless, but she still tried to numb herself as she started reading.

Anger and resentment—along with the guilt and shame she couldn't suppress—crept forward, even as she tried to remain clinical and approach it the way she would one of her own cases. It read just like the previous letters, three of them over the past six months. To someone who didn't know the sender, it would sound like a love letter, fondly recalling their time together.

But it wasn't. It was a letter from the Fishhook Rapist, the predator who'd evaded capture for almost a decade.

The predator who had started by abducting her on her way home to her dorm room at George Washington University all those years ago. He'd let her go the next morning, drugged and disoriented, carrying a permanent reminder on the back of her neck.

Maggie felt herself sway and clutched the table as she read the last line. It was different from any of the previous letters.

The Fishhook Rapist was coming back to DC. And he was coming back for her.

Chapter Two

"You got another one?" Maggie's older brother, Scott, was scowling furiously, clenching his fists so tightly, the knuckles looked ready to break through skin. He was standing in the entryway to her row house a mere thirty minutes after she'd called him, which meant he'd broken a lot of traffic laws to get there.

Normally, Scott was all charm, all the time, with an easy grin and a swagger. But today, even with his eyes red from being ripped from sleep before dawn, he looked angrier than she'd seen him in a long, long time.

Their best friend, Ella Cortez, had arrived ten minutes earlier; she lived within DC and closer to Maggie's house. Maggie had called them instead of heading to the bar, and Ella had gotten in her car practically before Maggie had finished telling her what had happened.

Now Ella put a hand on Scott's arm and gave him a look Maggie could read as well as Scott could. *Go easy.*

The three of them had grown up together, back in Buckley, Indiana, and Ella might as well have been her and Scott's other sister. After Maggie's assault her senior year of college, they'd made a pact together. Throw out all their plans for the future and join the FBI. Stop this kind of thing from happening to anyone else.

But she couldn't even stop the man who'd hurt her.

Maggie tightened her jaw, tried not to let them see her fear. "Yes. But the letter was different this time. He said he's coming back to DC. He said he's coming back for me."

"What?" Scott shouted.

He ran a hand through his close-cut blond hair, and she could see him trying to rein in his fury.

Scott was a year older than she was. They'd always been close, but since her attack, he'd become even more protective. She'd expected him to worry less once she'd joined SWAT, but it was only recently that his new girl-friend had taught him to loosen up at all. That would change back now.

"Have the case agents taken the letter?" Scott asked. As a sniper with the FBI's Hostage Rescue Team, Scott was used to being able to take action. Not knowing who the threat was drove him crazy.

"Were those his exact words? That he was coming back to DC, coming back for you?" Ella asked. She was calmer, but Maggie still heard her worry.

"They just picked it up," she told Scott, then looked at Ella. "His exact words were, 'I'm coming home for our anniversary.'" She choked the words out. Even saying them made bile rise up in her throat.

Scott swore, and Ella paled, but she still nodded thoughtfully. "Home," Ella mused.

Her brother took a loud, calming breath, but rage still filled his eyes. "What do you think it means?"

Just like her, Scott had gravitated toward a specialty that would let him physically, personally, take down threats. On the outside, they didn't resemble each other at all, though they were only a year apart in age. Scott was a head taller than her at six feet, with blond hair and chocolate-brown eyes. She looked more like their younger sister, Nikki, with her dark brown hair and light blue eyes.

But inside, they were so similar, both of them attacking every challenge head-on.

Ella was different. She'd been the glue that had held them together, kept them from butting heads over the years. And while Scott and Maggie had gone into physical specialties with the FBI, Ella had wanted to understand. So she'd become a profiler with the Behavioral Analysis Unit. If there was anyone who had a chance of deciphering the Fishhook Rapist's motivations—and hopefully his next move—it would be her.

"What does it mean?" Ella repeated. "Well, it could be the obvious."

"That he was born here," Scott replied, nodding. "Okay. What else?"

"Well, we know he doesn't live here now."

Part of the reason the Fishhook Rapist had managed to evade capture for so long was because he moved around a lot. He claimed one victim a year, and never in the same place. His last victim had been in Florida, and the second letter Maggie had gotten had been postmarked from there.

The first one had come from Georgia, and the most recent one had originated in North Carolina.

"Then, what?" Scott demanded.

Ella frowned, her deep brown eyes pensive. "This guy is a narcissist. He brags about what he does. It's why he lets his victims go. He wants the attention, and he gets off on knowing the women he abducts can't identify him. His attacks have become the main source of pride in his life. So the location of his first attack—"

"You think he might see DC as home because it's where he assaulted me," Maggie broke in.

She'd gone to school here—and she'd even finished out her senior year after her attack, putting all her focus into her new goal of making it to the FBI—but then she'd moved back to her parents' house in Indiana for a while, wanting to put physical distance between her and the memories. When she'd made it through the FBI Academy, and they'd assigned her to the DC office, she'd almost backed out.

But she'd stuck with it, then worked her way onto the SWAT team. DC had truly become her home now. It made her sick that he thought of it as his, too.

Ella looked uncomfortable, but she didn't fidget or honey-coat anything. "Yes. It's the start of where he got his name."

The media had dubbed him the Fishhook Rapist after they'd gotten wind of what he did to his victims, branding them on the backs of their necks with the image of a hook. Maggie's hand tensed with the need to touch the puckered skin on her neck that would never be smooth, but she clutched her hands together.

Ella looked apologetic as she finished, "To him, this is home."

Nausea welled up, and Maggie sank onto her couch. Scott sat next to her, wrapping an arm around her shoulder. A few seconds later, Ella was on her other side, hooking their arms together.

"He can write as many letters as he wants, but he's not getting anywhere near you," Scott vowed, in the dark, determined tone he probably used on the job. It sounded convincing.

So did Ella when she added, "We're going to get him, Maggie. He's making a mistake trying to come back here."

She wanted to believe it. Wanted to believe that the

case agents, and her brother and Ella and all of her FBI and SWAT training were enough to keep her safe.

But that fear she'd pushed down for ten years rose up, strong and painful, like the feel of fiery metal on the back of her neck.

Maggie squeezed her eyes closed, grasping her brother and Ella by the arms. "I'm not supposed to be anywhere near the case."

"Doesn't matter," Ella said. She was a stickler for doing everything by the book—except when it came to a possible lead on this particular case.

"We're not waiting for that SOB to come after you," Scott agreed. "And we're not leaving this to the case agents, no matter how good they are."

Maggie nodded, tears welling up in her eyes at their loyalty. "It's time to go on the offensive."

WHERE WAS SHE?

Grant Larkin tried not to stare through the near-empty pub at the entrance to O'Reilley's, but he couldn't stop himself, the same way he couldn't stop himself from taking a peek at his watch. The team had been at the pub for a solid two hours, letting the adrenaline from the arrest fade.

Now daylight was rapidly approaching. Even though it was Saturday, and they got a break, a couple of them were heading out the door, along with the last of the cops who'd been in the pub when they'd arrived.

Maggie wasn't coming.

"What happened to Delacorte?" Clive Dekker asked, looking at Grant as if he would know.

Grant shrugged, but he'd been resisting the urge to call her for the past hour and find out. He'd been shocked when she'd agreed to join them, after six months of skipping out on anything social. Even more shocked by the way she'd looked at him while agreeing. As if she was as interested in him as he was in her.

He'd been drawn to her from the moment they'd met, nine months ago. For most of that time, he'd tried to keep his attraction hidden. They were teammates, a definite Bureau no-no. Lately, though, he hadn't been able to suppress it, and he knew she'd noticed. But she'd never looked at him quite the way she had tonight, as if maybe she wanted more from him. If only...

"Well, I'm calling it, before my wife sends out a search party," Clive said, then squinted, leaning closer to him in the noisy pub. "Is that your phone ringing?"

Grant grinned at him. "I think you're still hearing the aftereffects of that flash bang, old man," he joked. The team leader was thirty-nine, only four years older than Grant. But Clive was the oldest guy on the Washington Field Office SWAT team.

"Ha ha," Clive replied. "It's *your* hearing that's going." He slapped Grant on the shoulder as he maneuvered out of the booth. "That was definitely your phone."

Grant frowned and took out his FBI-issued Black-Berry. Clive was right. One missed call. Hoping it was Maggie saying she was on her way, he held in a yawn and dialed his voice mail.

The message was from the supervisor of his Violent Crimes Major Offenders, VCMO, squad. SWAT was his calling, but VCMO was his regular position at the FBI, the job that filled most of his days.

"We've got a situation," the supervisory special agent said in his typical no-nonsense way. "I need you back at the field office, ASAP."

That was the extent of the message. Grant swore as he slapped some money on the table to cover his drink, then told his remaining teammates, "Gotta go. I'll catch you guys on Monday."

"Hot date?" one of them asked.

"I wish," Grant said. And boy, did he. If only Maggie had shown tonight. "But that was my SSA. Duty calls."

It was a short drive back to the office, which was oddly busy for 5:00 a.m. on a Saturday morning. Not that this was a nine-to-five sort of job, but from the amount of agents gathered in one of the interagency conference rooms, something big had broken. Or they wanted it to.

It wasn't *his* VCMO squad in the conference room, so Grant strode past with only a curious glance inside. His own SSA was waiting in the drab gray bullpen, a scowl on his face as he marked up a stack of paperwork.

"Thanks for coming in," James said, not glancing up as he wrote frantic notes on whatever case file he was reviewing.

Judging from the way his rapidly receding gray hair was sticking out, and the heavier-than-usual shadows under his eyes, the SSA had never left yesterday. But that was pretty standard for James.

"What's happening?" Grant asked, wishing he'd stopped for a coffee instead of settling for the bitter junk they brewed in the office. He'd been up nearly twenty-four hours straight now, and he was heading for a crash that even caffeine could only hold off for so long.

"Hang on." James finished whatever he was writing, then pushed it aside and looked up at Grant, a deep frown on his face.

Discomfort wormed through Grant. In his gut, he knew that whatever was happening, he *really* wasn't going to like it. "What is it?"

James sighed and rubbed a hand over his craggy face. With three divorces under his belt, he was now just married to the job. He was a tough supervisor, and he rarely looked stressed. But right now he looked very, very stressed. "Take a seat. Let's chat."

Grant tugged a chair over and sat down. "Spit it out."

James smiled, probably because Grant was one of the few agents in his VCMO squad who would push him. But the smile faded fast. "You know the situation with the Fishhook Rapist case, right?"

Grant cursed. Everyone who worked violent crime knew the background on that case. A sadistic rapist who grabbed one woman a year off the street, drugged, raped and branded her, then let her go, too disoriented to provide a description of her attacker. There was never any useful forensic evidence.

The guy was way too smart. He surfaced only on September 1, when a new victim would show up at a police station or hospital somewhere in the country, branded with his signature. Then he disappeared again, until the following year, when he'd hit some other state and leave a new victim.

And he'd started with Maggie Delacorte.

That part wasn't general knowledge—they didn't advertise the names of the victims, and they tried to keep the press from getting too much information. They inevitably did, but somehow, the FBI had managed to keep Maggie's last name out of the media for a decade, along with the fact that she'd moved on to become a standout SWAT agent.

Inside the Bureau, however, a few rumors had gotten out over the years, and when he'd moved to WFO and landed on her SWAT team, he'd heard the whispers.

She worked harder than just about anyone he knew, and he was positive she didn't want one terrible incident in her past to color the way her colleagues looked at her, so he'd never said anything. To him, it didn't change a thing. Not about what he thought of her work, and definitely not about how he felt about her as a woman.

"Grant!" his boss snapped, and he realized he hadn't been paying attention.

"Sorry." He ran a hand over his shaved head, dreading whatever he was about to hear. They had a month to go before the guy was supposed to surface, so any news about him now could in theory be a lead to catch him. But judging by his boss's face, Grant didn't think that was it.

"I said, is this going to be a problem for you?"

"What?"

James let out a heavy sigh. "You know about the letters, right?"

"Letters?" Grant frowned and shook his head.

"The perp's been sending them to Maggie over the last six months."

Anger boiled inside. No wonder Maggie hadn't been herself lately.

Did anyone on the team know? He felt his frown deepening, certain she wouldn't have told any of them, no matter how close the team was.

"The case agents checked with the other victims," James continued. "None of the others have received anything. But Maggie got a new one last night." He looked at his watch. "This morning, actually."

Grant looked toward the bustling conference room. So that was why the other VCMO squad had gathered. Maggie must have found the letter when she'd gone home. Which explained why she'd never shown at the bar.

Now he really wished he'd called her, even though chances were, she wouldn't have asked for his help.

"This letter was different from the others. The others were psychological-sick, but meant to hurt from a distance. This one was a threat. And given *your* background…" James stared expectantly at him, not needing to finish his sentence.

Grant had worked in the New York field office for eight years before moving to WFO, and while he'd been there, he'd closed a serial murder case with unusual elements. Specific dates of attacks over a number of years, letters to one particular victim. In that case, it was a woman who had escaped.

"You think my experience on the Manhattan Strangler case—"

"Could help close this one," James finished. "Yes. Kammy Ming has requested you be moved to her squad for the duration of the case. Full-time. We're going to catch him before the next anniversary. There's no other option."

"He said he was coming back for Maggie, didn't he?" Grant asked, shades of the homicide case he'd closed coming back to him. The warm blood spurting on him as he'd driven the perp's knife into him. Carrying the victim out to the ambulance, then being shoved in with her to have his own wounds stitched up.

Grant had caught the guy four years after he'd started killing, but it had almost been too late for the woman he'd come back for. The thought of Maggie being loaded into an ambulance made him queasy.

"Look, Kammy wants your help," James said. "But if you being on SWAT with Maggie is going to be a conflict…"

Suddenly glad he was sitting down, Grant shook his head and hoped for once, James's intuition would fail him.

"Are you sure?" James persisted. "Because once she hears you're on the case, if she asks you about it, you still have to keep it all confidential. Can you do that?"

Could he? He wasn't sure. Worse yet, Grant was pretty sure Maggie had no idea he knew about her past. How would she react to him being on the case now?

Did he even want to be on this case? He didn't have to ask Maggie to know she wouldn't want him involved.

It was one thing to walk into dangerous situations with her—he trained with her and knew she could handle herself. But to go through all the details of what had happened to her a decade ago, back when she'd been a scared college kid? Being her friend now, feeling the way he did about her, did he have any right to dig into the worst day of her life, without her permission?

"Well?" James demanded, staring expectantly.

Then again, how could he sit by and not do anything when he had a chance to stop the man who'd hurt her?

Rage and determination filled him in equal measure, drowning out the nausea. "Yes, I want in on the investigation."

"Good," James said, standing up. "Then, get in the conference room. You start right now."

Chapter Three

"Why now?" Maggie asked as she walked into her living room. "And how long have you been up?" she added, noticing the pillows and blankets she'd put on the couch for Scott looked untouched. The guest room bed she'd made up for Ella was probably still made, too.

She glanced at her watch—10:00 a.m. Which meant she'd been in bed for about four hours. Not that she'd slept much. She'd spent most of the time trying every combat nap technique she'd learned from Scott, who'd trained with military special operations teams for his HRT sniper position. Still, every time she'd drifted off to sleep, she'd startled awake almost immediately.

Despite having gotten out of bed at five in the morning when she'd called them over, Ella and Scott looked wide-awake.

Ella handed her a cup of coffee. "We stayed up."

"What did I miss?" Maggie asked, looking back and forth between them. But neither of them needed to answer. She could tell from their faces. "You talked about how you were going to protect me, didn't you?"

"Don't be ridiculous," Scott said. "We both know you can take care of yourself."

"Thank—"

"But that doesn't mean we're leaving you alone," he

cut her off, putting a hand on her arm. "Get ready for some houseguests. Or pack a bag. And don't even think about arguing."

Maggie was both annoyed and relieved. If it was one of them in trouble, she'd be doing the same thing. They were a team; they always had been.

"Okay. But I want to stay here." They could take turns staying with her—she knew there was no stopping them—but she didn't want to bring trouble to their doorsteps.

Especially since neither one lived alone. Ella's fiancé, Logan, was a cop, and Scott's girlfriend, Chelsie—who'd moved in with him a week ago—was FBI. But neither of them had signed up for this, and although Maggie knew they'd help if she asked, she didn't want to drag them into it, too.

Scott looked surprised at her easy agreement, but he changed the subject, probably worried she'd change her mind. "Maggie, you haven't told Mom and Dad about the letters, have you? Or Nikki?"

"No." She took a sip of coffee, and the hot liquid burned the back of her throat, clearing her head. "And I don't plan to now, either. What are they going to do from Indiana, besides worry?"

She got ready to fight Scott on it—her parents had worried enough about her, ten years ago. She didn't want them repeating it now. And Nikki had only been twelve then, so they'd tried to keep the details from her. Nikki knew now—since the Fishhook Rapist had never been caught, she'd read about him in the news over the years. But Maggie didn't want her little sister to worry, especially not while Nikki was just moving into her first apartment, starting her first job.

"I agree," Scott said, surprising her.

"You do?"

"Yes. We both know Mom and Dad will just call you constantly, insisting you come home. And you don't need the distraction. We need to focus on stopping him. I want this September 1 to be just another day."

So did she. Getting together with Ella and Scott once a year, praying a new victim wouldn't turn up, was a tradition she'd love to forsake. But September 1 was never going to be just another day for her.

"Good," she said. "Then let's get started."

"You don't have access to the case file, do you?" Ella asked.

Maggie snorted. "No." She knew more details than the average victim, because the task force had asked her questions over the years. But they'd never let her officially investigate. She suppressed a shudder at just the idea. Even if it could help, the thought of looking through all the other victim files—and her own—made the coffee churn in her stomach.

"It probably wouldn't tell us a lot more than we already know, anyway."

She didn't have to say why. The news gave them enough details about where the Fishhook Rapist had been, and it was no secret he'd stuck to a pattern. Victimology and the crime itself hadn't changed.

He always struck once a year, on the same date. And he always chose the same type of woman: someone in her late teens or early twenties, with a slender build and long, dark hair.

Maggie touched the hair she'd cut into a bob years ago, after the second Fishhook Rapist victim had surfaced, looking too much like her. She'd worked hard on her physique, too. No longer was she thin and willowy, but lean and muscular.

She turned her back on Scott and Ella, in the pretense of heading for the chair in the corner, but really to give herself a second without being scrutinized to get her game face on. The face she used when she went into a SWAT call and needed a perp who weighed more than twice as much as she did to recognize her as a viable threat. She could do this. She could talk about what had happened to her, with the two people closest to her in the world.

Her bruised back protested as she sat. When she raised her eyes to theirs, she could tell Ella and Scott weren't fooled. In some ways, this would be easier with total strangers.

Clutching the arms of her chair too hard, she asked Ella, "Why now? Why isn't this year the same as every other one? Do you think he plans to target a new victim, too? Or just come back for me? And what—" She choked on the rest of the sentence, but she could tell Ella knew what she was going to ask.

What did he plan to do to her this time?

Ella settled onto the couch across from her, her face scrunched up, and Maggie knew what was coming. A detailed profiler's analysis.

Ella looked pensive as she started, "It was a sophisticated crime. He didn't leave us any forensic evidence, not even the first time. He was probably in his late twenties a decade ago. Young enough to fit in around a college town, but old enough to be self-sufficient, with his own vehicle and the ability to leave town permanently afterward without attracting attention."

Scott was nodding from his perch next to the couch as Ella continued, "He's closing in on forty now, and he's still grabbing women in college or just out of it. It's not as easy for him to blend in anymore. He's starting to realize he needs to think about changing his approach. He's starting to realize his pattern for the past decade has to change, at least in some ways. It's made him reminisce. And ten years is a significant number, in terms of standard anniversaries."

Intense lines appeared on Ella's smooth olive skin, and even her tone changed as she got into what Maggie recognized as her profiler groove. "To this perp, September 1 is more important than any standard anniversary. He's not married, never has been, and for him, this crime dominates his life."

She looked apologetic as she continued, "You're important to him because that day was the start for him. It probably wasn't his first offense, but it was the first time he used the brand." Her voice caught as she said, "And that's his signature. As he's been planning his next attack, he can't stop thinking about how it all started. He's looking for that same thrill, the way it was the first time he decided to act—the fear and excitement and—"

Ella closed her eyes again, and Maggie realized this was as hard for Ella to profile as it was for Maggie to hear. Ella had been there that day, when Maggie had stumbled back to their dorm room, drugged and only able to remember fragments of what had happened. Fragments were all she had today, and in some ways, she was grateful for that.

Scott was standing beside the couch, his jaw locked, his nostrils practically flaring, as he listened silently.

Maggie got up and walked woodenly to the couch, sitting beside Ella, who'd befriended her and Scott when she'd moved down the street from them when she and Maggie were in kindergarten. "It's okay. Keep going."

Maggie could hear determination, sorrow and anger in Ella's voice as she said, "It's hard for me to profile him objectively, Maggie. But I don't think he's planning to go after a new victim this year. I think he means what he says in that letter. I think he's coming back here just for you, to re-create what's in his mind from a decade ago."

"THE DATE OF the attacks has to mean something," Grant announced Monday morning.

He'd been saying it for two days now, and he was certain he was right. The problem was, he didn't know what it meant.

"Maybe." Kammy Ming, the SSA of the VCMO squad where Grant was on loan, still looked skeptical.

They were the only ones in the room now, but in an hour, it would fill up with the rest of the case agents. Kammy was already here because, as far as he could tell, she didn't sleep. He was here extra early because he needed to figure this out, for Maggie.

"Or maybe it's just the day he went after what he wanted," Kammy said. "Maybe it's important *because* it's the date of the attacks. Because it's when he abducted Maggie, so then it became his day for every future attack."

"Yeah, I know that's the prevailing theory," Grant said, rolling his shoulders, which were tight from spending the weekend sitting in an uncomfortable chair in a WFO conference room. "But you wanted me here because of my experience with the Manhattan Strangler case, right?"

Kammy nodded, but she was frowning, looking exhausted after a weekend without much progress. "There are some compelling similarities we can't ignore. But this isn't the same guy…"

"No," Grant agreed. "But in that case, the killer specifically waited for the anniversary of his mother's death to make a kill. Four years, and he was in control enough to wait a whole year in between attacks. With someone who has this sort of compulsion, a year is a long wait."

"Keep talking," Kammy said, tying her graying hair up in a bun as she stared expectantly at him.

She was as much of a workaholic as James. Was that going to be him in ten years? No balance, just the job all the time?

An image of Maggie immediately filled his brain. There was a heck of a lot more than work that he wanted to fill his days. And there was a heck of a lot more than just work involved when it came to solving this case.

"It's the same with this guy," Grant pressed. "He's systematic with the abductions, the branding, every single year. But he can control the urge until September 1 comes along. There must be a reason."

Kammy raised her eyebrows, sinking back into the chair next to him. "You have any ideas *why* the Fishhook Rapist would choose that specific day every year?" Before he could answer, she added, "Why did the Manhattan Strangler wait for the anniversary of his mother's death every year?"

"He was textbook. Overbearing mother he hated. He'd threatened to kill her for years, but could never bring himself to do it. After she died in a car accident, he treated the new victims as surrogates. So he waited for her anniversary for each kill."

Kammy nodded thoughtfully. "Trying to kill his mother over and over again, in the form of women who resembled her."

"Exactly. And the Fishhook Rapist chooses victims with a definite look, so it's possible he's modeling them after someone, too, but it could just be that he has a type. And given the rape, I think his motivation is different."

"Such as?"

It was 6:00 a.m. Monday morning, and they'd been going over the evidence practically nonstop since he'd been called in early Saturday. He was exhausted. But he didn't think he'd be able to sleep even if he wanted to. Every time he closed his eyes, he thought of the case. He thought of Maggie's case file.

He thought of Maggie, the way he knew her now. Light blue eyes bright with intelligence and determination, dark brown hair framing her heart-shaped face, lean body outlined with muscle, primed to rush into a SWAT call. And he thought of her the way he'd seen her in the photographs from her case file, taken at the hospital shortly after her attack. Smaller and much younger, hunched into herself, battered and broken. He never wanted to see her like that again.

Straightening, he shook his head. "I don't know. Maybe we should talk to a profiler—"

Kammy cut him off. "This case has been to the BAU. One of their senior people profiled him for us a few years ago."

"Okay, so what'd they say about the date of the attacks?"

"He said there wasn't enough evidence to be sure either way."

"But if we could figure out what it was, maybe it would help us track him."

Kammy nodded. "Well, you have any ideas, then go for it. In the meantime, let's work with what we know. Why's he coming back for Maggie?"

"Because he couldn't claim her," Grant replied immediately. To him, that one was obvious.

It had been the same with the Manhattan Strangler. He'd come back for the one woman who'd escaped him, the one woman he'd tried to kill who had managed to survive, against all the doctors' predictions.

Kammy's eyebrows drew together. "He *did* claim her. He raped and branded her like the rest—"

"Yeah, but look at her now." Grant cut Kammy off, not wanting or needing the reminder of what Maggie had endured. "She's SWAT. She didn't let him break her. And she was the first one he went after, the one with the most meaning to him."

"You think he knew her personally?"

"Probably not, but I think he watched her from afar for a while. I think there's a good chance he had a legitimate reason to be at the college back then."

"You mean a student?" Kammy shook her head. "The profiler was pretty solid on the guy being older than his victims."

"Maybe he worked there."

"Okay," Kammy said, "We can double-check. But they definitely looked closely at college employees back then. And I'm pretty sure we checked into anyone who moved after that attack, because we know he must have left between then and the following year, when he showed up in Mississippi. But let's go back to what you said about Maggie being different from the others."

Grant spun his chair back toward the conference table and took out eight of the nine victim files, handing them to Kammy. "The other victims. Look at their updates, the follow-ups. Look at where they are now. Every single one of them was derailed by the attack in some way. Either they dropped out of school, so they didn't end up in their planned profession, or they developed other problems like drinking or substance abuse."

Kammy started opening the files. "Okay, you're right about some of them. Two dropped out of school and never went back, which—you're right—seriously impacted their futures. One has a drinking problem and another one has had substance abuse issues, but she's clean now. Still, what about Marjorie? She—"

"Was on suicide watch on and off for two years after her attack."

"Danielle—"

"Dropped out of school, too."

"She's a doctor now," Kammy argued.

"She eventually went back to school. But it set her back about four years. And she's been vocal about her experience since then, including her struggle with panic attacks to this day."

Kammy stared at him. "This isn't all in the files."

"I did some digging. I know Maggie was his first victim, and ten years is an anniversary. But I think it's more than that. Maggie didn't just survive. She went into one of the most physical jobs in the FBI. Looking at her now, you'd never think she endured that. I think he's developed a sick obsession with her, with the idea of her and how he tried to leave a mark on her—psychologically, that is—and ultimately failed. I think he's coming back for her because he wants to break her."

Kammy snorted. "I know Maggie Delacorte, too, Grant. She's one of the toughest agents here. If he couldn't break her when she was twenty-two, how's he going to do it now, when she's SWAT?"

Grant shook his head, frowning. "I don't know." Which worried him a lot. Because the Fishhook Rapist was extremely intelligent. He had to be, to evade them for this many years, with this much Bureau heat on him. So he would have a plan in place.

Yet, he'd advertised that he was going to return for Maggie. He'd never returned for any of his victims. So they would never have expected it if he hadn't told them. Why would he do that? Unless it was part of his effort to break Maggie down.

"Well, whatever his plan is, we need to get to him before he gets near her. I don't care if she can take him down with her bare hands, I don't like this," Kammy said. "I don't like anything about this."

"Neither do I."

"We've got twenty-seven days," Kammy said. "And so far, zero leads."

"Then we'd better get cracking," Grant said, standing. "I'll get the number for the DC cops who handled the original case."

"Just remember," Kammy called after him, "You run into Maggie, and you say nothing."

"Not a problem," Grant said. He hoped she wouldn't discover that he was working the case until it was over. Until they'd put the Fishhook Rapist behind bars for good.

PEOPLE WERE STARING.

Maggie felt uncomfortable as she walked down the drab gray hallway toward the bustling bullpen where she worked at the WFO. Other agents avoided her eyes as she approached, but she could see them watching from her peripheral vision. As if they all knew.

The case agents for the Fishhook Rapist investigation worked out of the WFO, and it had been that way for a long time, so inevitably some rumors had gotten out. But never like this.

She jumped as someone clapped a hand on her shoulder, then spun around to face the office newbie, a tall, reed-thin guy a few months out of the Academy. Still all nervous excitement and no experience. Still too green to know when to keep his mouth shut.

He gave her an uncomfortable smile and said, "I can't believe the jerk is writing you letters. But they'll catch him. Don't worry."

Mind your own business formed on her lips, but she held it in and nodded stiffly back. Until now, only the longtime agents had seemed to know anything about what had led her into the FBI, and by the time they found out, they knew her well enough not to judge her for it. Six years at the WFO, and she'd never felt as though there was an invisible cloud of pity around her no one wanted to enter. It was why she'd almost backed out when the FBI had assigned her here in the first place.

Frustration and dismay filled her, and she gritted her teeth and tried to bury those emotions under anger. After ten years, the Fishhook Rapist shouldn't have this kind of power over her life anymore.

She wasn't going to *let* him have this kind of power over her life anymore.

She straightened her shoulders, and the newbie must have seen something in her eyes, because he stammered nervously about getting to work and hurried off.

"Maggie."

She turned at the sound of the familiar voice, and found Clive standing behind her, a grim expression on his normally friendly face.

"You know," she said, and her voice sounded weak and emotional. She cleared her throat and added, "Does everyone know?"

Did Grant know?

Clive's lips twisted with sympathy. "No, not everyone. But those of us who came in early today heard the case agents working. They had the conference room open, and they were going over the new evidence." He lowered his voice. "This is the first I've heard about the letters. I wish you'd said something, Maggie."

She shrugged, trying not to feel she'd somehow let him down. She knew he was aware of her history, because it had come up when she'd joined his team. But he'd made it clear then that her past didn't matter to him so long as it didn't affect her ability to do the job. And she'd proven, for four years now, that it didn't. "It wasn't relevant. It didn't affect my position in SWAT."

He gave her a small smile. "No, it didn't." The smile faded. "But with everything going on—"

Maggie put her hands on her hips. "You're pulling me from the team?"

"No. But I want you to think about whether it's the best place for you right now. If you want time—"

"I don't." She tried to force confidence into her tone and her expression. "The letters just mean there's more evidence to investigate. They won't affect my performance on the team."

Clive frowned, as if he could see through her. "We've been friends a long time, Maggie. I'm here if you want to talk. And if you need a break, we'll hold your spot. Don't worry about that."

"Okay." She nodded, a lump filling her throat. There were three SWAT teams at the Washington Field Office, and agents tended to stay on the teams for years—positions very rarely opened up, and waiting lists for tryouts were long. Clive offering to hold her spot was a huge commitment.

She needed to remember she had good friends here, and focus on that, instead of the unwanted attention she was getting right now from agents who barely knew her. "Thanks."

"Of course." He gave her a smile that looked a little

forced then headed for his own desk across the room, in the Organized Crime squad.

As he walked away, Maggie surveyed the other agents in the room. It hadn't been her imagination. There was definitely staring.

She dropped her bag at her desk, slid her gun and cuffs into her drawer and headed back down the hall toward the coffeepot.

Hopefully, Clive was right and only the agents who'd come in early today had learned about the letters. And hopefully, those agents would get over it, stop staring and not gossip.

But the thing she hoped for most was that Grant hadn't heard.

She had to believe the Bureau would catch the Fishhook Rapist this time. Before September 1. She refused to think anything else, no matter how dread filled her every time she thought about that date. No matter how the voice in the back of her mind sounded too much like a whisper from a decade ago, telling her, "This is going to hurt."

She had to believe it would all be over soon, and once it was, she wasn't going to let a few bureaucratic rules keep her from taking a chance with Grant Larkin. Assuming he wanted to take a chance with her. Assuming he hadn't learned all of her horrible secrets.

Please, please, don't let him know.

She chanted the words in her head as she reached the coffeepot. As she grabbed the carafe, Kammy Ming strode over, managing to project power despite her tiny five-foot frame.

"Maggie." Kammy greeted her in the subdued tone she seemed to save just for Maggie.

"Hi, Kammy," Maggie replied. "How's the case going?" She clutched the carafe too tightly, certain

Kammy wouldn't tell her anything. Kammy never told her anything.

But this time, Kammy carefully tugged the carafe from her hand, poured her a cup and said, "We worked all weekend. We're going to catch him."

A smile trembled on Maggie's lips as Kammy poured herself a cup, then faded as Kammy turned to leave, calling after her, "Your friend Grant has some good insights."

Grant was *on the case*? Dizziness washed over her, and she would have dropped her mug of hot coffee except a pair of large hands grabbed it and steadied her.

She looked up, and there was Grant, staring down at her with concern and guilt in his deep brown eyes.

He knew. He knew all the horrible details of what had happened to her. It may have been years ago, but that didn't change how men reacted when they found out. Especially men she was dating. Or wanted to date.

She stepped out of his grasp and braced herself.

"I'm sorry, Maggie," Grant whispered.

And right then and there, she knew anything that could have happened between them was over.

Chapter Four

"Get out of here."

"What?" Grant stopped rubbing his eyes and looked up at Kammy.

She was so tiny, she barely had height on him when she was standing, and he was sitting, but she glared like a pro. "You're no good to me if you're so exhausted you can't focus. Go home. Get some sleep. You've been here too long. Come back fresh tomorrow."

Grant started to argue, but Kammy reached for the file in front of him and closed it. Knowing she'd fight him if he tried to stay, he held up his hands in surrender and got to his feet.

As he trudged through the practically empty bullpen and into the equally deserted parking garage, he admitted she was right. He did need to recharge. Pure determination wasn't going to solve a case that had eluded dozens of other case agents and local police over the past decade. He needed to be at the top of his game, and to do that, a solid eight hours of sleep was in his immediate future.

He was already pressing the button to open his doors when he realized someone was sitting on the hood of his car.

Maggie stood as he approached, a familiar "don't mess

with me" glint in those pretty blue eyes, though she usually saved it for the dirtbags they arrested.

He hadn't asked her before agreeing to work on the case. That made him uncomfortable, but the fact was, even if she'd said she didn't want him on it, he couldn't have turned it down. Couldn't have sat by knowing he might have made a difference when the Fishhook Rapist was after Maggie again.

Grant rubbed the back of his neck and prepared for a fight. "You could have called me if you wanted to talk, Maggie. I would have come out."

She shook her head. "I wanted to do this without causing more gossip."

He cut her off before she could get going. "I should have told you. But I wanted to help."

"And you didn't think I'd prefer someone else work this case?" she said, straightforward as always. "We work some heavy calls together. Every time we clear a room now, are you going to think I can't handle it?"

"Of course no—" he started.

"Do you know how hard it is to be in this field office?" Strain filled her voice. "Knowing there's a squad full of agents who've read all about the worst day of my life?"

"I'm sorry." He'd thought about the strength it took to get through that, and the character it took to ignore the rumors. But he'd never thought about how she felt as a federal agent who investigated crimes all day long, to be part of a case file as a victim.

Probably because, even with what she'd gone through, he'd never thought of her as one. He'd always thought of her as a survivor.

"And do you know how much worse it is, knowing you've seen the evidence from my assault?" she whispered.

The information from her rape kit. It'd been one of the

hardest things he'd ever done, reading through it. And he'd read plenty of them over the years.

"They wanted my help," he said, trying to be honest with her. "It doesn't change a thing between us."

"You're wrong about that."

He stepped closer, reached out and lifted her hand, threading his fingers through hers. "I hope not." He stared into her eyes, trying to tell her with just his gaze how he felt.

Considering how surprised she seemed, it might even have worked.

But then she looked down at their locked hands and frowned. "I'm sure you'd love to think it doesn't make a difference, that it doesn't change how you view me. But believe me, it always does."

He tugged on her hand, bringing her closer, and forcing her to look up at him. "How many people have seen the case file?"

She shook her head. "*Knowing* what happened to me always changes how people look at me."

"I don't believe that." And he didn't. Everyone working the case had the highest respect for her.

He could tell she was about to argue, so he cut her off. "Maggie, I've known since I moved to the WFO."

Her jaw went slack, and her eyes widened. "What?"

"I work the violent crimes squads, and those squads share theories. Just because I wasn't on the case…" He shrugged. "I already knew."

"Why didn't you say anything?"

"Why would I say anything? You heard about me getting stabbed in the Manhattan Strangler case a few years back, right?"

She nodded, studying him as though she was trying to figure out whether or not to believe him.

"You never said anything about that."

"It's a little different."

"It's a lot different, I know. But just because something really bad happened to you a decade ago, that doesn't have anything to do with how I feel about you now."

He tugged her even closer, so there was barely any space between them. She was tall, so even though he outweighed her by almost a hundred pounds, he only had a couple of inches on her. She stared up at him, surprise and uncertainty in her eyes.

Then her gaze traveled down to his mouth and back up again, and there was something new in her expression, something that made him completely forget he'd ever been tired.

She was so different than anyone he'd ever known, and he'd had feelings for her practically since the day he'd started with SWAT. But he'd never made a move, even tried to keep his feelings for her hidden, because she was a teammate. He'd been wary of risking their friendship, wary of risking his place on the team where he'd just been accepted, wary of going in too soon and ruining his shot.

Then they'd become fast friends, and he absolutely knew there was no way he could ever have anything simple or temporary with this woman. And yeah, that was a little scary, too.

But right now, with her staring at him as if her feelings were just as strong, there was no way he could resist her.

She pressed her free hand against his chest, and it felt as if the world was moving in slow motion as she rose up on her tiptoes, and he leaned forward.

He brought his hand to the curve of her waist, marveling at how slender she was beneath all that lean muscle. His fingers slid up to the middle of her back, and he brought her even closer. His lips brushed lightly against hers, and he felt her sigh.

He could practically feel his whole world shifting beneath his feet as he made another pass over her lips with his, and then another, until her grip on his hand tightened, and she kissed him back, harder.

If he'd ever managed to keep his feelings for her hidden, the secret was definitely out now.

Then the door into the parking garage opened with a loud *bang* as it hit the wall, and Maggie jumped backward, fast.

The agent who'd come into the garage didn't even seem to notice them as he headed for his vehicle, but when Grant looked back at Maggie, she had taken another step back and was cursing under her breath.

Before he could say anything, she blurted, "That was a bad idea."

"I think it was one of the best ideas I've ever had."

He grinned at her, and she scowled back, her cheeks flushed. "Grant..." She shook her head. "We need to work together. Let's not make this messy."

"I'm okay with messy," he argued, moving toward her.

She held up a hand, and he stopped. "You're on my case. That changes things, whether you want it to or not. I need this guy caught before September."

Grant nodded, getting serious fast. "Okay." But come September 2, when they had the Fishhook Rapist in jail, he was going straight for messy, regardless of what it meant for his position on the SWAT team.

He'd been shocked when a spot had opened up as soon as he'd moved to DC—as though it was meant to be. The idea of leaving the team was like a punch to the gut. The guys—and Maggie—had become like family. A family he didn't want to lose. And the chance of getting onto one of the other SWAT teams without waiting *years* was minuscule at best. But the thought of not taking a chance with Maggie was worse.

"Do you have any solid leads on the case?"

He gaped at her. "Come on, Maggie. You know I can't tell you."

"Really?" Her hands went from being crossed over her chest to her hips. "Because you had no trouble breaking the rules a second ago."

"*You* kissed *me*," he argued.

"You sure about that?"

Was he? Jeez, he had no idea. "Look, Maggie, I promise you, we're doing everything we can—"

"I've been hearing that for a decade, Grant," she broke in. "And if this guy really is coming back for me, I want to be prepared."

Furious at the idea of the Fishhook Rapist getting anywhere near her again, he vowed, "We won't let that happen."

"Neither will I," she said, her battle face on. "So tell me something I can use."

He stared at her, at the stubborn set of her chin, and he knew. She was already investigating on her own.

He swore. "Maggie, this isn't your specialty. You should leave the case to Violent Crimes."

"Well, that's not happening. So help me or don't, but I'm still looking into it."

Worry gnawed at him. But he couldn't deny this was what he liked about her—her insistence on going full force at a problem.

As the only woman on their SWAT team, she could have gotten out of some of the particularly physically grueling jobs on an assignment, but she never did. Half the time, she volunteered for them. And they could always count on her to get it done, no question.

He took her hand, folding it into his before she could pull it back, and said, "Promise me if you come up with anything, you'll take me with you."

"Scott and Ella are helping me."

He should have realized. "Okay, fine. If you find anything, bring me or Scott. Agreed?"

She raised her eyebrows. "Take a guy with me? What about Ella?"

"She's a profiler, not an operator. Your brother is HRT. Promise me."

"Okay, I promise. I'm not stupid. I wouldn't chase after this guy on my own, not when he's after me specifically."

"Good." He looked down at their linked hands, then back into her gorgeous blue eyes. "We don't have anything solid yet, but if we find something, I'll share."

"Thank you." She eased her hand free. "I need to go."

As she walked away, Grant sighed heavily. When he'd been brought into this case, he'd promised he'd be able to uphold the confidentiality. Now, only a few days later, he was already promising Maggie that he'd break it.

The reality was, there was no way he could say no to her if she pressed him. And there was no way he could step away from the investigation, not when it was this important.

He had a bad feeling that before this case was over, his career was going to take a direct hit.

"WHERE WERE YOU?" Scott greeted her as she walked into her house.

Maggie jumped, even though she knew he'd be there, since his SUV was parked in her driveway. She'd given both Scott and Ella keys to her house, and they insisted on knowing her whereabouts every part of the day.

"I told you I was going to be late coming back from work." As soon as she'd gotten over the shock of discovering Grant was on the case, she'd decided to talk to him. That meant waiting around until he left, which hadn't been until nearly 7:00 p.m.

Then the whole drive home, she'd alternately berated and congratulated herself for kissing him. Yes, she'd wanted to do that for months. And she *had* been honest about how his being on the case changed things. Sure, if they'd somehow gotten around the problem of being teammates and started something serious, she would have told him about what had happened to her, eventually. But she would have given him the basics; she wouldn't have handed over pictures from her rape kit and every horrible detail from her interview with the cops a decade ago.

Even thinking about the fact that Grant knew such personal, painful things made a knot squeeze tighter in her chest.

Scott frowned at her. "You okay?"

"Yeah, I'm fine." She squinted at her brother, taking in the stress lines on his forehead that hadn't been there a few days ago, the dark circles under his eyes, then glanced at her watch. "You're early."

He turned away, saying, "Ella will be over in a bit. She was swinging home first to see Logan before he leaves for his shift."

Maggie's stomach growled, loudly, from being unable to eat much all day, and not wanting to go out for dinner and miss Grant leaving work.

"Ella's bringing dinner," Scott added.

Turning all the bolts behind her, Maggie hurried after him. "What aren't you telling me?"

"Nothing."

Maggie grabbed his arm, making him spin around. "Scott, what is it?"

He shuffled his feet, then sighed. "Nothing to do with your case. Don't worry about it."

He tried to pull his arm free, but she held on tighter. "I appreciate you and Ella trying to protect me, but I'd rather hear it straight. *What*?"

He smiled. "How is it that you always know when there's something I'm not saying, but I could tell Nikki I met an alien in the backyard and she'd believe me?"

Maggie rolled her eyes. Their younger sister had been coddled most of her life. A decade younger than Maggie, she'd already been the baby, but after Maggie's attack, the whole family had become even more protective of little Nikki. But for all her blind trust when it came to family, she wasn't a fool. Maggie and Scott had drilled safety techniques into her until she'd finally told them enough was enough, or she'd be paranoid about everyone she met. "She's not trained by the FBI. I am. And she's not *that* bad. So, spit it out."

"It has nothing to do with this case. I just bailed on some advanced defensive driving training I'd signed up for a long time ago. My supervisor isn't thrilled with me right now." Scott shrugged. "He'll get over it."

Maggie frowned, because this *was* about her. Six months ago, Ella had taken personal time and accepted a case on her own because she thought it was related to Maggie's abductor. Ella's supervisor had been surprisingly understanding, but Maggie knew it had cost Ella a lot of trust she'd worked hard to gain in the elite Behavioral Analysis Unit.

Now Scott was putting himself in a similar position. Again for her.

"Don't do that," Scott said. "I can read you just as well as you read me, sis. I make my own choices. And this really isn't a big deal."

She could tell he was lying, but she also knew it didn't matter what she said. There was no way her big brother—and one of her very best friends, to boot—was stepping one inch away from the case.

"Thanks" seemed so inadequate, but she didn't know what else to say.

He patted her arm as the growl of a convertible came closer. "I hear Ella. Let's eat and then figure out how to stop this guy for good."

"I'm on board with *that*," Maggie said, following him to the door to let in Ella, carrying bags of Chinese food.

An hour later, she, Ella and Scott sat cross-legged on the floor of her living room, surrounded by legal pads, laptops and discarded balls of paper.

"Okay, let's think about this," Ella suggested. "He picks a different state every year. These attacks are definitely specific, and he spends real time stalking the women first, which means he's not just flying out to a new state once a year. He's moving from year to year. So he's either got a job that allows him to travel without attracting notice, or he's got a lot of holes in his résumé."

"We've been through that," Scott said. "Salesman, pilot, trucker—"

"Trucker," Ella said, cutting him off. "What about a long-haul trucker? Maybe someone who's independent, who can pick his own routes. Because he definitely stalks his victims first. But a truck would give him a private location for the attacks and the branding. He could soundproof the back."

"I don't know," Maggie started, but Ella kept going.

"There's a reason the FBI put together that database

on Highway Serial Killers. The interstate travel means multiple jurisdictions that are harder to track, and the nature of the job means they're often around people who are high-risk victims."

"Sure," Scott said, "but aren't most of the victims who were in that database prostitutes? This guy goes for women who are at pretty low risk for being victims of a crime and at a high risk to himself."

Ella looked impressed. "You do listen when I babble about profiling, don't you?"

"Of course, kiddo," he said, using the nickname he'd had for her since childhood.

"I don't remember a truck," Maggie said quietly, and both of them got serious, looking over at her.

"Do you remember that part at all?" Scott asked.

Maggie had always told them both she couldn't remember much about her attack. And it was true. She just had fragments—nothing she'd ever thought would help in an investigation.

She recalled feeling dizzy as she walked out of the college party alone, as though she'd had way more to drink than just one beer. Then, later, being lifted off the ground after she'd tripped and fallen. A low voice, whispering in her ear right before the brand burned her neck. The vague sense of stumbling out of a vehicle before she dragged herself back to her dorm room.

She'd never remembered a face. Never remembered the assault itself. Nothing that would lead police to whoever had hurt her.

Even though she'd always felt some relief about that, she'd tried. She'd even let herself be hypnotized once, attempting to get back the details. But hospital staff and police experts had warned her that date-rape drugs like the one she'd consumed could eliminate huge chunks of time from her memory. They hadn't been surprised when she couldn't provide any details.

Still, for some reason she felt strongly about this part. "I only remember bits and pieces. I couldn't say for sure. But I just don't think I was in a truck."

"Well, a motel room is another possibility," Ella said. "Something off the beaten path a little, somewhere that charges by the hour and expects the sort of customer who'd prefer not to be remembered."

"Or he puts down roots, rents something for eight months then moves on to the next location and starts scouting," Maggie suggested.

"Which would mean he probably works odd jobs and has a résumé full of holes," Ella said. "And this perp is extremely intelligent. So in these odd jobs, he's either hiding that so he doesn't stand out, or he's noticed for it."

"I know the original profiler said he was antisocial," Maggie said. "So maybe he just keeps quiet."

"Yeah, maybe." Ella was frowning. "But we know he arrives sometime after September 1 in each new location, and he leaves before September 1 of the following year, probably at least a few months before, so he can pick out a new victim. So he's either choosing all short-term contract work, or he's suddenly going absent from these jobs and creating a trend."

"A trend we can track?" Scott asked skeptically.

"Probably not. But I'm not sure—"

"Or he's wealthy," Maggie cut in. "Wealthy enough that the money doesn't matter."

"Maybe," Ella said. "But the hook suggests something to do with water, so he could also have some sort of seasonal job in the fishing industry, something that ends before the fall."

"That makes a lot of sense," Scott agreed. "That hook has to mean something."

"Does it?" Maggie glanced between them, knowing her frustration was showing. "Or is he smart enough to do it to throw us totally off track?"

Her eyes were wet, and she blinked fast, hoping neither of them had noticed, but knowing they had. "What chance do we have of finding him? We don't even have the case files. Even the case agents—who worked nonstop all weekend—don't have any new leads."

"We're going to get him," Scott promised.

She nodded, hoping she looked as though she believed it. At work, she tackled every case assuming that if she just worked hard enough, she'd solve it. She tried to treat her own life the same way.

But year after year, the memories added up. Going through the same motions of gathering together and closing ranks with Ella and Scott. Watching the news even as they tried to stay away from it. Hoping that year would be different even when they knew it wouldn't.

And every year, it was exactly the same. Every year, she watched some new woman live out the same horrible thing she had, knowing that just like her, they'd only have partial memories. Knowing that just like her, they probably wouldn't be able to identify the Fishhook Rapist even if he walked right up to them.

In twenty-seven days, would the Fishhook Rapist walk right up to her? And if he did, would she know it before it was too late?

Chapter Five

Twenty days.

There were twenty days left until Maggie's attacker came back for her, and despite the best efforts of some of the most dedicated VCMO agents Grant knew, there were no new breaks in the case.

Despite his nonstop hours at work, poring over the evidence, he wasn't making a difference.

Grant slammed his fist against the wall of the van he was riding in, and the teammate seated next to him gave him a perplexed look.

"Grant!" Clive barked. "Get your head in the game."

"Sorry," he muttered, refocusing.

They were en route to a warehouse in a particularly bad area of DC, where case agents had determined a human trafficking ring was conducting business. Two of their supposed victims had already shown up in the morgue, burn marks on their bodies as apparent punishment before their throats were slit, and case agents expected more would surface unless they acted fast.

Maggie's squad had brought the warrants and the evidence, and requested SWAT for the potentially high-risk arrests. It was well after normal business hours, but surveillance indicated the personal vehicles of the three men listed on the arrest warrants were parked outside. The only three vehicles in the lot.

If SWAT was lucky, they'd be the only people inside the building tonight.

"They've got surveillance cameras everywhere, so we're hacking them and blocking the feed," Clive continued briefing them. "But if anyone's watching the cameras, they're going to know we're coming. So get your A-game ready, people."

Grant pushed Maggie's case to the back of his mind, but he couldn't help glancing at Maggie. She was squashed into the corner of the truck, and even in all her gear, she looked tiny next to the teammate they jokingly referred to as "Tank." Her dark hair curled around her chin underneath her helmet, and even with goggles dangling around her neck and buried underneath Kevlar and weaponry, she made his pulse pick up.

As the van bounced over potholes, she held her MP-5 and stared straight ahead, totally focused. And totally ignoring him, even though she probably felt his stare.

It had been that way for a week. It wasn't as if they weren't on speaking terms, but things were definitely strained between them, and had been since they'd kissed.

Still, he couldn't bring himself to regret it. Given the chance, he'd do it again.

He felt himself smile at the idea, and Maggie finally glanced his way as if she could sense the direction of his thoughts. But then she went back to staring straight ahead, which was typical for her right before a high-risk arrest.

Some of the guys worked off tension by joking around just before they went into a call—usually, he was one of them. Others on the team sat in silence. Maggie always seemed to be envisioning exactly how the raid was going to go.

It wouldn't surprise him if whatever she imagined was usually right—she tended to have a sixth sense on this kind of call. More than once, he'd watched her react to a threat before anyone else knew it was there, before there was any reason for her to know it existed. Some of the guys on the team called it "Maggie's Magic."

As they drove past the warehouse, giving them eyes on the target, he hoped for a little of that magic tonight. The quick look he had before the truck parked down the street was of a high chain-link fence topped with barbed wire, cameras mounted above the windowless doors, and three vehicles big enough to hold five people each parked close to the loading dock of the sprawling warehouse.

"Time to move," Clive said, nodding to the tech who was already typing away, preparing to black out the cameras.

Tank threw open the door, and six FBI SWAT agents jumped onto the street. As Grant fell into the front of the line, his adrenaline picked up. His regular position on VCMO was interesting and challenging, but SWAT—most of the time—was downright fun. Yeah, it was serious, but anyone who tried out for a SWAT team had to get a thrill from this kind of work.

As he took off down the street, he imagined anyone who happened to be in the decrepit building across the street looking outside and getting a shock. Normally, this area was pretty deserted after business hours, and for good reason. Even during the day, it wasn't the sort of place you'd want to wander into accidentally.

Just about every building on the block had been raided by FBI or local police or both at some point. But for every criminal they pushed out, another seemed to take his place. Gunshots weren't uncommon around here, but rarely did anyone call for help when they happened.

But six FBI agents decked out in combat gear, carrying heavy weaponry and a battering ram, running at full speed, had to make anyone with half a brain pray the targets were arrested quickly and without a fight.

Over his radio, the tech's tinny voice came through. "The target's cameras are down...now!"

Almost before he'd finished speaking, Clive was using bolt cutters on the lock keeping them on the wrong side of the fence. Then they passed through single-file and moved for the entry on the corner, the one with the least visibility for the occupants inside, and the best coverage for the agents, according to the blueprints they'd accessed.

As Clive fell to the back of the line, Maggie came up beside Grant, her MP-5 submachine gun up to cover him as he lifted the battering ram.

One solid hit, and the door flew inward, bouncing off the wall and almost closing on them again, until he smashed it back open with his foot. His night vision equipment lent an eerie green glow to the short, dark hallway, but it didn't illuminate any targets as Maggie stepped in first, moving past him quickly and off to his right.

Grant dropped the battering ram, raising his own primary weapon as he came up beside her. Then they were moving together, in a choreographed entry that felt like a thousand practice runs.

The rest of the team came in behind them, their combat boots clomping on the concrete floor as they moved quickly down the hall as a unit.

"Clear," Maggie's confident voice came through his headset as she opened a closet door on her side and checked it. Then they came up to the wide, open area that was the main part of the warehouse.

The agents began splitting off in twos, each into their own sectors. Much of the open warehouse space was filled floor to ceiling with boxes, providing plenty of places for targets to hide, and lots of places to clear. The area in his and Maggie's sector was open until it branched off down a separate hallway leading to offices.

Checking his peripherals because his teammates wouldn't be able to clear their sectors as quickly, Grant was surprised not to see anyone in the main area. Either the targets hadn't heard the entry—which they should have, with a battering ram—or they were hiding. Or everyone was in one of the two offices.

"Quiet," Maggie's voice whispered through his headset.

Too quiet was what he knew she meant.

He nodded once to acknowledge it, and then jutted his chin toward the door straight ahead. It was closed, but there was a light on inside. As they got closer, he could just make out a voice, and he strained to listen. It sounded like a scream, only turned down to almost nothing, as though it was coming from a TV.

"Possible target," he whispered as they both lifted their NVGs.

Maggie reached for the door handle with her left hand, keeping her weapon sighted with her right.

She turned the handle slowly, nodding as it moved on its own—meaning it wasn't locked. Then she shoved it open, giving him a view of one corner of the room, but no angle on the rest, as the muted scream became a high-pitched wail, full of pain. The soundproofed walls registered in his brain as a charred smell instantly filled his nostrils.

He watched Maggie's left hand go back to her weapon almost before the door opened, then watched her jaw go slack and her eyes go abnormally wide before her whole body froze.

Grant stepped sideways quickly, the rest of the room coming into view. The filthy, half-dressed woman on the floor, a man's knee pressed into her back as he held a lighter to her. Another man standing beside him, looking bored. And a third behind them, surprise on his face as he yanked up a pistol.

Grant heard himself screaming at the target to put it down, even as he lurched sideways, shoving Maggie out of the doorway and trying to sight his weapon at the same time.

He pulled the trigger, then something smashed into his chest, and he flew through the air as a pair of gunshots filled his ears. He slammed into the ground with enough force that it would have knocked the air out of his lungs, if he could actually breathe. His head hit the ground, and his vision dimmed as he gasped for oxygen and groped with his left hand for the source of the pain exploding in his chest.

From what seemed like a long distance away, he heard Maggie's voice screaming his name, and two more gunshots in rapid succession. Then a dark figure filled his vision, and he tried to blink it into focus, tried to lift the weapon he was pretty sure was still clutched in his right hand, as his fingers finally grazed over his chest and dipped into the bullet hole.

"GRANT!"

Panic filled Maggie's chest as she slung her MP-5 over her back, dropped to her knees and reached for the hand Grant had clasped over his chest. His eyes were rolled back in his head, but he kept blinking as though he was trying to focus, and gasping for breath.

Please let him be okay, a voice chanted in her head, as she tried to remember all the training that had become second nature over the past four years in SWAT. Never in those four years had she watched a teammate take a bullet.

"Where are you hit?" she yelled, even though she knew he couldn't answer her.

She didn't wait for him to try. Instead, she pushed his hand aside, relief flooding through her as she saw the bullet lodged near the top of his Kevlar vest. But that didn't mean it hadn't caused damage.

Forcing her hand underneath his vest, she searched for any sign the bullet had gone through. But there was no blood.

Still, it was possible he had a collapsed lung, or broken ribs, or...

"I'm okay." Grant interrupted her fears as he finally seemed to catch his breath and started to push himself up.

"Stay there," Maggie said, but he ignored her, getting to a sitting position and looking around, already back on task as he checked for new threats.

"Status? Maggie, status?"

Suddenly realizing the question was coming from both Grant beside her and Clive over her headset, Maggie replied, "Grant was hit in the vest." Her heart still raced as she tried to get it together, tried not to think about what could have happened, tried not to think about *why*.

She'd never let anything distract her from a mission before. Never let her history prevent her from doing her job. Until today.

There'd be plenty of time to berate herself later. Right now she needed to get her mind back on the mission.

"Three targets down. One victim needs an ambulance."

"And Grant?" Clive pressed.

"I'm okay," Grant told them both.

Maggie glanced at him where he sat on the floor, still wincing as he braced a hand against his chest. "Grant, I'm sor—"

"Not now," he said, getting to his feet with a lot more effort than it should have taken.

"Are you sure you don't need—"

"It'll be a nasty bruise. Nothing's broken. Let's check the room." He slung his own MP-5 over his back, grunting at the movement, and grabbed the Glock strapped to his thigh then moved toward the room.

Reluctantly, she unholstered her own Glock, better for close quarters than the MP-5, and followed, looking into the office.

Inside, the three men who were listed on their warrants were down for good, one from Grant's bullet and two from hers. The three traffickers had only gotten two shots off, the one that had hit Grant and another that had gone wide, passing over her right shoulder.

There was nowhere in the office to hide. The only other person in the room was the woman who'd picked herself up off the floor and was cowering in the corner, rocking back and forth. Surely one of the trafficking victims.

The smell hit Maggie as soon as she entered. Not the blood. The burning.

She fought back the urge to gag, fought the memory that tried to incapacitate her a second time. The same memory that had surged forward the instant she'd opened the door. A memory she hadn't even realized she possessed.

A memory that had very nearly gotten Grant killed.

She glanced at him, checking the pulses on the three men on the floor, even though they were clearly gone. It chilled her how close he'd come to dying outside this room.

He looked back at her, concern and a hint of pain in his deep brown eyes, and she couldn't hold his gaze.

"Our sector's clear," Grant said into his mic, and within the next few minutes, the rest of the team announced the same.

"We've got ERT, an ambulance and the coroner on the way," Clive told them. "They're less than a minute out. We're coming to you now."

Before the team made it into the room, Grant had checked the woman over for any serious injuries—and weapons, because you could never assume—and Maggie had cuffed the three perps with the zip ties looped on her belt. Dead or not, it was procedure.

The whole time, she tried not to breathe too deeply.

"You okay?" Clive asked Grant as he joined them in the office, the rest of the team behind him, looking shaken. This was the first time anyone on the team had been shot since before Maggie had joined four years ago.

"I'm good," Grant replied easily, already beginning to move around as if he hadn't taken a bullet to the chest.

Vest or not, at this range, that had to *hurt*. A few inches higher, and it could have been much, much worse.

Was he playing it down because that was a SWAT agent's way? Or because of her?

"What happened?" Clive asked.

Grant opened his mouth, but Maggie cut him off, not wanting to know what he was going to say. Not wanting him to tell Clive she'd frozen at a critical moment, but not wanting him to lie for her, either.

"It was my fault," she said, watching her teammates'

eyes widen behind Clive as they looked back and forth between her and Grant and the dead men on the floor.

Grant frowned, his attention darting to the woman in the corner of the room, and Maggie realized he'd put it all together.

Of course he had. He'd read all the details from her case file. He knew exactly what had happened to her a decade ago, every terrible detail. Including the brand on the back of her neck.

It had smelled the same today as it had ten years ago, when she'd heard a voice whispering in her ear, telling her something would hurt. As she'd struggled toward consciousness to find her head pressed against a cold, hard surface. A hand against the back of her head. A disorienting, numb feeling over her entire body, and complete confusion as a room slowly came into focus around her. A room she didn't recognize. And then a sudden, fierce pain at the back of her neck, and the smell of her own skin burning.

She tried to force back the memory, then looked up at Clive and blurted out words she never thought she'd say. "I need to leave the SWAT team."

Chapter Six

"I'm so sorry."

Maggie blurted the words as soon as Grant opened his door. The door she'd finally gotten the courage to knock on after standing on his front stoop for ten minutes in the glow of the porch light.

She'd never been to his house before, but she'd told Ella and Scott not to come over tonight, because she was going out with her SWAT friends. There'd be plenty of time to break the news to them later about her sudden career change.

Instead, she'd looked up Grant's address and made the surprisingly short drive to his house.

Grant opened the door wide and stepped aside. His voice was somber when he said, "Come in, Maggie." He sounded as if he'd expected her, as though maybe he'd been waiting up for her.

Nerves, guilt and regret mingled as she stepped inside, glancing around. His tidy little row house looked similar to hers on the outside, but inside it was very different. Hardwood floors instead of carpet, beige walls instead of the muted blues and greens and yellows she'd chosen. More sparsely decorated, but somehow it still felt cozy.

She followed him into the living room, and her eyes

were immediately drawn to a row of pictures over his fireplace. She couldn't stop herself from stepping closer.

One was clearly him in high school, because he was wearing a letter jacket. He'd been muscular even as a teenager, and he had his arms around two smaller boys, a tired-looking black woman behind them. The younger boys took after their mother where Grant, who seemed to have some strong Mediterranean heritage, probably resembled his father. Still, there was something so similar in their expressions, marking them as siblings. The pictures on either side were of those boys grown up, married, little kids on their knees.

Grant stood next to her, his shoulder brushing hers. "My younger brothers." He pointed to the pictures on the outsides of the little boys, pride in his voice. "And this is them now, with my nephews."

She looked back at the young boys, his brothers' kids, who looked like miniature versions of Grant, and an ache settled somewhere inside that she didn't want to acknowledge. She'd never really let herself think about kids, because she'd never been able to get anywhere near the point of wanting to have them with someone.

"And your mom?" Maggie asked, looking at the center picture again, the one where Grant's expression said he'd grown up fast. Too fast. Even as a teenager, the protective instinct nearly screamed from him. The same way it did now, on SWAT.

"Yeah. Not the greatest picture of her, but it was one of the first family photos we have from after my dad took off. I need to get something more recent up there before she comes to visit and gets mad at me for choosing that picture to put up."

He grinned at her, and she couldn't help it. There was something about the way he smiled, the way it made his eyes brighten, the way he seemed to grin with his whole face, every time, that always made her smile back.

But it faded fast. "Grant, I owe you—"

"Nothing." He cut her off, actually sounding as if he meant it. "You owe me nothing."

"I owe you a lot more than just an apology. I wish I could go back to the day Clive asked me if I wanted to take time off from SWAT and—"

"Stop it," Grant said, and it wasn't his words, but the fact that he actually put his finger over her lips that made her quiet.

The touch sent a tingling feeling outward over her face, and his expression changed, too. The serious veneer was gone, replaced with a mixture of emotions she couldn't begin to unravel. But worry and desire were definitely part of the mix.

His gaze dropped to her lips, and instead of moving his finger, he traced it slowly over her mouth.

Every pore on her body seemed to suddenly come alive as the tingling swept outward, down to her toes. She stepped back fast. "What are you doing? I got you *shot* today!"

He walked over to the oversize leather couch on the far wall and sat down. "You're human. Everyone makes mistakes, Maggie."

She stared down at him incredulously. "You can't be serious!"

"I've messed up clearing a room before."

"Did you get someone else shot?" she demanded.

"No. I got lucky." He leaned forward, taking his arms off the back of the couch where he'd rested them as though he was settling in for a long argument. "Ask any guy on the team, and I bet you'll hear the same thing."

She frowned. Maybe that was true, maybe not, but it

was irrelevant. Her actions had gotten a teammate shot. And it didn't matter that he was okay. It didn't matter that it had happened because of a memory she couldn't have predicted would rear its ugly head at exactly the wrong time. What mattered was that it had happened.

"If I hadn't quit tonight, I would have been off the team, anyway."

"You would have been talking to OPR," Grant countered. The Bureau's Office of Professional Responsibility, who would investigate tonight's incident, got involved whenever a firearm was used. "Just like you're doing now. But you'll come through this, and you need to *fight* for your spot on the team, Maggie. You belong there, and we all know it. Besides, I'm fine. No harm, no foul."

She gaped at him. "How can you be this calm about getting shot?"

"It hurt less than being stabbed."

A burst of laughter escaped. "You should be pissed at me right now. What's wrong with you? You should hate me!"

"It wasn't you who shot me," Grant said, still so calmly it was starting to piss *her* off.

"No, it was me who *got you* shot!"

"And I'm glad it was me who was hit." He leaned toward her and held out his hand. "Come here."

"What?" She shook her head, not moving. "Why?"

He rolled his eyes, stood up and peeled his T-shirt off, tossing it aside. "Look." He put his hand up at the top of his chest, where a huge purple bruise spread outward from a dark center to a lighter bluish color snaking toward his neck.

She'd seen him without his shirt on before, but always in training, surrounded by a group of other FBI agents, including herself, all keeping in shape for missions. Times when she'd purposely avoided looking. Nothing like the sudden intimacy here, alone with him in his home.

Her mouth suddenly felt dry. She couldn't stop her eyes from wandering over football-player shoulders, down biceps that bulged with muscle without even being flexed, to what should have been a six-pack but looked more like a twelve-pack.

Her fingers pulsed with the need to reach out and stroke the bruise, or the shiny, jagged scar that ran along his side—a present from the Manhattan Strangler. From there, she could trace her fingers up to the ridges of muscle on his abdomen. She could glide her hands over him until he truly forgave her for what had happened in that warehouse tonight.

"Maggie." He sounded amused, but when she forced herself to look up, heat lit his eyes.

"Sorry," she whispered.

He strode toward her, and common sense told her to flee, but he was standing in front of her before she could move, so close she could feel the heat from his body.

She bit her lip as she felt his hand close around hers, lifting it up. He placed it over his bruise, and just as her fingers started to open, he moved her hand back toward her.

In an instant, she realized why he'd told her he was glad it had been him who'd gotten shot. It had happened because she'd frozen, but if he hadn't shoved her out of the way, she'd have been the one with a bullet hole.

Her fingers drifted over the base of her neck, neatly lined up with the bruise on the top of Grant's chest. No vest would have saved her.

The knowledge left her suddenly cold. The cold intensified as Grant turned and walked away, grabbing his T-shirt off the couch and slipping it over his head.

When he settled back on his couch and gestured for her to join him, this time her feet moved slowly until she was sitting next to him. "That doesn't make me feel any better."

"Well, you're going to have to deal with it. And you have enough to focus on right now, so stop worrying. I'm fine. You're fine. And once you go through all the OPR stuff, we want you back. *I* want you back."

Maggie shook her head, but he insisted, "Don't decide now. But just so you know, everyone on the team agrees."

She was touched by their loyalty, and surprised. Because on SWAT, decisions about teammates had nothing to do with friendship, and everything to do with ability. But it didn't matter how they felt. She had to do what was right for the team, whether they saw it or not.

"I'm a liability." It killed her to admit it, but right now, it was true. And she didn't remember much at all from her attack, so how could she predict if that would happen again, some other memory getting triggered at the wrong time?

Grant took her hand in his. "Once this case is closed and you've got your focus back, you'll change your mind."

"You're too nice for your own good. You know that, right? You know it's not normal to ask the person who just got you shot to come back and cover you?"

"I'll let you cover me anytime you want."

More laughter snuck out at the completely out-of-character remark, and she shifted to face him on the couch. "Are you actually hitting on me right now? Because your pickup lines could use some work."

"Really?" He turned slightly, moving a little closer and

stroking his fingers over the palm of her hand, igniting her nerve endings with the simple touch. "The way you were drooling before, I thought it'd be okay."

"I was *not* drooling," she said, even as she felt heat in her cheeks. But she found herself smiling back at him.

How did he always do that to her? Even on a day like today, with everything going on, with the shooting and the memories and the guilt she was feeling? How could he still make her feel this ridiculous, giddy happiness?

"Maybe you're right," she whispered, suddenly desperate to feel his lips on hers the way they had been in the parking lot of the WFO a week ago.

She leaned toward him, fast, before she could change her mind. Moving in close, she pressed her mouth to his.

And just like the last time they'd kissed, all rational thought fled her mind, and she could only focus on Grant. The bunching muscles underneath her hand, the tiny rasp of stubble from his chin, the ridiculous softness of his lips.

She moved even closer, until she was plastered against him, and could slide both her arms around his neck. Until she could open her mouth, inviting his tongue inside.

He didn't hesitate, and the first brush of his tongue against hers left her desperate for more. She tried to lean even closer, and felt his hands slip underneath her thighs and lift her up onto his lap as though she weighed nothing.

She tried to wriggle closer still, and felt the rumble of his laughter as his hands locked on her hips and held her still. She thought she heard him mutter something about his self-control—or maybe it was hers—and then he was kissing her again, flooding her entire body with need.

She ran her hands down over his arms then underneath his T-shirt, wanting to feel his bare skin again, this time wanting to caress her fingers over all the muscles she'd seen earlier.

He sucked in a breath as her fingers followed the lines of muscle in his abdomen up to his chest, stopping just short of his bruise, and she flattened her hand there, loving the feel of his heart thumping madly underneath her fingers. She wanted more.

Wrenching her mouth from his, she panted, "Bedroom," then leaned back in, hoping he'd just stand up and take her there.

Instead, his hands moved up to her waist, skirting around the gun at her hip, and he didn't let her close the distance to his lips again. "Maggie," he whispered, his voice even deeper than usual. "Maybe this isn't a good idea."

Surprise and embarrassment flooded. What was she thinking? She'd gotten him shot, then tried to sleep with him in the same night?

She tried to move off his lap, but his hands were still tight on her waist, holding her in place.

Of course this wasn't a good idea. Now that Grant knew everything he knew about her past, it was only a matter of time before it colored the way he looked at her. And she wasn't the type to sleep with someone without being in a relationship. Not anymore. Not in a long, long time.

"I'm sorry," she muttered, dropping her hands off his shoulders. "Let's forget this ever happened."

GRANT CURSED AS Maggie flushed deep red, trying to get off him.

"I just meant the timing, Maggie. Not that I'm not interested." Which should have been pretty obvious.

She still looked mortified—and as if she didn't quite

believe him—so he slid one hand up her back until he could pull her toward him and capture her mouth with his again.

He'd intended to kiss her fast, just once more, then convince her that they should wait until after her case was solved. Because a relationship between them was complicated enough already, with work, and especially now, with the inevitable OPR investigation into today's SWAT call. But add in her flashback and everything happening with her case, and he didn't want to screw things up for later by jumping in at the worst possible time.

But as soon as his lips found hers, longing rocked through him, a reminder of everything he'd been wanting for the past nine months. Everything he'd been looking for since before he even met her. *Maggie.*

He must have said her name out loud, probably sounding as desperate as he felt, because she mumbled something in return, then brought her mouth to his again. A second later, she shifted, until he could feel her whole body against his.

And he knew right then that it would take way more willpower than he possessed to say no to her again. But he pulled away from her long enough to whisper, "How about you take this off?"

She blinked back at him, and he patted her holster so she'd know what he was talking about.

She looked a little disappointed, so he added, "I'd prefer to take the rest off myself."

She smiled, but he didn't miss the brief indecision in her expression before she unstrapped her holster.

As she leaned over to drop her weapon on his side table, he forced himself to say, "Maggie, we can—"

"Shut up, Grant," she replied, wrestling his shirt off and tossing it on the floor. Then she sat there staring at him, eyebrows raised, as if she was waiting for him to make good on his promise.

Remembering how she'd responded before when he'd stroked his fingers over her palm, he reached for her hand and pressed it to his lips, tracing a circle on her palm with his mouth and his tongue until she relaxed toward him. Then he stroked his other hand up underneath the back of her T-shirt, marveling that someone who could handle an MP-5 the way she did had such silky, soft skin.

She squirmed on his lap and took her hand from his lips, hooking it onto his shoulder as she leaned into him again.

Tilting his head, he kissed her harder, drawing her T-shirt up. Then he stopped kissing her long enough to slip it over her head. He got a brief glimpse of a blue satin bra the same shade as her eyes, and then her bare skin was against his, and he groaned.

She smiled back at him, a pleased smile that told him she knew exactly what she was doing to him right now, and then she dipped her head, and he felt her lips on his earlobe. As her tongue slid across his neck, he felt his self-control slipping further and further out of reach.

Frantic with the need to kiss her again, he slid his hand up her back, so he could glide his fingers through her hair and tilt her head back to his. Just before his fingers reached the back of her neck, he realized what he was doing. A jolt hit him at his mistake, and he froze.

He tried to recover and skip over her neck to just palm the back of her head, but it was too late.

Hurt showed in her eyes as she stood up. She bumped his coffee table hard enough that it was probably going to leave a bruise, but she didn't seem to notice as she grabbed her T-shirt off the floor and pulled it over her head.

"I'm sorry." He got to his feet, too, dread pooling in his stomach.

"And you said knowing about my past didn't change anything."

He shook his head, genuinely bewildered. "It doesn't."

"Right." She turned away from him, picking up her holster and strapping it back on.

"Maggie." He put his hand on her arm, and felt her muscles tense. "It doesn't change how I *feel* about you. I just didn't think you'd want me touching you there. That's all."

She looked up at him, hurt and frustration written on her face, but he could see the truth of his words register there, too.

She wore her hair short enough that it wouldn't be a hassle in SWAT, but long enough to cover the entire back of her neck. It was a logical assumption she wouldn't want any man touching the brand there.

She stepped backward, making him drop her arm. "If it really didn't matter, you wouldn't be thinking about that at all. You'd be focused on me. On us. On right now."

"That's not fair," he countered. "After what happened today—"

She cut him off, swearing. She was practically yelling, but she sounded more frustrated than angry when she said, "I'm so sick of this. Every year. Every single year, I'm just sitting around waiting to see who's next." She dropped onto his couch, something defeated in the hunch of her shoulders he'd never seen before. "And this year, it's me again."

He sat next to her, wrapping an arm around her shoulder even as she tensed up at his touch. "It's *not* going to be you again. This is all going to be over soon."

"It'll never be over." She turned her head, looking

away from him, then admitted, her voice cracking, "I *don't* like anyone touching my neck."

He could feel her arms trembling as she said, so quietly he had to lean in to hear, "I had to go back six times before I could manage to get the tattoo over it."

"But you did it."

"Yeah, well, I wasn't going to let him win. No way was I leaving that mark on my body."

She turned away from him even more, lifting his arm off her shoulder. But when he'd expected her to stand up and leave, she tilted her head down and lifted her hair.

He'd seen the pictures from the case file, when the brand was new. Red and angry, an ugly raised hook on her delicate neck.

Now the damaged skin underneath was still evident if you looked closely enough, but she'd had a tattoo—some Chinese letters—put directly on top of it. Something that must have been incredibly difficult to do, but that was Maggie. She never backed down from any challenge.

"What does it mean?" he asked, as she dropped her hair back down to cover the deep black symbol inked on her neck.

"Strength," she answered, getting to her feet.

"Good choice," he said as she turned to face him. It was probably the most appropriate thing she could have chosen. She was one of the strongest people he knew.

She nodded, and from the raw look in her eyes, he suspected she very rarely showed it to anyone.

"Can you tell me what you remembered today?" he asked. He'd planned to do it tomorrow, but he suddenly didn't want to make her talk about it at the office.

"I figured we'd get to that eventually," she said then sat back down at the far corner of the couch, away from him. She glanced at him briefly, then away. "Can you put a shirt on?"

"Okay." He picked up his T-shirt from the floor and put it back on, then settled in the center of the couch, giving her the distance she obviously wanted.

"It was the smell." She was looking straight ahead, not at him, but he could tell she was wearing her SWAT-ready expression.

"I figured," he said softly. Scent was one of the most powerful triggers for memory.

"I thought I'd remembered everything I'd ever get back about that day—which wasn't much," she said, then shook her head, and her voice was stronger, more detached when she continued. "But today I remembered a room. I'd never been there before. It was…fancy. My head was on a table, a really cold table." She frowned, looking pensive, and then finally nodded, adding, "I think it was marble."

A marble table? Definitely not a pay-by-the-hour type motel or in a vehicle. Which lent credence to his theory that the person who'd done this had actually lived in DC when he'd attacked Maggie, and that he hadn't just been passing through searching for a victim.

"The room was blurry. From the drugs."

Grant tried to ignore the fury that rose up as Maggie talked, at the idea of anyone drugging her, hurting her. But it rose up like bile in his throat.

"I'm not sure I'd recognize it if I saw it today. But there were pictures on the wall, big ones, nice frames. And carpet under my knees. Thick carpet. I think it was a large room." She shuddered when she added, "When I screamed, it echoed."

"Do you remember anything about him?" Grant asked, trying to keep the anger out of his voice.

But she must have heard it, because she turned and looked at him. He thought she was going to say something—not about the case, but about his reaction—but after a long pause, she just shook her head.

"He was behind me. With the—with whatever he used on my neck. I think I passed out again after that." She paused. "I still don't remember him."

"Well, this could help," he told her. "These are new details. And I think…"

"What?" she demanded when he cut himself off before he blurted out his case theories.

"It could help."

"I told you all that, and that's all you're giving me?"

"You know I'm not supposed to—"

"What?" she interrupted. "Make out with a teammate?"

Even though he knew she was pissed, he couldn't help smiling at that. "Well, yeah, that, too."

"Come on. You already know I'm investigating. We have twenty days." She looked at her watch "Make that nineteen. I may not be VCMO, but I spend my days investigating some nasty stuff, too. Don't waste resources. Tell me what you're thinking."

Despite the voice screaming in his head that this was a really bad idea, screaming that she was using his feelings for her to get case information she'd never have access to otherwise, he told her. "I think he started in DC. I think you were the first one he marked, but not his first victim."

She frowned back at him. "Yeah, Ella thinks that, too, about him having a history of rape. Not necessarily about DC."

"Well, I think whoever he started with was someone in his life, and that her attack is why the date is significant."

She stared back at him, nodding slowly. "Maybe."

"If I'm right—"

"There could be a way to track him," she finished.

Chapter Seven

Maggie was sitting up in bed, her hand already gripping her gun, before she'd even identified what had woken her. Her heart thudding, she glanced at her alarm clock—6:00 a.m.

Below her, from outside, a car door slammed. Her bedroom faced the street, but there wasn't a lot of traffic quite this early, not where she lived.

Getting out of bed, she moved beside the window, lifting the slats on the blinds to peer outside. She saw Grant walking up her drive at the same moment she heard movement from inside her house, on the first floor.

Where her overprotective brother had spent the night on her couch. He'd been there, half-asleep, when she'd gotten home from Grant's house last night. For once, she'd managed to avoid his questions and go straight to bed.

She doubted Grant had already been to work, or had a break in the case, which meant he was probably stopping by on his way to the WFO. And that meant he either wanted to talk about her quitting SWAT or what had happened between them last night.

She felt momentarily frozen watching him stride up her driveway, until she heard another thud from downstairs. Probably Scott preparing to confront any approaching threats.

Cursing, she let the blinds drop and ran down the stairs. "Scott, it's just—"

Before she'd finished speaking, her brother had swung open the front door and tucked his gun into the waistband of his pants. "Grant."

"Scott, hi." Grant held out a hand for her brother, looking surprised.

"Scott and Ella alternate staying with me until this whole thing is over," Maggie reminded Grant, her words coming out too fast, and she felt herself flush as his gaze locked on hers. After last night, even his eyes on her gave her goose bumps.

Scott gave her a questioning look as he shook Grant's hand, and she remembered she hadn't told him that Grant was working the case.

"Come on in," Scott said, stepping back and rubbing his eyes. "You guys have a call or something?"

Grant frowned as he walked inside. "No. Didn't Maggie tell—"

"Is there something new with the case?" she asked, willing him not to tell her brother she'd left SWAT.

"No. I'm sorry. I just, uh—"

So he'd come by to clear the air about last night. After she'd told him the details of her flashback, things had suddenly felt awkward in a way they never, ever had with Grant. Not until he'd started investigating her case. She'd had a desperate need to get out of there, so she had, quickly, with barely a goodbye.

She'd known seeing him in the office today was going to be uncomfortable. She should have figured Grant would do this.

"Sorry I ran out on you last night," she said, hoping her

brother would assume the "you" she was talking about was plural—the whole team. "It was a long day."

"Sure, that's okay," Grant said slowly.

Maggie tried to appear nonchalant when Scott looked at her.

Grant was terrible at deception. He'd be an awful undercover agent.

It was a good thing he'd gone into VCMO and SWAT, where he could use his size and pissed-off expression to terrify the criminals, and his easygoing, contagious smile to reassure the victims, or charm his way into a tight-knit SWAT team. Or into her affections.

"I'm going to grab a coffee," Scott said in an obvious move to give them privacy. "Nice to see you, Grant." As he walked past Maggie, he raised his eyebrows, and she knew she'd be getting grilled as soon as Grant left.

"You, too," Grant called after him, then quieter, to her, "You haven't told him?"

"No," she whispered back. "But now I'll have to, because it's pretty obvious something's up." She shook her head at him, moving closer so her brother wouldn't overhear. "You're a terrible liar."

"He caught me off guard."

"I told you he was staying with me." Suddenly conscious of the fact that she was wearing pajama pants and a snug tank top without anything underneath, she crossed her arms over her chest. Instead of asking him why he was there, she said, "Can we talk later?"

"Yeah, I wasn't thinking about your brother being here. I totally forgot. I just wanted to see you, to—"

"To clear the air about last night," she said, staring at the collar of his T-shirt, where a hint of his bruise was visible. "I get it. But things are fine between us, okay?"

"No, I came by to apologize."

Surprised, she looked up at him, and he stepped closer still, close enough that she could smell his citrusy after-shave. She resisted the urge to breathe deeply, resisted the urge to lean into him the way she had last night. She'd gotten him shot, and now *he* wanted to apologize? "About what?"

"My timing."

She could feel herself gaping at him as he continued, "I waited nine months to do that. I could have waited another three weeks, until this case was over. I'm sorry."

"You waited nine months," she said slowly, "to—"

"To kiss you."

The flush she'd felt the second he walked through her door doubled. "We *met* nine months ago."

He grinned at her. "Yeah, I know. I walked into that first SWAT meeting, and you introduced yourself, and that was it."

"Introduced myself? I flipped you."

It was standard ops to prank the new guy. And since she'd joined the team, one of her teammates' favorite ways to initiate the newbies was for her to walk up, hold out a limp hand for them to shake, then promptly flip them to the ground.

In the three years before Grant joined that she'd been part of the team, she'd gone along with it because she found it was a good way to stop any preferential treatment before it could start. Drop a guy on his very first day on SWAT, and he wasn't likely to go easy on her just because she was a woman.

The four guys she'd flipped before Grant had been pissed off and embarrassed, but they'd gotten over it and become her friends. Grant had actually pulled her down with him. When they'd landed, with her braced on top of him, he'd looked stunned for a second, then offered her a hand as he'd gotten to his feet, laughing.

Oddly enough, that was the moment she'd fallen for him.

"Yeah, well, I like a woman who knows how to be in control. Besides," he said, leaning close to whisper, just as she heard her brother walk back into the room behind her, "I'm okay with you being on top."

She stammered something unintelligible as he backed up, nodded at her brother and walked out the door.

"What was that about?" Scott asked.

"Nothing," Maggie answered, but her voice came out way too high.

"Uh-huh," Scott said, "nice try. What's going on?"

Hoping she wasn't still blushing furiously, Maggie turned around. "Work stuff."

Scott snorted. "Come on. What's happening? And while you're telling me what's up with Grant, you want to fill me in on what you told Nikki?"

"Nikki? What are you talking about?"

"She called. Asked me about coming to visit in a few weeks. She wanted to be here September 1. I thought maybe you'd said something—"

"No way," Maggie said. "I didn't tell her about the letters. Did you?"

"No. And I told her to stay home, obviously. I said she should focus on her new job and getting settled in her new place. But I was surprised she volunteered."

"She's growing up." It *was* surprising, though, not because Nikki was insensitive, but because they'd always tried to keep her far away from their horrible September 1 ritual. And Maggie wanted to keep it that way.

"Okay, well, she'll probably call you. I told her not to come, but I don't think she was ready to give up."

"I'll handle her," Maggie said.

"Okay, and what about Grant? I don't know the guy all that well, but he was acting unusually cagey. And he knows about the Fishhook case? What didn't he want to say in front of me? If there's something about the case you're keeping from me—"

"It's not that. I mean, yes, I remembered something new about what happened to me, but it doesn't help with the case."

"You remembered more?" Scott sounded surprised. "Are you sure it won't help us? Because whatever it is, I don't want to be in the dark on this, Maggie. I can't help if I don't know everything."

"He wasn't here about the case. Although he's been assigned to it."

Scott's eyes narrowed with suspicion. "Is there something going on between you two?"

"I'm off SWAT," she blurted, not needing an overprotective brother to mess up her already rocky love life. And she definitely wasn't ready to talk about whatever was happening with Grant.

"What?" Scott set his coffee down, his face going pale. "What happened yesterday? Are you okay?"

"I made a mistake. It was bad, and I'm going to have to answer for it with OPR." Before he could dig for details, she added, "I quit the team."

She tried not to think about what that meant. Sure, she was dedicated to her regular work on the civil rights squad, but she *loved* SWAT. She had from the moment she'd been accepted onto the team.

"What? Maggie, what happened? I'm sure you can—"

"I'll give you the awful details later, okay?" She dreaded the idea of telling him about those ten crucial seconds when she'd frozen. HRT training was even more intensive than SWAT, and her brother had never made the kind of error she'd made today. On top of his ever-present worry about her, she didn't want to see disappointment on his face.

She ducked her head as he stared at her as if he could read the answer on her face if he looked long enough. Suddenly wishing Ella were here instead of her brother, Maggie sighed. At least with Ella, if she said she needed a little space, she'd get it. With Scott, *not* telling him something just made him even more persistent.

But for once, he backed off. She could tell he had a hard time getting the words out as he said, "Okay. Just tell me if you need anything. Ella, too." He squeezed her arm. "We're here for you. We always will be."

Tears stung the backs of her eyes as she nodded. They'd stuck by her for a decade, changing the whole course of their lives and joining the Bureau because of her. Every September 1, they dropped everything to be by her side. Now they were secretly investigating the Fishhook Rapist case with her because she couldn't leave it to the case agents.

Meanwhile, she was making errors at work she'd never, ever allowed herself to make before. Errors that would threaten not only her place on SWAT, but if she wasn't careful, her place in the Bureau, too.

And if she let Scott and Ella, they'd go down with her, like a sinking ship.

"WHAT DO YOU WANT?"

The woman peering suspiciously at him looked nothing like the picture Grant had in a police file from thirteen years ago.

She'd only opened her door an inch or two, so he held his badge a little closer to her, and repeated, "I'm with the

FBI. I wanted to ask you a few questions about a crime you reported a long time ago that might be connected to a current investigation."

She shook her head, limp peroxide-blond hair swinging. "I never reported any crime."

"It was a sexual assault report."

"Oh." Her shoulders slumped, and she glanced quickly behind her, then opened the door wide. Instead of inviting him in, she came outside, shutting the door behind her. Folding her arms, she said, "I don't want my kids to hear this." Then she squinted at him and asked, "What do you want to know about that? It was a really long time ago." Her shoulders lifted. "They never figured out who did it."

"Is there anyone *you* suspected?" Grant asked hopefully.

This was his third stop this morning. It would have been more, but only a handful of the possible matching cases had victims still in the area.

It was actually a little scary how many rape cases in the five years prior to Maggie's assault happened on or around September 1 in the DC area. He'd been able to narrow it down to the Fishhook Rapist's victim type— women in their late teens to early twenties, with long, dark hair. Which had given him three possibilities.

So far, no one he'd talked to had been able to give him anything new. Shana Mills, the woman standing in front of him now, was his most likely option, but even she was just a slim possibility. Given how under-reported rape was, chances were that even if his theory was right, and the Fishhook Rapist had assaulted women before he'd gotten his media name, they probably wouldn't have a police report for it.

"I don't have any ideas," Shana replied. "Not any more than I did back then. I was drugged. To be honest, I wasn't even totally certain what had happened until the doctors confirmed it."

"So you don't remember anyone?"

"No."

He glanced at the notes he'd jotted from the police file. Three years before Maggie's assault, Shana Mills had been drugged and raped. He'd almost missed it when he'd been digging through the DCPD's files, because she hadn't gone to the hospital until September 2, and the official police report hadn't been filed until later.

The investigation had been almost nonexistent, because the police had little to go on. Shana didn't remember her assailant; he'd worn a condom, and Shana had woken up in the basement of a frat house the morning after a big party. Lots of possible suspects, lots of potential witnesses, but no one had seen a thing, and the evidence hadn't been there.

"What can you tell me about Jeffrey Hoffmeier and Kevin Sanders?" Those were the only names listed in the police report who were possible suspects in his current case, since they were the only ones with a personal connection to Shana. That was assuming Grant's attempt at a profile of the Fishhook Rapist was right. It wasn't his specialty, but he'd put together a solid profile before, with the Manhattan Strangler, so he had to trust his gut.

He also had to hope for a break soon, because they were running out of time. There were exactly two weeks left until September 1, and with every day that passed, Grant got more anxious.

Shana shrugged at his question, and Grant tried to imagine her the way she'd looked in the police file. Back then, she'd had long brown hair, blue eyes and a lean frame. Even though to him she hadn't really resembled Maggie, he had to admit the basics were the same. For a serial rapist, the women definitely fit a "type." Now they looked nothing alike.

Shana's overdyed hair hung around an unremarkable face, and she seemed wrung out, with none of the energy and determination that practically seeped from Maggie.

"Jeff was my ex. We'd broken up a few weeks before."

"The police report says you saw him that night? He was at the party?"

"Yeah, he showed up, begged me to take him back. I refused. Again. He left, I think with some other girl."

"You see him after that?" Grant asked.

"A couple of times. We actually got back together, real briefly, about six months later, but it didn't last long at all. Maybe a week or so."

"Why didn't it work?"

Her face twisted with distaste. "He was cocky, obnoxious. Rich-kid syndrome, my roommate called it. I'm not even sure why I went out with him in the first place, except he was cute."

"What about Kevin?"

Shana scowled. "*That* guy creeped me out. I tried to get a restraining order against him, but police said they needed some kind of threat or something first."

"He was stalking you?"

"Yeah. He was angry that I wouldn't go out with him. And his daddy was some kind of big deal, so he seemed to think if he bragged about that enough, I'd suddenly go out with him."

"Was he still hanging around after your attack?"

"Oh, yeah. He hung around until I graduated and moved away. Then I guess he moved on to someone else."

Grant looked up from jotting notes. "You know who?"

"No. I just assume he did. That's how those guys work, right?"

"Usually." Grant shut his notebook and gave her his full attention. "Anything else you can tell me about that night? Anything at all?"

"I told the police everything. Everything I could remember, anyway. I don't even know how I got the drugs. My drink, I guess, but I always got my own."

"At a frat party, it could have been in the keg, or with whoever was mixing drinks or—"

"Canned beer," Shana said. "That's what I was drinking. I wasn't stupid. Friend of mine had been dosed a few weeks before."

That was news to Grant. "What was her name? Did she file a report?"

"She didn't get raped. I was with her when she started feeling weird. We took her to the hospital."

"They figure out who drugged her?"

"No. It happened at another party. But she was drinking whatever was handed to her."

Grant frowned, wondering if there could be a connection, and wondering how Shana had been dosed. "Anyone else hold your beer for you?"

"I don't remember. It was more than a decade ago. I've been married, divorced, married again, and had two kids since then. Not to mention gotten my degree, worked for four different companies, lived in two other states before I came back here. I don't remember who might have held my drink thirteen years ago."

Grant nodded, not really surprised. "Have you seen Kevin or Jeff in the last ten years?"

"No." She studied him more intently. "What happened to me back then sucked, but how could it possibly be connected to a current case? I mean, it was probably some frat guy who took advantage of the fact that I was unconscious in his basement, right?"

"I'm just running a theory," Grant said, handing her his card. "But if you think of anything else, or if you have any other ideas about that day, can you give me a call?"

"Yeah, okay," Shana said. She tucked his card in her pocket, where Grant figured she'd forget about it within the hour, and probably toss it in the wash with her jeans. Without a backward glance, she disappeared inside.

Grant probably would have forgotten about most of his chat with Shana, too, except something nagged him until he got back to the office and opened Maggie's case file again. He skimmed over the details of what she remembered from her assault.

College party. She'd been there with friends and a boyfriend. Her friends had left early, then she'd fought with the boyfriend, so she'd headed back to the dorm alone. It was on that walk back when she'd been taken.

Grant kept reading, then his heart rate picked up when he read the details about her being drugged. The only thing she remembered drinking at the party was canned beer, beer she'd opened herself.

Just like Shana.

Chapter Eight

Maggie rubbed her eyes, trying to focus on the report she'd been filling out for the past few hours. She should have been able to knock it out in half an hour, but her vision kept going unfocused; her mind kept wandering to the Fishhook Rapist case, and then suddenly another hour had passed.

At least the office had mostly emptied out, and there weren't a lot of agents there to witness her struggling over simple paperwork. Her civil rights squad supervisor had finally left, after asking her no fewer than three times if she needed some time away.

She'd told him no just like she had last week, and last month, when he'd first learned about the letters. But if two more weeks passed and they still had no idea about the identity of the Fishhook Rapist, maybe she should do it. The FBI would offer her protection, of course, but maybe she should just take off, head somewhere far, far away.

Hide. Go to ground, and pray he wasn't savvy enough to follow.

Gritting her teeth, Maggie closed the file and turned off her desk light. As appealing as the idea sounded, she knew she'd never do it.

Because no matter how much the thought of facing

her attacker again terrified her, she wasn't twenty-two anymore. She wasn't drugged and helpless. If this guy really planned to come for her again, he'd be facing down a trained SWAT agent armed with every weapon the FBI had issued her.

And come September 1, there was no question she'd be surrounded by Ella and Scott like always. She suspected that Ella's fiancé, Logan, a seasoned police detective and Scott's girlfriend, Chelsie, an FBI negotiator, would be there, too. Knowing Grant, whether she asked him or not, he'd show up with a small arsenal and plant himself directly in front of her.

What chance did the Fishhook Rapist really have?

Maggie sighed, getting up from her desk. It didn't matter how much she told herself that; it didn't even matter how logical it was. Because every time she so much as thought about September 1, her hands started to shake.

Even the idea of walking into the parking garage right now—despite the fact that no one who didn't possess FBI credentials could get in there—made her irrationally nervous.

Get it together, she told herself.

Her phone trilled, and she jumped, instantly chastising herself for letting her fear override common sense. "Maggie Delacorte," she answered.

"Hey, Maggie, it's Nikki."

Nikki. Maggie closed her eyes and tried to make her voice cheery. She didn't want her little sister worrying about her. She'd tried hard for so long to keep this from touching Nikki, and she didn't plan to stop now. "How's the new apartment? And when do you start your job?"

"The apartment's great," Nikki said. "And I start in a few weeks. So I was thinking I have time to come and stay with you and Scott for a little bit. I figured maybe the three of us—and Ella, of course—could go out on September 1." Her voice turned hesitant. "You know, do something fun."

It was sweet of her sister, especially since the whole family babied her, and she probably could have gotten away with acting completely spoiled. But she never had.

Still, Maggie didn't want her anywhere near DC right now. She also didn't want her worrying. "That's nice of you, Nikki, but work is really busy right now. For Scott, too. The timing won't work, but I'm going to make a trip home next month. See your new place."

"Okay," Nikki said slowly. "Well, I would stay out of your way. I just thought—"

"Thank you. Really. But another time, okay?" Maggie said, knowing the strain was starting to come through in her voice.

"Okay," Nikki conceded. "Is everything all right?"

"Just busy," Maggie lied, and she had a feeling her sister could tell. "I'm actually still at work. Can I call you later?"

"Sure." Her sister sounded disappointed. "Let me know if you change your mind."

"I'll talk to you soon," Maggie said, feeling relieved as soon as she hung up the phone.

A hand clapped her on the shoulder as she put the phone in her purse, and she turned, startled.

"Sorry," Grant said, and put a steadying hand under her elbow.

"It's okay," Maggie said, easing her arm free. "I'm just a little jumpy tonight."

He frowned at her, looking worried, but all he said was, "Can I ask you some questions?"

"Okay." She studied him more closely, the dark circles under his eyes, the rolled-up sleeves on his dress shirt that showcased muscular forearms. Even though she was used to seeing him in his office clothes, he looked more natural in his SWAT getup. Maybe because he was built like a linebacker, khakis and a button-down never looked quite right on him.

Looking back to his face, she noticed the tight line of his lips, as if he was about to do something he didn't want to. "It's about the Fishhook Rapist case, isn't it?"

"Yeah. I'm sorry. I'm just trying—"

"No, it's fine." She tried to keep the exhaustion out of her own voice, knowing that Grant had been working more hours than anyone in the office since he'd been assigned to this case. Knowing that it was for her. "What is it?"

"The night you were drugged, your report says you were drinking beer out of a can. Is that right?"

Maggie gritted her teeth and nodded.

"Do you remember if you had anything else? Or if anyone could have—"

"You're wondering how I was drugged?" When he nodded, Maggie shook her head. "I'm not sure. Back then, I didn't know the things I do now, but I was relatively street smart. I didn't take drinks from people at parties, or let anyone I didn't know hang on to it, or leave it anywhere. I opened it myself. Best guess is that someone dropped the drugs in without me noticing."

Grant frowned. "Hmm. Okay. Are you sure no one got it for you?"

"Well, my boyfriend did, but I opened it."

"Do you know the names Jeff Hoffmeier or Kevin Sanders?"

"No. Why?"

He seemed disappointed, but not surprised, by her answer. "Just running some theories. Thanks."

As he turned to go back to the conference room, Maggie grabbed his arm and felt his muscles tense at her touch. "Are they suspects?"

"Not right now." She thought he was going to say more, but Kammy walked into the bullpen, her eyes narrowing when she saw them standing close together.

"Maggie," Kammy said, nodding at her, then she looked pointedly at Grant.

"Back to work it is. Thanks, Maggie."

When Kammy turned and headed off to the coffee-pot, Maggie touched his arm again before he could follow. "Grant."

"Yeah?"

She stared up at him, not sure what she'd actually planned to say. She saw him in the office every day, but lately it had felt different. Even standing in front of him now, doing something as impersonal as touching his forearm, felt intimate.

She had a sudden flashback to the feel of his hands clutching her thighs as he lifted her onto his lap, the feel of his body pressed tight to hers, his heartbeat thundering against her palm. Heat spread through her.

It must have shown on her face, because his pupils suddenly dilated as he stared back at her.

Her voice came out huskier than usual when she blurted, "Uh, why don't you come over after you finish here? We can talk."

"Sure," he said, sounding surprised. He glanced at his watch, and when he looked up at her again, there was anticipation in his eyes. "Probably an hour or two?"

"Whenever," she said, then watched him hurry back to the conference room, knowing he'd thought she wanted to talk about what had happened between them last night. Or maybe start right back up where they'd left off.

She tried not to feel guilty as she walked to the parking garage. Because he was in for quite a surprise when he did arrive at her house, and that's not what she was after at all.

WHEN IT CAME to work, Grant had never been able to do anything but go all-in. He couldn't help himself. With his cases, it was all or nothing. It had gotten him in trouble a time or two, namely during the Manhattan Strangler case.

If he'd waited for backup the way he'd been told to, he probably wouldn't have ended up in the hospital getting stitches for a nasty stab wound. He wouldn't have ended up with the censure in his Bureau file, or ultimately decided it was time to transfer to a new field office for a fresh start.

Then again, if he'd waited for backup, the victim surely would have died. And the Manhattan Strangler probably would have gotten away yet again.

So he'd never been able to regret his actions. Not on that case, and not on any job where he went in strong, the way SWAT let him do as their designated door-kicker.

But in his personal life, he was a little more restrained, particularly when it came to relationships. He'd had a few that had approached serious, but he'd never felt that all-consuming need to dive in, the way he did with his cases. Not until Maggie.

Which was probably why he was standing on her doorstep right now, instead of home in bed. Because she might have been purposely vague about why she wanted to talk to him tonight, but he'd realized exactly why she'd invited him over.

She wanted to grill him for details about the case. Details he was supposed to keep confidential.

Swearing, Grant lowered his fist from the door instead

of knocking, but it opened, anyway. And suddenly the cars in the driveway made sense, because it wasn't Maggie who answered, but her friend Ella Cortez.

A feisty profiler in the Bureau's Behavioral Analysis Unit, who'd shown up with Maggie a few times at O'Reilley's. He didn't know her particularly well, but he'd seen her name in Maggie's police file from a decade ago. Ella was one of the friends who'd left the party, thinking Maggie was safe with her boyfriend. She'd been the one to call the police the next morning when Maggie had stumbled back to their shared dorm room, bleeding and branded on the back of the neck.

"Ella, hi," he said.

It almost seemed that she could read what he was thinking, but she just said evenly, "Grant."

Then she stepped backward and led him toward the living room, where Grant saw a group of people gathered. "Come on in. We've been waiting for you."

His eyebrows rose. "I didn't realize it was going to be a party."

"Sorry about that," Maggie said as she came toward him, dodging an open pizza box on the floor.

She'd changed out of the dress pants and stiff, short-sleeved blouse she'd worn at the office into curve-hugging jeans and a well-worn T-shirt that looked more *Maggie.* His fingers itched to touch the soft cotton, to caress the skin underneath.

As he stared at her, probably broadcasting his every thought for the entire room, she lowered her voice. "I figured if I told you—"

"I knew what you wanted to talk about." He was trying to stop staring at those gorgeous blue eyes of hers, but ever since he'd realized her attraction to him might actually come close to how he felt for her, he seemed to have lost all his willpower. "I just didn't realize you expected me to break protocol in front of a crowd."

She turned red, but Scott came up behind her and said, "You don't have to worry about that. Nothing you say leaves this room."

The serious, massively protective, big-brother expression on Scott's face made Grant get his act together. He stood a little straighter and ripped his attention away from Maggie. "Quid pro quo?"

"Absolutely," Scott answered. "We'll share everything we're thinking. But I've got to tell you, it isn't much. We don't have the access you do. But you know we're not going to sit idly by on this one."

"Neither will I," Grant said, and he knew his conviction—and probably the strength of his feelings for Maggie—rang in those words. "I'll do whatever it takes to get this guy."

Scott stared back at him a minute, then simply nodded, but Grant could see in that minute he'd won Scott's approval.

"Let's get going, then," Scott said.

Ella had already sat down in a chair in the corner, beside a guy who looked about Grant's age. He had gruff, hard features, dark, close-cropped hair and the intuitive stare that immediately labeled him as law enforcement.

"Logan Greer." The man stood and introduced himself with a hint of a drawl. "I'm Ella's fiancé and a detective with the DC PD."

"Nice to meet you," Grant said.

"Hi, Grant," the last person in the room called from the floor, where she was jotting notes in a legal file with one hand and holding a slice of pizza in the other.

"Chelsie," he replied. Chelsie Russell was a willowy blonde who worked in the WFO and had an ancillary position as a negotiator. When he'd first met her, she'd seemed stiff and quiet, but she and Maggie were friends, so he'd learned she actually had a pretty good sense of humor and a decent break at the pool table.

"So we've got a couple of tactical agents, a profiler, a negotiator and a detective," Grant summed up. Not to mention his experience on the violent crimes division and Maggie's work in civil rights cases. "Let's see what we can come up with here."

He tried to ignore the voice buzzing in the back of his brain telling him this was going to end like the Manhattan Strangler case, with yet another censure in his file for disobeying orders.

He glanced at Maggie and found her looking gratefully at him. Suddenly, he didn't care what the case did to his file, so long as the other part of the Manhattan Strangler case didn't come back to haunt him. Because he couldn't bear to watch Maggie get hurt.

Just the thought of it made his chest tense up until his breathing felt unnatural.

Forcing himself to focus, he found a spot on the floor, helped himself to a slice of pizza and told the group the details of the Shana Mills case. "She didn't show up at the hospital until September 2, but she was assaulted on the first, thirteen years ago."

"Okay." Scott sounded skeptical. "What happened in the two years in between, then? Other victims who he didn't brand? On the same date?"

"Maybe, but none of the other cases I looked at had any similarities. And if there was no branding, I'm not sure the date matters."

Ella started shaking her head and leaned forward, so Grant cut her off. "Look, I'm no profiler, but the date is significant for a reason, right? Don't you think there's a good chance it was the date he assaulted the person he actually *knew*, the one he really wanted to hurt? Originally?"

Ella frowned, grooves appearing between her eyebrows. "My theory is that the date is important because it's when he finally took the step he'd fantasized about for years. It's when he finally abducted someone, and everything that came after that. And he wanted to keep doing it. That's why he's coming back for her. Ten years have gone by. Ten years to build up the sick obsession of his first target. Ten years, and suddenly he's not having such an easy time fitting in around these college students. He's looking for a replay of when it all worked for him."

Her voice was strained, and as her fiancé put his arm around Ella's shoulders, Grant realized how hard it was for her to profile Maggie's case.

"I think you're wrong."

Everyone stilled and stared back at him at the announcement, probably because Ella was a heck of a profiler. Even he knew it, and he'd never worked with her.

"You were there when it happened. You're too close to see it clearly."

She jerked back as though she'd been insulted, and he quickly added, "I'm sorry. I just think the date has to be more significant. Otherwise, why wait so long? If it was really just about when he started, why not make it the first of every month? Or every six months? There's still a pattern in that, and then he's not forced to wait a whole *year*. It's got to be more. It's got to be *personal*."

Silence greeted his argument, and Grant cursed himself for his word choice. The September 1 a decade ago was extremely personal to everyone in this room.

It was Chelsie who finally spoke up. "Why this case? Why Shana Mills?"

"She's pretty sure someone drugged the beer she was drinking. Beer in a can, that she opened herself."

"So what?" Ella said, then held up a hand when he started to continue. "Yeah, I know that's what happened to Maggie, but what does that tell us? That both perps were savvy enough to get close to their victims without being noticed. Doesn't make it the same person."

She was right, but something about this file brought his investigative instincts to life.

"Then there's this." He handed Ella the copy of Shana Mills's picture he'd taken from the case file.

Her eyes went from the picture to him and back again. "Okay," she admitted, "there's a certain type here. Same basic look as all the Fishhook victims."

Maggie, who'd been mostly silent and still during the exchange, reached over from where she'd been standing, arms crossed in the corner, and took the picture. She frowned. "You think she looks like me?"

The truth was, he didn't. Not in the ways that mattered. But when it came to the basics—the long, dark hair with the off-center part, the light blue eyes, the slender, toned figure—the similarities were definitely there.

"It's a type," Ella spoke up. "The kind of similarities this guy might be looking for." She looked at Grant. "It's still not a sure thing. Scott's right about the two-year wait."

"You think he would have started the branding the very next year, if my theory is right?" Grant pressed, genuinely wanting Ella's opinion. She knew this kind of killer better than he ever would, regardless of how close she was to the case.

She fiddled with the diamond on her finger, seeming to have an internal argument, before she finally said, "Not necessarily. You could be right about there being more victims who weren't branded in between, and then the date might not be as important. Or it's possible he waited, put together his plan, found a location, did practice runs."

"Practice runs?" Logan asked, sounding as if he wasn't sure he wanted to know what that meant.

"Victims he killed. Or victims he didn't think would ever report, even with a brand. Prostitutes, for example."

"So what do we do with this?" Scott was tapping his foot incessantly, which made him seem desperate to move, and move now.

"It's just a theory," Grant said. "Two names came up in Shana's file. I'm going to run them down."

"Jeff Hoffmeier and Kevin Sanders," Maggie said.

"Yeah." He squinted at her, surprised she'd remembered the names he'd mentioned at the office. "*I'm* going to run this down," he emphasized. "If it leads anywhere, I'll loop you in."

Maggie looked as if she was going to argue, but Scott cut her off. "We're trying to go at this from the traveling angle. How does he move around so much, and what does that mean for his occupation? We're considering trucker, contractor, independently wealthy—"

"Wealthy," Grant interrupted. "The marble table."

"What marble table?" Chelsie asked, setting her pen down and staring up at him.

Grant swore as he looked over at Maggie, then started to apologize.

"It's fine," she said. "I haven't had a chance to tell them all the details. I had a flashback. I remembered room details. I wasn't thinking about what it meant for the profile, but the room I was in was nice. It wasn't some dive hotel. It was someone's house."

Ella stood. "Maggie, that's huge. That means he *did* live here ten years ago. When he talked about *home* in his letter, it wasn't a figure of speech. We need to start looking at anyone who lived on or around campus back then who moved within the year."

Maggie sighed loudly. "That's been done several times over the years. Besides, the number will be huge. With all the colleges around here, the population shift is enormous. And if he left in the summer right before the following September, it would be when a whole graduating class left."

"Yeah, but he was older," Ella said. "He wasn't a college student. That I'd bank on. Although…"

"What?" Scott demanded.

Ella looked at Grant. "If you're right about Shana Mills, he could have been a student *then*. Probably not an undergrad, but maybe a grad student or a teaching assistant or something."

"Okay." Grant's energy level, which had been hovering around zero when he'd arrived, suddenly spiked. This was the best lead he'd had yet. And if it wasn't the ex-boyfriend or the stalker, it was probably someone in Shana's life. Someone who'd been in DC thirteen years ago, and who'd been here ten years ago, but had left sometime after September 1 of that year.

Even though he didn't have any solid evidence to back up the connection to Shana Mills, he knew he was onto something.

He glanced at his watch—9:30 p.m. Kammy would probably still be at the office. "I need to go. Let me know if you come up with anything. And I'll tell you what happens on my end with the interviews of those two guys."

Maggie nodded, but there was something in her expression…

Grant looked at Scott. "Can I talk to you in private for a second?"

Maggie didn't seem happy about that, but Scott nodded. "Yeah, okay."

"I'll be in touch," he promised everyone as he followed Scott down the hall and to the front entryway, where there was a modicum of privacy.

"We're sticking close," Scott told him before he could say a word.

"Good." Grant pulled a card out of his pocket and handed it over. "Just call me if you need help. I'll be here. The same is true of any of the guys on the team. They all love your sister."

As soon as the words were out of his mouth, Grant felt as if someone had sucker punched him.

"You okay, man?" Scott asked.

"Yeah, fine." He tried to shake off the realization that had just hit him, but the knowledge rattled around in his brain even as he tried to focus. "Look, this perp knows Maggie is SWAT. He must."

"Which makes him an idiot," Scott spat. "I mean, believe me, I'm not leaving her alone, but she doesn't need me. You should know—you see her working on SWAT."

"That's the thing," Grant countered. "He's *not* an idiot. He has to be really intelligent to have pulled this off for a decade."

"So you're thinking, what? That he doesn't actually plan to get close again? You thinking a long-distance shooting?"

Grant swore at that idea, which had never occurred to him. "No. Talk to Ella, because she knows this stuff better, but I don't think so. But he's *obsessed* with Maggie, fixated on her in a way he's never been on any of the others. So he must have a plan to get near her. Unless maybe his plan is purely psychological? Break her down by giving her reason to believe he's coming after her, then stick to his normal pattern and grab someone else?"

Scott nodded, looking grim. "Well, we're going to assume he's serious. But you could be right. Every year, waiting for a new report..." Scott shook his head. "It's really hard on her. If she's focused on this threat against her, and that's where the manpower is, and then he hurts some other woman..."

"I know."

"Thanks for helping out," Scott said.

"Of course."

Scott slapped his arm and walked back toward the living room, his steps slow, as if he didn't want to talk to Maggie about the possibilities Grant had suggested.

Grant stepped outside but before he'd made it off the stoop, Maggie ran out, closing the door behind her.

"I just told your brother—"

"To keep an eye on me," Maggie said, interrupting him. "I get it. Look..." She trailed off, studying him. "Are you okay?"

A smile slipped out as he stared back at her. "Yeah, I'm okay." He stepped forward, until they were standing close to each other.

He didn't know how deep her feelings for him ran. She was attracted to him, and they were friends, and at least to some extent, she was using his feelings for her to get his help on this case. But was there more?

He lifted his hand, stroked the side of her cheek, and she leaned her face into his palm. He moved a little closer, until he could feel her breath on his chin. Until he could lower his lips and press them lightly to hers, try to show her what he'd realized, what he wasn't ready to say out loud.

He was in love with her.

Chapter Nine

When Maggie walked back into her living room, every-one was staring at her. Everyone but Logan, who was staring resolutely at the wall, obviously wanting no part of whatever was about to happen.

"What?" she demanded.

"What's the deal with Grant?" Ella asked, a smirk on her face that Maggie recognized all too well.

"Nothing," Maggie answered, knowing her voice was giving her away. "We're friends. You know that."

"I also know when you're lying to me," Ella answered, still looking smug. "I've known you way too long. You really think you can keep secrets from me?"

"I like him," Scott put in, and Maggie gaped at him. "What? I do."

Over the years, Scott had taken his big-brother role with both her and Ella a little too seriously, especially when it came to guys, and even more so since her attack. He'd gone easier on Ella, and he'd approved of Logan, but Maggie didn't think anyone had ever passed his test for her.

"Well, that doesn't matter," she started, but Ella cut her off.

"I wondered how long that was going to take."

"What are you talking about?"

Ella leaned forward, grinning, and in the chair beside her, Logan made "sorry my fiancée is nosy" gestures so animated that Maggie couldn't help but laugh.

Ella glared briefly at him, then continued, "The times you invited me along with your SWAT team to O'Reilley's, I could tell you were interested. And so was he." She looked pleased with herself when she added, "I wondered how long it would take for you two to finally admit it."

"Well, it doesn't matter," Maggie said again, settling back on the couch beside her brother and crossing her arms over her chest to signal that the discussion was over.

"Why? Because he's a teammate?" Chelsie asked.

"He's not a teammate anymore," Maggie said, and stopped Scott before he could jump in as she knew he wanted to, telling her she'd get back on SWAT. She definitely didn't want to get into that discussion. "Grant's investigating my case, so that's the end of it."

"He's trying—" Ella started.

"I don't want to talk about it," Maggie blurted, and her friends went silent, because she rarely refused to discuss anything. "It's not happening, so just leave it alone."

Scott and Ella shared a glance that Maggie purposely ignored, and then Logan spoke up, clearly trying to change the subject. "Look, this isn't my specialty, but given what Grant was suggesting about that Shana Mills case, if the perp actually knew her, is there any chance he knew Maggie, too?"

Ella sat straighter beside him, instantly serious, and started shaking her head, then paused, looking pensive. "He wouldn't have been someone in Maggie's life. But if she was the first one he didn't know, it was a change in tactics, so it's possible he was around the periphery."

"What do you mean?" Scott demanded, leaning forward, the muscles in his arms bulging.

Ella looked at Maggie. "The thing Grant said about your drink. We know this guy stalked you. He would have done that with all of his victims. If he got close enough to slip drugs into your drink while you were holding it, maybe he talked to you. Maybe you knew him in some way—not well, maybe not even well enough to know his name, but enough to recognize him when he walked past you."

Numbness started to fill Maggie, and she recognized it as the coping mechanism she'd adopted whenever the discussions turned to areas she didn't like. Usually it happened when talking to investigators about specific details, not with her friends. But the idea that she might have known the person who had hurt her, even in some small way?

The numbness evaporated, and cold swept over her in its place, a light-headed feeling she tried to replace with anger. "So you think I could recognize him now?" she asked, and her voice sounded as though it was coming from far away.

Concern wrinkled Ella's face, but she nodded. "It's possible. I think you should ask Grant to take a look at pictures of any of his suspects."

Maggie nodded, even as discomfort overwhelmed her. It was bad enough that Grant was investigating, and hard enough to discuss the case with him—as though it didn't hurt her to think about him digging into the worst day of her life. She really didn't want to dig through it with him.

But if it meant catching the Fishhook Rapist, she'd do it. Because no matter how hard she tried not to dwell on it, she knew exactly how long she had left. Thirteen days, two hours and six minutes until it hit September 1.

And then the Fishhook Rapist would be back for her.

MAGGIE COULDN'T WAIT any longer.

She'd been sitting at her desk, staring at her files, for over an hour, waiting for Kammy Ming to finally call it quits and head home. So she could talk to Grant alone. But the WFO had pretty well cleared out, and Grant and Kammy were still cloistered in the conference room, going over the case.

Her stomach rolling at the idea of what she was about to do, Maggie stood, moving through the dark and empty bullpen toward the conference room fast, before she could back out.

When she opened the door, Grant and Kammy stared back at her with surprise. They were sitting across from each other at a long conference table that was covered in open case files, boxes and laptops. A whiteboard at the far end of the room was inked up with notes, and a map pinned next to it had red circles and writing that Maggie didn't need to get close to to read. She recognized the locations instantly. The nine credited attacks of the Fishhook Rapist, scattered across the country.

She tried not to look at the files as she headed for the far end of the room where Grant and Kammy sat. Grant stood as she approached, and she couldn't help herself from glancing over the contents on the table. A box full of information on the fishing industry. Stacks of college attendance records from all across DC from a decade ago. Victim case files.

Over the years, Maggie had been tempted to try and reach out to the other victims, try to piece together what they knew. Try to get answers. But she'd resisted. Not just because it would have been completely against protocol, but also because she didn't want to go over every tiny, insignificant thing she could remember, or the big hole in her memory. So how could she ask someone else to do it?

As she reached Grant's side, Maggie forced herself to look away from the case files before she spotted her own. She knew what was in it, and she didn't want or need to see it. She had enough memories.

"We're doing everything we can," Kammy told her, sounding worn-out, and beneath the seasoned investigator's voice was something that sounded an awful lot like defeat.

"What is it, Maggie?" Grant asked, as he closed the file next to him, which had to be hers.

She tried to keep the emotion out of her voice as she told him, "I want to look at pictures."

"What pictures?" Grant asked, just as Kammy said, "You need to leave the investigation to us."

How was she going to do this without letting Kammy know Grant had been sharing information with her? Frustration filled her, because she couldn't wait around to talk to Grant in secret. Keeping her personal investigation segregated from their official one was limiting resources. What if not working together prevented them from finding the Fishhook Rapist in time?

"If there's a chance this guy started with someone he knew before me, maybe he hung around me when he was stalking me. Maybe I could recognize him."

Kammy glared at Grant. "I know James talked to you about confidentiality—"

"It's not him," Maggie said. "I'm an agent, too. I can't sit back and leave this to someone else. I'm looking into it myself."

For a split second, Kammy looked furious, but Maggie

could see her making a concerted effort to rein it in as she said, "There's a reason you weren't assigned this case, Maggie. You're too close to it, and you know it."

"I can help," Maggie snapped. "I want to look at the pictures. I don't want to be sitting in my house, hoping this guy won't come back for me in thirteen days, because you were worried about bureaucratic procedure!"

Kammy stood, and even though Maggie had eight inches and probably thirty pounds on her, she suddenly understood why Kammy had a reputation as someone not to cross. The full force of her glare was intimidating.

But Maggie was SWAT—or at least she had been— and she glared right back.

Grant held his hands out and said calmly, "Look, this is on me. I told Maggie my theory. I asked if she recognized the names from the Mills file. No sense in spreading our resources thin if she knew them. She didn't, but let's see if the faces ring any bells. Okay?"

Kammy turned on Grant again and gave one curt nod, and Maggie knew her outburst had just put a dent, not in her career, but Grant's.

Ashamed, she opened her mouth to apologize, but Grant held out a file before she could speak.

"Here," he said. "This is the stalker, Kevin Sanders. He look familiar?"

Her hands shook as she took the file from him, and she braced herself. But when she stared at the picture of Kevin Sanders from thirteen years ago—blond hair, cocky smile, college sweatshirt even though he'd already graduated—she felt nothing. No sudden burst of recognition, no painful memories. Nothing.

She looked harder, willing something forward. They already knew he was a stalker, and if Shana Mills was the original victim, he had to be first in the suspect line. If it was him, they would have a name, a person to hunt down.

Finally, she looked up at Grant and shook her head. "I don't recognize him."

"That's okay." Grant closed the file and set it down. "We're still going to check him out." He handed her a second file. "The ex-boyfriend, Jeff Hoffmeier."

She opened it fast, expecting nothing, but hoping for... something. But just like Kevin Sanders, he didn't look familiar. He was scowling slightly, which made what would have otherwise been a good-looking face seem ugly and angry. His dark hair was buzzed close to his head, and his eyes were strikingly blue. He had apparently already graduated a few years earlier when he'd been dating Shana, but he still looked like a college kid in the picture. A typical college kid.

She started to shake her head and hand back the file when a voice from her past whispered in her head, *What are you drinking?* The same voice that she remembered from one other time, telling her, *This is going to hurt.*

She gasped, and the file slipped from her hands, spilling its contents all over the floor.

"Hey." Grant's hand locked on her arm, and the voice in her mind faded. "You recognize this guy?"

Kammy leaned toward them across the table, looking expectant, a phone already in her hand, as if she was ready to call in the rest of the team.

"Uh, I don't know." Her voice shook, and Maggie tried to get it together. She reached down for the file, and Grant stopped her.

"I got it." He set the file on the table. "Did he look familiar?"

"Let me look again."

"You want to take a break?"

"No, I'm fine." She gritted her teeth and opened the file on the table, taking out just the picture. She focused hard, studying Jeff Hoffmeier more closely.

He had a strong, angular face, an aristocratic nose and a strong jawline. He'd probably had an easy time getting dates, if he didn't scowl the way he was doing in the picture. But no matter how intently she stared at him, willing the memory back, she didn't recognize him.

So why had that memory rushed forward when she'd looked at his picture?

Was it even a real memory? She had no recollection of the Fishhook Rapist ever talking to her before the abduction, no recollection of him asking her about her drink, even though he'd obviously dosed it. Had the investigation created false memories?

She knew it could happen. She'd seen it firsthand in her own cases. The further back an incident was, the harder the memories were to access. The more details a victim had about the possible suspects, the more likely she was to talk herself into believing something just because she needed answers.

Was the same true of Maggie, despite her FBI training?

"Do you know him?" Kammy asked, and Grant said, "Give her a second." Their voices seemed distant as she kept staring desperately at Jeff Hoffmeier.

Finally, she set the image down and shook her head. "I'm not sure. He gives me a bad feeling, but he doesn't look familiar."

"What does that mean?" Kammy asked, sounding frustrated. "You think this is him or not?"

Grant glared at Kammy, but when he turned back to her, his expression was even and calm. "What about him gives you a bad feeling?"

"I'm not sure. I think I had a memory when I looked at his picture, but it was just a voice. And I can't be certain…" She sighed heavily, infuriated that she couldn't say more. She'd always been grateful that she couldn't remember much from the attack itself, but suddenly she wished she did.

"I'm not sure *why* that happened. Maybe it's him, or maybe something about him just reminds me of the guy. I don't know." She heard the anguished frustration in her voice and tried to even it out, like the professional she was. "Maybe when you talk to this guy, I should go with you."

"No," Grant barked.

"If it's him, and he sees me, he might—"

"No," Grant cut her off. "We'll look into him more closely, see if he's even a possibility. If he looks good for it, we'll bring him in, and if there's a reason for you to get involved, you can do it through the glass."

"That's not—"

"It's not happening," Kammy said softly, and Grant looked as though he might burst an artery.

"Okay, look—"

"We're not tipping our hand on this." Grant seemed to be working hard to keep his voice calm. "Once we narrow in on a name, there's going to be a pattern, and it might take a little time to dig up, but it will be there. We're not letting anyone know they're on our suspect list until we show up at their door to slap the cuffs on, got it?"

Maggie frowned, unable to deny the logic there. She definitely didn't want him running, if it was him. "Okay, then why haven't you started digging into information on these two already?" They had to be at the top of the list, if Grant's theory was to be believed. "I can—"

"We had some other leads today that looked good," Kammy said. "But they didn't pan out."

"What were they?"

"They didn't pan out," Kammy repeated tightly. "But Grant is right. If Hoffmeier is the guy, then he's lived in all the locations on the board." She gestured vaguely behind her at the map with the bright red circles. "And we'll find that."

Maggie nodded. Their plan made sense. "Okay." She pushed a stack of files aside and settled into the chair next to where Grant had been sitting until she walked into the room. "I'll help."

"No way," Kammy burst out.

Maggie crossed her arms over her chest and gave Kammy her best SWAT stare, the one that said she wasn't backing down. "You want me out of here, you're going to have to drag me. And I've got to warn you, you're not going to have an easy time of it."

"Are you kidding me?" Kammy let out a stream of curses more creative than Maggie thought the uptight woman knew.

"I'll track locations," Maggie insisted as she tried not to look at Grant. She could see him out of the corner of her eye, staring at her with an expression she couldn't quite read.

Anger? Worry? Disappointment? Probably all three, and she didn't want to think about what her actions were doing to his reputation within VCMO, or how they were going to impact his feelings for her.

"Fine," Kammy said tightly. "But you research what we hand over, and nothing else. Any more than that, and I don't care about your personal stake in this. The rules exist for a reason, and you step any further over the line, and I'm putting it in both of your files. Got it?"

Maggie nodded, the fear of harming Grant's career weighing on her more than the chances of hurting her own. And from the perceptive look in Kammy's eyes, she knew it.

"You take Sanders," Grant said, handing her the file.

"I want—"

"I'll deal with Hoffmeier," Grant interrupted. "Kammy was already digging into other people in Shana's life who might be involved."

Maggie looked up at her, where she was still standing, looking irate. "You find anyone?"

"No." She dropped into her seat, wrestled her jet-black hair streaked with gray into a knot and added, "I'm still looking, though."

"Thank you."

Kammy frowned at her. "I respect your work here, Maggie, or I wouldn't let this—" she gestured around her at the files "—slide. But watch your step. If you want to be involved with this in any capacity, you need to stop your side investigation. I don't want you running across this guy unprepared."

Maggie nodded, hoping she looked convincing. Kammy's argument was logical, but no way were Ella or her brother stopping, which meant she wasn't, either.

Kammy's eyes narrowed suspiciously, so Maggie grabbed the Kevin Sanders file and started working.

It didn't take long before her heart rate picked up, and she began to wonder whether her reaction to Jeff had actually been a delayed response to seeing Kevin Sanders's picture. He'd served two stints in jail in the past five years, both for sexual assault.

Neither were in states where Fishhook Rapist victims had appeared, but they were in between attacks, so they could have been en route to a new state. She sat straighter, sifting through information faster, looking for a connection.

An hour later, she sank back in her seat and shook her head, trying not to dwell on her disappointment. "It's not Kevin Sanders."

Grant looked up from his own laptop and rubbed his eyes. "Why not?"

The dejection sounded in her voice when she told him and Kammy, "At the time of the third victim's attack, he was in lockup for drunk driving. Thirty days. There's no way it was him."

"I haven't come up with any other likely possibilities from Shana Mills's life," Kammy said, slumping back against her chair. "How's your luck, Grant?"

Maggie turned toward him expectantly, but one glance at the weary slump of his shoulders and her hope for a break in the case faded, especially as he shook his head.

"Jeff Hoffmeier is a real possibility."

"What?" Maggie sat straighter, grasping his arm before she realized what she was doing. She quickly pulled her hand back. "What do you mean?"

"He was living in DC ten years ago. After that, I have no idea."

Maggie frowned. "You can't track him? He has to have owned property, or gotten a driver's license or—"

"I can't track him," Grant said. "It's as if he just disappeared. And it happened sometime after September, ten years ago."

Chapter Ten

Grant had finally lain down in bed when the doorbell rang. He stared up at the ceiling in the darkness, sighed, then threw on a T-shirt and went to the door, feeling every step. It had been a very long, frustrating day, and the verbal warning from James—who'd had a call from Kammy about him and Maggie—had capped it off.

He opened the door, already knowing who was standing on the other side, and turned around, telling her, "Come on in."

"I'm sorry—"

"Stop apologizing," he told Maggie as he led her to the living room, squinting as he flipped on a light.

He turned around and faced her, discovering that she looked more worn out than he felt.

"I didn't mean to wake you. I just wanted to apolo—"

"Maggie," he said. "If you're going to start every visit to my house with an apology, it's going to get old fast. You want to come by, then come by because we're friends, and you want to see me. Come by because we're—" he paused, then settled on "—more than that, and you just want me." He grinned to let her know he was at least partly teasing, and finished, "Just don't say *sorry* one more time."

She fiddled with the hem of her blouse, stuck her hands in her pockets, took them out again and crossed them over her chest. "Okay. Sure." She glanced over his T-shirt and boxers, and added, "I didn't think you'd be sleeping."

It was still early evening, but he'd put in so many late nights during that past two weeks, he'd finally crashed.

"Long day," he said, settling onto the couch and gesturing for her to join him. "You're here to find out where we are on the case, I assume." He'd leaned his head against the back of the couch and closed his eyes, so he didn't know if she nodded or not as he felt her sit down next to him, but he continued, "Jeff Hoffmeier's name pops up a few times, but it's sporadic, and it's not giving us places of residence."

"What about his family? They're still in town."

Slowly, Grant opened his eyes and looked at her. She'd sat closer than he'd realized, and he could see the strain on her face that got worse with each day closer to September 1.

"I thought you were going to stay away from this." That had been their agreement, after she'd helped them the night before at the office. Kammy had insisted she stay away from Hoffmeier, and she'd agreed. Grant had known she wouldn't stay away from the investigation entirely, but he'd thought she'd conceded to focus on her safety, and let them run down the lead. Apparently, he'd been wrong.

Before she could reply, he swore. "Maggie, please tell me you didn't talk to them."

"I didn't give my name. I called, claimed to be from the alumni association, asked for contact information for him."

Grant sat up, suddenly wide-awake and furious. "Are you kidding me? Are you trying to sabotage this investigation?"

She leaned toward him until they were mere inches apart, looking furious herself. "You know me. You know I wasn't going to leave this to anyone else."

"I was checking into Hoffmeier," he growled. "I told you to leave it alone."

"Yeah, well, you're not my boss."

"Your boss told you to leave it alone, too."

"Too bad," she said. "I called. It's done. And they gave me the runaround, said he wouldn't want to be in the directory listing, even when I pushed for just a phone number to ask him myself."

Grant rubbed his forehead, where a headache was rapidly forming. "You're going to get yourself hurt," he said quietly, trying to keep the anger out of his voice. And he was successful. Because what came through was worry.

He felt her hand close on his, and even though he'd seen up close in SWAT what she was capable of doing with those hands, all he could focus on was how tiny they were, compared to his.

"I didn't go anywhere near him, and I don't plan to, even if I'd learned where he was. I made a phone call. If anything had come of it, I would have…"

"What?" he pressed when she paused. "Called Scott and taken him over there?"

"No," she replied. "I would have called you. I understand that I have a target on my back. I'm not going to put anyone else in danger by going near a possible suspect who's out to get me, and probably willing to take other people down to get to me. But that doesn't mean I'm going to sit home, boarding up my windows and praying someone else finds him, after a decade of dead ends. Come on!"

Grant tried to forcibly keep the words in that wanted to burst from his mouth. When he felt he had it together, he told her, "I'll pay the family a visit tomorrow."

"What about not tipping your hand?"

"If Hoffmeier is living in DC right now, he doesn't have his name on any lease. Which means he's either off the books somewhere, or his family is putting him up. They've got some serious political connections, and they're not going to scare easily, but they're also not going to want bad press attached to the family name. I'm going to use that."

"How?"

"Maggie, trust me, okay? I've run a lot of investigations like this. I understand why you can't back away, but just let me run with Hoffmeier."

"We've got twelve days, Grant," she said softly, nervousness in her eyes that he hadn't seen on even the diciest of SWAT calls.

He stroked her hand. "If we don't have someone in custody by August 31, the FBI is putting you in protective custody. And I'm taking a break from the case to be on the detail." That last part hadn't been approved, but it didn't matter. Whatever it took, he planned to be there for her.

She gave him a forced smile. "That's sweet of you, Grant, but I've got SWAT training. If he gets anywhere near me…"

"I know." He made sure he put conviction in the words, wanted her to know he believed them. "But this guy is smart, and I'm not willing to take chances. Neither is anyone in the Bureau. I didn't even need to request this. The word came down from way above me."

She was silent a minute, and he wasn't sure if she was digesting that, or trying to come up with an argument, but he spoke up first.

"Even if it wasn't an official order, Maggie, you know every single guy on our team would have taken personal time to stand by you on September 1. This SOB would have had to go through an entire team of SWAT agents to get anywhere near you."

Tears welled in her eyes—something he'd never once seen—and he finished, "But it's not going to come to that. We're going to get him."

She nodded. Then she reached up and put her hand on the back of his head to pull him to her, and softly kissed him. She leaned back again before he'd really registered what was happening. "Thank you."

She'd never let go of his hand, so he used it to tug her closer, until he could wrap his arm around her shoulder. He knew she cared about him, and she was attracted to him, but beyond that? He really had no idea. And now was the wrong time to find out, but when she rested her head in the crook of his arm and relaxed against him, it felt right, like something a girlfriend would do.

"When I was a teenager, my dad left."

Maggie shifted, apparently surprised by the change in conversation, but he kept his arm around her shoulder and drew her back against him.

"It was sort of out of the blue for all of us. My parents never had the most solid marriage, but they never argued, either. There was just this…distance. Then my dad just left. Middle of the night and everything. Packed up one suitcase and bolted. Left everything else behind, including his family."

Maggie's fingers tightened around his, telling him

she was listening carefully, even though he couldn't see her expression.

"I get postcards and phone calls every so often, but for all real purposes, he just washed his hands of us. Never got an explanation, either. I think that's the part that eats my mom up most. But the timing…" He sighed, remembering the changes that had come swift and unforgiving during his sophomore year of high school.

"We lived in the city. New York. We were already struggling, but without the second income, we had to move, and where we ended up was bad. Real bad. With a big gang presence."

"And they took one look at you and wanted you to join," Maggie guessed, reminding him she'd seen the picture on his mantel.

Even in high school, he'd looked like the kind of muscle a gang might want to use. "Yeah. My younger brothers weren't quite my size, but they tried to jump all three of us in. I worked hard to keep us all out of it."

"And what happened?"

The memory made him tense. "Vinnie was okay. It wasn't easy, but he genuinely wanted nothing to do with it, so even though it wasn't exactly simple to keep them off our doorstep, at least we were only fighting on one side there. But Ben—he's the baby of the family, in seventh grade then—he was interested. I honestly thought we were going to lose him to them. I'd all but given up, when one of his friends was killed in a drive-by. It scared him straight."

"They seem to be doing pretty well now," she said. "From your pictures, I mean."

"Oh, yeah. Vinnie's still in New York, but way up north now, and Ben moved out to Chicago a couple of years back."

"And you stayed in New York."

"Well, that's where the Bureau assigned me."

She twisted to look at him. "You requested it, though, didn't you? As your office of preference?"

Once an agent made it through the FBI Academy, they got to request the field office where they wanted to be placed. It was considered sort of a joke, because rarely did anyone seem to actually get their office of preference, but he had. "Yeah. Well, at the time, my family was still there, and I wanted to…"

"Make a difference," she finished.

"Sounds a little corny, I know, but—"

"It doesn't sound corny at all," she said.

"Well, I didn't get gangs, which honestly, I'm kind of glad about—I'd had plenty of that—but I've been in VCMO my whole career so far. I wanted to try for SWAT in New York, but there was never an opening. So when I came here and a place opened up right away, it seemed like it was meant to be."

"Maybe it was."

He stared down at her, looking back earnestly, and he knew he'd probably never get a better opening. "I feel the same way about meeting you."

She jerked backward, eyes wide, and dread overtook him. He'd pushed too much, too soon.

"Grant, you know…" She sighed, cutting herself off. "There's been something…more than friendship… between us all along."

"There has?" She'd felt it right away, too?

"Yes. But things have changed."

"Why?"

"You look at me differently now," she said softly, slipping out of his grasp and standing.

He got to his feet, too. "Maggie, that's just not true."

"I know you don't want it to be, but it is. I could feel it, before, when you kissed me."

Because of his mistake with her neck. He tried to argue, but she talked over him.

"That one day has affected *everything* in my life ever since. I joined the FBI because of it, I take a personal day every September 1 because of it, and every relationship I've ever had has tanked in one way or another because of it."

Her voice wavered, but there was certainty in her eyes as she said, "It's been ten years. I need to get to the other side of this. And I can't do it with you. Not with everything you know, with everything you've seen in my case file. I'm sorry," she finished quietly, then she turned and headed for the door.

MAGGIE SQUEEZED HER eyes shut and pressed a hand against the ache in her chest as she opened her car door.

From behind her, another hand reached out and slammed it shut.

As she whipped around, a woman out jogging paused and let out a cat call, then raced on past as Maggie realized Grant had followed her outside, in boxers, a T-shirt and bare feet.

She blinked, hoping Grant couldn't tell she was seconds from crying, and tried to turn her back on him. Just get in her car and drive home. Put this whole day behind her.

He took her arm and spun her around, something fierce in his expression as he told her, "The only thing that's different now is my feelings for you have gotten stronger, Maggie. If you're not interested, fine," he said, although his voice broke on the last word. "But if you're really worried I see you as somehow *less* because of what happened to you, that's just not true."

She pulled angrily out of his grip. "Look, Grant, maybe I've been giving you mixed signals, because I *am* interested. You know it. But it doesn't matter! What happened before—"

"When I almost touched your neck and I froze?" he asked bluntly.

"Yes." Some part of her actually wished he'd done it, that she'd had her inevitable panicked reaction. Maybe then she'd be able to admit to herself, once and for all, that it wasn't going to ever matter how the guy responded to learning about her past. That it was *her*. That she was never going to be cut out for a normal relationship.

She gulped and hung her head, not wanting him to see that fear in her eyes. Because if anyone might, it was Grant.

"I just didn't want to hurt you," he said softly.

"You saw me as damaged," she said, and preempted the response he was trying to give, adding, "Maybe I do, too."

"Maggie." He put his hand under her chin, forcing it up so she was looking at him. "I don't think that. You're one of the strongest people I know. And you must know that about yourself, or you'd never have had the confidence to go out for SWAT."

"That's different."

"It's no different—"

"Yes, it is. Romantically, men find out and they look at me as if I'm…tainted." She hated even saying the word, hated believing it was true. But decent men, men she'd been interested in enough to go out with, had suddenly changed when she told them. They'd begun looking at her as though she was a victim, and worse, as though she was somehow a different person than before. Unintentionally, she was sure, but to her—being on the other end of it—that didn't matter.

"Oh, Maggie," Grant sighed, and he sounded so sorry for her, she just wanted to leave.

She reached for her door handle again, but he drew her hands to his chest.

"The only person tainted by any of this was him. You came out of that stronger." His face was as serious as she'd ever seen it as he told her, "That's my theory on why he's threatening to come back for you, and not any of the others."

"I was first," Maggie said, feeling her shoulders slump with sudden exhaustion.

"Sort of," he said. "The first with the brand, anyway. But I don't think that's really why. I said from the start that it's because he couldn't break you. It's why his sick little obsession with you didn't end that day. You were too strong for him. You always will be."

She stared up at him, the anger and weariness fading underneath hope and fear that mingled together in equal measure.

He must have seen it, because he insisted, "What happened to you changes *nothing* about how I feel about you."

She blinked at him, her pulse beginning to race. "Prove it."

He went completely still for a few seconds that seemed to stretch out forever, then he peeled the keys out of her hand, hit the lock button and put his hands on her face, leaning in.

A car driving by honked, and Maggie jumped. "Not here."

"Okay." He bent down and with one smooth motion, picked her up and tossed her over his shoulder.

She was so surprised, she let out a burst of laughter, and suddenly the tension that always seemed to fill her broke apart. But nervousness quickly settled in its place.

They were back inside before she had a chance to figure out how to handle her anxiety. Then he was setting her down and bringing his hands back up to cup her cheeks, his thumbs caressing her skin before his lips slowly descended on hers.

Just like the other times he'd kissed her, she marveled at how soft and gentle his lips were. It was such a contrast to the hard muscles in his arms that she felt as she ran her fingers upward to tangle around his neck.

They stood there for a long time, his mouth pressing softly and sweetly against hers, his tongue teasing the seam of her lips, until she couldn't take it anymore, and she pushed up on her tiptoes and wound her leg around his.

Finally, he slid his hands down her back, pausing just long enough to unstrap her holster and set it on the mantel. Then his hands drifted lower, gripping her thighs. Pinpoints of pleasure danced over her skin where he touched her, and he lifted her up. As soon as she wrapped her legs around his waist and thrust her tongue into his mouth, he turned, heading straight for the couch.

Ripping her mouth from his, she panted, "Bedroom," then stared back at him, waiting, hoping he wouldn't stop the way he had the last time she'd made that request.

Instead, he smiled at her, one of those huge grins she'd always been drawn to, and strode down the hall as though he couldn't get there fast enough. He flipped on the light in his bedroom, and she had a brief impression of framed art on the wall, an open closet filled with suits on one side and cargos and T-shirts on the other, and a king-size bed.

She expected him to place her back on that bed, but

he turned around and sat on the edge, so she was sitting on top of him. He didn't give her time to decide if that was because he was afraid she wouldn't like someone over her; his hands slipped underneath her blouse and started stroking the curve of her waist. He ran his tongue along the outside of her ear, and need pulsed through her.

"Grant," she moaned, shocked at how desperate she sounded as she grabbed fistfuls of his shirt and tugged it over his head.

"Mmm," he responded, then turned back and fused his mouth to hers, simultaneously unbuttoning her blouse and sliding it off her arms.

As soon as it was off, she arched into him, loving the feel of his skin against hers. His hands started to head back to her waist, so she took hold of them and directed them to the button on her pants.

He undid them fast, then flipped her over onto her back, standing up and pulling the pants slowly down her legs, his gaze traveling the same path.

She propped herself up on her elbows to watch him there in nothing but his boxers, and when his eyes met hers, the pure desire she saw made her smile. In that instant, she was absolutely certain he wasn't thinking of anything in her past. Only her. Only right now.

She crooked her finger at him, and he smiled back at her, a smile full of anticipation and want and something else, something powerful that told her this was going to be more than a fling between friends. That maybe she'd found something much, much stronger.

Her breath caught as he lowered himself slowly on top of her, until she couldn't wait any longer. She had to wrap her arms and legs around him and arch up to meet his mouth.

Practically the instant his lips touched hers, a sudden ringing jolted her out of the moment.

He swore and glanced at the phone lit up on his nightstand, then down at her, then back again. Letting out a few more curses, he rolled over, bringing her with him so she was lying on top of him and making her laugh as he whispered, "Shhh," and picked up the phone.

"Work," he said, his voice suddenly serious and grim as he answered. "Grant Larkin."

Maggie could hear just enough to tell it was Kammy, but not enough to know what was happening. But there was no mistaking the all-business expression that wiped away the desire that had been on Grant's face seconds before. "Okay, I'm heading there now," he said, and hung up.

"What is it?" Maggie asked, propping herself up on her elbows so she could look down at him.

"The Hoffmeier family is taking a little impromptu vacation. There's a flight plan scheduled on their private jet leaving in less than an hour. I've got to go meet the plane." He pressed a fast kiss to her lips, then sat up, lifting her with him. "I've got to go."

Chapter Eleven

Grant was pissed off as he bullied his way onto the private airfield, using his Bureau credentials, his badge and his best SWAT scare tactics. What timing that the Hoffmeiers had to suddenly decide to leave DC. Really, really bad timing for him. And particularly suspicious timing for them.

"Heading to Florida, are you?" Grant called as he approached the midsize Cessna private jet being loaded with baggage as a man and woman stood beside it, looking impatient.

They both turned as he approached. The man was late sixties, with a shock of white hair and the kind of grimace on his face that looked as if it was permanently embedded there. Despite the warm August weather, he was wearing a lightweight suit. Beside him, the woman looked a few years younger, but she'd clearly tried to stave away the years with plastic surgery and dye. The result was too-plump lips, too-high eyebrows and unnaturally blond hair. She'd topped the look off with a candy-pink skirt suit, a floppy hat and oversize sunglasses.

"It's so lovely this time of year in Naples," Lorraine Hoffmeier replied, while her husband just scowled.

"I thought this was the rainy season," Grant said as he reached them and held out a hand. "Grant Larkin, FBI."

Lorraine took his hand limply, looking sideways at her husband, Frederik, who ignored it entirely.

"This is a private airstrip," he snapped.

"Not to me," Grant said, glancing over at the pair of men loading up the Hoffmeiers' luggage. It was going to take a while. "Long trip?"

"We're—" Lorraine started, but Frederik cut her off.

"If you have a business question, you can go through my office," Frederik said, peeling off a shiny business card and handing it over.

Grant pocketed it without a glance. "I don't. I have a family question."

Lorraine shuffled on tall heels that couldn't have been comfortable in the eighty-degree heat, and Frederik snapped, "I don't know what you think you're doing, harassing my family, son, but I know people over at the FBI. Whatever you're here for, it's not sanctioned, and your supervisor will be hearing about it."

Grant gave him a hard smile in return. "My supervisor is aware that I'm here. The Hoffmeier name has come up in connection with a case. I have a few simple questions for you, so that *I* don't have to kick this up to the next level."

Frederik turned to face Grant, leveling him with a look that had probably served him well in boardrooms for the past forty-five years. But this wasn't a boardroom, and Grant didn't intimidate easily.

"I know my rights. I don't have to answer a thing," Frederik said.

Grant shrugged, as though it didn't matter to him either way. "You don't. I can reach out to your employees, business associates and other family members next. Maybe they'll be more willing to cooperate in our investigation. Especially when they learn what we're investigating."

"I keep an attorney on retainer, son. I don't think you or the FBI wants a slander suit." His voice was hard and steady, but his jaw quivered.

Beside him, Lorraine had hunched down, and she'd crossed her arms over her chest.

"It's only slander if it's not true," Grant reminded him, then shrugged again and started to turn. "I'm surprised you don't even want to know what the investigation's about."

"What's it about?" Lorraine burst, like he'd gambled she would.

He turned slowly back around. "It's a serial rape case."

Lorraine turned so pale Grant thought he might have to catch her if she fell over, and Frederik sounded insulted when he said, "This is outrageous!"

"Obviously, you're not suspects," Grant said with the friendliest smile he could manage. "But your son has a connection to one of the victims, and we think he might be able to help us identify the person who did it."

Frederik's lips thinned into a straight line, but it was Lorraine who stiffened and said, "Jeffrey would not associate with a rapist. And I'm afraid he's unavailable. He's been living abroad for many years."

"Oh, I didn't say Jeffrey associated with him," Grant said, choosing his words carefully. "But he might have some key information to point us in the right direction."

Lorraine shook her head. "He's not here."

"That's okay. I just need some contact information." Grant took out a pen and notepad. "Phone number, address. I won't take much of his time."

Frederik and Lorraine stared at one another, seeming to have a silent communication, until Frederik gave one brief nod, and Lorraine pulled out her phone with shaking hands. "All I have is a cell phone number." She read a number off to him, which he jotted down.

"What about an address?"

Lorraine shook her head. "He moves around a lot. You know how some kids backpack across Europe?" She waved a still-shaky hand, encrusted with rings, in the air. "He never got over it."

"Where was he living the last time you talked to him?" Grant asked, trying to keep the annoyance out of his voice.

"I really don't know," Lorraine said, a long-simmering frustration in her tone. "He told me he was in Europe. That's all. I gave up trying to get more from Jeffrey a long time ago. The boy likes his privacy."

"Is he planning to come back to DC this summer?"

"Summer's about over, son," Frederik said, seeming to get his equilibrium back.

"I know. But September seems a perfect time to visit DC."

Lorraine's eyes narrowed, but confusion knitted her brow, as if she suspected there was more to his words, but she didn't know what. Beside her, her husband just frowned.

"You have the number," Frederik spoke up. "Now we need to get on our way." He turned toward the two men who'd almost finished loading the plane. "Let's get moving!"

The pilot who'd just come over from the closest building in time to overhear Frederik's demand, looked at them, then at his clipboard. He held out a hand to Frederik. "Just the three of you, sir?"

"Not him," Frederik said.

"I thought there were three passengers?" the pilot asked.

"Sorry I'm late!" someone called from behind him,

and before Grant turned around, he saw Lorraine smile widely and Frederik's scowl deepen.

The woman walking toward them in an expensive-looking skirt and blouse made Grant feel light-headed.

He must have been gaping because she tilted her head, gave him a perplexed look and asked, "Are you working security for my father?"

"Claudia Hoffmeier," he said. He'd known the Hoffmeiers had a daughter, younger than Jeffrey by six years, but he'd never seen a picture.

"That's right." She stood there, giving him an obvious appraisal.

He was probably staring right back, although his expression had to be a little more of the just-seen-a-ghost variety.

Claudia Hoffmeier had dark hair that hung halfway down her back, sky-blue eyes and a trim, athletic figure. Her gaze was direct, her stance assured, and her neck long and elegant, although he doubted hers sported a hook on the back. But she looked a lot like Maggie. A lot like eight other pictures stapled to case files.

He did the math in his head, realizing she was the same age as Maggie, too.

Various scenarios ran through his head, and he wasn't happy with any of them. It seemed pretty doubtful that Jeff Hoffmeier's name would come up in connection with a rape case, and his sister just *happened* to look like the victims. But what sort of deranged personality raped women who resembled his little sister? What would the motivation be? Some misplaced revenge for a sibling rivalry? An inappropriate attachment? Both?

"What?" she asked, sounding amused. "We know each other?"

"No," he said, his voice not quite right. "But I think there's someone in common we both know."

"Oh, yeah?" she asked, just as Frederik stepped forward and grabbed her arm. "Who's that?"

"Maggie Delacorte," he said, taking a chance and wishing he'd done more background on Claudia.

The smile instantly dropped off her face, and she stumbled, though he couldn't be sure if it was his question or her father yanking her away.

"Uh, sorry, no," she said, shaking her head. "I don't think so."

"Does Jeffrey know her?" he asked, getting louder and following as Frederik dragged Claudia toward the plane.

Lorraine moved more slowly, looking between them.

"I don't like this line of questioning, son," Frederik said, spinning and holding his hand up.

"Dad," Claudia said. "It's fine. Who are you, exactly?"

"Grant Larkin, FBI."

Her forehead furrowed as she studied him for a moment, and then she reached into a purse that probably cost more than he made in a month and handed him a card. "I have no idea if Jeffrey knows this woman, but I doubt it. He's lived abroad a long time. But whatever this is about, we're happy to help."

She tapped the card he was holding, and he finally glanced down at it. Claudia Hoffmeier, Attorney-at-Law, General Counsel for Hoffmeier Financial.

"Go ahead, Dad," she said, ushering him toward the jet, then looking back at Grant. "You have questions, feel free to give me a call, Mr. Larkin."

Then she and her parents boarded the plane, and Grant moved back, heading numbly toward his own vehicle, still staring at the card and pondering Claudia Hoffmeier's reaction.

Did she recognize Maggie's name? Did her parents know their son had done something they should be worried about? *Was* Jeffrey really living abroad?

Putting the card away, Grant doubled his speed. He needed to go to the office, call the number Lorraine had provided for Jeffrey and see if he could get a lead on where it pinged to, and check out the entire Hoffmeier family.

GRANT CURSED AS he hung up his cell phone, wishing he was using a landline he could slam down, maybe a few times. "Out of service," he told Kammy.

She looked unsurprised as she nodded at him from across the conference table at the WFO.

He'd called her back there after visiting the Hoffmeiers, and he could tell she'd been planning to make it an early night, just like him. She'd swapped the suit she seemed to own in every shade of black, blue and gray for linen pants and a T-shirt, and scrubbed her face clean of makeup. It should have made her seem more approachable, but somehow she still looked every bit the hard-driving FBI supervisor.

"You think Lorraine Hoffmeier gave you a dead number on purpose?" Kammy asked.

"I don't know. When I asked about Jeff coming back to visit in September, she gave me this look that said she knew I was alluding to something, but she didn't know what. The father and sister, on the other hand..."

"You think they're knowingly covering up for a serial rapist? That would make them accessories. If she's a lawyer—"

"I think they suspect. And I think they're trying to distance themselves from him, protect their family name.

It's why I was hoping they'd cooperate, so if it *does* turn out to be him, they'll look like they have clean hands."

Kammy braced her elbows on the table and leaned forward. "Let me ask you a question, Grant. Something here stinks, that's for sure, but we've only really connected Jeff Hoffmeier to Shana Mills. What if she's the only victim? Maybe the family found out and suggested he take to backpacking in Europe."

Grant swallowed his instant reaction, which was to argue, and thought about it. "Well, assuming we're talking first-degree sexual assault, statute of limitations in DC generally runs out after fifteen years. But he didn't leave right after Shana's attack. He left DC ten years ago, after Maggie's."

"Maybe the family found out later?"

"It's possible, but that's some coincidental timing."

"Unless he really is in Europe. In which case, he's not a possibility at all. If he's here, he's stayed way below the radar. You think the family's supplying him with wads of cash? He'd have to stick to places that weren't running credit checks. That means no house rentals, nothing. You think a kid with his background is living that low to ground?"

"Or the family money supplied him with forged documents," Grant suggested, then he did pound his fist on the table. "I should have pushed harder, not let them get on that plane."

"We had no reason to compel them to stay," Kammy reminded him. "And the sister is a lawyer, so she knew that, even if the parents didn't."

"Oh, Frederik Hoffmeier knew. That's the other thing. He handed me a business card, tried to kick me off the airfield as soon as I showed up. Had no interest in even hearing what case I was investigating."

"He owns a big, successful business," Kammy said. "I'm not sure that's a smoking gun. This guy has been investigated before."

"Yeah, I know," Grant said. "Securities fraud. It might not have stuck, but you'd think going through an investigation again would worry him. You'd think he'd want to at least *pretend* to cooperate. Besides, even after I told him it was family-related, he didn't want to talk to me."

"Again, that's not a cry of guilt. You're suggesting that this man knows—or at least suspects—his son has abducted, raped and branded nine women in the past decade. That's some pretty strong family loyalty."

"I've seen it before," Grant said. "I'm sure you have, too."

She sighed and nodded. "Yeah. But for something this serious and long-running? I'd say he'd be the exception. And what about the sister? An intelligent, high-powered lawyer who's willing to keep her brother's sick secret? Especially when it involves him attacking other women, ones who look like her?"

"A high-powered lawyer who works for the family business," Grant reminded her. "A thirty-two-year-old woman who reacted when I said Maggie's name."

"Who reacted when you said my name?"

Grant looked toward the door of the conference room as Maggie strode in, wearing the gray dress pants and short-sleeved blouse she'd shown up in at his house. But his mind instantly flashed to how he'd seen her last: stretched out in his bed in nothing but a dark blue bra and panties. Her hair haloed out behind her on the bed, her lips swollen from kissing him.

Maggie flushed, and he realized his thoughts must have been showing, so he quickly looked away, before Kammy saw, too.

Kammy glanced back at him suspiciously, but Grant fiddled with the file in front of him until he was sure he had control of his emotions, then he looked up, all business, and told Maggie, "Claudia Hoffmeier."

The very next call he'd made after talking to Kammy on his drive over to WFO had been to Maggie. She'd still been waiting at his house, and he'd fought the instinct to call Kammy off and just go home to Maggie. The idea was so appealing, even the thought of her waiting in his house made his body heat up.

But the case was too important, and he was onto something with Jeff Hoffmeier. He was sure of it.

Maggie frowned as she walked around the long table and sat down next to him. "The name doesn't sound familiar."

Grant reached for Kammy's open laptop and turned it toward Maggie. "This is her." The picture was from the Hoffmeier corporate website, and for the millionth time that night, Grant wished he'd looked it up on his phone on the drive over to the airport.

Maggie studied Claudia's photo, either not noticing or not commenting on the similarities between them. Finally, she shook her head. "I don't recognize her. What's the connection?"

"She's your age. And look at her bio. She went to your college at the same time you were there."

"So did thousands of other students. She said she knew me?"

"She claimed she *didn't* know you. But she definitely reacted when I said your name. And it hasn't been in the papers, so there's no reason for her to recognize it."

"And you think, what?" Maggie asked. "That she knows her brother is the Fishhook Rapist?"

"I think she suspects," Grant said, just as Kammy mused, "The Fishhook Rapist."

"What?" Grant glanced over at her.

Kammy dug through the file in front of her, then set the picture of Jeffrey Hoffmeier on the table. "How does a rich kid get a name like that?"

Maggie paled a little, but she said, "You mean why the brand of a hook?"

"Exactly," Kammy said, clearly uncomfortable as she stared back at Maggie. "What connection does he have to the fishing industry?"

"Maybe it's random," Maggie suggested. "Something to throw investigators off track?"

"No," Kammy said adamantly. "The profiler we had look at this a few years back said this hook is his signature. You know what that means, right?"

"It's the thing he's compelled to do. It matters to him," Maggie replied, her tone professional, as though it wasn't her own case they were discussing. "So it must mean something. There has to be a connection. You're right." She looked questioningly at Grant.

He frowned. "We can search for a connection, but I think we should put our resources into finding this guy. Let's talk to Interpol."

"We need more than your gut to get Interpol involved," Kammy said.

"Okay, fine. I don't think he's in Europe, anyway. I think he's here."

"And what if you're wrong?"

The question came from Kammy, but Grant looked at Maggie. If this were any other case, he'd push to follow his instincts, but it wasn't any other case. For him, this one was all about Maggie. And he'd never be able to forgive himself if they let the Fishhook Rapist slip through their fingers because they were following his stubborn lead on the wrong guy.

"What if I tried calling Claudia?" Maggie suggested.

"She's on a flight to Florida," Grant reminded her.

"Yeah, but it's a private plane. She could have her cell phone on."

"What are you hoping to gain from that?" Kammy asked.

"Shock value. See if we can figure out how she knows me."

"She's a lawyer," Kammy reminded her. "I don't think—"

"A lawyer," Maggie repeated, looking pensive.

"What is it?" Grant asked.

"See if you can find a picture of her from college."

"I'll try," Grant said, dragging the laptop toward him again and starting a search.

"I took a prelaw class right before my senior year. There was a girl in my class—I can't remember her name—but we did a project together. We weren't friends or anything, so I don't remember a lot about her, but I do recall we did well on that project. She suggested I could intern at her family's company—that I should apply once I finished my undergrad degree. It was so long ago, and after…what happened…I decided not to go to law school, anyway, so I totally forgot about it."

Maggie had once planned to go to law school? Grant glanced sideways at her, surprised. He knew her decision to join the FBI had come because of her assault, but he couldn't imagine her doing anything else. She was such a natural on the SWAT missions, and he assumed she ran case investigations with the same intense, focused tenacity.

"You think this girl was Claudia?" Kammy asked. "Did you ever meet her brother?"

"It's possible it was Claudia." Maggie shook her head. "I just don't remember. It was only a weeklong project. And it was ten years ago. It was the very end of the summer semester and I didn't end up taking more prelaw classes my senior year, so she fell off my radar. But as for meeting her brother? If I did, it wasn't through her. We never talked outside of class. I was surprised when she mentioned the internship thing."

"So you never interviewed for it?" Kammy pushed.

"No."

"I've got her," Grant said, turning the computer so Maggie could see the grainy yearbook image. It was amazing what you could find on the internet.

He pointed to the girl at the end of the dorm picture. "That's Claudia, from ten years ago."

Maggie squinted at it, her teeth catching her bottom lip, and Grant forced himself to stop staring before Kammy suspected there was something between them—if she didn't already.

"Is that her?" Kammy pushed.

"It could be," Maggie said slowly, not sounding certain. "This picture looks sort of familiar."

"What about the company? Hoffmeier Financial?" Grant asked.

"Hoffmeier Financial? That's what their family business is called?" Maggie's eyes drifted upward, and he could tell she was trying to remember. "You know, it might be her, then. I remember the company didn't sound like a typical law firm, so I asked about it, and she said it wasn't a law firm at all. But she said they had a lawyer on staff, and that she had the position lined up as soon as she graduated."

Grant nodded at Kammy. "Claudia has been working for her father's company since she graduated from law school."

"What about Jeff?" Kammy asked. "They promised Claudia their general counsel position, but nothing for him?"

"Well, he obviously hasn't worked there in the past decade," Grant answered. "Before that, I don't know. He would have been twenty-eight a decade ago, so it's possible he worked for the company before he left for Europe, assuming that's what he did."

"And if he didn't actually go to Europe, maybe he quit when he dropped off the map a decade ago." Kammy nodded. "It's worth checking out."

"When exactly did he disappear?" Maggie asked, her hands clutched too tightly in her lap.

"December is the last time his name shows up on ownership documents," Grant said, "So a few months afterward."

"What did he own?" Kammy asked. "A house?"

"An apartment."

"Not a likely spot to bring his victims, then," she concluded.

"What about the parents' house?" Grant suggested.

"That would be risky," Kammy said. "But worth looking into, I suppose. Maybe they were away. Let's dig deeper on Jeff and see what we can find."

"Thanks for coming back in," Maggie said softly.

"Whoever it is, we're catching him. And if it is Jeff, and his family knew, I don't care how connected they are. We'll make sure they pay for it, too."

Grant nodded at Kammy, pleased by the intensity in her voice. "Let's get to it." He tried to sound confident, but he'd already spent time hunting for Jeff and hadn't come up with any solid leads.

Praying tonight they'd find the break they needed, he told them, "I'll check into his connection to the company."

An hour later, he stared at what he'd found, surprised. "Jeff *did* work for Hoffmeier Financial. He went to college out of state—where he apparently spent most of his time partying—and then moved back and started working for his dad. I've got some buried arrests from that time period, and from when he was at school. Apparently Dad kept having to bail him out of trouble."

"What kind of arrests?" Maggie asked.

"A couple of DUIs, some resisting arrest and assaulting a police officer charges related to cops breaking up a party at his college fraternity house back in Palo Alto when he was still a student. Plus a handful of other charges, mostly minor stuff, but a few assault charges that got pushed under the rug once he moved back to DC after he graduated. Not sexual," he clarified. "Mostly seems to be him getting into bar fights."

"So what happened? Why did he leave the family business?" Kammy asked.

"It seems that Frederik Hoffmeier got sick of his son's work ethic and kicked him out of the company."

"What was his position while he was there?" Maggie wondered.

"Vice President," Grant replied. At her raised eyebrows, he added, "Hoffmeier Financial had three back then, and from what I can tell, Jeff's was mostly in name only."

"So he got kicked out of the family business and left DC," Kammy summed up.

"No," Grant said, "He got kicked out of the family

business, and hung out in DC for another year, dating college girls and blowing through his trust fund."

"What's that?" Maggie said just as he was about to tell them more about Jeff's wastrel lifestyle.

"What?" Grant asked, glancing at her.

Her whole face had tightened as she leaned toward his computer.

"I found an old archived image of the Hoffmeier website, listing executives."

"In the corner," Maggie said, her voice as tense as her expression.

Grant leaned closer, too. "The logo. That's weird," he realized. "It looks like the current logo was cut in half from this original one." He clicked to enlarge it and then felt his jaw drop.

"It's him," Maggie choked out.

"How do you know?" Kammy asked, standing up and moving behind them to see the screen.

Grant pointed. The current Hoffmeier Financial logo resembled the top half of a family crest, but the original logo had been the entire thing. And the bottom half of the crest contained three distinct fishing hooks.

Chapter Twelve

Maggie glanced around her at the near-empty WFO office and then opened the picture of Jeff Hoffmeier on her computer screen. Except for the initial reaction she'd had to him, she still didn't recognize him.

Yet for her, the hooks on the family crest—and Hoffmeier Financial's sudden logo change about a decade ago—cinched it. Jeff had to be the Fishhook Rapist.

Kammy and Grant were theorizing that he might have actually used something with the family crest on it to make the brand. On her own, Maggie had told Ella about it, and she agreed, saying it was a good bet Jeff had used the crest because he harbored hatred toward his family for cutting him out of the business.

From an investigative perspective, the fishhooks had led them off track, because the FBI had long theorized the rapist was in the fishing industry. The reality was that the Hoffmeier family *had* been in fishing—but centuries ago, back in Germany.

From a psychological perspective, Ella had told Maggie that Jeff had probably used the hook as a way to try to implicate his family. Not that he was trying to get himself—or them—caught, but that he got a sick thrill out of branding something so intimately connected to the family that had rejected him onto the women he was trying to mark with a type of ownership.

Ella had also been the one to point out that Jeff's firing from the company business had happened only two years after Shana Mills's attack. He'd gotten away with that assault, giving him the confidence that he could do it again, and a plan had started to form in his mind. At least that was Ella's theory.

She'd continued to profile that he probably particularly resented his brunette, blue-eyed sister, for getting the place he thought he deserved as the firstborn son. That, too, would have happened within a year of Jeff's being pushed out.

So Maggie already fit his "type." She looked like both Shana Mills and Claudia Hoffmeier—the two women he simultaneously loved and hated, in different ways. And the rest of the known Fishhook Rapist victims fit, too. But Ella thought Jeff might have targeted her specifically because he learned his sister had offered her a job at the company that wanted nothing to do with him.

It made her sick just thinking about it, especially if Claudia knew—or suspected—what he'd done to her afterward, and said nothing. And there was a good chance she had, since the Hoffmeiers had cut the family crest in half, using only the top part for their company logo, after he'd begun his attacks.

Grant and Kammy had been back to talk to Shana Mills, to see if she had any idea where Jeff might be, and to get more insight into that relationship. Grant had returned from the visit convinced that Shana had been his first rape victim, and that he'd gotten power out of the fact that drugging her prevented her from realizing it was him. He hadn't told Maggie that; she'd overheard it.

It had instantly made her think about what else she

knew about Shana and Jeff's relationship: that they'd dated again after Shana's rape. Maggie's whole body chilled at the idea that Shana hadn't realized she was going out with the same man who'd hurt her.

It was bad enough that Jeffrey Hoffmeier was a rapist, but what kind of sociopath dated the woman he'd assaulted, secretly feeling empowered because she didn't know? The answer was the kind of sociopath she wanted behind bars for the rest of his sorry life.

But when she'd pushed to find out everything else Grant and Kammy knew, she'd learned that with only three days left until September 1, it wasn't enough. It wasn't anywhere near enough.

Staring at Jeff's picture all the time wasn't telling her anything new, either. Because just like Shana, she didn't remember the person who'd hurt her. And it wasn't doing her any good obsessively staring at him, hoping a memory would surface. The reality was that even if one did, it probably wouldn't help them find him now.

Closing the image, Maggie shut down her computer and headed for the conference room. It had become her last stop of the day. Sometimes the whole team working the case was there, but often Maggie stayed late, waiting until everyone had gone home except Kammy and Grant, who were working later and later each night as the deadline drew closer.

Her own supervisor had already approached her and told her that in two days, if they didn't have Jeff under arrest, they were putting her in protective custody. Even though she was officially off the team, she still felt like a SWAT agent, and she hated the idea of needing protection. But she wasn't about to turn it down.

Before she reached the conference room, Maggie's phone rang. Halting midstride, she checked the readout, then turned the other way, down the hall where the coffeepot was situated, for a little privacy from the few remaining agents in the bullpen. It was the investigator from OPR.

"Hello," she answered, hearing her nerves come through in the single word.

"Agent Delacorte, this is John from OPR. I'm sorry to call you in the evening."

"That's okay. I'm still at the office," she said, trying to calm her voice. OPR calling her meant they'd made a decision about the incident that had caused her to leave SWAT.

"I wanted you to know that we came to a decision. The incident will go in your personnel file," he began, but she'd expected that.

It was the least of her worries.

When she didn't say anything, just waited, her breath stalled, he continued, "Your teammates think very highly of you. Every one of them spoke up on your behalf."

Her eyes got watery at the idea that all the guys still wanted to work with her, that they still trusted her in a firefight after she'd frozen at such a critical moment. That included Grant, even though he was the one who'd paid for her error, but she realized that part didn't surprise her. Grant always stood by her.

The thought stuck with her even as John continued, "Until the investigation into the Fishhook Rapist is concluded, you're to stay on only your civil rights squad duties. However, after that time, you're free to rejoin SWAT."

They'd cleared her.

Maggie gasped, then stuttered, "Th-thank you."

"Don't thank me," John said. "Thank your teammates. They were very convincing that you're an asset to SWAT.

Between them and your excellent record there over the past four years, we agree."

Relief washed over Maggie stronger than she'd expected as John hung up, and she doubled over with the knowledge that she hadn't let the Fishhook case destroy her SWAT career.

It didn't mean she'd be going back, though. When the Fishhook case was over, there was going to be another stumbling block: Grant.

She had no idea how to define their relationship, but there was no question they had one that went beyond the scope of teammates. She wasn't willing to give up whatever was developing between them, which meant one of them would have to leave SWAT.

Maybe a spot would eventually open up on another team, but it was rare. And it wouldn't be the same. Her SWAT team had become like family.

The very idea of leaving left a knot in her chest, but Maggie straightened, vowing to worry about it later. Right now, she needed to find out the status of the case.

She hurried through the bullpen, past the only two agents still cloistered in their cubicles, and into the conference room. The room was an organized mess. The files and documents covering every surface seemed to have tripled in the past week as they tried to hunt down Jeff Hoffmeier.

Grant and Kammy sat in their usual seats at the far end of the room, and both looked up at her with bloodshot eyes as she entered.

"What happened?" Grant asked, standing.

"Nothing. I just heard back from OPR."

"I'll give you a minute," Kammy said, getting tiredly to her feet. When Maggie started to protest, she added, "I need caffeine, anyway, or I'll be down for the count."

She headed out the door, closing it behind her, and Grant was instantly at Maggie's side. "How did it go?"

"They told me you spoke for me."

"Of course."

"You're not worried—"

"What?" Grant cut her off. "That you'll have another flashback to a memory you didn't even know you had, when responding to a SWAT call? What are the chances of that? Probably as slim as my MP-5 misfiring."

"That could happen," Maggie said.

"Exactly. Or Clive could have a heart attack on a call. But the chances are much higher that none of those things will happen, so why lose one of the best members of the team?"

"You think I'm one of the best members on the team?"

"And the cutest," he teased, then got serious. "I do, but it was Clive who told OPR that part."

Wow. Her team leader thought she was one of his best agents? That was high praise from Clive. "Well, it's official, but I'm not sure what I'll do. You know, with everything between us…"

She stopped as Kammy came back in the room, practically gulping from a coffee mug.

"We'll figure it out," Grant said, pressing his hand against her upper arm before he returned to his seat.

Maggie followed more slowly, more torn than ever. She'd felt vindicated to hear she was still on the team, then conflicted because of Grant, and now even more conflicted hearing how her teammates viewed her. She couldn't deny whatever was happening with her and Grant. If they were going to be serious, one of them had to leave the team. She'd been there for four years, so it seemed only fair that it be his turn on SWAT now. But how could she leave the team after their vote of support?

Pushing the worry to the back of her mind, Maggie focused on the more immediate problem. "Do you have anything new?"

"A new reason September 1 is Jeffrey Hoffmeier's date of choice," Kammy said.

"What do you mean?"

Kammy gestured to Grant, and he said, "I kept digging for old information about Jeffrey from eleven years ago, when his family pushed him out of the company, and I found a press release. It announced that Jeffrey was leaving the company as VP and named some other guy who was taking his place. It was dated September 1."

She felt a wave of hot anger, "So he's using part of the crest to punish them, and that—plus Shana Mills's attack—is why he picked September 1? Because it's a date that ties to both Shana and Claudia and his family?"

"Looks like it," Grant said.

"Have you been able to track him?"

"Well, we've confirmed that he had a pretty sizable trust fund, although what happened to it all is questionable," Kammy said. "We think at least some of the money went into foreign banks and was hidden under shell companies. We've got some of our White Collar agents digging around, but they're not likely to be able to untangle that mess in the next three days."

"Claudia Hoffmeier isn't answering at the number she gave us, and neither are her parents," Grant said, clearly frustrated. "And we're trying to get some warrants to get the family property information—whatever we can't dig up on our own—but it's not happening."

Maggie nodded, angry but unsurprised. She was sure it was Jeff Hoffmeier now, but what did they have, evidence-wise, really? A lot of conjecture, some suspicious timing and a family crest with an element that, while it wasn't typical, definitely wasn't unique to the Hoffmeiers.

"What about the property we do know about?" Maggie asked. "He must be in DC at this point."

How close had he gotten to her? Maggie shuddered, thankful Grant was looking at Kammy and didn't notice.

Kammy set her empty coffee mug down, seeming significantly more awake. "The Hoffmeiers have a house in the city, and another in horse country in Virginia. Claudia has one here and an apartment in Maryland, where her boyfriend lives. Beyond that, we don't know, but we've already found a couple of shell companies with Frederik's name on them, so we're digging deeper there."

"But even if you find something, you can't get on the property," Maggie summed up.

Grant glanced at her, and the expression on his face told her that if the deadline hit and they hadn't caught the guy, procedure was going right out the window.

She started to shake her head at him, then realized there was no way he'd be kicking down doors on September 1, because he'd be wherever *she* was, standing beside her. Or, really, knowing Grant, he'd be standing in front of her, wearing Kevlar and holding a Glock.

A smile quivered on her lips, and he looked back at her questioningly, but she didn't get a chance to say anything, because her phone rang again.

She glanced at the readout and rolled her eyes. "Scott," she told them. "I'm running late. He probably expected me at the house two minutes ago and is panicking."

She stood and hurried out of the conference room to answer, not wanting to distract them any more than she already was by constantly seeking out updates. "Hey, Scott, I'll be leaving the office in a few minutes, I promise. I just—"

"Don't leave," Scott said, panic in his voice that made fear creep along her nerve endings.

"What's wrong?"

"I'm not at your house," Scott said, and it was so obvious he was trying not to worry her that it was making it worse.

"Why not? What happened?"

"There was a break-in at my house," Scott said, and his voice got choked up as he finished, "Chelsie was shot."

Shock made her go rigid, then pain seemed to explode in her chest. Her voice came out too high when she asked, "Is she okay?"

"I'm driving to the hospital right now. I'll call you with an update. All I know so far is that she's in surgery."

Maggie ran over to her cubicle and grabbed her purse. "I'm on my way to meet you."

"No," Scott replied. "Call Ella. Ask her to come over tonight and stay with you, okay?"

"Scott, I want to—"

"I can't stay with you every second at the hospital, Maggie. And that place is busy. I don't want someone coming in with a weapon and walking you out of there—"

"It's not September 1," Maggie reminded him. "That date *matters* to him. A lot. How would he even know about Chelsie, anyway?" Her legs wobbled and she sank onto her chair. "Did—"

"It's not him. They got a description from my neighbor, who happened to be out running at the time." Scott lived quite a distance from his closest neighbor, out in the country in Virginia. "The person who broke in was black. Not this Hoffmeier guy."

"Is it connected to what happened a few months ago?" Maggie asked. Chelsie had been targeted by some men with major resources, and Scott had been shot in that house protecting her. But she'd thought that nightmare was over.

"No. Local police called me, and they're pretty sure they know who it is. It looks like he was after money. He's a known druggie, and this isn't his first offense of this type."

"So let me come—"

"No," Scott said, his tone harsh and final. Then he said more calmly, "Please don't make me worry about you, too. I know my hospital scenario is me being overly paranoid, but humor me. Just call Ella. Promise me you won't go anywhere until you hear from her, and I'll let you know when Chelsie's out of surgery."

She heard Scott's tires squeal and then his car door slam and realized he must have arrived at the hospital.

"Okay," she promised. "Please call me when you know anything."

"I will," Scott said and hung up.

Maggie's hands shook as she did the same, then immediately dialed Ella. It went straight to voice mail, so she left a message telling Ella to call her, then walked slowly back to the conference room.

Grant lurched to his feet. "What happened?"

"There was a break-in at my brother's house. Chelsie was shot."

"Is she okay?" Grant reached for the holster he'd set on the cabinet behind him. "You need me to drive you to the hospital?"

Beside him, sympathy and frustration warred on Kammy's face.

"She's in surgery," Maggie said, walking to the end of the table and taking a seat. "Scott's going to call me when he knows anything. But I'm going to stay here until I hear from Ella."

"Good idea." Grant, who knew about Scott's and Ella's

determination not to let her out of their sight unless she was with other FBI agents, nodded approvingly. Then, ignoring Kammy, he slung an arm around her shoulders and gave her a hug. "Chelsie's almost as stubborn and strong as you are. She'll be okay."

"I hope so," Maggie said, then straightened, determined to distract herself. "I don't suppose anything new came up while I was on the call?"

"Actually," Grant surprised her, "I was running down a hunch, and I did find something."

"It's good," Kammy said, leaning toward them. "This might be enough to get us a warrant on the properties, if we follow the trail far enough."

"Or maybe some new places to look," Grant suggested.

Maggie's heart rate spiked. "What is it?"

"Since we weren't having any luck with Jeff's name showing up in any of the cities where the attacks occurred, I started checking into other family members." He leaned back in his seat, looking proud. "I got a hit. Another name that showed up in every city, at all the right times."

Shock pulsed through her. Had they been wrong? Had she been unable to recognize Jeff Hoffmeier because it wasn't actually him? Had her reaction to his picture been because he resembled the actual perpetrator, some other member of his family?

"Who is it?" Maggie choked out.

"Jeff's cousin. Different last name, which is why Hoffmeier didn't come up for us."

"What's his name?" Maggie asked. "Do you have a picture?"

"Yeah." Grant typed away on his computer, then turned it around.

A picture labeled Jasper Grimes filled the screen, and

he looked a lot like Jeff Hoffmeier. Slightly more angular features, bigger nose, not quite the same bright blue eyes. But close enough that it would explain her reaction to Jeff. Except...

She looked over at Grant. "I don't recognize him."

"No." Grant shook his head. "It's not him. Sorry, I should have been more clear. Jasper Grimes was in a car accident eleven years ago. He was badly injured. He made it through, but with severe brain trauma. He'd been living in a medical facility in Maryland ever since. It's not him using that ID."

"It's Jeff," Maggie realized. "He hasn't been in Europe. He's just been using his cousin's ID to stay under the radar."

"Exactly," Grant said. "Credit checks were fine, because Jasper's still alive—his ID is still good. And Jeff looks similar enough. So that's why we see Jeff popping up randomly in the states every few years. He uses his own ID to access his trust fund in some in-between state where there's no connection to the Fishhook cases, then keeps traveling and goes back to Jasper's ID."

"So," Maggie asked the most important question, "does Jasper Grimes own property in DC?"

"Let's find out," Grant said.

He and Kammy started searching, while Maggie tried not to think about how Chelsie was doing.

Finally, Grant sighed and glanced over at Kammy, who shook her head.

"Either he's not using Jasper's name here, or he's buried it under one of his dad's shell corporations. I can't find him."

Maggie tried not to feel discouraged. The information could still lead them to him. She had to think positive.

But all she could think of was the anniversary looming

over her. Three days from now, she wouldn't be gathered with Scott and Ella, praying no other victim would show up in the news reports.

She'd be surrounded by federal agents, in some undisclosed location, under protective custody.

If Jeff Hoffmeier couldn't find her, who would he go after instead? And how would she ever forgive herself when she heard that name?

Chapter Thirteen

"Come home with me."

Grant's request was met with silence from Maggie, as she stared up at him, seeming to only half comprehend.

They were still at the WFO, an hour after Kammy had gone home. An hour after the rest of the office had completely emptied out. Grant had promised himself he'd wait until she heard back from Scott about Chelsie before suggesting it, but it wasn't doing either of them any good being at the WFO.

The office was dark except for the conference room, which looked as though a tornado had hit it, dropping Fishhook Rapist detritus everywhere in its wake. Not exactly what Maggie needed to be surrounded by while she waited to hear the status of her friend's condition.

And although Grant was still searching for leads on the Jasper Grimes ID, he was heading rapidly for a wall of exhaustion, and he knew it.

"What about—" Maggie started, but jumped when her phone rang. She grabbed it, stress in her voice as she answered. "Scott? How is she?"

Grant tapped her arm, and Maggie hit speaker.

"She made it out of surgery." Scott's weary voice came over the speaker sounding tinny and far away.

"Thank goodness," Maggie said.

"There were no complications. The bullet went straight through, so she lost a lot of blood, but it didn't nick anything vital on its way. She got lucky."

As lucky as anyone who got shot could be, Grant thought, taking Maggie's hand in his.

She gave him a shaky smile, her eyes watery, then looked back at the phone. "She's going to be okay?"

"Yeah," Scott said. "But I'm staying with her here overnight. Not exactly protocol, but the FBI credentials are good for something."

"Good," Maggie said. "Did they catch the guy who did it?"

"Not yet." Scott's voice was instantly hard and angry. "But the police chief stopped by the hospital personally, and he tells me they're running down all of this guy's haunts. He's supposed to call me as soon as they have him in custody."

"Okay," Maggie said. "Let me know. And tell Chelsie I'm thinking about her, when she wakes up."

"I will," Scott said. "Am I on speaker? Is Ella there?"

"Uh, no," Maggie said. "I'm still at WFO. I called the BAU office and was told Ella's in a late meeting, so I'm waiting until she gets out to go anywhere."

"Do you need me to—" Scott started.

"No," Grant said. "I'm here with Maggie. If we don't hear from Ella soon, Maggie can come back to my house. I won't leave her alone."

"Thanks, man," Scott said, relief obvious in his voice. "Call me if you need anything."

"Don't worry," Maggie said, squeezing Grant's hand. "Just focus on Chelsie."

She hung up the phone and turned toward him. "Let me try Ella one more time."

He nodded at her, taking in the tension of her jaw, the

deep shadows under her eyes that hadn't been there six months ago. He stroked his fingers over hers, silently praying that they'd catch Hoffmeier and end this all for good.

He missed the light that used to come into her eyes when they did SWAT training, the easy way she'd joke with them at O'Reilley's after a call. He hated watching this weigh on her, and ten years was far too long.

Worry filled him, the fear that even having identified Hoffmeier, they wouldn't be able to catch the guy. He realized after a moment that he'd squeezed Maggie's hand even tighter.

She looked questioningly at him, and he lifted her hand to his lips, pressing a kiss on her knuckles that made a smile lift her face and a little of that light he loved come into her eyes.

"Go ahead and call Ella," he said, instead of telling her what was on his mind. "See if her meeting is over."

She dialed, then shook her head a minute later, looking frustrated as she set her phone down. "She's still not picking up." Nerves strained her voice when she said, "Do you think something's wrong?"

"I think her meeting is going late. Or maybe the profiler you called forgot to give her the message. She thought Scott was with you, right? She was planning to just go home. Maybe she's there, and she's got her phone in the other room or something, and can't hear it."

"Yeah, but maybe I should call Logan. Just to make sure." She checked her watch, then looked at Grant. "He's at work now. I didn't realize it was so late. You're probably exhausted."

He was, but that didn't matter. "I'm fine. Come on." He stood, pulling her up with him. "You can just as easily call Ella again from my house."

He'd expected her to drop his hand, but instead, she turned it and threaded her fingers through his as she tucked her phone in her pocket. "Okay. Getting out of here—" she gestured around her at the case information "—sounds really good."

"Let's go," he said, heading for the conference room door, their linked hands swinging between them making him ridiculously happy even with everything that was happening.

They'd almost reached the parking garage when Maggie's cell phone rang. She whipped it out of her pocket. "Ella," she said, pressing the phone to her ear.

Then she ground to a sudden halt. Her face went unnaturally pale as a stream of what sounded like gibberish to Grant burst from her phone.

"What is it?" he asked, wrapping an arm around her shoulders in case she was going to fall.

She held up her hand, listening to whatever Ella was telling her, as foreboding traveled up Grant's spine, raising goose bumps along the way.

"No, no," she finally spoke into the phone. "Scott's at the hospital with Chelsie. Break-in at their house. Chelsie's okay." There was a pause, then she sobbed, "I'm so sorry."

He watched her trying to get it together as Ella said something else, then Maggie assured her, "I'm with Grant at WFO. I won't leave his side. We've got three days. We know September 1 is too important to him, and the FBI is putting me in protective custody the day before. Go. Check on Logan. Call me when you know."

"What happened?" Grant asked as soon as she hung up.

Maggie's voice was barely above a whisper as she told him, "Ella is on her way to the hospital. Logan and his partner were called to the scene of a crime, where they were ambushed. Logan was hit." A sob escaped as she said, "They don't know if he's going to make it."

"This isn't random," Grant realized.

"It's my fault," she sobbed, and before Grant could argue, she finished, "It's the Fishhook Rapist, trying to take away the people who've always been beside me, so I'll be isolated. So I'll be all alone when he comes back for me in three…" She glanced at her phone, and he saw that it had just hit midnight. "Make that two days."

Chapter Fourteen

Maggie crossed her hands over her chest, a stubborn tilt to her chin Grant recognized from SWAT calls. "I'm not putting you in danger, too."

"Well, I'm not leaving you alone," Grant said, "and you know it. Would you feel better if I called the rest of the team? We can all camp out at my house. Or we can get the FBI to start the protective custody now."

"No," she responded instantly, standing her ground at the dark entrance to the WFO parking garage, where she'd halted as soon as she realized what Ella's call meant. "I'm not going into hiding, not with Logan and Chelsie in the hospital. Scott or Ella might need me."

"There's nothing you can do for them right now," Grant said, but he knew that trying to make her go anywhere while her brother and best friend were in trouble wasn't going to happen. Especially not when she was this angry.

At least she was furious and not terrified. Or at least, that's what she was letting him see.

"I've got two days until he comes for me," Maggie reminded him.

"I'm not sure we can count on that," Grant said. "Maybe he anticipated the FBI putting a detail on you, and he's trying to strike early. Why would he go after

Logan and Chelsie today if he wasn't coming after you for another two days?"

"They were both shot," Maggie burst out. "They'll be in the hospital at least that long. And it's the psychology of it. He's been playing mind games with me for months, with those sick letters. This is more of it. He's drawing everyone I love away from me, and I'm not letting you put yourself in harm's way, too."

"You don't have a choice," Grant said softly, folding her hand into his. Her slim, pale fingers looked so small and delicate next to his bigger, darker hand.

"Ella and Scott have been beside you for ten years. They're long-term staples in your life he would obviously anticipate. But Hoffmeier doesn't know about me. And look, I think we should assume the worst, but honestly, I agree with you about the date. We know September 1 is symbolic to him. I'm not sure why he went after your friends early, but I think he's tied to the date. I think he'll wait for it. Assuming the whole thing isn't one huge mind game."

Which he wasn't going to count on, but he couldn't rule it out. He'd wondered from the very beginning how the Fishhook Rapist planned to overpower a trained FBI SWAT agent. Maybe he never planned to do that at all. Maybe he was hoping to break her from a distance.

"So then—" Maggie started.

"So nothing," Grant said. "We prepare for the worst, just in case. Let's call the rest of the team and at the very least, put them on standby."

He could tell she was in the middle of an internal debate. Finally, she conceded, "Okay, let's just text them and tell them we might need them. I don't want to call everyone out of bed on a false alarm."

"Done," Grant said. "In the meantime, we're not going

anywhere near your house. And on second thought, in case for some reason I'm on his radar, we're not going to mine. We'll go to a hotel. Even if he can find us, he won't risk getting himself caught by trying something with that many people around."

Maggie nodded slowly, her shoulders relaxing a little, but worry was still written all over her face. "That makes sense."

"Logan and Chelsie will pull through." Grant tugged her toward him until she put her arms around his back and rested her head against his chest. "You have to believe that."

"If they don't, it will be my fault."

"Bull," he said. "What happened to them was *not* your fault. And there's no way you could have predicted this. Not even Ella predicted this, and that's part of her profiling gig, figuring out what these guys will do next."

"Yeah," Maggie said, "But I should have—"

"What? Not let anyone close to you because some psycho fixated on you?" He hugged her tighter, and emotion seeped into his voice, all the worry and anger and love he was feeling right now. "Even if you'd tried, Maggie, that never would have worked. Not with Scott or Ella and not with me."

She lifted her head and told him, "Just don't get yourself shot for me again. Got it?" Her tone was lighter, as if she was trying to make a joke, but it didn't hide her concern.

"You need to stop worrying about that. It happened. It's over. And I'm fine."

As she stared up at him, looking unconvinced, she was so close, he couldn't resist. He tried to tell himself he was reassuring her as much as himself as he bent his head and brushed his lips softly over hers.

Her arms moved from his waist to his neck as she kissed him back. Unlike the previous times they'd kissed, where it quickly turned passionate and sent his libido rocketing out of control, she seemed as content as him to let their mouths linger, slow and tender.

Even after a full day in the WFO bullpen, she smelled fresh, a faintly gingery scent he associated solely with Maggie. She tasted like the best coffee he'd ever drunk, and her body fit against his with no space between them, like a puzzle piece.

When he finally eased back, the stress on her face had faded a little, and she even gave him a hesitant smile. "Let's get to that hotel."

If only circumstances were different right now, those words would have him running for the door.

She must have sensed it, because she shook her head at him, took his hand and led him into the empty parking garage.

Even though it was connected to an FBI building and there was no way Hoffmeier could have gained access, Grant's eyes swept over the open space, lingering in the dark corners, as they approached his car. Then he checked in the backseat before hustling her into the car and climbing in beside her.

"Not taking any chances," she observed, and she was glancing around the lot, too, as he put the car in gear and pulled out onto the street.

It was after midnight, but the streets were still clogged as he drove through the tourist district. He picked an expensive high-rise hotel near the Virginia border he knew had solid security, because they'd helped with the detail for a government function shortly after he'd joined the team.

Beside him, Maggie smiled approvingly as he bypassed the valet, taking a ticket and parking the car himself. They didn't have luggage, but he usually kept a duffel bag with extra clothes in the trunk, and he took the spare weaponry from his lock box and added it to the duffel.

There was no way Hoffmeier could have followed them from a nonpublic FBI building all the way to the hotel, but still, Maggie kept glancing around nervously until they'd checked in—under his name—and settled into their room on the thirtieth floor.

Grant dropped his duffel bag in the corner as Maggie sat down on the oversize chair by the floor-to-ceiling window. She kicked off her combat boots and leaned back in the chair, closing her eyes.

If it weren't for the stress radiating from her and the horrible reason they were here, this was a page out of Grant's dreams. Alone with Maggie in an absurdly decadent hotel room.

As though she could read his thoughts, her eyes opened, and she studied him. "Let me ask you something serious."

"Okay." Grant sat on the very edge of the king bed close to her, suddenly realizing it hadn't occurred to him to get a room with two beds. He hadn't even noticed it until just now.

"How can you get over what happened in that SWAT call so easily?"

"Maggie, we don't—"

"Seriously, Grant. I need to know. I mean, I'm glad it hasn't ruined things between us, believe me, but getting shot is a big deal. You just shrugged it off as though it was a blank in a training exercise."

"Well, I figure with all the crap life throws at you,

you can either choose to let it drag you down, or you can focus on the good stuff."

She leaned forward, propping her chin in her hands. "Really? And it's that easy?"

"If it's not, I hit the gym and get some sparring in. An hour in the ring kicking the heck out of a substitute—or a punching bag—also does the trick." He grinned at her.

"Now, that I can see," she said, glancing at his biceps. "So you hit the gym after that warehouse bust?"

"Nope."

She looked surprised, and maybe a little pleased, so he clarified, "Didn't need to. I meant what I said before, Maggie. You froze. It was a mistake, and an understandable one, given the situation. It was, what? Ten seconds? It just happened to be the wrong ten seconds. Honestly, I was just relieved that I got you out of the way."

She attempted a smile, but couldn't quite do it, so he added, "And then I went home and bought more stock in Kevlar."

She gave a small laugh, which he'd hoped for, and he said, "But when you asked if it was that easy? Yeah, most of the time it is. The stuff with my brothers was hard. It was so much work, every single day, trying to keep the gangs off our steps, trying to keep Ben from going to them. Not to mention just being in that house. Everything was falling apart, the rats were so bold they came out in the daytime, my mom was a mess, my dad was gone."

His shoulders tensed, remembering those days. "I spent a couple of years just mad all the time, and it got old. It probably helped with the gang stuff, and keeping my brothers in line, but it got to the point where *I* didn't like being around myself. And that's just not who I am. I'm not that pissed-off guy, angry at the world."

Maggie got up and sat beside him on the bed, leaning against him until he put his arm around her shoulder. "You do have a pretty good angry face, though," she teased.

"I do?"

"Yeah. You should see the way you glare when we go into a SWAT call. I wouldn't want to be the crook on the other side of that. This big, buff guy running toward them with an MP-5 after he's smashed the door in? No way."

"Buff, huh?"

"Like that's news," she said, nudging him. "So tell me. What happened? You got tired of being mad, so you just stopped?"

"Close enough. Things started turning around my senior year of high school. Mom got it together, got a better job. We moved somewhere a lot safer. I stopped worrying about Vinnie and Ben and started worrying about getting into college. And I just made up my mind that I might not be able to do anything about the hardships life throws at me, but I can control how I react to them."

He stopped, suddenly embarrassed. "I sound a little bit like a public service announcement, don't I?"

"Maybe a little," she joked. "But it's a good outlook. It's one of the reasons I fell for you, you know?"

His pulse picked up. "That first day I walked in to meet the SWAT team, you mean?"

She turned so he could see her clear blue eyes gazing up at him. "That's when it started." Her tone got more serious, quieter. "It's just gotten stronger."

He stared back at her, and even though he knew this was the wrong time, he couldn't help himself. "It's gotten stronger for me, too, Maggie. If I could, I'd go to the Bureau right now and tell them I can't be on your team anymore because we have a relationship that's way more than professional. If I could, I'd tell everyone I know that we'll never be able to work on the same squad again, because it would break the rules. Because I'm in love with you."

She stared at him, surprise in her eyes, and her mouth opened soundlessly.

He put his finger over her lips before she could figure out what to say. "You have other things to think about right now. I don't need you to say anything. I just wanted you to know."

She closed her eyes, as though she was working it out in her head, and he prayed he hadn't just blown it. "I realize it's too soon—"

"Shhh." She grabbed the front of his shirt and drew him toward her. She kissed him softly, twice, then leaned back to stare at him, looking so serious. Then she leaned in and pressed her lips to his once more.

Certainty flooded him in that moment. She might not feel as strongly about him, yet, but she'd already told him she'd fallen for him. He just had to give her more reasons to keep falling. And that would be easy, since he'd do anything for her.

Maybe she knew what he was thinking, because she grabbed his hand and pulled it up and around.

Realizing what she was doing, he let his hand go limp, so she could control it completely.

Her chest rose and fell faster as she placed his hand on the back of her neck, then slid her fingers down his arm until they were resting at his elbow.

He could feel the raised and puckered skin beneath his palm, but he could also feel the silky smooth skin on either side. He kept his touch light, skimming his fingers upward into the base of her hair then back down, under the edge of her blouse and back again.

She had such a soft, delicate neck, but like everything else about Maggie, there were strong muscles underneath.

Pain and anger that someone would dare do this to her flooded him, and he tried to shove it aside, because he knew it wasn't what either of them needed to focus on in this moment. Instead, he thought about what it meant for her to let him do this, and the wonder of that.

Her hand dropped off his elbow onto his knee, and she raised her head, unshed tears in her eyes as she looked at him, but with relief on her face.

He slid his hand from around the back of her neck to cup her cheek and touch his lips once more to hers, then she whispered, "I think we *are* going to have to talk to the Bureau."

It wasn't exactly a declaration of love, but it was close.

She was in love with Grant Larkin.

She smiled and snuggled closer to him in the ridiculously huge hotel bed, feeling lighter than she had any right to feel with everything that was going on. She knew the heavy weight pressing on her would return as soon as she emerged from the dreamlike half sleep she was still in, and so she resisted wakefulness.

It wasn't hard with Grant next to her. She wasn't exactly small, but he made her feel tiny and protected. His head was barely an inch from hers on the pillow, his body seeming to somehow surround her with one hand tucked around her waist, holding her close.

Exhaustion had hit her last night so hard and fast, she'd barely gotten under the covers before falling asleep fully dressed. Apparently, Grant had shed his button-down, and the heat from his bare chest warmed her, keeping her in that sleepy haze even after she opened her eyes.

She studied his features as he slept—from the thick eyebrows, the big nose, the generous lips, to the sandpapery scruff coming in on his chin. He had a strong, hard profile, but in sleep—just like when he grinned at her in a training exercise—he didn't look intimidating.

Instead, he made her feel safe. He made her feel happy. He made her want to move forward with her life, to start a new chapter where the past no longer haunted her.

It would always be there. It had defined her for so long, in ways both good and bad. But last night, when his hands had skimmed over her neck, and all she'd felt was *Grant*, she'd realized that he was right about her. She *wasn't* broken. And she was ready for more, with him.

His eyes opened slowly, something intimate in the depths of his deep brown eyes as he smiled sleepily at her, and she knew. This was exactly how she wanted to wake up every day.

Her hands were tucked up between them, one of them clutched in his hand. She let her other hand drift down, over the bare skin of his chest, where the bruise from that bullet was just a splotch of yellow now. It was barely visible against his light brown skin. Another day or two, and it would be gone entirely.

Another day or two...

The comfortable, sleepy haze lifted, and Maggie's body tensed up. "Where'd I put my phone?"

He brought the hand resting at her waist around, and she saw he had her cell phone clutched in it. "It'd been a long day," he said, his voice rumbly with sleep. "I was worried we wouldn't hear it unless it was close."

He handed it to her, and she moved just enough to look at the readout. No missed calls. But it was earlier than she'd thought, barely 5:00 a.m. She'd only slept a few hours, and somehow she felt more rested than she had in weeks.

"I should call the hospital, check on Logan and Chelsie."

When she just stared at the phone, not moving, Grant asked, "You want me to make the call?"

"No." Chelsie was supposedly stable. And whatever Logan's status right now, Ella deserved to hear from her. "I can do it."

Before she could dial, the phone rang, startling her.

The readout just read "Private Number." Probably the hospital. "How are they?" she answered.

"They?" a voice came over the phone that locked her muscles and sent fear racing through her.

She must have looked panicked, because Grant leaned in close, propping up on one elbow and leaning down so he could hear, too.

Her hands trembled, but she turned the volume up and tilted the phone a little so he could listen.

"You mean *her*, don't you?" that voice from her nightmares continued. "Or are you talking about Logan and Chelsie? Tsk, tsk."

"What do you want, Hoffmeier?" Maggie demanded, and her voice came out stronger than she'd expected as Grant took her hand in his.

There was a pause, then he responded, "You figured that out, did you?" A hint of unease sounded in his voice, but it was gone when he said, "Too bad you didn't figure out my plan sooner, isn't it?"

"You're not going to get away with this," Maggie said, wondering how he'd even gotten her cell phone number. Was he close?

She couldn't help looking at the huge window across from the bed, behind Grant. The thick, heavy curtains were drawn, no way for Hoffmeier to get line of sight if he was across the street peering down a rifle scope.

Hoffmeier laughed, a nasty, ugly sound that seemed

to skitter over her skin, making her feel dirty. "I already have."

"What are you talking about?" she asked, her dread swelling. Had Logan died?

"You have forty minutes," he told her, his voice eerily calm and confident as he gave her an address that sounded vaguely familiar.

"His parents' country house," Grant mouthed.

"You come to me, alone," Hoffmeier said.

She wanted to laugh back at him, to scoff and call his bluff, except he sounded too confident, too certain she'd agree. And she knew, deep in her gut, that he'd found a way to win again.

"Aren't you going to ask why you'd do that?" he mocked.

Grant's jaw tightened, and Maggie could tell it was taking everything in him to stay quiet, to let Hoffmeier believe she was alone right now.

"Why?" she asked, and her voice shook.

"Because I have something you want."

There was a brief shuffling noise, then her sister's voice came over the line, high-pitched, scared and speaking at warp speed. "I'm so sorry, Maggie. I came to DC, anyway. I knocked on your door, and you weren't home and then I was on my way back to the hotel and he grabbed me. I didn't—"

"That's enough," Hoffmeier said, and Nikki was gone.

Maggie sucked in a breath that didn't seem to contain nearly enough oxygen and choked out, "Leave her alone! I'll be there, I promise. Just please don't hurt her."

"Come alone," he repeated. "I even *think* you have backup, and she's dead. *After* I give her a token on her neck to match yours."

Maggie's hand tightened around the phone, panicked

for the baby sister she'd always tried to protect from this evil. "Don't touch her," she barked, terrified that it was too late.

"Forty minutes," he reminded her, then hung up.

Chapter Fifteen

"Hang on," Grant said as Maggie leaped out of the bed, tangling in the covers and almost pitching herself to the floor.

She righted herself, tossed him her phone and ran for her boots, lacing them up fast. "Look up the address, would you? Get me directions." She checked her watch, and there was panic in her voice when she choked out, "Forty minutes! I can't make it in forty minutes, not even if I speed the whole way."

Grant pulled his shirt on, punching the address into her phone as he groped for his own shoes with his other hand. "Just wait a second, Maggie. Let's call Clive, have him get the rest of the team on the move."

"There's no time! That's the whole point. They can't gear up and get out there that fast, either. And it's in the middle of nowhere, that much I know. We have no time for a tactical plan, and he'd see them coming from a mile away. This is Nikki's life. I'm not risking it."

"Maggie," Grant pressed. "We train for this."

She strapped on her holster, then raced over to his duffel bag, unzipping it. Ignoring his comment, she asked, "You have an ankle holster? Something I can take as a backup?"

"Nothing that won't show," he said. "But I'm your backup."

"No," she answered, the way he'd known she would. She was in full-on panic mode, desperate and not thinking straight.

He yanked his shoes on, then hurried to her side and grabbed her arm, making her pause.

"Grant, I have to *go*."

"Just hang on a second, okay? You can't run right into his trap. That's going to get both you and Nikki hurt."

She froze at his words, and her arm tensed under his hold.

"It's going to be okay," he reassured her, but she shook her head.

"I don't think it is," she whispered. "I have to play by his rules. I can't let him do to Nikki what...what he did to me."

It was unspoken, but hung in the air, that it might already be too late.

"We need to treat this like a SWAT call," he said, trying to reason with her, but the truth was, they *didn't* have a lot of options. Not on that timetable, and not with the location he'd provided.

Even if they called the rest of the team, the houses—estates, really—where the Hoffmeier family had their second home was deep in Virginia horse country, where neighbors were miles apart. Worse, land there was flat enough to see for miles. The team would only be able to drive in so far, and they'd have to hoof it from there. By the time they arrived unseen, it would probably be too late.

Still, if everything fell apart, it would be good to know they were on the way.

Maggie stepped back and yanked her blouse down

over her gun, her movements jerky and panicked. "I'll call them on the way."

"Okay." He strapped on his own Glock, then took out his MP-5. He dumped out the contents of his duffel, then stuffed the gun back in, zipping it up. "But I'm going with you."

Her head swiveled toward the door and back, desperation still in her eyes, her body twitching with her obvious need to move. "You heard him—"

"I'm not a full SWAT team. It'll be easier for me to sneak in with you."

She shook her head. "I have to *go*."

"Fine. We can argue on the way," he said. "Let's move."

"WATCH THE LIGHT," Grant warned.

Instead of stopping as the light at the intersection turned from green to yellow, Maggie slapped Grant's siren on the roof of his car and flew through it. Honking and the squeal of tires filled the air, and she just pushed down on the gas, taking the corners dangerously fast.

She called on every bit of the special defensive driving training she'd taken at the FBI's training facility at Quantico as she raced through the outskirts of DC. It wasn't even 6:00 a.m. yet, but here, commuters were already out, ladder-climbers getting an early start, and political assistants prepping for the day ahead.

"You can't stay there once we get close," Maggie said, keeping her attention totally on the road, watching the sidewalks in her peripheral vision for jaywalkers.

Panic threatened, like a river about to burst through a levee. How had he gotten close enough to her house to spot Nikki? And how had no one noticed Nikki had left Indiana for DC?

Sitting beside her, Grant said, "When we're close, I'm going to get down in the backseat."

"He'll see you!"

"No, he won't," Grant replied, sounding calm. "You'll stop the car far enough away. He's not going to be looking in the backseat. To do that, he'd have to get close enough to have his back to you, and he's not stupid. He's going to make you come to him. So you leave me in the car. I'll come after you."

There was such confidence in his voice, such certainty. She'd heard it plenty of times in SWAT calls, and he'd always been able to back it up. But today was different, in so many ways.

"Maybe you should just get out before we drive close enough for him to see the car," Maggie suggested. She knew the area where Hoffmeier had called her to was nothing but open spaces and gently rolling hills. For her to stop where he couldn't see the car would be too far away for Grant to help.

"No," Grant replied. "But that's where Clive will be."

"Don't call Clive," she burst when Grant started to dial his phone. "Hoffmeier knows what I do. What if he's sending me here as a test? What if he's not there at all? I could show up and find a note on the door, sending me to some other property his parents own under that shell company. Meanwhile, he's got a camera set up there and knows I've brought backup and he kills Nikki!"

"That's really elaborate," Grant reasoned. "Most criminals think basic."

"Well, it was pretty elaborate to hire a druggie to break into Scott's house and shoot Chelsie. It was pretty elaborate to hire a couple of guys to open fire into a crime scene with police detectives there. Who knows who else he's hired? Who knows who else he's got with him, watching the area!"

"Your sister said she came to DC on her own. She couldn't have been here long, which means this wasn't his original plan. Not this part. So he's working at least a little bit on the fly here. He hasn't had a lot of time to work all the details out."

"Yeah, but this guy has gotten away with it for a decade! He's not stupid." Maggie whipped around another tight corner, then finally, finally, she was on the I-66 West freeway heading out of DC. It was an hour's drive to the location he'd named, in the best traffic conditions. Even speeding like a maniac, she wasn't sure she'd make it in Hoffmeier's forty-minute time line.

She knew that was the point. He wanted to give her no time to react, no time to come up with a counterplan. He wanted to make her panic, so she wasn't thinking clearly when she arrived. So he'd have the upper hand.

It was working.

"No, Hoffmeier isn't stupid," Grant agreed, still sounding calm; he might've been in the WFO office, planning SWAT details. "But his goal is to get you there. And I bet those guys he hired were purely about throwing cash at people who already had records. There's no way he'd invite strangers into this part. This is about him. And it's about you. He's counting on you to react emotionally."

"I know," she told Grant. "But what choice do I have? This isn't just another SWAT call. This is my sister. I'm not taking any chances."

"Our team is the best," Grant said, still sounding way too calm, as he put the phone to his ear. Then she heard him talking to Clive, going over the details, warning Clive to stay at a distance until they'd checked the place out.

The truth was, Clive and the team wouldn't make it until past the deadline, anyway. The hotel had been a solid twenty minutes closer to Virginia than Clive and her other teammates, who lived on the opposite side of DC. By then, she'd know for sure if Hoffmeier's plan was more involved than it seemed, if he was planning to send her somewhere else. By then, she'd have eyes on Nikki. By then, hopefully, it would all be over.

If it wasn't, there was a good chance she'd need the team. She couldn't risk bringing them too early and alerting him, but thinking like a civilian and playing entirely by his rules could get everyone hurt. She had to have a contingency plan in place, and besides Grant, Scott and Ella, she trusted her SWAT team the most. If she didn't make it, she wanted Nikki safe.

Before she knew it, Grant had put his phone back in his pocket. "The team is coming," he said calmly as she picked up her speed even more. "It's going to be okay."

She bit back her instant response. There was no reason to take out her fear and anger on him, not when he was putting his life in danger for her and Nikki. Not when she cared about him the way she did.

What if she never got the chance to tell him?

"Grant, I need to tell you…" She took a deep breath, wishing she could actually look at him when she said she loved him for the first time. But she couldn't. She was going ninety-five on the freeway, racing around the other vehicles with her siren blaring.

"Tell me later," Grant said, and from the tone of his voice, she could tell he knew it was about their budding relationship.

"But just in case—"

"You don't need a *just in case*. We're both coming out of this, and you can tell me when your sister is safe, okay?"

"Okay," she said, because right now, she needed both of their attention focused on saving Nikki.

But the words sat heavy on her tongue. She prayed he was right, and she would get the chance to say them.

The reality was, she'd do whatever it took to get Nikki away from Hoffmeier. And if she had to trade her own life to do it, she wouldn't hesitate.

Her hands gripped the wheel even tighter, and the farther they got from DC, the lighter the traffic got, giving her room to increase her speed even more. Beside her, Grant had one hand braced on the door handle, but he didn't say a word as she picked it up to over a hundred miles an hour.

He got his duffel bag from the backseat and removed his MP-5, then crammed the empty duffel under the front seat. He set the MP-5 in the backseat, where he'd be climbing before too long.

"You have any other weapons?" she asked, even though she shouldn't need them. Chances were, Hoffmeier would try to get her to lay her gun down. But all she needed to do was get close enough. Her training with the FBI's SWAT team meant her hands were deadly weapons. Assuming she didn't freeze the way she had in the warehouse the second she saw Hoffmeier with her sister.

"I've got the obvious," Grant said. "Wrench for changing a tire, pen knife."

"Pen knife," Maggie said. "Can you put it in my pocket?"

Grant reached into the glove box and took out a small folding knife, then slid it into the pocket of her slacks. "He'll probably search you."

"He gets that close, and I won't need the knife," Maggie said darkly, praying it was true. Praying that if she got the chance to pull her Glock on him, her trigger finger wouldn't shake the way her entire body did every time she so much as thought about seeing Hoffmeier face-to-face.

"That's my girl."

"You're right about that," she said seriously, taking her eyes off the road for just a second to look his way, hoping he understood the subtext. He wanted her to wait to tell him she loved him, fine. But at least this way, if the worst happened, he'd know.

He squeezed her knee as she took the exit onto M-50 and glanced at the dashboard clock. If she could keep her speed up on the country highway, they might actually make it.

Just as that thought hit, Grant's phone rang.

"It's Clive," Grant said, picking it up and talking to their team leader a minute. Then he told her, "I'm leaving the call open," and he stuffed the phone under the middle seat. "He'll be able to hear us," Grant explained to her. "If he has to, he can call HRT, and they can come in by helicopter."

Maggie nodded mutely. If Chelsie hadn't been shot, Scott would have been with HRT right now, armed with a sniper rifle that could take out Hoffmeier from half a mile away. All assuming he'd have been able to mobilize and find an unseen location by then, and assuming Hoffmeier came out into the open.

But the deeper into the country they traveled, the more she realized how smart Hoffmeier had been in choosing his location. A distance shot wasn't going to happen here.

If he was going to be taken down, it would have to happen up close. And she was the only one who'd be able to get close enough without endangering Nikki.

"This is the road," she finally said, terror settling

deep inside as she followed the GPS onto a smaller country road.

The scenery was gorgeous: deep green, rolling plains dotted with grazing horses and the occasional estate. It was also the perfect place to hide a kidnap victim. Even if a scream echoed here, who would hear it?

"I'm getting in the back now," Grant said.

She slowed her speed a little as Grant unfastened his seat belt and climbed into the backseat, settling down on the floor, where there was no way Hoffmeier would see him without standing close to the car. She glanced over her shoulder and saw he had one hand lingering near the holster, holding his Glock, and his MP-5 clutched in his other hand.

"Here we go," she said, turning onto a driveway so long it could have been its own private road. She slowed even more, rolling down her windows so she could hear as she passed large, empty fields meant for horses.

She studied two huge outbuildings as she drove past, but continued on toward the looming main house straight ahead. It was ridiculously ornate, lined with perfectly groomed shrubbery, columns highlighting the entryway. An empty truck was right up front.

Maggie squinted at the house, still a solid five hundred feet away up the drive. "I don't see him," she whispered.

The boom of a voice—*Hoffmeier's* voice—startled her so badly she jerked the wheel, almost veering off the drive.

He was using a bullhorn, she realized, even though she still didn't see him. But he was here.

"Stop the car," he ordered, so she did, planting her foot on the brake, but not putting the car in park.

Her hands shook around the wheel as she waited for more, as she squinted at the house, trying to see any sign of where he was. Something glinted in a front window, and she stared until her eyes hurt, but she couldn't tell what it was.

"Toss your gun out the window," he said, and his voice made the nerve endings in her neck fire to life, almost as if they were preparing for the pain of another brand.

When she hesitated, he snapped, "Don't make me ask again."

Maggie undid her seat belt and unholstered her Glock, holding it out the window so he could see, then dropped it.

"Good," he said, sounding pleased and confident, as if he'd always known it would come back to this, to him in charge. "Now, your backup weapon."

She held up her hands and shook her head, assuming he was staring at her through binoculars.

"Of course you brought a backup gun," he said. "Let's motivate you."

A pained scream echoed through the bullhorn, bringing tears to Maggie's eyes, and Grant's whisper barely penetrated her fear.

"Under the seat."

Reaching down, she picked up his Glock, then held it out the window and tossed it as tears tracked down her cheeks. She didn't bother to wipe them away. He wanted to be in charge, and as much as everything in her resisted, she needed to show him he was. She needed to let him think this would break her. Needed to get him to let her close enough to bring him down. Her hands clenched into tight fists on her lap, where he couldn't see them.

"Very good," Hoffmeier said, and there was that flicker again, in the front window.

Was it open? Maggie wondered.

"Now there's just one more thing," Hoffmeier continued, "and then you can drive up to the house. You follow all my instructions, and I'll let Nikki walk out of here. You know it isn't her I want."

Maggie stared at the house, her jaw trembling, and not because she was trying to let him see fear, but because she couldn't control it. Because she knew exactly who he did want. And she knew exactly what he wanted from her.

"You don't follow my instructions, and I'll shoot her right now, you understand?"

All she could do was nod desperately and wait.

"Tell Grant to get out of the car," his voice boomed.

Maggie froze, terror lodging in her throat. What was he going to do to Grant if she told him to do it? What was he going to do to Nikki if she didn't?

"Tick tock," Hoffmeier mocked.

Before Maggie could figure out what to do, she heard the back car door open.

"Grant, don't," she warned, and her voice came out a desperate whisper, but she was too late.

A flash of light exploded at the front window, with a sharp crack that sent birds flapping from a grove of trees behind the house. Next to her car, Grant dropped to the ground, and dark red spread across his chest.

"Now you can come get Nikki," Hoffmeier said, opening the front door and stepping outside, a pistol pointed at her sister's head.

Chapter Sixteen

"Grant!" Maggie cried, her foot automatically lifting off the brake. The car rolled forward, and she stamped her foot back down, glancing over her shoulder. "Grant," she pleaded again through the open window.

On the ground, Grant lay flat on his back with his right arm splayed out beside him, completely still, not responding. Maggie knew the amount of blood seeping through his shirt meant if he wasn't already dead, he would be soon.

Panic raced through her, the desire to leap out of the car and check his vitals. To press her hands into the wound and try to stop the bleeding.

"Tick tock," Hoffmeier called, startling her.

She looked back at him, where he held a bullhorn in one hand and Nikki in front of him. Then she glanced once more at Grant and gulped back a sob. This time, he wasn't wearing any Kevlar. This time, there would be no "do overs."

"Now!" Hoffmeier screamed. "Or Nikki pays, too!"

Praying Grant was still alive—and that Clive had heard them over the open phone line in the car and was coming—Maggie pressed on the gas, stopping right in front of the porch.

Up close, she could see that Nikki's hands were bound

together in front of her. She was wearing shorts and a T-shirt, and although she was clearly terrified, she was alert, and Maggie didn't see any obvious injuries. She hoped there were none she couldn't see, no brand already seared into Nikki's neck.

Nikki's lips moved, and although Maggie couldn't quite hear her, she read the words. "I'm so sorry."

Hoffmeier dropped the bullhorn on the ground, drawing her attention to him. He looked older than the pictures she'd seen of him, and the years hadn't treated him well. If the idea that people's psychology eventually showed up on their faces was true, he was a prime example.

He still had the good bone structure, but there were more lines on his face than he should have had at his age. The smug, vile smirk that looked stamped on his face overrode any charm he might have once possessed.

But he was still in good physical shape. Maybe more so than he'd been a decade ago, judging by the muscle outlined on his bare arms. Even if she could get close, he wouldn't go down easily.

"Get out of the car, slowly," Hoffmeier said, "and don't try anything."

She turned off the engine and stepped out, her hands up over her head, an overriding fury surging inside.

He waved the hand holding the gun at her, and Maggie's calves tensed the second his weapon left Nikki's temple, but he was too far away to rush.

His eyes narrowed, and he pressed the gun back to her sister's head before he demanded, "Lift your shirt. Are you wearing a holster?"

Every time he spoke, she had to resist the urge to cower. Even with him right in front of her, no flashbacks raced forward, but his voice was imprinted on her memory like a brand of its own.

"Yes. For the gun you made me toss." Her voice came out shaky, and she moved slowly, lifting the side of her blouse so he could see her holster was empty. The weight of the pen knife in her pocket seemed abnormally heavy, and she hunched a little, hoping he couldn't tell she had something there.

"Good," he said, not seeming to notice. "Let's go inside, then." His tone was suddenly jovial, as if he was inviting her to brunch. He backed toward the house, dragging Nikki inside with him.

Her sister's gaze locked on hers as she was yanked inside, such guilt and regret there, the same things Maggie felt herself whenever she thought about the Fishhook Rapist.

She cast one more desperate glance over her shoulder, but in the distance, she could see that Grant was still prone on the ground.

She looked farther down the road, but there were no SWAT vehicles barreling down on them. She needed them right now, for Grant. Yet, if they showed up, Hoffmeier would surely kill Nikki.

Her vision clouded with tears, Maggie followed them inside.

Hoffmeier and Nikki backed through a long entryway into a formal living room, and Maggie walked a few paces behind, her hands up by her ears. The second she entered the room, her eyes were drawn to the elaborate painting on the wall, inside a gilded frame. Then they were pulled to the antique coffee table with the ball and claw feet and the beautiful marble top.

The place where he'd forced her to her knees and branded the back of her neck, tying them together forever. On top of the table was a circular piece of metal attached to a short pole, and as Maggie squinted at it, she realized what it was. A modified family crest, one hook soldered to raise above the rest.

Her whole body shuddered, and Hoffmeier's lips slowly spread. "You remember," he whispered.

This is going to hurt. This is going to hurt. This is going to hurt.

The words chanted like a record set too fast that she couldn't turn off, until she wanted to curl into a ball and slap her hands over her ears. Only it wouldn't help, because the voice was in her head.

"I hoped someday you'd remember what we had," he said, and Nikki suddenly stiffened and snapped, "Stop it!"

Hoffmeier drew the pistol away from her temple then slapped it across her cheek, making Nikki's head whip sideways and blood trickle from her lip.

It snapped the world into focus for Maggie, and she straightened her spine. "I'm here. Time to let Nikki go."

Her voice sounded stronger, and Hoffmeier's smile faded. "Not yet. I know what you do for the FBI, Maggie."

He shifted to the side, yanking Nikki with him, and behind them, Maggie realized there were two mahogany chairs in the middle of the room. "A place for us to talk," he told her. "You sit in the one on the right. There are ties there to make sure you do as you're told."

"Don't do it," Nikki burst out.

Maggie shook her head at her sister, willing her not to antagonize him. "What assurance do I have you'll let Nikki go once I do what you want?"

His eyebrows lifted. "You'll just have to trust me. What choice do you have? Don't do what I say, and I pull the trigger." He tapped the gun barrel against Nikki's head.

"And then I kill you," Maggie vowed, her voice dark and so ominous even Nikki's eyes widened.

"Oh, I probably won't shoot her in the head," Hoffmeier said conversationally. "But a kneecap maybe. Somewhere really painful, that'll never heal right."

He swept his free hand grandly toward the chair, as though he was presenting something at auction, and Maggie moved slowly toward it.

If she could just get close enough, get him to lift his gun away from her sister's head...

But as she stepped toward them, Hoffmeier yanked Nikki off to the side, away from the chairs. So they were both out of striking range.

Nikki mouthed, *No.* But what choice did she have? Maggie picked the zip ties off the chair and sat down.

"Loop it around your wrist and the chair arm," Hoffmeier instructed. "Hurry up."

It was awkward, but Maggie managed to get one arm fastened to the chair, then she held up her free hand with the other zip tie and shook her head. "I can't do this with one hand."

"That's okay," he said cheerfully. "Nikki will finish it." His tone turned menacing. "And you'll sit still. If I could hit your boyfriend in the heart from five hundred feet, I can hit your sister in the head from three." He smiled, a crazy glee in his eyes as he added, "Dad taught me to shoot skeet when I was five, but it never interested me until recently."

Pain wrenched through her at the mention of Grant, and Maggie pushed it aside. She had to focus on Nikki now.

She had to watch for any chance to escape, because yes, Hoffmeier really wanted her. So he might well just let Nikki go once he had her immobilized. By the time

Nikki could get help, he could plan to knock Maggie out with something, load her in the trunk and be long gone.

Yet it was equally likely he'd keep Nikki right here, use her to make Maggie tame, to get her to do whatever he wanted.

Maggie tried to numb herself, tried not to think about what he might want, as Nikki approached. Maggie kept her eyes on Hoffmeier, looking for any moment that his gun might move away from Nikki. If she had the chance, it didn't matter that the chair was attached to her wrist. She'd bring it with her when she tackled him. It was awkward, but it weighed less than her fifty pounds of SWAT gear.

Nikki reached her side, and her own hands, already tied together so tight her wrists were raw, fumbled with the second zip tie. Her fingers trembled as she closed the zip tie around Maggie's other wrist. The whole time, Hoffmeier just stared back at her, barely blinking, his bottomless blue gaze unnerving.

"You okay?" Maggie whispered, and Nikki nodded.

"Enough sisterly love," Hoffmeier said. "Take the other seat, Nikki."

"No," Maggie burst. "Let her go!"

"I will," Hoffmeier said, then waved Nikki over. "Eventually. Right now, I need her here to keep you in line. I know you, Maggie," he purred. "You were always a fighter."

She wrenched at the ties, bile rising up in her throat. She didn't remember the assault; did that mean she'd fought him back then? Or was he just referring to her using his attack as motivation to join SWAT?

Nikki's head moved back and forth between them. "Leave my sister alone."

"Listen to that," Hoffmeier said. "I guess Nikki here

is getting a backbone. I like that in a woman." He sighed dramatically. "Too bad for her that I'm already way too obsessed with her big sister to bother with the knockoff version."

Maggie scowled at him, then glanced at Nikki and hoped she wasn't making an irreversible mistake. "Do what he says." Instinct told her he would only hurt Nikki to force her hand, that he was being honest about wanting to hurt Maggie, not her sister.

"No," Nikki said, and her jaw jutted out as she stepped in front of Maggie. "My sister has her team of SWAT agents on the way and they're going to—"

"Now!" Hoffmeier bellowed.

"Nikki, please. Just do it," Maggie begged, and with one last worried glance at her, Nikki sat in the other chair.

Hoffmeier kept his gun aimed at her, and he stayed carefully away from Maggie as he walked to the far side and secured an extra zip tie to the one around Nikki's wrists, so she was latched to the second chair.

Only then did he turn his gun on Maggie and move closer, murmuring, "I've been waiting so long for this."

Maggie fought off the panic building inside her and prepared herself. Keep coming, she willed him, hoping that if he gave her the chance, she wouldn't freeze up.

But the nearer he got, the faster her breath came, the louder her heartbeat thudded in her eardrums, the more terror clouded her vision. Was this the end for her and Nikki both?

GRANT GROANED AND rolled to his left, uninjured side, trying to push himself off the dirt. His right arm hung limply at his side, blood dripping steadily down it.

He'd waited until Hoffmeier had disappeared inside with Maggie and Nikki to try to move at all, not wanting

Hoffmeier to realize he'd survived. The way his shoulder throbbed and pumped blood, that survival was still in question.

Fighting dizziness as he got to his knees, Grant managed to get his button-down off. He swore as he slid the shirt off his damaged right arm and got a good look at the injury.

As a SWAT agent, he had basic medical training, the sort of thing a soldier learned for the battlefield. But he didn't need it to know his injury was bad. Really bad.

His shirt was soaked through with blood, and so was the ground below him. He had to stop the flow, or he was going to die of blood loss way before backup arrived.

Awkwardly, he managed to wrap the shirt around his shoulder, getting it above the bullet hole. Using his good hand and his teeth, he tugged the knot tight enough that the blood slowed to a stop.

His right hand immediately started to tingle and as he pushed himself to his feet, he swayed and almost fell. Realizing he didn't have a weapon anymore, Grant stumbled as he looked around, finally spotting his Glock a few feet away in the dirt. He walked unsteadily over to it, a wave of dizziness sweeping through him as he bent down to grab it off the ground.

His hand shook around the handle, and he knew the gun wasn't going to do him any good. His body was already shutting down from the blood loss. The likelihood of being able to pull the trigger with Hoffmeier standing close to either Maggie or Nikki and actually hitting Hoffmeier wasn't strong.

Nerves rose up, for Maggie, for Nikki, for himself, and he tried to think the way he would on a SWAT call. Stay calm and focus.

He shoved the gun in his holster, clenched his teeth

against the pain and headed for his car, up by the house. If he could just get to the cell phone, he could tell Clive to call HRT, get them airborne immediately. If he was really, really lucky, Clive and the rest of their team were already close, and they'd arrive in time to stop Hoffmeier from carrying out whatever plan he had for Maggie and Nikki.

New pinpricks of pain skittered up his arm as it began reacting to the blood flow being cut off. It meant he'd successfully tied off the wound, which would buy him some time, but it also meant that arm was completely useless.

Reaching the car, Grant braced himself against it. He reached for the door handle, then moved his hand away. He'd have to get down on the floor and reach under the seat to search for the phone, and if he bent back down, there was a good chance he wouldn't get up again.

Normally, Grant would have skirted the front entry of the house and moved around the side, peering into the windows and getting a lock on the subject and the hostages before he made a move. But with Maggie inside and knowing his time of being any help at all was fading fast, he climbed onto the porch and looked into the house. The door was open, and he could see a long, ornate entryway, but not Maggie or Nikki. Not Hoffmeier.

He had to get to Maggie now, while there was still something he might be able to do. Hopefully, she wouldn't even need him, but since he'd come up close to the house, he hadn't heard anything from inside.

He was careful with every step because he was feeling clumsy from blood loss, and he didn't want to stumble, make noise and give himself away. But fear skyrocketed as Maggie's anguished voice screamed out, "You said you wanted me! Leave her alone!"

Flattening himself against the wall, and vaguely registering that he was smearing it with blood, Grant peered around the corner and into the large living room. At the far end of the room, Hoffmeier had his back to Grant. Maggie and Nikki were each tied to a chair in front of him. Hoffmeier was leaning toward Nikki, running the hand not clutching his gun over her face, but his attention was entirely on Maggie.

Maggie's eyes suddenly widened, and he realized she'd spotted him. He ducked his head back around the corner just in case her reaction gave away his presence.

Dizziness hit again, and he closed his eyes briefly. Was he going to be able to help, or would he just get them all hurt?

Grant willed his body to hold out a little longer and carefully peeked around the corner again. There was no way he could use a gun right now, but he didn't need his arm for pure, brute force. He tried to signal Maggie, but had no idea if she knew what he was telling her.

"I don't want her," Hoffmeier told Maggie. "And now that you're here—" he gestured to her, tied up in the chair "—I don't need her."

Instead of the terror Hoffmeier had probably expected to see on Maggie's face, fury raced over her features. "What do you want?" she barked. "I'm here. But it sure seems like you're too scared to get close, even with me tied up."

"Maggie," Nikki whispered, but Maggie ignored her, her eyes lasered in on Hoffmeier.

Grant couldn't see his face, but his whole body visibly stiffened. "I didn't think you'd have figured out my name, but it was going to come out. It was always going to come out. I had everything planned out perfectly," he bragged, his gun hand drifting down as he talked to Maggie.

Although Maggie just continued glaring, Grant knew

her. She was waiting for him to get more distracted, to move the gun a little bit more away from Nikki.

"Your sister doesn't matter. She wasn't even part of the original plan, but she sure did make it easier when she showed up at your door. She really looks like you, you know? I was just going to leave her here, tied up, until someone came and got her. She would have been fine, but she's unimportant. Expendable, if you didn't follow my instructions, if I needed her to make you behave. Your boyfriend doesn't matter, either, although him I kind of wanted to kill. You belong to me!" He bellowed the last part.

"After ten years, I knew it was time. The perfect time." He laughed. "I never actually planned to wait until the first to come for you, but I needed you to believe that. We were going to have two perfect days together, and then I was going to call your brother on the first, tell him where to find us. On our anniversary."

In that instant, Grant realized the rest of Hoffmeier's plan. From the look on Maggie's face, so did she. This was his end game.

"We were going to be together forever, Maggie," Hoffmeier purred, and he moved a little more, obviously wanting to revel in Maggie's reaction to that news.

It was a huge mistake. And Grant knew Maggie. He knew she would take advantage of that error.

So the second he saw it, he didn't wait for her signal. He just raced as hard and as fast as he could into the room.

He watched Maggie's feet shoot out and lock around Hoffmeier's knees the instant he moved the gun off Nikki. She used her legs to yank him down hard.

Hoffmeier flew backward, his arms lurching up, and

his head smacked the floor as the gun blasted a hole in the ceiling, dumping plaster on top of him.

Tied up, Maggie didn't get her feet clear fast enough, and her chair slammed down, too, rolling sideways, right after Hoffmeier. He swore and swung his gun back around fast, looking furious and only a little disoriented from the fall.

Grant had a brief vision of Nikki uselessly fighting her bonds, of Maggie scrambling to right herself, before he pushed off and dived the final distance straight at Hoffmeier.

Chapter Seventeen

Grant landed on top of Hoffmeier, and he heard the air whoosh out of Hoffmeier's lungs. Then the gun blasted off again, with deafening effects, right beside Grant's ear.

His right shoulder screamed in pain as Grant reared back and smashed his left fist into the space between Hoffmeier's shoulder and his chest. Hoffmeier's eyes went wide with pain, but the gun didn't fall, so Grant hit again, swallowing back nausea at the movement.

This time, the gun dropped out of Hoffmeier's hand, but Hoffmeier got smart and twisted underneath Grant, smashing his own fist into Grant's wounded arm.

Searing pain raced down his arm and across his chest, and he was pretty sure something in his shoulder tore. Trying to ignore it, Grant flung his right arm wide, knocking Hoffmeier's pistol out of reach.

Blackness threatened at the edges of his vision, and something damp that had to be blood escaping his makeshift tourniquet splattered like big raindrops onto Hoffmeier. He willed his body to keep going, to stay conscious long enough to get rid of the threat, to get Maggie free.

Beside him, on the ground, he could hear Maggie frantically trying to get her arms unhooked from the chair, without success. Then she seemed to give up on it and just spun, pushing the chair backward so her feet were pointed toward him.

Grant used his good arm to propel himself up off Hoffmeier enough to give her a target, and she didn't hesitate. His whole body was wrenched sideways along with Hoffmeier as Maggie kicked up and out, meeting Hoffmeier's chin with her foot.

The strike effectively knocked both of them out of her reach, but it slowed Hoffmeier down, and Grant pushed up to his knees, trying to get another hit in.

Before he could, Hoffmeier recovered, shoving Grant off him. He scrambled to his feet, glanced at the gun in the corner, then back at Grant, who was hauling himself up on Nikki's chair.

It felt as if Grant was moving in slow motion, inch by painful inch, but he must still have seemed like a threat to Hoffmeier as he finally hauled himself to his feet.

Because instead of running for the gun, Hoffmeier glanced desperately at Maggie one last time, then swore and ran the other way, out the door.

"Grant! Grant!" Maggie sobbed.

He was staring in the direction Hoffmeier had disappeared, but it wasn't until he looked back at her that her fear subsided. His arm looked bad, but when Hoffmeier had hit him and the wound had opened up again, she'd thought he was going down for good.

He looked steadier on his feet now, and his shoulder had stopped bleeding. "How hurt are you?" she asked.

"I'll make it," he said, and dropped to his knees beside her.

"I didn't know if you—" she started.

"I know," he said, and his words slurred a little, then

he seemed to make a conscious effort to sharpen them. "I'm sorry. I couldn't let Hoffmeier see I was alive."

"My pocket," she said, moving closer so he could get access. "The knife."

"Got it," he said, and fumbled for it, finally getting the knife out and open.

As he cut awkwardly at the zip tie, she studied his face, looking for signs he was worse than he was telling her. Then she glanced at Nikki, still tied to the chair, who had silent tears running down her face.

"You okay?" Maggie asked.

"I'm fine," Nikki answered. "He didn't hurt me, he just hit me the one time to make me scream when..." She choked back tears. "I'm so sorry. And then he fired the rifle and..."

"It's okay," Grant told her. "I'm tougher than I look."

Nikki actually laughed a little through her tears, probably because Grant looked pretty tough. Then she stared at Maggie. "Are *you* okay?"

"I'm fine," Maggie said. It was Grant she was worried about. And Hoffmeier getting away, disappearing for another decade.

As soon as Grant got the zip ties sliced open, Maggie lurched for the landline, knowing that Grant needed help soon. Instead of calling an ambulance, she called Clive. "Where are you?"

"Two minutes out, max," he answered.

"Go faster," she begged. "Grant needs medical attention now. He was shot, and I need you to get him airlifted out of here to the closest hospital."

"I'll make it," Grant told her, giving her a weary-looking smile as he shuffled over to her sister on his knees and set the pen knife against her zip ties.

"Where's Hoffmeier?" Clive asked.

"He ran." She glanced at Grant, cutting her sister free, and then at the doorway. Could she wait for Clive? Or would Hoffmeier get away again? With his resources, would they ever find him?

She looked at the marble coffee table where he'd pressed her head a decade ago, and at the metal brand he'd made, still lying there.

Would he get away again, make a new brand? Keep trying to punish his family for their perceived wrongs against him? Keep hurting young women, to try and give himself some kind of sick power?

"Go," Grant said. "Get him. End this for good."

Over the phone, Clive said, "Here we come. We're at the drive."

"Go now," Grant said. "Don't let Hoffmeier get away."

The squeal of tires sounded outside, and Maggie jumped to her feet. She heard Grant's voice call after her, "Be careful," as she ran as fast as her feet would carry her out the door.

The living room opened up on the other side into an expansive kitchen, and the back door was hanging open. Maggie might have thought it was a trick, except the wide, flat land that had been a challenge before was now a benefit. She spotted him, running flat-out across the expansive field behind the house, away from the SWAT agents' vehicles descending on the front where his truck was parked.

He glanced back at her, and in that instant she realized she'd left her gun behind, that it was just her and Hoffmeier again. The way it was ten years ago.

She pushed down her emotional reaction and tried to think like the SWAT agent she'd become. She had the upper hand this time.

She took off as fast as she could after him, her combat

boots smashing through the thick, immaculately groomed grass. Her lungs burned as she pushed herself harder, and the distance between them began to close.

He looked back again, stumbled when he saw how close she was getting, and then turned, heading in the other direction, around the back of the house, toward an enormous man-made pond.

Maggie followed, and just as Hoffmeier looked as if he was going to change direction again, Maggie realized she was close enough. She pushed off and flew through the air toward him, landing hard and taking him down with her.

They crashed into the muddy ground at the edge of the pond, Maggie on Hoffmeier's back, and she scrambled to get to her knees. To push him down flat and get his arms behind his back. It occurred to her in that moment that she'd left her handcuffs back in the hotel room, but it didn't matter, because he suddenly flipped over, getting her beneath him.

"It's not finished," he panted, sounding out of breath and injured.

He was heavier than he looked, and with the back of his head pressed against her face, Maggie got a whiff of his expensive cologne, and it took her back ten years. The same smell, the same voice, the same man.

Instead of immobilizing her, it filled her with fury. "Yes, it is," she swore, pushing right back, trying to shove him off her. She thought she'd succeeded, but he managed to grab hold of her, and they both flipped over the edge of the pond.

She'd expected it to slope slowly downward, but instead it abruptly dropped off, and it was much deeper than she'd thought. Together, they sank down, and kept going, toward the muddy bottom.

Maggie twisted, trying to pull out of his grasp, but his other hand closed desperately around her arm, dragging her down with him. Her lungs screamed for air, and her eyes opened, filling instantly with water and grit.

She could make out Hoffmeier, not fighting to get back to the surface at all, just letting himself sink, trying to hold on to her.

Wrenching her legs in front of her body, she kicked hard, her feet connecting with his stomach. Air bubbles flooded all around her as his grip slipped, and she got free.

Knowing he wouldn't want to go down without her, Maggie swam hard for the surface, her muscles shaking now since she'd gone into the water without getting a breath. Finally, finally, she broke the surface.

She sucked in air over and over, coughing as she swam for the edge of the pond, not sure how they'd drifted so far so quickly. In the distance, she saw Clive running toward her.

She was close to the edge when he surfaced, gasping for air and grasping for her. His flailing arms gripped her hair, then slid down to the back of her neck as he pulled her under.

Maggie twisted frantically, turning to face him, and jammed her fist as hard as she could into his throat.

His eyes bulged, and his limbs thrashed as she watched him breathe in a mouthful of water.

She pushed for the surface, looking back in time to see his limbs slow then stop, and then he sank toward the bottom of the pond, his eyes and mouth wide and unmoving.

It was over. Maggie burst to the surface and gratefully drew in more air. She swam hard for the shore, until finally, her fingers dug into the dirt at the edge of the pond, and Clive was hauling her out of the water.

"Where's Hoffmeier?" he asked.

She blinked grit from her eyes and peered over the huge pond, toward the spot where he'd sunk. "He's gone."

"Good," Clive said. "Then we need to get back to the house. The medical helicopter is coming. Grant's in trouble."

"What?" She whipped her attention back to Clive.

"He lost a lot of blood. He needed a surgeon—and maybe a transfusion—ten minutes ago."

Maggie ran as fast as she could toward the house, still gasping for breath. Clive ran alongside her, and she could tell by his strides that she wasn't at her usual speed. She pushed harder, frantic to get back to Grant. She heard the roar of blades as the helicopter landed on the Hoffmeier estate's lawn.

Maggie watched two of her teammates race toward it, carrying an unconscious Grant between them. Nikki ran out after them, looking around until she spotted Maggie, then gestured for her sister to hurry.

Maggie ran faster, and Nikki gripped her arm, pushing her into the helicopter with Grant before it lifted off. The huge house faded below her, the forty-foot-wide pond soon becoming nothing more than a speck.

But Maggie barely noticed as she took Grant's limp hand in hers and sobbed, "You need to fight. I have something important to tell you, and you promised I'd get the chance as soon as this was all over."

Grant didn't move, his face and lips abnormally ashy, and Maggie held on tighter. "I love you," she said just as the monitor beside him let out a long, flat, final-sounding beep.

Epilogue

Maggie paced back and forth in the hospital waiting room until Nikki pushed her into a plastic chair.

"I should have stayed," Maggie said for what felt like the millionth time since they'd been in the Hoffmeier house two days ago. She'd gone over and over it in her mind, that moment she'd chosen to chase after Hoffmeier instead of staying beside Grant.

"He told you to go," Nikki reminded her. "So stop beating yourself up."

"She's right," Scott said, and Maggie glanced over at him, his hand clutching Chelsie's.

"You need to stop beating yourself up about all of it," Chelsie ordered. "And don't look at me like that. I'm fine."

Chelsie had been discharged a few hours earlier. She was moving more slowly, and she'd be off work for two weeks, but doctors didn't expect any lasting problems from her injury.

"Logan's fine, too," Ella put in, probably seeing guilt still on her face.

Maggie glanced from Ella to Logan, sitting close together on the uncomfortable hospital couch.

Logan nodded his agreement. "My injury just looked bad. But head wounds always bleed like crazy. And hey, we caught the three guys Hoffmeier paid off for those hits."

Maggie couldn't help smiling a little. Only someone in law enforcement could make light of having a bullet graze his head. But he was right—the injury itself had been minor, and he'd actually been released within a few hours.

"And it really worked out for me," Chelsie joked, wiggling her left hand, where a brand-new diamond sparkled.

Next to her, Scott rolled his eyes. "I already had the ring. But seeing you in the hospital, I just couldn't wait."

"See?" Nikki said. "Everyone is fine. And it's finally over."

"It will be," Maggie agreed.

Local police had dragged the Hoffmeier lake and found Jeff's body. And his family had been forcibly returned to DC to answer questions.

Apparently, Lorraine had been completely ignorant of her son's criminal activities. She'd simply thought he was spoiled and difficult. She'd had no idea he'd left DC ten years ago at her husband's insistence. She was back home in DC, cloistered alone in her house and avoiding the press camped out in her yard.

Frederik and Claudia were in custody, awaiting a hearing on bail. Clive predicted it would be denied, because of their resources and the amount of money they'd thrown at Jeff ten years ago, to make him go away. They were being charged as accessories in nine sexual assaults, and four assaults on law-enforcement officials, along with obstruction of justice, and a slew of other charges. Even if only some of them stuck, they'd pay.

Both had initially insisted they really thought Jeff had been in Europe the past ten years. But the Hoffmeiers were well-known in DC, and the story had broken quickly in the press. A witness had come forward, a friend of Claudia's from college, who'd said Claudia had tearfully confessed that she suspected her brother had raped Maggie. She'd confessed to telling her father, who'd changed the family logo and paid Jeff to stay away from them. Apparently, Claudia had gone back to that friend a few days later and said she was wrong, and that police had caught the real offender.

Back then, since Maggie was the first to be branded, and there were no other known victims, the friend had believed the story. Since Maggie's full name had always been kept out of the press accounts, she claimed she'd forgotten all about it until she saw the recent news.

Whether it was true or not, her going to police had broken Claudia's silence. There was some question to how much the Hoffmeier family actually knew, and how much they'd only suspected, but they'd known enough. They should have turned Jeff in a decade ago, and they could have prevented eight other women from going through what Maggie had. Instead, they'd changed the Hoffmeier Financial logo to get rid of the hook images that matched the brand on her neck. Instead, they had tried to protect the family business, and the family name.

Nikki squeezed her hand. "I talked to Mom and Dad this morning at the hotel. Apologized for telling them I was spending the week with friends, instead of letting them know I was coming here. I know they told you when they got here, but they are really proud of you, you know? For getting through this. For finding the guy and stopping him for good."

Maggie smiled back at her, but her feet tapped nervously on the floor of the surgical area waiting room. What was taking so long?

"He'll be here," Scott said.

Then the door to the waiting room opened, and he was. Maggie sensed everyone getting to their feet, but she couldn't be certain, because she was already running across the room. She stopped just in front of Grant, resisting the urge to throw her arms around his neck and just hang on and never let go.

He looked awful. His skin was still a little ashy, and pain was etched on his face, his right shoulder looking lumpy under his hospital gown from the bandages. The nurse pushed his wheelchair into the room and as soon as she left, he scolded, "Don't look at me like that. If all goes well, they'll release me tomorrow. I'll be kicking down doors with SWAT again in no time."

He winked at her, and Maggie felt a grin break free, then she did lean down and throw her arms around his neck, only lightly, barely touching him.

He squeezed back, with more strength than she'd expected after having his heart shocked back into rhythm on the helicopter, then being rushed here for a blood transfusion and surgery to repair his shoulder.

"How long?" she asked him, leaning back to look at his face.

"Probably six months," he replied. "The shoulder is going to need some rehabilitation."

Most SWAT agents would be furious at that much time away from the team, at the prospect of that much work to get back into fighting shape. But this was Grant, and he said it not only like a guarantee he'd do it, but with his typical good-natured attitude.

Nothing ever kept him down. It was one of the things she loved best about him.

At that moment, she realized he'd never even heard her say it. He'd almost died for her and Nikki, and he didn't really know how she felt about him.

She must have gone pale, because he said, "It's okay. I have a plan."

"What's your plan?" Scott asked him. "You taking some time off to heal, and having Clive hold the spot for you on the team?"

"Not exactly," Grant said, looking up at her.

He patted the chair next to where the nurse had left his wheelchair, and Maggie sat, as he folded her hand in his. It was funny how natural that already felt.

"You're not leaving SWAT?" she asked. "Because I—"

"No." He twisted a little in his chair so he was facing her. "But I talked to Martin two weeks ago." He was the leader of the second SWAT team at WFO. "One of his guys is transferring to the LA field office in April, and I asked about taking that spot."

"No," Maggie said. "You waited so long to get on a team. It's not fair that you be the one to—"

"I talked to Clive last week, too," he said. "I told him I wasn't going to be able to stay with the team. I didn't say why—I figured I'd wait until you and I talked about it first—but he knew."

Maggie blushed at the idea that the team already knew what was happening between her and Grant before she'd had the chance to tell them, but they were practically family. It shouldn't have surprised her. "Did Martin guarantee you a spot on his team?" She held her breath.

"No."

"Then I should be the one—"

"But he'll give it to me," Grant insisted. "As soon as I get through rehab and can prove to him my shoulder's back to one hundred percent." He brought her hand up to his lips and pressed a kiss to it. "It's perfect timing, Maggie. I should be through the rehab right when a spot opens up. I'll get it."

She grinned at him, not believing they might actually be able to date and still both have a place in SWAT. Although she'd miss running into missions with him by her side. "Are you sure?"

"I'm determined," he said. "I don't give up on something I want." He smiled back at her and asked, "It worked on you, didn't it?"

"Oh, yeah." She leaned in to kiss him, and just before her lips met his, she corrected, "But I think it was me who went after you until you couldn't resist any longer."

His mouth covered hers, showing her that determination. When he kissed her like that, she could almost forget he'd been shot. She could almost forget all of it. When he kissed her, there was a lightness in her soul that she'd never had before.

"Mmm," she mumbled against his mouth a few minutes later. "Don't ever stop that."

He smiled back at her, a glint in his eyes that promised he'd do more than that as soon as he healed up.

Suddenly remembering where they were, Maggie glanced over her shoulder and saw that everyone had cleared out to give them a little privacy.

But she didn't need it. She was ready to tell everyone, including the Bureau, that she and Grant were forming their own team now.

Before she could say it to him, he stroked his hand down her cheek and asked, "How are you doing?"

She knew exactly what he was asking. Four hours had passed while she'd waited frantically to hear about Grant's condition. Another two days had gone by while she sat in this waiting room with Scott, Nikki, Ella, Chelsie and Logan for Grant to be well enough to leave ICU.

Now it was September 1. A day she'd never thought

would be anything but painful, even after they'd finally caught Hoffmeier for good.

She squeezed his hand and told him honestly, "It's a good day today. A really good day."

He leaned down to kiss her again, and she pressed a finger to his lips. "You haven't let me finish what I was trying to tell you before," she told him softly.

Realization washed over his features, then a slow smile spread across his face, even before she said, "I love you, Grant."

Then he did kiss her again, and his lips were full of promise.

Today was the first day of a new start for her. A fresh new life with Grant, and she was going to grab hold with both hands and never let go.

*   *   *   *   *

THE SAFEST LIES

DEBRA WEBB

This book is dedicated to my two beautiful daughters. Like the heroine in this book, you are strong, amazing women!

Chapter One

Winchester, Tennessee
Friday, August 9

Sadie Buchanan had never been to Winchester before. The closest she'd come was Tullahoma and that had been years ago when she was first assigned to the Nashville area. A joint task force conference at the Arnold Air Force base had required her attendance for a day. Frankly, it was unusual for an agent to end up in this area, much less request a retrieval. The kind of trouble that required her participation rarely happened in small towns. Most of her assignments took her to the larger metropolitan areas around the state or deep into the desert or the mountains.

In any event, whenever an agent was in trouble, she went in.

She parked in front of the Franklin County sheriff's office. Extracting agents from dangerous situations hadn't exactly been a part of her plan when she started her career, but within two years of her first field assignment she found herself doing exactly that after one particular mission. The assignment as well as the agent involved had been high profile, garnering her the full attention of the powers that be. During that fateful mission she as well as the Bureau discovered her knack for getting in and out with particular ease. From that point forward, she had been focused on training for moments like this one. It wasn't the sort of task just any agent felt comfortable doing. Success required a very particular skill set.

Go in, attain the target and get out alive.

Her father always said that everyone had a gift. Evidently, this was hers. It hadn't failed her yet. She had no intention of allowing it to start today.

Inside the brick building that housed the sheriff's department and county jail, a female desk sergeant greeted her.

"Special Agent Sadie Buchanan." Sadie showed her credentials to the other woman. "I'm here to see Sheriff Tanner and Agent Ross."

"Good morning, Agent Buchanan. Down the hall and to the left," Sergeant Rodriquez said with a gesture toward the long corridor beyond her desk. "They're waiting for you in the conference room, ma'am."

Sadie thanked the sergeant and headed in the direction she'd indicated. One thing she had noticed about Winchester already and it was barely ten o'clock in the morning—it was a couple of degrees hotter than Nashville. The town was attractive in a quaint sort of way, surrounded by a lake and bordered by hills and woods. Most folks would see those hills and woods as nature's perfect landscape. What Sadie saw in all that natural beauty were places to hide. Lots and lots of potential hiding places.

Not a good thing when attempting to locate a target.

She opened the door to the conference room and walked in. Four people waited for her but only one that she recognized: Special Agent Deacon Ross. He, too, was assigned to Nashville. They'd only worked together on one occasion, but he had a stellar reputation. The last she'd heard he had taken an extended leave of absence.

Maybe the rumors that he might not be coming back were just that—rumors. He certainly appeared to be involved in this case.

"Agent Buchanan," a tall, dark-haired man at the head of the table said as he stood, "I'm Sheriff Colt Tanner. We're glad you could come." He extended his hand.

Sadie gave his hand a shake. "Happy to help, Sheriff."

"This is Chief of Police Billy Brannigan." Tanner gestured to another man. This one had brown hair and eyes and looked as much like a cowboy as the sheriff.

Brannigan extended his hand across the conference table. "Good to meet you, Agent Buchanan."

"Likewise, Chief." Sadie accepted the gesture and turned to the next man in the room. "Agent Ross." She offered her hand.

Ross gave her hand a shake and then turned to the woman at his side. "This is Cecelia Winters."

Sadie extended her hand once more, this time toward the petite woman with the fiery mane of red hair. "Ms. Winters."

Winters brushed her palm briefly against Sadie's but didn't speak. Since she had the same last name as the target, Sadie assumed she was a wife or other family member.

"Why don't we have a seat and get started," Ross suggested.

Sadie pulled out a chair and sat down as the others resumed their seats. A couple of files and a stack of maps lay on the table. Not exactly the typical setup for a tactical mission briefing but she'd gotten the impression this one was different than her usual assignment. She didn't have a problem with different. As long as it didn't get anyone killed. Sadie was yet to lose a target once she had attained him or her.

"I imagine," Ross said, "you were briefed on the situation we have."

"I only just returned to Nashville late last night from an assignment in Memphis. I'm afraid the details I received are sketchy at best. I assumed I would be fully briefed when I arrived."

This would certainly be her first briefing with a civilian present who was totally unrelated to the official aspects of the investigation. She had a feeling this assignment was going to become more and more unusual.

"A particular group of extremists in the Franklin County area was pinpointed more than two decades ago. Gunrunning was suspected to be a major part of this group's activities. Over the past few years suspicions of their involvement with kidnapping, possibly related to human trafficking, have surfaced. My former partner, Jack Kemp, investigated this group when it was first discovered but at the time there was not enough substantial evidence that the members were involved in anything criminal or illegal to pursue any sort of operation. Just over nine years ago that status changed, and Jack came back for a second look. During the course of that assignment he disappeared. Recently, new information about what happened to him has come to light. In part, that information was obtained through a civilian informant. Like most of us, Jack worked with a number of civilian informants."

"One of those informants is Levi Winters," Sheriff Tanner added. "Levi has recently gone missing and we suspect this group may be involved."

Brannigan didn't add anything. Sadie was undecided as to whether his continued silence was a good thing. Perhaps his involvement was only for informational purposes. The target was likely outside his official jurisdiction.

"Is the Bureau opening a new case in the area?"

Seemed a no-brainer. But Sadie was not up to speed on the happenings in Franklin County. The more Ross talked, the more she understood that he had friends in high places and that was why she was here. "Or is this one off the record?"

The men in the room exchanged a look, which answered the question without anyone having to say a word.

"To a degree," Ross admitted, "the retrieval is off the record. There appears to be some hesitation about reopening the case involving the group known as Resurrection. Personally, I think we're caught in the middle of a war between the Bureau and the ATF, leaving us blind. We're hoping any information Levi may have will help pull this all together. But," he qualified, "finding him is our primary goal."

Making it doubly important that she brought him back alive. Sadie considered the other woman at the table. The hope in her eyes was impossible to miss. Right now, Sadie could walk away and that decision would not adversely affect her career since this mission was off the record. She could stand up, walk out that door and never look back rather than risk her life for some informant whom she did not know and had no idea if he was actually credible.

Chances were, if she made that decision, the informant would die.

And though that decision would not prove unfavorable to her career, it would prove immensely unfavorable to her conscience.

"Let's have a look at what I'm up against."

Tanner went first. He explained that he had not en-countered any trouble with members of this group—at least none of which he was aware. The members of the so-called Resurrection group were anonymous. Any who lived amid the community kept quiet about their involvement. Neighbors, friends, possibly even family had no idea about their participation. The tac-tic was actually fairly common and had been used for centuries by one secret group or another.

Brannigan spoke for the first time, agreeing with Tanner's summation. The Winchester Police De-partment had not run into trouble with anyone who claimed to be or who was thought to be involved with this extremist group. The crime rate in the county was comparatively low. Rumors regarding the group known as Resurrection leaned toward the idea of ex-treme or doomsday-type preppers. Part of the prob-lem was that there appeared to be an offshoot fringe group known only as the *others* who were far more dangerous. More primitive and violent.

Ross took over from there. "We've contacted a source within the ATF but we don't have anything back from him just yet. He can only help us so much without crossing a line. Whatever else we do, we can't keep waiting and risk losing Winters. Ulti-mately, the hope is that the Bureau and the ATF will initiate a joint task force, along with local law enforcement, to look more thoroughly into what this group is doing. As I said, for now, our immediate focus is on extracting Winters."

Sadie understood perfectly. "If the Resurrection or this offshoot group has him, we need to get their attention. Obviously—" she scanned the faces at the table "—you don't have the location where he's being held."

Tanner tapped the stacks of maps. "There are certain areas we feel are the more likely places but, no, we don't have a damned clue."

"And there's no time to conduct the kind of search required to locate a needle in a haystack," Sadie suggested. "Time is our enemy." She set her gaze on Ross's, knowing he would understand the goal. "We need their attention. I would recommend a news bulletin about a missing federal agent last seen in the Winchester area. Keep it ambiguous for obvious reasons. Give my description but not my name." She shifted her attention to Tanner. "I'll start with the most likely place and beat the bushes until they find me."

"You want them to find you?" Tanner looked uneasy as he asked the question.

"We don't have time to locate and infiltrate any other way. Prompting them to find me will be much faster and far more efficient."

"Isn't that far more dangerous, as well?" Brannigan asked.

"Yes." Sadie saw no point in whitewashing the answer. "But it's the only way to accomplish our goal in a timely manner."

"Agent Buchanan is highly trained for exactly these sorts of situations," Ross assured all present.

Judging by the expressions Tanner and Brannigan wore, his assurance did little to alleviate their reservations.

"You're suggesting going in without backup," Brannigan argued. "The only thing I see coming of that is two hostages needing extraction."

Sadie acknowledged his assessment with a nod. "That is a possibility. But, Chief, you can trust me when I say, if I wasn't experienced and completely confident about this situation, we wouldn't be having this conversation. I know what I'm doing. I understand the risk and, based on what I've heard so far, I am not overly concerned."

"I may be able to help."

All gathered around the table turned to the woman who had spoken. Cecelia Winters looked directly at Sadie even as the men in the room started to argue with her announcement.

"Not happening," Ross stated unconditionally, tension in his voice, his posture and the set of his jaw.

"He's right," Tanner agreed with a firm shake of his head.

"This whole thing is far too risky as it is," Brannigan added.

Sadie ignored them all. Instead, she focused on

the woman who had made the statement. "How do you believe you can help?"

Cecelia blinked at Sadie's question. "The people in this town know me. They know what happened to me—to my family. Nothing is secret anymore. If I spread the news, they'll believe me. They will pass it along far more quickly than something reported in the news. Not everyone around here trusts the news."

"Cece," Ross argued, "your getting involved could only complicate matters."

Sadie got the picture now. Ross and Cecelia were a couple. He didn't want her anywhere near the line of fire. A personal connection more often than not spelled trouble when it came to an assignment like this one.

"Help from most any source can be useful, but Ross could be right," Sadie said, not to change the woman's mind but because it was true.

The hard look Ross sent her way shouted loud and clear that he wasn't happy with how she had responded to the offer. Too bad. He wanted Sadie to do a job, an extraction—a very risky extraction. Why wouldn't she use any available resources?

"Levi is my brother," Cecelia said. "I want to help." She glanced at Ross. "I need to help."

"You understand that when this is over, there could be a backlash?" Sadie needed her to comprehend the long-term ramifications of any step she might opt to take. Sadie didn't like getting civilians involved but it seemed as if this one was already eyeball deep in the situation.

"I do. The past decade of my life has been one long backlash. I think I can handle a little more."

Ross obviously didn't think so.

Sadie stared directly at him. "Is this going to be a problem for you?"

She didn't like problems. Especially those that came from the people who were supposed to be on her side.

He held her gaze for a moment before saying, "I guess not."

"Good." Sadie turned back to Cecelia. "You tell whomever you believe will get the word out the fastest that the agent who was working with your brother showed up and was going around town asking questions." She shrugged. "Trying to help, but now she's suddenly gone missing and you're worried about her."

Cecelia nodded. "I can do that."

"The most likely starting place?" Sadie asked, looking from one man to the next.

"The church," Ross said. He glanced at Cecelia as he spoke. "We have reason to believe the Salvation Survivalists were working with the primary group in some capacity. They were housing weapons most likely intended for the Resurrection group, but we don't have solid evidence of that conclusion. The ATF is looking at that aspect along with numerous others but, as we've established, they're taking too damned long and they're not sharing."

"But you're certain the two are or were connected."

"We are," Ross said.

Tanner and Brannigan agreed, as well.

"Then that's where I'll start." To Cecelia she said, "You put the word out about me asking questions." She shifted her attention to Tanner. "Make sure the local news reports a missing federal agent. No name, just a description," she reminded.

Tanner nodded. "I can make that happen."

"I'd like to familiarize myself with maps of the area, particularly around the church."

Ross spread the maps on the conference table and started the briefing regarding landscape. Sadie took her time and carefully committed the maps to memory. One of the things that made her good at her job was her ability to memorize maps and recall landmarks. For a girl who grew up in the city, she was a damned good tracker. As good as any hunter she'd ever worked with and she'd worked with a few.

More than anything, she paid attention. The old saying that it was all in the details was more often true than not. The details were crucial. One didn't need a photographic memory to recall the details. She just had to pay attention.

"What about the church?" Sadie considered the map of the area around the church, which appeared to be well outside town. "I need some additional history on the church."

"My father started the church about thirty-five years ago," Cecelia explained. "He was a very cruel man, capable of anything. He had many devoted followers who turned to my older brother, Marcus, after our father's murder. There are those who still believe one or both to be messiahs of a sort. I'm confident the most deeply devoted know far more than they've shared. If they hear about you, you better believe the word will go where you want it."

Ross pushed a folder in Sadie's direction. "This will give you a good overview of what we know. It's not complete by any means, but it's as much as anyone knows."

Sadie opened the file and skimmed the first page. "I'd like some time to go over what you have and then I'll drive out to the church, hide my car and start digging around. If I'm lucky, someone will come looking for me in short order."

"For the record," Chief of Police Brannigan spoke up again, "I still think this is a bad idea."

Sadie wished she could convince him otherwise but to an extent he was correct. This was most likely a bad idea.

But their options were limited. Sometimes the bad ideas were the only feasible ones.

Chapter Two

Dusk was settling way too fast. Sadie had knocked on doors in the vicinity of the church—not that there were that many. She'd asked straightforward questions, calling the group she sought by name. Then she'd driven to the now-defunct church of the Salvation Survivalists and she'd started poking around.

Breaking in had been a breeze. The ATF and the FBI had gone through the building numerous times and though every entrance had been secured, the lock on the back door was damaged. All of ten seconds were required to rip the crime scene seal away and finagle the thing open. As easy as taking candy from a baby.

It was possible a couple of days might be required to garner the attention she sought. Not good for her target. Levi Winters might not have a couple of days. On the other hand, it was possible he wasn't a hostage at all and was happily ensconced among friends deep within this suspicious group. His sister, Cecelia, was convinced he was a hostage, but sisters didn't always know the whole story.

Sadie's sister certainly did not.

She and her sister had never been friends. Maybe it was the ten years that separated them in age or the fact that her sister had chosen a path Sadie despised. Pricilla Buchanan was a criminal defense attorney. Her entire existence was focused on undoing what law enforcement personnel like Sadie risked their lives to do. Of course their mother insisted they were both angels, but she was wrong. Their mother wanted to see good in everyone. Pricilla was not good. She was self-centered, self-serving and indifferent when it came to justice.

Sadie kicked aside thoughts of her older sister as she strolled the halls of the extremist church whose followers still refused to speak ill of their most recent infamous leader. The man, Cecelia Winters's older brother as it turned out, had been hiding smuggled guns. He'd sworn he had no idea how the weapons had ended up in the secret underground hiding place beneath the church. He'd gone so far as to attempt to claim the weapons had been there since before his father died almost nine years ago. Talk about a scumbag. Then again, apparently his father had been an even bigger lowlife.

Ross and the others suspected Marcus Winters had been holding the stockpile of weapons for the Resurrection. Despite the seriousness of the charges he faced, Winters refused to spill his guts. Whomever Marcus Winters was protecting he was too damned afraid to make a deal, even for the promise of a new life in witness protection.

The moment he'd been arrested he had shut down like a dying cell phone battery and hadn't spoken since.

Anything that might provide clues about a connection between the church and the gunrunning extremist prepper group was long gone. The tunnel between the church and the Winters home was set for demolition. Cecelia mentioned that she intended to sell the place the moment it was released from evidence. She wanted to wash her hands of that ugly past as soon as possible and who could blame her? Based on what Ross had told Sadie, the woman had already paid a high price for standing up against her family.

Sadie followed the directions she'd been given to find the tunnel area. Mostly she was killing time. The longer she hung out in the area the more likely she was to run into what she was looking for. At least that was the hope. If she were really lucky things would happen as quickly as she hoped.

Ross had given her a piece of information to use as leverage once she had infiltrated the group. His contact from the ATF insisted this would be immensely useful. She'd gone into missions with less, but this felt a little slim by any measure.

The entrance to the tunnel was barricaded. Sadie turned and headed back in the direction she'd come.

She took the stairs two at a time and returned to the church's main sanctuary.

There was nothing else to be done here. She turned for the front entrance and stalled. A man sat on the very back pew. His hair was gray—not the white gray, the silver gray. It poked from beneath a fedora. A full beard did a hell of a job of camouflaging his face. He wore overalls and a button-down, long-sleeved shirt, no matter that it was as hot as hell outside. It was difficult to assess if he was armed. Her view of him from the chest down was blocked by the back of the pew in front of him. From a merely visual perspective he appeared reasonably harmless.

Sadie, however, was too smart to assume any such thing based on appearances.

"You must be that missing fed."

Though he said this in a low, rusty-with-age voice, it seemed to echo in the hollow sanctuary. Not particularly threatening and yet with simmering power.

"That's me. Sadie Buchanan."

"I hear you and a fed friend of yours have been looking for me."

Obviously, he meant Deacon Ross. "I don't know about anyone else and I definitely don't have any friends around here, but I've been looking for someone. That's a fact. Can't say whether that someone is you."

She dared to walk toward him, one step at a time down that long center aisle. The rubber soles of her hiking boots were quiet on the wood floor.

"What is it you think you're looking for, Ms. Buchanan? Or should I call you Agent Buchanan?"

Sadie sat down at the pew in front of him, turned in the hard seat to face him. "Sadie is fine. After yesterday, I doubt that anyone considers me an agent anymore—except maybe for the purposes of prosecution."

The story that she was an agent on the run was the best cover she could come up with given the circumstances and the shortness of time.

"Nine years. Stellar record. Up for promotion," he said, his gaze steady on hers, "the way I hear it. That's a lot to give up for whatever it is that brought you here, Sadie."

So the man had friends in the right places. Only a handful of people in this town knew her name and none beyond the four with whom she had met in the sheriff's conference room were aware of her background. She shrugged. "I should have gotten that promotion two years ago. And you're right, nine years is a long time to watch men like my SAIC write his own definition of justice. Besides, my daddy was a firm believer in a man—or woman—having the right to live his life the way he wanted and to bear arms. I suppose I have him to thank for my hard-headedness."

The man's gaze hardened. "As interesting as this conversation might prove to be, I don't like wasting my time, Sadie. Why don't you tell me what it is you think I need to hear?"

"I appreciate that you looked me up, Mister…?"

"Prentiss," he said, "Rayford Prentiss."

"Mr. Prentiss," she acknowledged. "The trouble is—and I mean no offense to you—I really need to speak with the man in charge. It's urgent. We don't have a lot of time."

He held her gaze for a long moment of thickening silence. "You don't look like the sort with a death wish," he finally said.

Sadie smiled. "Not if I can help it. What I have, Mr. Prentiss, is some information about a joint task force mission that will prove more than a little devastating to the Resurrection. If you and your friends take me in, I'll give you the heads-up you need to survive the storm that's coming—assuming you know what I'm talking about and have the authority to take me where I need to go."

A crooked smile lifted one corner of his bearded mouth. "First, I know precisely what you mean and I have all the authority I need. The real question is, why on God's green earth would I believe that foolish story?"

"Well, my motive is somewhat personal, Mr. Prentiss. I will tell you that I've gotten myself into a bit of trouble and I don't see any ready way out, so this looks like as good an option as any other. My daddy always said planning for the future was smart business. I need to disappear for a little while, Mr. Prentiss. I think you and your friends can make that happen. You do me a favor and I'll do one for you."

Prentiss chuckled. "I really am flummoxed, Sadie. You appear quite sincere and yet I'm not certain I believe you. Be that as it may, we'll play your little game. After all, it took considerable courage to start this thing." His gaze settled heavily on her and this time there was no mistaking the promise there. "Rest assured, whatever this is, if you're lying to me, you will not like how this ends."

"Great." Sadie pushed a smile into place and sat up straight. "Then we have a deal."

Another of those long moments of silence elapsed with him staring at her. "It appears we do."

He raised a hand and people seemed to come out of the woodwork. Four men, all armed. "My friends will see to your transportation. Goodbye, Sadie."

When he stood and walked away, she couldn't help wondering if this mission would end right here, right now. These guys could kill her and no one would ever know exactly what happened, much less who did the deed.

Wasn't that the way it always was?

The door closed behind Prentiss and she stood, glanced from fierce face to fierce face. "So, who's driving?"

"Take off your clothes," the one nearest her said.

She laughed. "I never take off my clothes on the first date."

He aimed his weapon at her. "Take them off now."

One of his pals stepped forward and tossed a bag on the floor at the end of her pew.

"There are clothes in the bag," the one who appeared to be in charge and who held his aim steady on her announced.

"Well, if you insist."

Taking her time she toed off her boots, peeled off her socks, then unbuttoned her shirt. When the shirt, the boots and socks were in a neat pile next to the provided bag, she shucked her jeans and added them to the pile next.

When she reached for the bag, the man with the gun at the ready protested, "Everything comes off."

She figured that would be his next order. Sadie reached behind her and unhooked her bra. She allowed it to fall forward and drop to the pile. Then she swooped off her panties and added them unceremoniously to the rest.

The man nodded and she reached for the bag. Inside was a pair of gray sweatpants and a white tee. No underwear. No socks. Thankfully there was a pair of plastic flip-flops. The cheap kind found in bins near the checkout counter at discount stores. She donned the provided outfit and slipped her feet into the flip-flops.

The man who'd brought the bag grabbed her things and put them into the empty bag. She hated that her cell phone was in that bag. Besides a gun, it was the asset she depended upon most.

Oh well.

"Let's go." The man with a bead on her motioned

with the barrel of his weapon toward the back of the church.

"What about my car?" she asked as they marched toward the rear exit.

"A friend will pick it up and dismantle it for parts."

She stalled and glared at the man. Was he out of his mind? "Wait just a minute. That car cost—"

"You won't need it where you're going."

THE DRIVE TO their destination took half an hour, give or take a minute.

Sadie had counted off the seconds and minutes, in part to distract herself from the sorts of thoughts that wanted to crowd into her brain. But mostly because it was important to maintain a sense of location. Half an hour from the church was a reference anyone coming to her rescue could use to facilitate the task.

Except there was no one coming. This mission was basically off the books. Ross and his friends would get worried when they didn't hear from her in a couple of days but there wasn't a whole lot they could do other than beat the bushes and rattle a few cages looking for her. Finding her would be difficult if not impossible. The tracking devices in her cell phone, in the soles of her shoes and in her bra were who knew where. Unless someone had been watching her and followed this caravan, she was probably out of luck as far as backup was concerned.

Frankly, she had been surprised by their vehicles. She'd expected big four-wheel-drive trucks caked with mud and decked out with gun racks. But that wasn't the case at all. The two vehicles were both new top-of-the-line SUVs. Sure, they were four-wheel drive, but they were sleek and almost elegant looking—unlike the men inside.

The younger of the group had been tasked with her personal security. He'd secured her hands behind her back and dropped a cloth bag over her head. He sat in the back seat with her. Another one drove. The other two men were in the second vehicle, with Prentiss, no doubt. No one in this vehicle had said a word en route. Music had played just loud enough to prevent her from noting another reference—any sounds in the areas they drove through. Animals, trains, construction, whatever.

When the vehicle rolled to a stop and the engine cut off, the music died. The doors opened and low voices rumbled around her. Beyond the voices was quiet. No city sounds. No traffic sounds. Not even any animals.

Fingers wrapped around her upper arm and tugged her from the center section of the back seat. A hand guided her feet so she wouldn't break her neck climbing out. When she was steady on the ground the sack was dragged from her head.

Her first thought was that she had gone back in time. The towering stone walls made her think of the ones surrounding a castle she'd visited in Edinburgh,

Scotland. The walls were massive, at least thirty feet high. There were what appeared to be guard towers built into the wall. A large, square stone structure stood in the center of the expansive grounds that were like a quad on a college campus without all the fancy landscape. Like the primitive keeps she'd seen in her travels, the windows were tiny in proportion. There were other buildings beyond the larger one, but she could only see the rooftops in the distance.

She stared overhead. Frowned. There was no sky.

She scanned what should have been the sky for as far as she could see. Steel and some sort of panels stood high above her. Reminded her of a massive warehouse. But no clouds or sun or anything else that said *sky*.

Wherever they were, they were not outside. But the SUVs had rolled to a stop right here. She glanced over her shoulder at the one she'd only just emerged from. The ride had seemed to stay on level ground. There had been no downhill or uphill movement. The ride had been smooth but not so smooth that she wouldn't have noticed a change in elevation. There could have been an elevator somewhere that brought them below ground. But that didn't seem right, either, since they hadn't stopped long enough to roll into any sort of elevator until a minute ago, when the engines shut off and they got out.

The man behind her nudged her forward with the muzzle of his weapon. She took in as much of what she could see as possible, committed it to memory as they moved forward. Wherever they were, the place was certainly fortified for battle. If they were underground as she suspected, she supposed the purpose was for surviving a nuclear attack. Additionally, being underground would explain why the feds and local law enforcement hadn't already spotted the compound from the air.

By the time they rounded the corner of the largest building she'd seen so far, only two of the men remained with her. Prentiss and the other two had gone in a different direction. The one with the gun at her back kept her moving forward with the occasional nudge. Beyond the large building were increasingly smaller ones. Along the east side of the wall the smallest structures were numbered. They sat in a long row like cabin rentals at the lake. Only there was no lake—not that she'd seen so far anyway—and this was no vacation. The long, low building that stood the farthest west from the center of the grounds had no windows and appeared to be their destination. The squat roofline told her it was one story. She saw only one entrance along the front, assuming what she was looking at was the front.

The second of the two guards unlocked and opened the door. Number one nudged her to go in. The guards followed close behind her. An immediate left took them down a long white corridor lined with doors on either side. No windows on the doors, either. Midway down the corridor, they stopped at a door and number two guard unlocked it with a few clicks of the keys on the control pad. Once the thick door pulled outward, Sadie understood this would be her accommodations for now. Until they decided what to do with her, she imagined.

"I'm supposed to be meeting with the man in charge," she reminded number one.

"Tomorrow."

The door slammed in her face.

She turned around. A dim light came from around the perimeter of the room. There was a steel cot, a toilet hanging on the wall with a sink formed in the tank. Just like the ones she had seen in the few prison cells she'd visited.

With a quick drawing back of the covers, she checked the mattress, ensured the sheets weren't tainted with anything she could see or smell. Fabric smelled clean enough. She paced the small room and considered her options. There had been four men with Prentiss. She hadn't seen any others when they arrived but that didn't mean there weren't hundreds around here somewhere. There was no accurate body count for this group.

If the Resurrection was like most of these extremist groups, there would be several hundred on-site. This was obviously a headquarters. The setup was too good to be anything else. The Bureau had been gathering information on extremist groups like this for decades. But this one had somehow managed to stay under the radar. The members didn't talk. Fear, she imagined. It was human nature to talk about the things in which one was interested. Being a part of something like Resurrection would typically provide bragging rights for those who had a penchant for the extreme. But there was no bragging from these members.

Their silence made them even more dangerous. Restricted the available intelligence to gather, making the jobs of Sadie and others like her far more difficult. Law enforcement personnel depended upon informants and the information garnered on the streets. When information stopped flowing, it was impossible to find footing in a given situation.

Sadie braced her hands on her hips and moved around the room again, this time more slowly. She considered the walls, thought about the door when it had opened. The walls were likely made of concrete just as the door was. Thick concrete, eight inches at least. The floor and ceiling of this building appeared to be the same as the walls. The smooth, cold finish of the concrete was interrupted only by the small blocks of light around the walls near the floor. The cot was metal, the sheets a thin material more like paper than fabric. No good for constructing a hangman's noose. She turned back to the door. The lock wasn't the usual residential sort. It was electronic and required a code.

Getting out of here wouldn't be easy. If she was really lucky, Levi Winters was in this same building. Assuming he was a hostage. Hopefully, he would know a way out and would be willing to go with her.

That was the problem with being underground or, perhaps, burrowed into a mountainside. Getting out was generally somewhat complicated.

She'd been in tighter spots, Sadie reminded herself.

All she had to do was find her target and she would locate a way out of here.

It was what she did.

Chapter Three

The woman was trouble.

Smith Flynn studied the screen monitoring her movements. She paced the six-by-eight cell as if the journey might end some other way the next time she turned around. She hadn't stopped since being placed inside. This restless behavior was for the benefit of anyone observing.

He had watched her arrival. She had walked into the compound, shoulders back, chin held high, all the while discreetly surveying everything in her field of vision. Sadie Buchanan was neither afraid nor uncertain. Her arrival at this compound was not by accident any more than was the timing of her appearance. She was on a mission.

Whatever she was doing here, unfortunately she was his issue now.

He did not like unexpected issues. Even fearless, attractive ones like Sadie Buchanan.

"What's your take on this new development?"

The voice drew Smith from his musings. He

turned to Prentiss. The older man had been running the group known as the Resurrection for a very long time. He rarely had much to say but when he spoke anyone within hearing distance listened—not because he was so articulate or interesting, but because they wanted to live. Prentiss did not take disrespect well.

"She has an agenda," Smith said, not telling the other man anything he didn't already know. "It'll take some time to determine what that agenda is."

Prentiss nodded, his attention fixed on the screen. "I don't like killing women. There's something innately wrong with a man killing a woman. It's a sin like no other, except for killing a child. Any man who would kill a woman or a child is lower than low." His gaze swung to Smith. "But, if you tell me she's lying, I will kill her."

Smith didn't waste time pretending to consider the situation. "I can tell you right now that she *is* lying. No question there." He turned his attention back to the screen. "The question is why. We'll need that answer before you kill her."

Prentiss nodded. "You're right. Until we have the answer, she belongs to you. Do with her what you will, just get the truth for me."

"I always do."

The old man stood and headed for the door. Smith waited until the door closed before turning back to the screen. He wondered if this woman had any idea just how much trouble she was in. Whatever she thought she'd come here to do, she had made a most regrettable mistake.

He exited his cabin, locking the door behind him, and crossed to the detention center. No one questioned his movements. They knew better. The door was unlocked and opened for him as if he was a king. Once inside he said to the guard, "I'll be using interview room two for an hour or so. Bring me Levi Winters."

"Yes, sir."

The guard hustled away to do Smith's bidding. Smith took the short corridor on the right and then an immediate left where six interview rooms waited. Each room was equipped with very specific instruments for persuading answers from those who had the misfortune of ending up in one of the spaces. Before going to interview room two, he stepped into the observation room and checked the monitoring system.

Two minutes elapsed before the guard entered interview room two. He settled the prisoner Levi Winters into the chair on the side of the metal table facing the hidden camera. Once Winters was secured to the bolt in the concrete floor, the guard exited. Smith considered Winters for a longer moment. He was younger than this woman who'd gotten herself invited to this ultrasecure place.

More important than any other aspect of this prisoner, he was scared. Scared to death.

THEY WERE PROBABLY going to kill him now.

Levi's whole body felt as cold as ice. There was no telling what they had planned for him this time. That bastard Flynn had done things to him, made him talk when he didn't want to talk.

Levi closed his eyes and lowered his head. He was doomed. All he'd wanted was to find the truth. To prove to his sister that he wasn't a bad guy like their brother, Marcus. He'd let her down so badly already it hurt to think about it. Even under the circumstances. He hadn't helped Cece the way he should have so he'd decided to prove the whole truth about their daddy and all that he and Marcus had done, like ordering the death of the FBI guy, Jack Kemp.

Jack had been good to Levi. He'd made him feel like his life mattered—like he mattered. Levi had wanted to be like him. And then the guy had disappeared.

What nobody knew was that Levi remembered the night their mother had died, no matter that he'd been nothing but a little kid. She and that bastard who was their father had been arguing so loudly and so desperately—arguing, screaming and crying. Then suddenly the arguing had stopped. Levi had crept out of his bedroom and to the top of the stairs. Their momma had lain at the bottom of the stairs. The crying had started again, only that time it was

Levi. The only thing he remembered after that was Cece holding him and their grandmother screaming. Eventually she had calmed down and taken them home with her.

The certainty and hatred that had sprouted that night had grown and grown but before Levi could work up the courage to do what needed to be done, their younger sister, Sierra, had killed the old bastard. It should have been Levi. He should have killed that devil and taken care of the family when their older brother, Marcus, had not. But Levi had been weak. He'd been weak and afraid. He'd let Cece down and now he was going to die without having made up for the past.

He wished he could see Cece one more time and tell her how sorry he was. She had paid the price for all of them.

The door opened and Levi froze. It would be him—the one the other prisoners called the Interrogator. Levi's body shuddered at the idea of what he might have planned for him this time. Why had he screwed up so badly yet again? All he wanted at this point was to go home. To show his sister how much he loved her and to start doing the right thing with his life.

He wasn't like his father or his older brother. Evil didn't swim in his blood.

He just wanted to go home.

Smith Flynn walked into the room. He had the lightest gray eyes, almost transparent. That and his blond hair almost made him look like some guy from Norway or Sweden or something. He didn't look like anyone from around here. He was tall, six-four at least. And strong. You could tell he pumped iron. But he hadn't laid a hand on Levi. He had other ways to induce pain. He used equipment and his words. He knew the things to say to strike terror in a man.

Before Levi could stop himself, his gaze flitted to the far end of the room where the metal cabinets stood. Inside those locked doors were instruments he hoped to never see again. Evidently he wasn't going to be so lucky. Flynn wouldn't be here otherwise.

The worst part about the whole damned mess was that this guy wanted some truth from Levi, but he didn't have anything to trade for his life or even for a little more time free of torture. Levi had nothing. He had come to this place to prove something. All those years ago when he'd first joined the Resurrection so Jack Kemp would see how smart he was, he'd made a mistake. Truth was he'd let Jack use him. He'd needed that father figure Jack represented so badly. Levi would have done anything to impress him. But he'd gone too far.

All he'd done was gotten into trouble. Now he was likely going to get dead the same way Jack had.

Levi would end up in hell with his damned daddy.

"We have a new problem, Levi."

Fear tightened around his neck. Even the man's voice had a way of terrifying anyone who happened to be stuck in the room with him. Deep, dark, dangerous. Fear twisted inside Levi. Why didn't this Interrogator just kill him and get it over with? He didn't want to die but he couldn't take this much longer.

"I already told you I don't know anything. I only came here to find the truth about an old friend. I swear that's it. The whole story. The truth. There's nothing else."

"Jack Kemp," Flynn said. "You told me that before. Tell me again why you think Kemp came here?"

"He was from the FBI," Levi said. No point pretending he could hide anything from this bastard. The Interrogator had ways of digging stuff out of him. "He asked me to help him get information about the group called the Resurrection, but I went too far."

"Meaning you joined the calling all those years ago? Nine or so years ago, am I right? You did this to help your friend."

Levi nodded. "But Jack disappeared before I could tell him anything. I figured y'all found out what he was up to and got rid of him."

"Your brother, Marcus, was responsible for what happened to him, Levi. If you had seen the news recently, you would know this. He confessed."

Levi was surprised that Marcus confessed to giving Jack to those crazy people. The only way he would have admitted to anything was to save his sorry ass. Hurt twisted in Levi's chest. "What about my sisters? Did you see anything about my sisters?"

Flynn directed that icy glare at him. "Do I look like I would waste my time keeping up with your sisters?"

Levi blinked, bit his tongue so hard he tasted blood. He wanted to hurt this guy. But he'd heard all about him—the Interrogator. The one who got the answers for the Council. The one who knew how to cause pain. Fear snaked through Levi. He shouldn't have come back here. He'd wanted to help…but he'd just made another mistake. Jack was dead by now, no question. Marcus was in jail. God only knew about Sierra. Hopefully Cece was okay.

Flynn placed a photo of a woman on the table. "Do you know her?"

The woman had black hair and eyes nearly as dark, like a raven. Her skin was dark, like she'd lain on a beach all summer. She was pretty but he hadn't seen her before. He shook his head. Prayed that was the right answer because it was the only one he had. "No. She doesn't look familiar."

"Are you certain? Think carefully, Levi. If you lie to me, it will be much worse for you."

"I swear to God I don't know the woman. I have never seen her before."

Flynn said nothing for a long moment. Levi's chest felt ready to explode with tension. Why the hell didn't the bastard just go ahead and tell him he was a dead man? If death was coming, he'd rather know now and brace for it. He was sick of these games. He did not know this woman. He did not know any other information related to the FBI or this damned place or any damned thing else that mattered. His foot started to bounce, making his shackles rattle.

He forced himself to still. Losing it wouldn't help his situation.

"I believe you, Levi." Flynn withdrew the photo, tucked it away in a folder. "My true concern is that she appeared here only a few days after you."

Agony welled inside Levi. "I don't know why. I don't know her. Why don't you ask her?"

"Not to worry, I certainly will. I think I might know why she's here but I need to be certain."

Levi blinked. He didn't have a damned clue where this was going or what this woman had to do with him. He just wanted to go back to his cell and be left alone. He didn't want the Interrogator opening up those cabinets over there the way he'd done before. Pulling out his torture tools and making Levi nearly piss his pants.

Ever since he was a teenager, Levi had thought that to some degree he was brave. He'd thought he was the kind of man who did the right thing. A sort of hero. At least he'd wanted to be. He'd hoped he could be a hero for his sister Cece and help her prove her innocence…but he hadn't helped. And he damned sure wasn't a hero. He wasn't even brave.

He was a coward.

Nothing but a stinking coward.

"Can I count on your help, Levi?"

Levi snapped his focus back to the man. He swallowed back the bile that had risen in his throat and tried to slow his pounding heart. "Yeah, sure. What do I have to do?"

"I haven't worked out all the details just yet. We'll talk again soon."

The man stood and walked out.

Levi sagged in his chair. Squeezed his eyes shut and thanked God he'd survived a second encounter with the Interrogator.

Whatever he wanted, Levi could do it. He would do it. At this point obedience was probably the only way to stay alive. Cece would want him to stay alive. She would. He knew this without question. His sister would absolutely want him to do whatever necessary to stay alive.

Even if he was the worst kind of coward.

SMITH RETURNED TO his cabin and turned on the security feed to watch the woman.

She had stopped her pacing. Had decided to conserve her energy. He suspected she was above average in intelligence. Certainly she was cockier than the average agent. Her dark hair and eyes, the olive skin, gave her an exotic appearance. Beyond the superficial, she looked strong. Undeniable curves, but not soft. Lean. Toned muscle. This was a woman who worked hard to be prepared.

Her claim of possessing useful information was not a particularly original tactic. Her methods of getting their attention, however, were damned original. To garner the attention of Prentiss himself, then get herself picked up by members and brought here this way was ingenious. And extremely risky. Whatever she wanted, it was important. Important enough to risk her life.

Reconnaissance teams had been doubled and were out there now, patrolling and watching for trouble. No matter that the team that had brought her here had ensured they weren't followed. Her clothes and personal items had been removed before she left that godforsaken church. That level of motivation demanded careful consideration.

It was possible a tracking device was implanted somewhere on her slim body but the initial scan had not picked up on anything close to the surface. Her clothes and cell phone had been cleaned. As he'd anticipated, her phone was more or less a blank slate. Anything incriminating had been wiped. It had been reduced to a mere tracking device. This was a very well-trained agent.

Rather than take the risk the initial scan had missed something, he picked up a secure internal line and called Medical. "Run deep scans on Prisoner Buchanan. Send the results to me ASAP."

Smith ended the call, his attention still focused on the woman. He watched as she whirled around at the sound of her cell door opening. She didn't resist when the guard cuffed her hands behind her back and then escorted her out of the confining space. Smith followed the monitors, watching her move down the long white corridor and out onto the quad. The two crossed the common area and entered the smaller medical building. Smith switched to another camera and followed their movements inside.

The guard took a position at the door leading to Imaging while the waiting technician assumed custody of the prisoner.

"Remove your clothing," the tech ordered.

Buchanan glanced around the room, noted the imaging equipment and then did as he asked without question. The top came off first, revealing high, firm breasts and a narrow waist. As the sweatpants slid down her hips and thighs, Smith's gaze followed. Despite his own training, his body tightened. Her shape was undeniably attractive. Gently rounded hips and long legs sculpted by hours of running. Her long hair hung around her shoulders, the only remaining shield she possessed.

The quality he found most surprising and interesting was that she stared square at the male technician without the slightest flinch. She was not shy or afraid.

Smith continued to observe as the scans were accomplished. On a second screen, he monitored the results. There was no indication a tracking device or other electronic object had been inserted or implanted. She was clean.

His curiosity roused. This woman—this Federal Bureau of Investigation agent—had walked into a compound filled with heavily armed and well-trained extremists. In truth, the people here were more mercenaries than preppers. She had done this while completely unarmed and with no way to call for backup or hope to escape.

Sadie Buchanan was either telling the truth about her agenda for being here or she was completely insane.

He would know the answer soon enough.

Chapter Four

Saturday, August 4

Sadie opened her eyes. Darkness crowded in around her, jolting her heart into a frantic run.

For a moment her brain couldn't assimilate where she was. Air refused to fill her lungs.

Then she remembered. Compound. *Resurrection.* Trouble.

She froze.

What had awakened her so abruptly? A sound. The slightest brushing of fabric against fabric as if someone had come far too close to her huddled position on this rock-hard cot.

She dared to take a breath and the subtle scent of leather and wood whispered against her senses. Adrenaline burned through her once more.

She was not alone.

Forcing herself to relax, she peered into the darkness. Slowly but surely her eyes filled in the dark form sitting on the edge of the thin mattress, barely centimeters away. Whoever it was sat perfectly still, didn't even breathe.

Someone had come into her cell, had walked the half-dozen steps across the small concrete room and sat down on the edge of her cot. The door opening should have awakened her but it had not. Had they put something into her food?

She never slept so heavily.

"What do you want?" She said the words then waited for a response, holding her breath for fear she would miss some part of the answer, assuming an answer came.

"Why are you here, Sadie Buchanan?"

Male. His voice was intensely deep, and...*dangerous*. She couldn't stop the shiver the sound elicited.

Grabbing back her usual unflappability, she fired back, "You already know the answer to that question."

A grunt was his immediate reaction.

She ordered herself to relax. Where was her usual fearlessness? It was something for which she didn't typically have to search. Granted he had startled her from sleep in the middle of the night. Then again, she couldn't be sure what time it was. It could be morning for all she knew. Without a window with which to judge, she couldn't make an accurate assessment. There had to be something in the food she had dared to nibble at. She had known better but hunger sometimes overrode experience.

"Why are you here, Sadie Buchanan?" he said once more.

The words were harsher this time. His patience was thinning, and he obviously didn't like repeating himself. Well, she didn't, either.

"Like I told your friends, I have information that could help your cause. I came to make a deal."

He laughed. There was zero humor in the rough noise. "If you were half as smart as you apparently believe you are, Sadie Buchanan, you would know that people like us don't make deals."

The full depth and breadth of her courage finally reared its head. About time. "Well, now, that's not entirely true, Mister...?"

"Flynn. Smith Flynn."

Her brain instinctively searched her memory banks. No Smith Flynn was found there. "Perhaps you're unaware of the deals those in charge make quite often. Deals with a certain South American gunrunning cartel. The recent shipment was detained by the feds and local authorities right here in Winchester—assuming we're still in the Winchester area. And that's only the beginning of your troubles. Things are not going to go so well for your friends if you refuse my generous offer of help."

He appeared to contemplate her warning for a time. If she was really lucky, his curiosity would trump his logic.

"What happened recently," he said, his voice still somehow disturbing to her senses, "was an unforeseeable stroke of good fortune for *your* friends, but it won't happen again."

Sadie was the one who laughed this time. "You really believe all those stored weapons were found in those underground tunnels at the church by accident? A lucky break for the feds?"

His tension shifted to the next level; she felt it in his posture even if she couldn't see him in the darkness. Though their bodies weren't touching, tension crackled between them. He was as edgy as she was. She squinted, peered harder through the darkness. Her eyes had adjusted more fully to the darkness allowing her to see that he had lighter hair. Blond, she calculated. Maybe gray. She couldn't say for certain.

"You have proof it wasn't?"

The next step was a risky one. Other than Levi Winters, she had no names of members except the one she was saving as the ace up her sleeve. "I know what the local authorities said. A heads-up took them to the church. The Winters family meltdown was secondary. They were already going there anyway. The church had been on their radar for a while. The goal was to hit when it counted. We both know how that turned out."

He considered her statement for long enough to make her doubt herself.

"I can't decide, Sadie Buchanan, whether you actually have relevant information or if you simply have a somewhat complicated death wish. If exiting this world is your goal, putting your service weapon to your temple would have been far easier."

"I can assure you, Mr. Flynn, I do not have a death wish." She was winning this round. "What I have is information you and your friends can use. But I can't force your interest." She relaxed into the thin mattress as if she'd said all she had to say.

"I will be watching you, Sadie Buchanan. If you're lying, you will regret your actions far more than you can imagine."

She reached out, her hand landing on what felt like his upper arm. The muscles there were like steel but she suspected that had nothing to do with him not being relaxed and everything to do with serious workouts.

"Tell me about you, Smith Flynn. What's your story? What are you running away from?"

He snagged her hand, clutched it in his own. "Why would you think I'm running from something?" His thumb found her palm and stroked the tender flesh there. "You don't know me."

His touch unnerved her, which was the point. "How can you be certain I don't know you? No one is invisible, Mr. Flynn."

The mattress shifted and fabric rustled as he leaned close. His face came so near to hers she could feel his breath on her skin. Her own ability to breathe stalled.

"I know this because you have never seen my face.

A name is only a name. It's the face—the eyes—that tell the story, and I will know yours."

With every ounce of courage she possessed, she forced herself to turn fully toward him, putting their mouths mere millimeters apart. "Then show me your face and we'll know for certain."

She felt his smile. "You are very brave, Sadie Buchanan. Or perhaps you are more naive than I thought."

"I thought you had me all figured out, Mr. Flynn."

"So did I."

He drew away and she dared to breathe again.

"You have a command performance this morning, Ms. Buchanan." The mattress shifted again as he stood. "I hope for your sake you pass the series of tests you are about to encounter. If some part of you recognizes that you're in over your head, you might consider quitting now. I'm confident the Council would be willing to permit a quick, merciful death if you confessed the truth before wasting more of their time."

"I'm not a quitter, Mr. Flynn." Sadie dropped her feet to the floor. "If you knew me at all, you would know this."

The next sound she heard was the door closing and then locking.

Just to be sure he was actually gone and not waiting in the darkness, she stood and moved around the walls of the room, reaching out to ensure he wasn't standing in the center of the dark space.

She leaned against the door and closed her eyes. He might be right about one thing—there was a very strong possibility she was in over her head.

THE GUARD USHERED her out the exit. This one, like the ones yesterday and the men who had accompanied Prentiss, wore a camouflage military uniform. The boots were military style, as well. Outside, Sadie squinted at the light. It seemed so bright she had to remind herself it wasn't the sun. There was no sky because this place was underground somehow.

"Where is this place?" she asked the man ushering her along. "Underground? In a cave?" If it was a cave, it was a really large cave. Maybe it was built into a mountainside. That would explain how they'd driven directly in and why the facility had not been located by any sort of aerial surveillance.

As usual, the man ushering her along said nothing. Even when he'd opened her cell a few minutes ago, he hadn't spoken. She had gotten up from the cot and walked out, grateful to escape the concrete box.

"If we're underground…" Sadie stopped, causing him to almost trip over her. "Technically I don't need these cuffs. Where would I go if I ran?"

He glared at her, grabbed her by the upper arm and steered her forward.

"Where are we going?"

Still not a word.

The smaller buildings, almost like cabins, captured her attention again. Living quarters for those in charge, she surmised. Somewhere around here there would be a barracks for those members like the one escorting her this morning. She wondered about the man who had come to her cell sometime during the night. He probably lived in one of those private quarters.

"Were you on duty all night?"

Still no answer. He walked forward, his gaze straight ahead.

"A man came into my cell." She almost stumbled trying to look back over her shoulder at the mute guard as she spoke. But she was glad she did. He made the slightest little flinch in response but quickly schooled his face. She couldn't decide if he'd felt a fleeting hint of concern that she might fall or if the idea of the man who visited her unsettled him somehow.

"He tried to scare me."

No reaction.

"But he didn't scare me. If he'd intended to kill me, he would have."

"There are worse things than dying."

His fingers wrapped around her upper arm once more and ushered her toward a building on the left. The sign posted by the door read Clinic. She wanted to question him about the comment, but he ushered her through the entrance and walked away before she could. A woman wearing a white uniform took charge of Sadie.

"The guard will wait for you outside," the nurse, doctor, whatever she was, explained.

The woman, her black hair slicked back in a tight bun, led the way to a plain white room with an exam table as well as a side table loaded with medical equipment. Sadie decided the woman was a nurse or technician. She checked Sadie's temperature and then led the way back into the corridor.

In the next room, there was yet another examination table. A stack of neatly folded sweatpants and a tee sat on the table. Beyond that was a curtain—the type that would hang over a shower.

The nurse pulled a key from her pocket and removed the cuffs, then gestured to the curtain. "Take off your clothes and shower. Use the soap in the bottle."

Sadie didn't argue. She took off her clothes, got into the shower and washed her hair and body as instructed. When she'd finished and stepped out of the shower, the woman—nurse, whatever she was—waited by the exam table. She wore an apron, a face mask and gloves. Stirrups now extended from one end of the table.

"We'll do your exam now."

No point in arguing. Sadie climbed onto the exam table and placed her feet in the stirrups. A close physical examination followed. She rolled Sadie onto her side and checked her back and buttocks. She scanned her arms and legs, hands and feet. Her face and scalp. Then she did a pelvic exam.

Sadie grimaced. "You looking for anything in particular?"

They had scanned her thoroughly yesterday. This seemed a bit overkill.

The woman peeled off her gloves and tossed them into a trash receptacle. "Put on your clothes."

Sadie complied. When the fresh sweats and tee hung on her body, the nurse recuffed her and led her back out the front entrance to where the guard waited. From there, he led Sadie toward yet another building, this one about the same size as the clinic. The sign on the door read Council. The building was like all the rest, gray, like concrete. Austere. This one was a one-story like the clinic and the detention center.

As soon as they stepped inside the building Sadie understood this was a place of importance. The floor was carpeted. Something commercial with low pile, but enough to quiet footsteps. The walls weren't a stark white as all the others had been. This was more of a beige.

"What did you mean when you said there were worse things than dying?"

"Wait here." He steered her toward the waiting bench. "Maybe you won't have to find out."

Sadie sat on the bench against the wall and watched as he walked away. She ignored the idea that he had a point about there being some things worse than dying. For now, she preferred to focus on more optimistic scenarios. She had a feeling she was on a dangerous precipice. Whatever happened in the next few minutes would determine her future. One slip either way and she could go over the edge completely.

Minutes passed. Three, then four and five. Eventually ten. Sadie crossed her legs, uncrossed them and then crossed them again. She swung her foot up and down. Someone in this place was watching her. She might as well show them how thoroughly unimpressed and utterly bored she was.

A door on the opposite side of the corridor, a few yards beyond where she sat, opened. A different guard—she recognized the camo uniform but not the face—strode to her, pulled her to her feet and shepherded her toward the door he'd exited. The room was fairly large. A long table stood across the far end; seven, no eight men were seated on the other side. One chair sat on this side of the table. Sadie suspected that chair was for her. The guard nudged her forward, confirming her suspicion. When she'd taken a seat, he waited behind her.

Most of the men were old and Caucasian. Not a particularly big surprise. There was one, however, who was not so old. A few years older than Sadie. Maybe forty. Blond hair. Piercing gray eyes. He stared at her, as did the others, but there was something about his stare that penetrated far deeper. They wore civilian clothes. Jeans, short-sleeved shirts— some button-down, others pullovers—and hiking boots. Except for one.

Of all those present, the only person among them

she had seen before was the man named Prentiss. He wore the same style overalls and long-sleeved shirt he'd worn in their first meeting. No fedora this time.

He spoke first. "Agent Buchanan, you've created quite a stir around here." He glanced side to side, acknowledging his colleagues. "We're mostly in agreement as to what should become of you. There's a single holdout, preventing a final decision."

Sadie made a face. "I'm not sure I understand, Mr. Prentiss. You haven't heard what I have to say. Maybe you're not interested in protecting your assets and followers."

He stared directly at her, his glare as deadly as any weapon she'd ever faced. "I don't think you understand, Agent Buchanan. We have no interest in anything you have to say. We have our doubts as to the worth of anything you might have to offer and we've decided we have no patience for whatever game you're playing."

Not exactly the reaction she'd hoped for. Time to throw out the ace up her sleeve. "Mr. Trenton Pollard." She scanned the faces as she said the name, looking for a reaction or some indication that one or more of those present recognized the name. Everyone seated at the table—except the younger man—had shoulder-length hair, a full beard and mustache, hiding a good portion of their faces, but not one of them outwardly flinched, grimaced or so much as batted an eye.

"The Bureau and the ATF," she went on, "have

targeted Resurrection with the intention of taking down those in power, starting with you, Mr. Prentiss. They consider you the weak link in this group. The necessary information to accomplish this feat will be provided by Mr. Pollard. It's my understanding there's more than simply your location, far more, he plans to share."

All eyes stared at her.

Good or bad, she'd shown her hand—her only hand. Now the ball was in their court.

She had nothing else.

Except what she could make up as she went along. She'd always been fairly good at improvising.

The men whispered among themselves, save the younger one. He sat staring at Sadie without saying a word or even glancing at anyone else. That he still watched her so closely had begun to get under her skin. She kept her attention on the others, hoping all that going back and forth was in her best interest.

Finally, a hush fell over the group and Prentiss settled his attention on her once more. "Agent Buchanan, we still have reservations about your decision to come here with this so-called warning. Though I will give you this, you have our attention. Still, my question to you is what could you possibly hope to gain?"

Now for the improvising. "I screwed up." She shrugged. "I had an opportunity to pad my bank account and I took it. I see no reason to share the dirty details. Sadly, two days ago I found out an investigation had been opened and my assets were about to be frozen. I moved a few things around but there was no way I was going to be able to disappear quickly enough. I needed someplace to go ASAP. Someplace they wouldn't be able to find me. Since they haven't been able to find you in all this time, I figured we could help each other out. The information would buy my way in. Then I found out Pollard is about to spill his guts. I'm assuming your organization has a backup plan for disappearing."

"I fear you have overestimated your worth, Agent Buchanan."

Well, hell.

"I regret that you feel that way." She stood.

There it was. The no-go she had hoped wouldn't be thrown out. Still, he had mentioned a holdout. Maybe, just maybe the game wasn't over yet.

When no one said anything else, she offered, "Since there's no place for me here, I guess I'll just have to take my chances trying to outrun the Bureau's reach. I wish you well in doing the same. They are coming, Mr. Prentiss. Trust me on that one."

A remote smile tugged at the old man's face. "Perhaps you should have done your due diligence when weighing your options, Agent. You see, once you're here, there's only one way to leave."

She didn't need a more detailed explanation.

The Council had decided her fate.

Death.

Chapter Five

"What happens now?"

As usual, the guard said nothing while he steered Sadie out of the building. She hadn't actually expected him to answer her question, but she needed to try. He was the one person who had spoken to her besides Prentiss, even if it had been only once.

And there was the man who had visited her in the dark of her cell.

Definitely wasn't the guard. His voice was different. He smelled different, too. This close it was obvious her guard wasn't freshly showered like the man who'd sneaked into her cell. The stranger who'd made that middle-of-the-night appearance had smelled clean, like soap—the kind of soap used by a man who cared how he smelled. His hair had been lighter, as well; a blond or maybe a gray.

Frankly, she hadn't encountered anyone else who met the smell-good criteria. She thought of the blond man in the room where her appearance before the powers that be had taken place. He had seemed nearer to her age. Considering his light-colored hair, he could have been the one, though she hadn't been close enough to him during the questioning to pick up on his scent.

Didn't matter, she supposed. They hadn't bought her story so living past this moment was growing more and more unlikely. Not exactly the way she had seen things going. She was still breathing so no need to give up just yet. There might be time to turn this around.

"Are you supposed to kill me?"

Her guard just kept walking, shepherding her along as he went. He wasn't so old. Early forties, maybe. It was difficult to tell. He was tall, reasonably muscled. He looked fit. The woodland greens uniform molded to strong arms and legs and a broad chest. His complexion wasn't as pale as she would have expected considering this place—wherever the hell it was—appeared to be sheltered from the sun. Now that she thought about it, the old men who'd sat around the table, the younger one, as well, had good coloring. They either had tanning beds around here someplace or these people spent time in the sun outside these walls.

But where?

Gardens? Fields? Wasn't part of the doomsday prepper thing attaining self-sufficiency? They either raised their own food or bartered with others of like mind.

"If I'm going to die, why not talk to me? It won't matter in a little while anyway, right?"

Despite her urging, he kept his mouth shut. He led her beyond the quad and all the buildings that seemed to circle the place where she'd been questioned by the group of elders or leaders. The final building they approached wasn't really a building. It was more like a massive carport. SUVs and trucks and a couple of military-type vehicles were parked beneath its expansive canopy. On the far end a long low building with half a dozen overhead doors connected to the covered parking. Vehicle maintenance, she supposed.

The guard didn't stop dragging her along until they were beyond the parked vehicles. Several small metal domes dotted the ground. At first she thought of underground gasoline tanks, but that didn't make sense since four huge tanks stood next to the maintenance building. Maybe the aboveground ones were water tanks. There had to be a water supply in here somewhere.

Her guard ushered her to the nearest dome and opened it. Beneath the metal dome was a steel wheel, the kind you would see on a submarine door. Grunting with the effort, he twisted it to the right and then raised the lid-like door upward. Beyond the door was a ladder that disappeared into the ground.

The guard straightened and reached for her secured hands. When he'd removed her restraints, he gestured to the ladder. "You go on now."

She looked from the hole in the ground to him. "What's down there?"

He stared at her a moment. "You'll see."

"Really? You couldn't think of anything more original than *you'll see*?" She ordered her heart to slow its galloping. This was that moment, the one where she had to decide if she was going to cooperate or make a run for it.

She glanced around. There was no readily visible place to run. Her guard didn't appear to be armed but that didn't mean that others who were close by weren't. Besides, where the hell would she go? And there were those guard towers.

"Running won't do you no good."

He didn't need a crystal ball or to be a mind reader to recognize what she had on her mind. "Tell me what's down there and I'll get out of your hair."

With a big put-upon breath, he said, "There are people like you down there."

"Prisoners?" She stared him directly in the eyes. He nodded.

"Are they dead or alive?" That was the big question now.

He shrugged. "Does it matter? Like I told you, there's some things worse than dying. This is one of them."

He said a mouthful with that. So much for rescuing Levi Winters. Then again, maybe he was down there, too. "Well, thanks for the heads-up."

It was now or never. If she was going to make a run for it—

"You see that hole in the wall to your right?"

His words yanked her attention back to him. "What hole?"

Even as she asked the question, a small square opened and the barrel of a rifle extended from the wall. Apparently there were guards monitoring the walls of this place from numerous vantage points, not just the obvious towers she had seen. Running would definitely be a waste of time.

"If you run, you're dead."

Made her decision considerably easier. "Got it."

Sadie put a hand on the ladder and swung one foot, then the other onto a rung. When she'd scaled down about four rungs, the squeak of metal on metal drew her attention upward as the hatch-type door closed. She drew in a big breath and let it go. Nothing to do now but see if there were any other living humans down here.

Thankfully it wasn't completely dark. Emergency-type lighting, dim though it might be, was placed along the downward path. When she reached the bottom of the ladder, a good twenty feet below the hatch, a long tunnel lay ahead of her. More of that dim recessed lighting kept the darkness at bay. The temperature was far cooler down here and there was that earthy, musty smell in the air.

Speaking of air, it was obviously pumped down

here somehow. She took another breath. Hoped like hell it was anyway.

"You're the first female we've had down here."

Sadie whipped around at the muttered words. The man stood only inches from her. How had he sneaked up on her like that? Her instincts were generally far more in tune with her surroundings.

"Who are you?" She kept her shoulders square and met his curious gaze without flinching.

Unlike the men in the compound, this man was as pale as a ghost. His hair was a stringy brown and hung down around his hunched shoulders. His clothes were like hers, sweats and a tee, only his looked old and were filthy and ragged. His feet were bare and dirty.

"George." He licked his lips. "What about you? Got a name?"

"Sadie." She braced to make a run for it but decided to hold off until she got a better indication of his intentions. It wasn't as if there was any real place to go and George here likely knew the place like the back of his hand.

"Sadie." He rolled her name around in his mouth as if he were tasting it.

She glanced around again. "What is this place?"

"The big dig." He chuckled, the sound as rusty as his teeth.

She forced her lips into a smile. "Like in Boston. I gotcha. Where are you digging to, George?"

He shrugged one of those bony shoulders. "Wherever they tell us to."

"They tell you things?" She jerked her head up toward the hatch at the top of the ladder.

"Orders. Yeah. They send 'em down along with food and water."

Thank God. That was her next concern. "So they feed you. That's good."

Another of those spasmodic shrugs. "Enough to survive. Most of the time anyway."

Well, great. Just great. "What now, George?"

"Can't say for sure. You work until we hear different." He started forward into the tunnel.

"Work?" Sadie walked alongside him. The tunnel was wide, plenty wide enough for about three people to walk side by side. Overhead, wood and steel supports kept the ground from caving in. This was no slipshod operation. Some amount of engineering know-how had gone into what they were doing.

"On the dig, of course. We're working on a tunnel headed south to Huntland. Already got one finished to Winchester."

"Sounds like a sizable operation."

He croaked another of those rusty laughs. "The Resurrection's got big plans, Sadie."

Clearly. "How many workers are down here?"

"About twenty."

"They're all prisoners?"

"Yep. Some of us were part of them before we

screwed up. I guess getting put down here was better than the alternative."

That remained debatable. "What about those who weren't part of the Resurrection?"

"Some were taken from the outside for their knowledge or skill and put down here."

"Knowledge?"

"Contractors. You know, builders. A couple ex-military guys who were assigned to the air force base."

A point she would need to pass along if she ever got out of here. "You have tools and equipment?"

"Sure." He glanced at her, his brown eyes sunken and hollow. "Lots of tools."

Sadie followed him down the length of the first tunnel and then they hit a sort of fork in the road, except there were about four different ways to go. He took the fork farthest to the left.

"Do you dig up to the surface, creating an egress or access point?" This could be a good thing.

He shook his head, deflating her hopes. "Only so far up. The rest is up to them. They do that part from above. We're not allowed to get too close to the surface."

Nevertheless, that meant those areas were closer to freedom. "Sounds like they've got it all figured out."

Her escort grunted an agreement.

The sounds of metal clanging and low voices rumbled in the distance. "We're almost to the dig where we're working now."

Ahead, the outline of bodies moving came into focus. Men wore helmets with attached lights. They swung pickaxes, hefted shovels and other digging tools. A battery-operated jackhammer rattled off. Sadie surveyed the cacophony of activity.

"This is what I'll be doing?"

George stopped and faced her. She did the same. "You give me those flip-flops you're wearing and I'll tell you."

She could do that. They were a sort of one-size-fits-all and pretty much worthless as foot protection went. "Sure."

As soon as she kicked off the footwear, he snatched the thongs and tugged them onto his grimy feet. When he'd finished, he looked directly at her and held up his end of the bargain. "We'll get the word—usually don't take long, I'd say between now and tomorrow—then we'll know whether you're a worker or supplies."

"Supplies?" A frown creased its way across her forehead. Deep inside she had a very bad feeling this was the worse-than-dying thing the guard had mentioned.

"Sometimes they stop feeding us. Like when we don't get as much done as they want. Some of us get sick and can't work as fast. They punish us then. If you're supplies, then you'll be the emergency food."

Oh hell.

He shrugged those bony shoulders again. "You'd be surprised how long even someone as skinny as you will last."

She glanced around. Said the only thing she could think to say in response to that unnerving statement. "Doesn't seem as though you have any way to keep your *supplies* from going bad."

"No need. We wouldn't eat you all at once. We always keep supplies alive as long as possible. Take an arm or a leg, then another when that one is gone. It works out pretty good. By the time the supplies is dead, we can finish off the edible parts before they start to rot."

Made an eerie kind of sense, she supposed. Unless you happen to be the main course.

No one paid much attention to them as they arrived at the worksite. The man who'd served as her guide—George—handed her a pickax and motioned to a spot for her to start. Sadie walked wide around the other workers and started hefting the ax. She couldn't help glancing over her shoulder now and then just to make sure no one was watching her. Most of the group looked like the man who now sported her flip-flops. Baggy, ragged clothes. Long, stringy hair. Filthy. Pale and weary looking.

Now that she had arrived they didn't talk so the only sounds were the pecking and scraping at the earth. The rattling jackhammer. And in those rare moments of silence, the breathing and grunting. During the next few minutes several things crossed her mind. Where did they sleep? Relieve themselves? And if she was the only female to show up, would she be raped if she tried to sleep?

Maybe she would ask George the next chance she got.

A loud sound like the single dong of a doorbell echoed through the rhythmic poking and pecking and grunting. She glanced around, her attention settling on George. He put down his shovel and started back the way they had come. The other workers looked from George to her before going back to work.

Apparently the news had arrived. Maybe dropped down from the top of that ladder the way she basically had been.

Her fingers tightened on the handle of the ax.

She supposed she would know soon enough if she was to be a permanent worker or emergency supplies.

SMITH WAITED FOR Prentiss to show up.

He'd asked for a meeting with the man immediately after the Council questioned Buchanan. The old man had decided to take his time. He knew Smith was not happy with the decision and he wanted him to wallow in his frustration.

Smith crossed the Council's private meeting room and stared out the window. For more than three decades the Resurrection had been clawing its way into this mountainside. Back then there had been only whispers about a group of doomsday survivalists sprouting up in Franklin County. No one really knew or understood what they were. Smith wasn't sure if even those early leaders of the small group understood what they would become over time.

Smith shook his head. They had become something entirely different from what they once were—from what they were supposed to be. Preparing to survive mankind's destruction of himself was one thing, preparing for a war with those not like-minded was something else altogether.

But things had escalated in the past decade. Now it was about power and greed for the few rather than the safety and survival of the many.

"Making you wait was unavoidable."

Smith turned to face the man who had entered the room. Rayford Prentiss was an old man now, but that didn't stop him from being utterly ruthless. Age had not mellowed him at all—in fact, it had done the opposite. He was as mean as hell and cared nothing for human life.

Prentiss poured himself a hefty serving of bourbon and lifted the glass to his lips. Smith watched, his patience thinning all the more with each passing moment. But he would not allow this bastard to see his mounting discontent. He couldn't let that happen until the time was right.

Soon, very soon. Sooner than Smith had anticipated.

The Buchanan woman's arrival and the name she had tossed about was a warning. Something was about to go down. Smith needed to prepare. To do that, information was required—information from Buchanan. Dropping her into the hole had been premature. The move was a blatant challenge against what Smith had suggested.

"You're displeased with my decision about the woman," Prentiss announced as he poured himself a second drink.

"She obviously has connections. Those connections could prove to be valuable."

Prentiss sat the bottle of bourbon back onto the credenza and belted out a laugh. "Because she spouted the name of a man who has been gone from here for years? If she had connections, she would know that Pollard is likely dead and buried. Of no use or threat to anyone."

"Maybe, maybe not. Either way, you're missing the big picture, old man." Smith strode toward him. "How much longer do you believe you can continue to rule these people like a dictator?"

"You believe you would be better as the head of Council."

It wasn't a question. Smith purposely made no bones about his feelings. He wanted Prentiss to know that his days were numbered. Far more so than he realized. Smith had to bite back the smile. Everything was going to change and this greedy bastard had no idea what was coming.

"You're the only one left who believes in your vision. No one on the Council agrees with your methods. They merely tolerate you out of respect for what once was."

Anger sparked in the old man's eyes. "You mean your father? I've gone too far beyond *his* vision of what the Resurrection was?"

Smith gritted his teeth for a moment. "Don't compare yourself to my father."

Prentiss moved in closer, glared up at Smith, his fury barely held in check. "You were gone for ten years. You only came back when you heard he was dead. If he hadn't named you to the Council with his dying breath, you would be in the tunnels where you belong."

The one thing that had gotten Smith through the past two years was knowing that in the end—when this was all over—he would be able to look Rayford Prentiss in the eyes and tell him the truth that no one else could know. The shock alone would likely kill the old son of a bitch.

Smith lived for that day.

Prentiss cleared his face of emotion. "You would have me change my decision about the woman."

Another statement. "You can do as you please, including change your mind."

No one questioned Prentiss. At least no one except Smith. His first month here, Smith had drawn the line in the sand. So far, Prentiss had not crossed it. He blustered and stomped all around it, but he was careful not to push too far. There were too many who remained faithful to the memory of Avery Flynn.

Prentiss wouldn't risk a rebellion. Not at this crucial juncture.

"And why would I change my mind?"

"Buchanan could prove useful," Smith said. "She
didn't pull that name out of thin air. Consider how
few people know what that name stands for."

Smith had him there and he knew it. Trenton Pollard had been an ATF agent. He was the only one
to burrow in so deeply without being discovered.
Fury roared through Smith at the memory. Pollard had burrowed deep into Resurrection. Almost
took them down and then he disappeared. Except
he hadn't gone far. Like the FBI agent Jack Kemp.
He'd ended up buried not far from here. But Prentiss
didn't know that for sure. No one except Smith knew.
Although Kemp had been a casualty of the Winters
family, he and Pollard had been after the same goal:
the end of the Resurrection.

They weren't the first but they were the most
memorable—the ones who had infiltrated the deepest.

Until now.

Prentiss made a face of dismissal. "I have my
doubts as to any potential use she might prove to
have."

"Are you willing to take that risk?" He wasn't.
Smith was well aware that his bravado was merely
for show. Particularly now that the possibility had
been publicly brought to his attention. He would
never give Smith that kind of ammunition to use

against him if he turned out to be wrong. "At the very least she could prove a valuable bargaining chip in the future."

"Very well. For you, I will change my mind. But the risk is yours. If she becomes a liability, she will be your liability."

The two stared at each other for a long moment. Smith imagined Prentiss wished him dead. The feeling was mutual.

But not just yet.

"One day, old man, you'll learn to trust my judgment."

Prentiss made a scoffing sound. "Perhaps."

The old man walked out, leaving Smith staring after him. Rayford Prentiss would know soon enough.

Smith summoned the guard who had been assigned to Buchanan's security. He wondered if she would ever understand that she owed her life to him. If the two of them survived what was to come, he would see that she recognized what a serious error in judgment she had made coming to this place.

What the hell had she been thinking?

What had the Bureau been thinking?

He supposed it was possible this was some sort of rescue mission. Maybe for Levi Winters, though Smith didn't see him as a valuable enough target to risk the life of an agent.

Whatever had brought her here, she had put a kink in his timeline.

Now he was left with no choice but to make drastic adjustments. Otherwise everything could go wrong. The past two years of his life would be wasted.

That could not happen.

Chapter Six

Sadie did as she had been ordered and kept digging but part of her attention remained on the man coming toward her. Most of the other workers glanced her way but none dared to stop and stare. They wouldn't risk being caught slacking. The men in charge, George and three others, didn't mind bopping a slacker on the head with a shovel or nudging them in the kidneys with an ax handle. Judging by the scars on some of the workers, things could get a lot worse.

Whether it was survival or just the hint of control that came with being in charge, George and his peers appeared to take their positions very seriously. Maybe there were perks not readily visible. Obviously it wasn't clothes or a good hot bath or more to eat. Everyone in this hole looked the same as far as their state of health, ragged attire and level of filth went.

George stopped a couple of steps from her. "Come with me."

The best she could estimate she'd climbed down that ladder about two hours ago. Already blisters were forming on her hands and her muscles ached from hefting the ax. As much as she didn't look forward to days or weeks or months of this sort of hard labor, she would take that any day of the week over becoming the rest of the crew's dinner.

"Why?" Might as well know now. The whole crew would hear the news soon enough. Why keep everyone in suspense?

"They want you back up there." He jerked his head upward.

Sadie's knees almost gave way on her. "I have to go back up the ladder?"

She framed the question in a less than optimistic manner since the rest of the workers were listening. No need to rub in the idea that she was out of here. If she sounded hesitant or worried maybe they wouldn't feel so bad that they weren't the ones climbing out of this hole. Then again, there was no way to guess what waited for her up there.

There are some things worse than dying.

Still, she preferred continuing to breathe over the alternative.

"Let's go," George said rather than answer her question.

She tossed her pickax to the ground and followed the man back through the long, dimly lit tunnel. He didn't speak, just walked along, his newly attained flip-flops clacking in the silence.

When they reached the ladder, he squinted his eyes to look at her. "Somebody up there must have plans for you. Once you're down here, you don't usually go back up."

She thought of the man who had visited her in the dark and then of Prentiss. If either of them wanted her back, it couldn't be good. She would know soon enough, she supposed. If Levi Winters was still alive, he was obviously up there. She hadn't seen him down here.

"Guess so." She shrugged.

He nodded toward the ladder. "Thanks for the flip-flops."

She resisted the urge to tell him that if she had anything to do with it, he and the others would not be down here much longer. But she couldn't take the risk. Not to mention, at this point she couldn't guarantee anything. So far this mission had been an epic failure.

"Sure."

She climbed the ladder. As she reached the upper rungs the hatch-type door opened. The guard—the same one from before—waited for her. She blinked repeatedly, then squinted against the brighter light. Maybe it was coming up from the dim lighting, but she realized that the lighting was very similar to sunlight. More so than she had realized. Maybe there were solar tubes or some other discreet way of pumping in sunlight without being easily detected by anyone flying over the area.

The guard closed the hatch and glanced at her feet. He didn't ask what happened to her footwear. He probably had a good idea.

He ushered her away from the small field of domes. She decided since she'd only seen one access point while she was down there, all the other domes must be for pumping air into the tunnels.

"Where am I going now?"

He probably wouldn't tell her but it didn't hurt to ask.

As she'd expected, they continued forward without him responding. When they reached the detention center, they kept walking. Once they were beyond the Council building where she'd been questioned, they reached the area with the row of smaller buildings. He steered her toward the one marked with a number nine. At the door, he knocked and waited.

Sadie's fingers and palms burned and she wished she could wash her hands. The blisters stung. Her gaze drifted down to her feet. And they were filthy. Her pink toenails looked out of place on those feet.

The door opened and the blond man from the group who'd questioned her today stood in the threshold.

He nodded and the guard walked away. "Come inside."

This he said to Sadie. His voice was deep, curt. His silvery gaze unflinching.

Sadie did as he ordered, crossing the threshold and entering unknown territory. Nothing new. Encountering the unexpected was a major part of her mission history. If she and Levi Winters were lucky, this mission would flounder its way to success while they were both still breathing.

Her host closed the door behind her. The cabin-like structure was basically one room. A bed, table and chairs, and a small sofa were the only furnishings. On the far side of the room was a small kitchenette. A door beyond the kitchenette likely led to a bathroom. Next to the bed was a smaller table that appeared to serve as a desk since a laptop sat atop it. All the comforts of home, she mused.

He pulled out a chair from the larger, round table. "Sit."

She sat.

Rather than secure her in some manner as she'd expected, he moved to the other side of the table and sat down, his clasped hands settled on the tabletop.

"You present quite the quandary, Sadie Buchanan."

She had been told this more than once, usually by a superior at the Bureau. The words rarely turned out to be a compliment. More often, she was reminded of proper procedure and other prescribed protocols.

"Tell me what I need to do to rectify whatever the problem is." She placed her hands on the table, wanted him to see the blisters. "I'd like to know I have a place here."

He stared at her for a long while without saying more. She decided he was even closer to her age than she'd first thought. Thirty-five or thirty-six, maybe. He was tall, looked strong and his skin was unmarred by scars, unlike many of those she'd seen above and below ground in this compound. Obviously, he'd never been in a lower-level position.

"I don't trust you."

He said this in scarcely more than a whisper and still the sound startled her. He hadn't spoken in so long, she was caught completely off guard. And there was something else. The harsh whisper was somehow familiar. She studied his blond hair and then she leaned forward, putting her face closer to his, and she inhaled deeply, drawing in his scent.

It was him.

The man who had visited her in the darkness. *Smith Flynn.*

She eased back into her seat. "If it makes you feel any better, I don't trust you, either, Mr. Flynn."

He smiled. The expression was so scant she might not have noticed had she not been staring at him so intently.

"You would be wise to be grateful for my intervention on your behalf."

She met his intent stare with one of her own. "So you're the one who had me yanked back out of that hole." She hummed a note of surprise. "Interesting."

Made sense, she supposed, since she'd been brought directly here.

"Is that your way of saying thank you?"

She stared directly into those silvery eyes for a

long moment before she answered, opting to give him a taste of his own medicine. "Should I be thankful?"

He glanced at her blistered palms. "I can send you back, if you prefer. The rest of the Council recommended you for emergency supplies."

Damn. She moistened her lips, tried her best not to show how immensely grateful she was not to still be in that hole. "That won't be necessary. I am thankful you rescued me, Mr. Flynn. I suppose I'm a little worried about why you would go against all the others."

"You need a bath, Agent Buchanan."

He pushed back from the table and walked to the door. When he opened it, her guard still waited on the other side. "Get her cleaned up and put back in her cell," Flynn ordered.

"Yes, sir."

Sadie didn't wait to be told what to do next. She pushed to her feet and headed for the door. When she stood next to this man who had saved her for now, she hesitated. "Will I see you again?"

"If you do as you're told, you will see me again."

She walked out, followed the guard in his camo uniform. As usual, he said nothing. Relief sagged her shoulders. She was tired and hungry. Maybe after the bath she would be allowed to eat.

She decided to go broke on information. "I haven't seen Levi Winters. Is he in solitary or something?"

The guard didn't respond.

"He's been here longer than me," she went on, as

if he'd spoken. "Maybe he's already assigned to a job. I didn't see him at the big dig."

At the door to the detention center, he finally looked at her. "You don't need to worry about anyone but yourself. That's the way you stay alive. You do what you're told and you don't ask questions."

She nodded. "Got it."

Inside, he took her to another room, not her cell, and ordered the female in the white uniform there to see that she got cleaned up. This was only the second time she'd seen another woman. When her guard had left, Sadie turned to the other woman. "Hi."

The woman looked her up and down. "After your bath we'll do something for those blisters."

Sadie followed her to a large room that was mostly a huge shower. Three freestanding tubs sat to one side. Hooks along the wall were likely for towels. The other woman turned on the water in one of the tubs and then she left the room. More than ready for cleaning up, Sadie walked over to the tub and started to undress.

The woman returned with a towel, more of the ugly sweats and a pair of sneakers. "Size seven?" She glanced at Sadie's feet as she asked the question.

Sadie nodded. "Yes, thanks."

"Don't linger too long," the woman said. "When you're done, come back to my office."

Sadie nodded and thanked her again. The woman disappeared.

The extra-warm water felt amazing as she stepped

into it. She ignored the burn when it covered her hands. A sigh slipped from her lips as she permitted herself a moment to relax. She had earned it by God. The woman had said not to linger so she didn't. She washed her hair and smoothed what appeared to be homemade soap over her skin. When she was finished, she dried off and pulled on the clothes. Still no underwear and no socks, but she was grateful for something more than flip-flops.

She exited the shower room and walked in the direction she'd come. The only other door went into the woman's office. It looked more like an exam room. The woman got up from her desk and gestured for Sadie to sit in the only other chair.

Sadie watched as she gathered gauze, tape and some sort of salve. "You're a nurse?"

The woman glanced at her. "I am."

She was young. Midtwenties, Sadie decided. "They let you go to nursing school?"

The woman paused in her work of applying salve to Sadie's palms.

Damn, she'd obviously asked a question she shouldn't have. "Sorry. I was just curious."

"I had just finished nursing school in Tullahoma when they brought me back here."

Sadie held her gaze. "Oh."

The other woman's attention flitted away as she wrapped gauze around Sadie's right hand. "I thought I didn't want to come back but then they told me I'm getting married this year." Her face lit with a smile. "I was happy then."

Sadie moistened her dry lips. The young woman had gotten a taste of freedom during nursing school and she hadn't wanted to come back so they had dangled a carrot. "Who's the lucky guy?"

"His name is Levi. We met a long time ago but then he left. I never forgot him. I always told my father I missed him."

"Levi Winters?" Was that possible?

She nodded. "You know him?"

Sadie gave her head a slight nod rather than flat-out lie. "Who's your father?"

"Rayford Prentiss." She beamed another smile. "The head of the Council. He has many children here. Of course, we're all grown up now. My father says it's time for more children."

The picture cleared for Sadie. The Resurrection numbers were dwindling and Prentiss intended to plump up the population.

"Are there lots of married couples here?"

"Some, yes. But more are getting married this year. Some of us will be moving out, integrating into the outside communities. It's—" She snapped her mouth shut and her face paled as if she'd only just realized she had said way too much to a prisoner.

"I understand," Sadie said quickly. "It's a great plan. Mr. Prentiss is a visionary."

The other woman's smile returned. "He is. I

didn't want to see it when I was younger, but I see it clearly now."

Sadie wondered if the powers that be at the Bureau and the ATF had any idea what Prentiss was planning.

The man had his sights set on far more than this compound.

SMITH RAN HARD, pushing for another mile. There were times when he left the compound for Council business but this was the only way he left the compound on a daily basis. He ran six miles every day. Did the rest of his workout in the rec center at the compound. But when he ran he needed the freedom he couldn't get within the center running around and around a track. To find that freedom he ran through the woods. He had a route that took him through the areas where he was less likely to run into another human. Only once had he encountered another man and he'd been a hunter with no desire for small talk. He'd been on a mission that involved prey of the four-legged kind.

Smith made his usual quick stops. Leaned against a tree in one location and pretended to check his right shoe. There was nothing on the ground at the base of the tree. Nothing tucked into the moss. Then he moved on. His next stop was the sparkling stream that bubbled out from the mountainside. He knelt on one knee and cupped his hand for a drink. The water was crystal clear and cool despite the heat of the late summer days. He scanned the rocky bottom of the stream as he drank. Nothing. He sipped the water and then moved on. There was one final stop, the rocky ridge where he stopped again. This time he tied his shoe. There was nothing tucked between the stones.

No message.

He had been certain there would be something. A warning of some trouble headed his way. Or of some planned rebel uprising. The one time that had happened had secured once and for all his position on the Council. This time, however, he'd expected news of Sadie Buchanan's true mission. Some word of other trouble he should anticipate. But no message had been sent.

There could be only one explanation. Buchanan's mission was off the books, in all probability unsanctioned.

She was on her own.

Damn it. He couldn't take care of a rogue federal agent and complete his own mission. He was already on thin ice with Prentiss.

The memory of Avery Flynn carried a great deal of weight, as did his warning when a rebel faction had planned a takeover. But Prentiss remained more respected. If a choice had to be made between the two of them, Smith would not likely come out on top.

There was one other thing he could do. He could go down to the church and find the most recent newspaper. A message went into the classifieds only if there was no other option. If his contact had felt he was being watched in the woods, he would not leave a message at any of the regular drops.

Smith headed in that direction at a steady pace. His destination was just over three miles so less than half an hour was required to make the journey. He would have been able to go much faster if not for the winding, rocky paths through the woods. The paths were ones used by hunters and hikers, nothing made by anyone who belonged to the Resurrection.

He and the others were careful not to make new paths and to stay on the ones made by others. Slowing as he approached the church, Smith surveyed the area to ensure no one was about. The church was now defunct. Marcus Winters and his sister Sierra had been outed by their sister, who had recently been released from prison.

That was the way of secrets. They could only be kept for so long before they were found out.

His secret wouldn't keep much longer. He could not accommodate this unforeseen hitch. There was no leeway in his schedule for Sadie Buchanan and whatever trouble she had dragged in with her.

The church was empty as he'd expected. He walked to the road and checked the paper box that hung beneath the official mailbox. With the local newspaper in hand, he strode back to the church and sat down on the front steps. He opened the paper and carefully skimmed the classifieds. Nothing.

But the name Trenton Pollard had been a clear warning. He tossed the paper aside and stood. Some-

thing was happening and he needed to be able to prepare for whatever that something was.

What if his contact had been compromised?

There was no way to know.

Smith heaved a breath and returned to the woods.
He picked his way back to a familiar path and jogged
for a couple of miles. In the two years since going undercover he had not been faced with a situation like
this one. But he'd understood this time could come.
His contact could be compromised. The man was
older; he could very well have fallen ill or died. Time
would be required for a replacement to be situated.

The only question was whether or not Smith had
the time.

He slowed to a walk when he was within a mile
of the compound. For now there was little he could
do beyond moving forward as if Sadie Buchanan had
not suddenly appeared.

The Levi Winters issue had apparently been rec-
tified. Prentiss had decided to use him as a breeder.
Smith still found that abrupt decision strange. Had
that been the beginning of whatever was happening?
Perhaps Sadie Buchanan was not the real problem.
Maybe it was Winters.

His brother, Marcus, had been a reliable ally for
many years. Levi had been an on-again, off-again
dabbler. He had been involved with Jack Kemp—yet
another reason Smith couldn't understand Prentiss's
sudden decision to keep him for any purpose.

Smith ensured he was not being followed as he

ducked into the camouflaged pedestrian entrance to the compound. Whatever Prentiss was up to, he would keep it to himself until he was ready to move. He never shared a strategic move that involved security with any of the other Council members, much less Smith. He was far too paranoid.

There was nothing to do but remain vigilant and see how the situation played out.

Prentiss was a very astute man. He had not hung on to his position as leader of the Council by being naive or weak.

Smith supposed he should be grateful he had managed to abide the man this long. Certainly he could claim at least one record.

No one else had ever lived a lie right in front of Rayford Prentiss for this long.

Chapter Seven

"Where are we going now?"

Sadie felt grateful for the bath and the clean clothes and in particular for the salve and the bandages on her hands. But she still had a mission to attempt completing. She needed to find Levi Winters. Obviously he was still alive if Prentiss had planned his marriage to one of his daughters. Sadie decided not to try to figure out if the woman was his biological child. The idea that the old man could have dozens of children by different women made her feel ill, especially if the women had not been willing participants in the endeavors.

"The cafeteria."

Her attention slid back to the man at her side. The rumble in her stomach warned that it had been way too long since she had fueled up. No question. But maybe the trip to the cafeteria was about a new job for her. Just because she was being taken there didn't mean she would be allowed to eat.

"To work?" she asked since her guard seemed a bit more receptive to answering questions now.

"To eat."

This time her stomach growled loud enough for him to hear, too.

He grunted. She supposed that was as close to a laugh as he would permit, but she didn't miss the glint of humor in his eyes.

They entered the detention center. This time their journey took them to the left when they reached the connecting corridor that led to the cells on the right. At the end of the left corridor a set of double doors stood, the word *Cafeteria* emblazoned across the pair.

At the doors he hesitated. "Go to the serving line. Get your food and sit down. Eat and don't get into trouble. I'll be back for you in fifteen minutes."

She nodded her understanding and walked through the doors. Her guard didn't follow. There was probably a separate cafeteria for the people who belonged. There were maybe a dozen people, all wearing the same attire as she did, seated around the four tables. When she stepped up to the serving line, the man behind the counter grabbed a plastic tray and dumped beans, bread and something not readily identifiable but green in color onto the tray.

Sadie accepted the tray and walked toward the tables. Stainless steel water pitchers and cups sat on each table. The other prisoners were male. Not surprising since the number of females she had met

were few and far between. The other prisoners eyed
her suspiciously as she passed. She caught snatches
of conversation about working in the fields or the
laundry facility. There was one who sat alone at the
table farthest from the serving line. He stared at his
plate, visibly forcing his spoon to his mouth, chewing and then repeating.

Relief swam through Sadie. It was Levi Winters.
Even in the baggy sweats and with his head bowed,
she recognized him. She headed for his table, pulled
out a chair and sat. Before she spoke, she reached
for the pitcher and poured herself a glass of what
appeared to be water. Just plain water, she hoped.
Hopefully not laced with some drug to keep them
under control. She still believed the man—Flynn—
who had come into her room in the middle of the
night had only been able to do so without her knowledge because she had been drugged with a mild sed-
ative.

When she had downed a bite of bland-tasting
beans and dry bread, she glanced at her tablemate.
"You okay, Levi?"

He glanced up at the use of his name, stared at
her for a moment. "Do I know you?"

She shook her head. "My name is Sadie. Your sister Cece sent me."

Hope lit in his eyes. "Is she okay?"

Sadie smiled. "She's doing great. Her name has
been cleared and they've sorted the truth about what
really happened when your father was murdered."

Cece had given Sadie a specific message for Levi. "Cece wanted you to know that everything is fine and none of what happened was your fault. She just wants you safe and back home."

His hopeful expression fell, and he stared at his plate once more. "They'll never let me go."

"Do you want to marry the girl?"

His head came up, his fearful gaze colliding with Sadie's. "I don't even know her. Prentiss said when I was a kid my father promised me to him for one of his daughters. He said if I didn't do exactly what was expected of me they'd put me in the tunnels." He shook his head, shuddered visibly. "I've heard about what happens to the folks who end up down there."

Nothing good. Sadie knew this firsthand. She glanced around. "Don't worry. I'll get you out of here. Just stay calm and trust me."

A frown furrowed his brow. "I don't know who you are but you're crazy if you think we'll get out of here alive. No one does. You either do what they say, or you're never seen again."

Sadie gave him a reassuring smile. "Like I said, just stay calm. Do as you're told until I tell you different."

His eyes rounded, his attention shifting over her shoulder.

Sadie glanced back just in time to see a man coming toward her. He didn't look happy. In fact, he looked angry. She stood, putting herself between Levi and the threat. "You have a problem, pal?"

The man stopped, evidently surprised that she stood up and faced him. He glared at her. "I'm going into the tunnels, because of you." He stabbed a finger into her chest. "You're damn right I have a problem."

He called her one of those truly ugly names that no woman ever wanted to be called and then he spit in her face.

Sadie swiped away the spittle with the sleeve of her sweatshirt. "I hate to hear that, but I didn't make the decision. Mr. Prentiss probably did. Why don't you take it up with him?"

His face blanched at the mention of Prentiss's name. Sadie gave herself a mental pat on the back for the quick thinking.

The man glared at her a moment longer, then walked back to his table. Sadie dragged her chair around to the end of the table and sat where she could see the rest of the people in the room. She snagged her tray and pulled it down to where she sat and forced herself to eat. Food was necessary to survival. She tasted the water—it seemed okay so she drank it down, quenching the thirst that had been dogging her since she arrived.

One by one the other prisoners in the cafeteria got up, tray in hand, and readied to leave. On their way to the tray drop, they passed Sadie, flinging whatever food they hadn't eaten at her.

She ignored them, kept shoving beans and bread into her mouth. From time to time when the food hit her in the face she flinched, but otherwise she showed no outward sign of discomfort or fear. They were all ticked off at her now. She had been pulled back from the tunnels and one of them was going in. They likely believed it was only because she was a woman. The truth of the matter was, Sadie had no idea why she'd been pulled out of the tunnels. Luck? Not likely.

"I wish I was as brave as you."

Sadie glanced at Levi. She gave him a reassuring smile. "You're doing pretty damned good, Levi. Cut yourself some slack. And don't worry, we'll be out of here before you know it."

He shook his head. "You don't understand."

Judging by his defeated expression he was more worried than relieved to know she was here. "What is it that I don't understand? I came here to find you and get you out. I will make it happen."

He swallowed hard, his throat seizing with the effort. "They're listening. I couldn't tell you. I had to do what I was told." He stood, picked up his tray. "I'm sorry. Really sorry."

As Levi walked away Sadie wondered how she had allowed her defenses and her instincts to fail her so thoroughly. She'd made an elementary mistake. One that would likely carry a heavy cost—like her life. She should have considered that Winters would have been brainwashed or indoctrinated to some degree by now.

"Well, hell."

She stood to take her tray to the drop zone but her

guard appeared. "Leave it," he said, his expression as unreadable as his tone.

Sadie deposited the tray back on the table and followed the guard out of the cafeteria. The corridor was empty. The prisoners who had thrown food at her had either returned to their cells or were back at work. The guard led her back to her cell. He held her gaze a moment before he closed and locked the door. She could swear she saw a glimmer of regret in his eyes.

If the guard was feeling sorry for her, she was definitely screwed.

SMITH STEPPED OUT of the shower and dried his body. There had to be a reason he hadn't been given additional intelligence about Sadie Buchanan via his contact. The name she had tossed out, Trenton Pollard, was a code phrase warning that trouble was headed Smith's way. But there was nothing else. No message at any of the usual drop sites.

He pulled on clean jeans and a freshly laundered shirt. The dress code was fairly simple for Council members. They wore whatever they liked. Most moved back and forth between the compound and the outside community. But not Smith. He stayed here. Didn't take chances by lingering in the community.

The guards wore the camo while the workers were issued the sweats. Only those in supervisory positions or who served on the Council were allowed to wear civilian attire. The clear distinction was one of the things Flynn hated most about this place... this life.

No one should be made to feel inferior to others. One's way of life should be based on choice, not a dictatorship led by one insane, self-centered man. How the hell had so many been drawn into this life? Then again, the world was changing, and those interested numbers were dwindling.

A knock at his door drew his attention there. He finished lacing his boots and stood. "Enter."

The door opened and one of Prentiss's personal bodyguards, this one named Mitchell, stepped inside.

"Mr. Prentiss would like to see you in his private quarters."

The old man rarely summoned Smith unless there was a Council meeting...or trouble. Smith's gut said this was the latter.

"Tell him I'll be there shortly."

Mitchell gave a quick nod, then left, closing the door behind him.

Smith walked to his desk and checked the monitor on his laptop. Buchanan was in her cell. Her bandaged hands and clean sweats told him she'd behaved herself during her cleanup. There were no posted complaints of trouble involving her.

She presented a conundrum. Did he tell her who he was or did he wait for her to admit why she was really here? Her provided story wasn't cutting it for him. There was something more she was hiding.

Prentiss hadn't swallowed it, either. Smith's move

this morning had bought Buchanan a little more time, but he couldn't be certain how long that time would last. He had hoped to receive word from his contact this morning to give him some sense of direction. His best course of action at this point was to hold out for any intelligence that filtered in over the next few days, assuming the trouble he worried was coming didn't show first.

Taking his time, he walked to the final cabin on Council Row and knocked on the door. When his father had been alive, he had lived in cabin one. Prentiss didn't like the idea of being that available. He wanted the rest of the Council in front of him, like a wall, protecting him from any danger that forced its way into the compound.

The bastard was a coward.

"Come in."

Smith went inside. The old man sat at his table, a steaming cup of tea in front of him.

"Join me," he offered with a wave of his hand.

Smith pulled out the chair opposite him and settled into it. "I'm good, thanks," he said, declining the tea.

Prentiss sipped his tea for a half a minute before saying, "The Council has had a change of heart."

Smith remained still, his face clean of tells. "Has there been a vote I wasn't informed about?"

Of course there had been. This was how Prentiss conducted business when he wanted something his way. He didn't bother arguing his point, he simply left out the people he felt would vote against him.

"It was an emergency and you weren't available." His gaze locked with Smith's. "Apparently you were on a run or a hike. Some communing with nature."

"I do the same thing every day," Smith reminded him. "Today was no different. You're well aware of my personal schedule."

"Except something occurred while you were out," Prentiss countered. "Your new pet project, Sadie Buchanan, confessed her real reason for being here and it was not that she required sanctuary. She has infiltrated our walls under false pretenses. She represents a threat to our security."

Dread coiled inside Smith. Buchanan hadn't looked as if she'd suffered any torture for information. He couldn't see her voluntarily coming forward with this new and startling information, particularly if it cast her in a negative light.

"Really. That's an interesting development. Why don't you tell me what happened?"

"She told Levi Winters that his sister had sent her here. Buchanan was tasked with coming here to rescue him. The information she fed us was nothing more than a distraction to cover her real mission."

"I'd like to question her again," Smith said. He stood as if the recommendation had already been approved. "I'm confident I can get her full story."

Prentiss held up a hand. "No need. A final decision has already been reached. We're turning her over to the *others*. Levi Winters, as well."

Smith kept his surprise to himself. "You selected Winters for your daughter—"

"The choice was premature. He failed his final test. We don't need his kind here."

"We do need more females. Buchanan wouldn't be the first one we've swayed to our way of thinking." It was the best argument and the most logical one he could come up with at the moment.

The old man eyed him for a long while before he spoke again. "You've been her champion since she arrived. Are you suggesting you've selected her as a wife?"

Before he could answer, Prentiss went on. "You've snubbed each of my daughters, but you would have this traitor? This outlander?"

"As I said—" Smith ignored his suggestions "—she may prove useful in a future negotiation. I have not considered her as a wife, only as a bartering asset."

Prentiss announced, "The Council wants her out of our midst."

"I don't agree, and I have an equal say on Council matters." Smith held his ground. He had a vote in all matters. Prentiss understood this, no matter that he despised the idea. The bastard would not force his hand.

Prentiss stood and walked over to his desk. He picked up a document. "It is decided. The decree is signed, and the message conveyed to the *others*.

There is nothing further to discuss. You missed a great deal by being out of pocket this morning, Smith. Perhaps you should rethink your schedule in the future."

"Decrees can be overturned," Smith said, dismissing the other man's declaration. "I'll speak to the Council members."

"There will be no further discussion on the matter. You will escort Buchanan and Winters personally. Tomorrow morning."

Smith stared long and hard at him. "What are you up to, old man?"

He held Smith's gaze, then he smiled. "We make our own beds, Smith. And in the end, we have no one to blame but ourselves for the lack of comfort."

The slightest hint of uneasiness trickled through Smith's veins. This was something more than Sadie Buchanan or Levi Winters at play here.

"At sunrise in the morning you will depart," Prentiss repeated. "You should be back before dark."

Smith didn't waste any more time arguing. Instead, he left and walked straight to the detention center. The guards didn't question him as he entered, nor did anyone attempt to stop him when he walked straight to Buchanan's cell and unlocked the door.

Buchanan turned to face him. She stood on the far side of the small cell as if she'd been pacing the too-confined space. Before she could school the reaction, uncertainly flared in her dark eyes.

He went straight to the point. "What happened today?"

There were ears everywhere on this compound but questioning her was not going to change what had already been done. As a Council member he had a right to know all the facts.

"What do you mean?" She shrugged. "I was pulled back from the tunnels, given an opportunity to bathe and then taken to the cafeteria."

His irritation flared. "Do not waste my time. What happened?"

Her arms folded over her chest. "I ran into an old friend. Gave him a message from his sister. She's been worried about him."

"What exactly did you say?" Fury had him clenching his jaw to prevent saying more than he should.

She heaved a big breath as if he were the one trampling on her last nerve. "I told him who I was and that his sister had sent me to rescue him. I also told him not to worry because I would be getting him out of here."

Well, that sure as hell explained a lot. He stared directly into those dark eyes. "So you lied. Your story was a cover for your real mission."

She gave a succinct nod. "I lied."

"Get some sleep. We leave at sunrise."

He turned his back on her but before he was through the door she asked, "Where are we going?"

He didn't bother glancing back. "To trade a mole for a lost rabbit."

Chapter Eight

Sunday, August 11

They knew.

What was worse, she had told the enemy herself.

Sadie closed her eyes and shook her head. She had royally screwed up this one. Flynn had called her a mole. He was taking her from the compound today to trade her for a lost rabbit. One of the Resurrection's own, obviously, who had been taken by another group or some other faction involved with their mutual black market business dealings.

Considering she was FBI, it was possible the lost rabbit was in holding with some branch of law enforcement. The local cops? The feds? She had gotten the impression that as far as Winchester and Franklin County law enforcement were concerned—at least until the takedown at the Salvation Survivalist church—the Resurrection was more a local legend than anything else. A bunch of local yokels with guns they picked up at gun shows and MREs they ordered from the internet.

But that was not the case at all. The Resurrection was a long-term, well-planned and -operated organization with powerful contacts and an extensive reach. At this point, local law enforcement was well aware that gunrunning was involved. In Sadie's experience, drugs and human trafficking oftentimes went hand in hand with the smuggling of weapons. Maybe these daughters of Prentiss's weren't his biological children. Maybe they were stolen children he'd raised in this damned compound.

Sadie paced the few steps to the other side of her concrete cell. She had to finagle an escape. There were people in this place who needed rescuing. There was Levi and the ones in the tunnels. And possibly all the women. Though she had only seen a couple, she suspected there were more. She exhaled a big breath. This situation was far bigger and more complicated than she or anyone else had initially speculated.

It was possible another federal agency, like the ATF or the DEA, knew more than the Bureau about this group. The sharing of information was limited to a need-to-know basis for the safety of any ongoing operations and embedded agents.

She needed more information. She exhaled a resigned breath. What she really needed was backup.

The swish and whir of the lock snapped her attention to the door.

Sunrise had arrived.

The door opened and Smith Flynn met her gaze. He didn't mince words. "Let's go."

She walked toward him, expecting the broad-shouldered man to step aside so she could move through the door but he didn't. He held his ground, staring down at her.

Apparently he had more to say before this party got started.

"From this moment until I tell you otherwise you will do no thinking for yourself. You will do exactly as I say, when I say. Understood?"

Anything to get out of this prison. "Understood."

"We walk out of here, you don't look at anyone, you don't say anything. You follow me and you do exactly as I tell you."

"I can do that."

He turned and headed along the corridor. She followed. As they left the cell behind and reached the exit of the detention center, she didn't spot her guard or any others for that matter. Outside was the same. Her instincts urged her to look back over her shoulder, to look around, but she resisted the impulse. Flynn had told her not to look at anyone. She decided not to test him this early in today's game. Whatever was going to happen from this point forward, she needed to proceed with extreme caution.

She had resigned herself to the idea that she might not be able to escape this place on her own. If she couldn't get out, she couldn't get Levi out. At least if she managed to lose Flynn at some point, she had a chance of getting help back here to rescue Levi.

At this point she was more than a little surprised that Flynn hadn't restrained her hands. They headed in the direction of where she had spotted all those vehicles parked. The tunnels were in that direction, as well. Her heart instantly started to pound. She did not want to end up back down there. If that was what was about to happen, she had to do something. At least try to escape. A final ambitious effort even if she was shot for her trouble.

She bit her lips together to prevent asking him if that was his intent, simultaneously bracing for fight or flight. He'd said she was being traded. Surely that meant they were leaving the compound. Then again, the guy in the cafeteria had been fired up because he was being sent to the tunnels in her stead. That was a trade, wasn't it?

Damn it. A rush of dread roared through her veins.

She was stronger than this. If she allowed the dread and uncertainty to get to her now, she would lose all semblance of control over the situation. She might not have much as it was, but she was still hanging on to a sliver. Whatever happened, she had to cling to that modicum of control.

When they reached the motor pool, he opened the rear passenger door of a black SUV. He reached inside for something. When he drew back he had two things, nylon wrist restraints and a black hood like the one she'd worn on the way here with Prentiss and his thugs.

Movement inside the vehicle had her leaning forward just a little. Someone was already in there. The black hood concealed everything from the shoulders up, making it impossible to say if the passenger was male or female.

Flynn held out the nylon restraint and she offered her hands, wrists together, for him to do what he had to do. When her wrists were bound tightly together, he dropped the hood over her head. A hand rested against her upper arm, ushering her toward the open SUV door. She climbed in and settled into the seat.

"Where are we going?" the other prisoner asked.

Sadie recognized the voice. *Levi.* Apparently, he either hadn't received the same lecture she had or he chose to ignore the order.

The door closed and a few moments later the front driver's-side door opened, the SUV shifted slightly and then the door closed again. She resisted the urge to lift her hood and make sure it was Flynn who had climbed behind the steering wheel. He'd secured her hands in front of her so she could certainly do so but, again, she resisted the impulse. If the situation went downhill from here it wasn't going to be because she gave it a shove.

She wanted out of here far more than she wanted to satisfy her curiosity. That Levi was with her was a genuine stroke of luck. If she could salvage this rescue operation, all the better.

The vehicle started to move. About a minute later there was a brief stop, then they were moving forward again. Sadie imagined they had stopped long enough for the doors or gate or whatever to open, allowing them out of the compound. Though she couldn't see to confirm the conclusion, her heart hammered at the idea that they could very well be beyond those suffocating walls.

For the next ten minutes by Sadie's count, they drove fairly slowly. The ride was smooth, making her judgment of the speed not as reliable as it could be. Again, the urge to lift the hood and look around nudged her. She wrestled it away.

At least for now.

"Get down on the floorboard!"

The shouted order startled Sadie and for a split second she couldn't move.

"Get down!"

She tugged at Levi's arm and then scrambled onto the floorboard. Thankfully he did the same.

The shattering of glass and the pop of metal warned they were under assault.

"Stay down as low to the floor as possible," she whispered to Levi. She felt his body flatten in an attempt to do as she said.

The SUV's engine roared and the vehicle rocketed forward. The momentum of the driver's evasive maneuvers swung their weight side to side, made staying down increasingly difficult.

"Stay down," she urged the man hunkered between the seats with her.

The SUV barreled forward, swaying and bumping over the road. Sadie concentrated on keeping her body as low and small as possible. This vehicle likely wasn't bulletproof. The shattered glass she'd heard earlier all but confirmed as much. A stray bullet could end up killing one of them.

If the driver was hit...they would probably all die.

The SUV suddenly braked to a hard, rocking stop.

Another shot exploded through the rear windshield and then a detonation of new sounds. Ripping, cracking, scratching...then a hard crash.

The SUV suddenly lunged forward.

"You can get up now."

Flynn's voice, definitely his voice though it sounded muffled. Sadie recognized it was the blood pounding in her ears that smothered his words. She scrambled upward, swept the glass she felt from the seat and then righted herself there.

"We okay now?" she asked. After what they had just gone through, she figured the rules had changed. Asking if they were out of danger seemed reasonable.

"For now."

"What's happening?" Levi demanded, his voice high-pitched and clearly agitated.

"We're okay," Sadie told him, hoping he would calm down rather than grow more distressed.

She felt his arm go up. She grabbed it, hung on.

"Don't do anything until he gives the order," she reminded. "We need to get through this."

At this point, she trusted Flynn on some level whether he deserved that trust or not. But they weren't in the clear yet. She couldn't be sure of his ultimate intent. There was a strong possibility that she and Levi were only valuable if they were still alive. His risky protection measures might be self-serving.

The SUV braked to another sudden stop. Sadie's pulse sped up again.

The hood covering her head was abruptly yanked off. "Get out," Flynn ordered.

He whipped Levi's hood off next and issued the same order to him. Sadie hurried out of the SUV. Levi came out behind her rather than getting out on the other side. The road was not paved. Dirt and gravel. Muddy. It must have rained last night.

She looked up, squinted at the rays of sunlight filtering through the thick canopy of trees overhead. They were deep in the woods but they were out of that damned prison. The dirt road seemed to cut around the edge of the mountain. To their backs was the mountainside, in front of them was a steep drop-off. As she and Levi watched, Flynn stood outside the driver's-side door and guided the still-running SUV to the edge of the road. He jumped back as the engine roared and the vehicle bumped over the edge of the road, crashing through the trees.

Exactly like the one that had been firing at them,

she realized, as the familiar sounds echoed around them. That was the reason for his sudden stop back there. The other driver instinctively attempted to avoid the collision, whipped the steering wheel and ended up going over the edge of the road and down the mountainside.

Sadie watched the man walking toward them. It wasn't until that moment that she noticed the backpack hanging from one shoulder. She didn't have a clue what was in that backpack, but what she did know was that they had no transportation.

She asked, "What now?"

"Now." He pulled a knife from his pocket and sliced through the restraints on her wrists and then did the same to Levi's nylon cuffs. Flynn's gaze locked back on hers. "We run."

THE COUNCIL HAD VOTED.

Fury roared through Smith as he moved through the dense underbrush as quickly as he dared. Buchanan had no trouble keeping up with him, but Winters was slowing them down more than anticipated.

"Keep up," he shouted over his shoulder. Buchanan shot him an annoyed look.

He imagined she had some idea that they were in trouble but he doubted she fully comprehended the magnitude of the situation. The Council had decided to terminate Smith's position within their ranks and, apparently, him. They would want him and the people with him dead as quickly as possible. No loose ends. No way to trace the murders back to them.

This was Prentiss's doing. No one else on the Council would have dared to speak against Smith. The old man had grown worried that the rest of the members preferred Smith's style of progressive leadership.

He had suspected this was coming. Smith had kept his cover intact far longer than anyone expected. Funny thing was, it wasn't until Buchanan showed up that Prentiss found the perfect leverage to use toward this very end.

Smith had two choices: save Agent Sadie Buchanan's life or attempt to salvage his cover.

His cover was shot to hell.

He led them deeper into the woods. Merging into the landscape was the only way they would make it off this mountain alive. For now, they had a head start. The three-man crew Prentiss had sent after them was down. If one or more survived, it was only a matter of time before he climbed up that ravine and called for backup. Staying on the road was out of the question. There were lookouts at certain points along this stretch of road and there was no other drivable egress in the close vicinity. Disappearing between scout stations was the only option. Moving back and forth and in a zigzag pattern was their only hope of outmaneuvering the enemy.

Reinforcements would come like panthers after prey. Until then, they needed to put as much distance between them and this location as possible. Prentiss would send his team of trackers and they would bring the dogs. Time was of the essence.

Smith knew these woods. He had grown up here and he'd spent most of his time cutting paths through this dense foliage. Over the past two years he had planned for this very moment. There was never any doubt about this moment. It would come and he would need an emergency egress. He just hadn't expected to be bringing two others along with him.

There were answers he would need eventually but there was no time for that now.

"Where exactly are we headed?"

Buchanan pushed up behind him. She was strong, fit. The only good thing about the additional luggage with which he was saddled.

"You'll know when we get there."

"Those were your friends back there, right?"

Before he bothered with an answer, she fell back a few steps. "Hang in there, Levi. We have to keep going."

"Why the hell are we following him?" Winters shouted. "He's one of them."

"That's a good point."

It was the total lack of sound after Buchanan's statement that warned Smith the two had stopped.

He did the same and swung around to face the latest hurdle in this unfortunate turn of events. He visually measured Buchanan before shifting his focus to Winters. "Do you know your way out of here?"

He waved an arm to the junglelike growth around them. "We're a lot of miles from the nearest house. You'll need water. I have water. A limited supply, but I have it."

Buchanan glanced at Winters, who now stood beside her. Then she looked up, probably searching for enough of the sky to see in which direction the sun was rising.

"We're heading south," Smith advised. "And we have a long way to go. When my *friends* back there—assuming there are survivors—get a call through to Prentiss... Even without survivors, he'll be expecting a check-in. When that call doesn't come, they'll pour out in droves to find us and they'll bring the dogs. We have to move as fast and as far as possible before that happens."

"Why should we trust you?" Buchanan asked.

She was no fool. She was ready to go but she held out, no doubt to prove to Winters that she was ultimately on his side. She hoped her support would gain his cooperation. If rescuing him had been her original mission, she likely wanted to make that happen. Understandable.

Smith shrugged. "You have no reason to trust me. But I'm going. I know the way. I have the necessary supplies. You can either follow me or you can find your own way. Makes no difference to me."

He pivoted and continued his trek through the shoulder-deep underbrush.

Fifteen seconds later he heard the two coming

behind him. They were moving fast, trying to catch up. Whatever Buchanan had said to Winters, she had lit a fire under him. Good. Smith had no desire to end up dead before he'd finished his own mission.

THEY WALKED FOR another three hours before he felt comfortable allowing a water break. There was a small overhang of rocks just up ahead. They would duck under there. It would be cooler close to the earth beneath the outcropping and their position would be hidden from anyone who might be catching up to them. So far he hadn't heard the dogs but that didn't mean someone wasn't out there on the trail. Prentiss would use every method available to him. Losing more control was not an option. Smith almost wished he could see the bastard's face.

He had his doubts about the physical condition of the three who had gone over the mountainside in the other SUV. He doubted any one of them would be capable of giving chase. A call for backup would require time. Forty minutes to an hour to prepare and reach the point where the three of them had abandoned the SUV.

He scanned the trees beyond their hidden position and listened intently. By now, it was more likely than not that search parties were out there. The dogs would ensure they moved in the right direction. The head start Smith had gained was the one thing he had on his side.

Smith downed the last of his water and tucked the empty bottle back into his pack.

"Where are we going?" Buchanan asked.

"To the river. The water is low this time of year but that will work to our advantage. We'll use the water to throw the dogs off our scent."

"I haven't heard any dogs," Winters argued. "Wouldn't they be after us by now?"

"When you hear them," Smith warned, "it'll be too late." He pushed up from the rock he'd used as a seat. "Let's get moving."

He held out his hand for their water bottles. He tucked each one into his pack and headed out. Buchanan didn't hesitate. Winters did but not for long.

Rested, Smith pushed a little faster. He wanted over this ridge and to the water's edge within the hour. He wouldn't rest easy until they'd put a mile or so wading through the water behind them.

Mosquitoes swarmed when he pushed through the foliage. He ignored the occasional bite. Behind him he heard his followers swatting at the irritating insects. The ground was rockier here, making him less sure-footed. Still he pushed as fast as he dared.

By dark he would reach the safe place where he would be able to use the emergency device that would summon backup. Smith had nothing against local law enforcement in Franklin County, or the neighboring counties, for that matter, but he had an obligation to ensure there was no breach in security. The only way to do that was to use the communication device he had hidden and to call his contact and no one else.

The rumble of curt conversation droned behind him. He didn't slow down or bother to look back. He couldn't force either of them to follow him. More important, he could not share who he was or his mission with either of them, either. If they were captured, Buchanan might survive torture without talking but Winters would not.

Besides, Smith saw no reason to share that information until absolutely necessary for his own protection, as well.

"Why did my sister send you to find me?" Winters asked the woman two or three steps in front of him.

Evidently, Winters had decided to question all aspects of his good fortune. Some people just couldn't be satisfied by merely being rescued from certain death.

Buchanan kept her voice low as she answered the question. Smith didn't catch all that she told the ungrateful man. Something about his sister being worried and the local police being concerned that the Resurrection group were a more considerable threat than they had estimated.

Smith could tell them exactly how big the threat was, but he had to get out of this situation first.

"Why you?" was Winters's next question.

Smith slowed, diminishing the distance between them. He would like to hear the answer to that one.

"That's what I do," Buchanan said, practically

under her breath. "I rescue other agents or assets who get themselves into trouble."

Well, well, he'd known the lady wasn't the average federal agent. Interesting that she was a rescue and retrieval specialist.

"I guess this time isn't working out so well," Winters said with a dry laugh. "Just my luck."

"We're not beaten yet," she protested. "I've never failed before. I don't intend to start now."

Smith hoped the lady was right.

Failure would mean a very bad end for all of them.

Chapter Nine

They had been walking for most of the day. Her sneakers were still wet from the slog through a mile or more in that narrow river. The water level had been low but hopefully it was enough to throw the trackers and their dogs off their scent.

The sun was going down and the trees were thick but it was still as hot as hell. Sweat beaded on Sadie's forehead. Her legs ached. She was in damned good physical condition but this went way beyond her usual workout. This was grueling. They'd been going uphill until the past hour. The downhill journey wasn't much better, just used a different muscle group. The under-canopy brush remained thick and the landscape was rocky.

She had tried to keep Levi calm and focused on moving forward but he was resisting more and more the farther they went on the desperate journey. She wasn't sure how much longer she could keep him cooperative. His misgivings were understandable, reasonable even. But they had little choice. Keeping ahead of the enemy had to be their priority.

So far they hadn't heard any sign of the dogs Flynn had worried about. Thank God. Their stoic leader had stopped several times and listened for anyone who might be following them. He hadn't heard or spotted anyone yet. She hadn't, either, and she was keeping her eyes and ears tuned in as keenly as possible. She did not want to be captured by those bastards. Chances of surviving beyond the trip back to the compound were way less than zero.

If they were caught, they were dead.

"How far now to the destination you've targeted?" She had to admit, she was damned tired, not only physically but of blindly following orders. But she would keep going until they reached some semblance of safety or until she found reason to do otherwise.

"It's a ways yet."

Flynn said this without looking back.

Something about his nonchalance bugged the hell out of her. "Define *a ways*."

He stopped. She almost bumped into his broad back. He wheeled around, his glare arrowing in on her and she stumbled back a step.

"We've been lucky so far, let's not screw that up now. We'll get there when we get there. Just keep moving and stay quiet."

He gave her his back and started forward again.

So much for getting an update. Sadie trudged after him.

"I'm done." Levi glanced covertly at her. "I know where we are now. I just want to go home." He jerked his head toward the faint path Flynn left in his wake. "We can't be sure what he's got planned. I'd feel better taking my chances on my own from here. I can do it. You should go with me."

Sadie slowed, keeping pace with Levi. She glanced at the man disappearing deeper into the woods. "You sure about that, Levi? If they catch us, it's doubtful we would survive. Let's get through this night and we can decide how we want to move forward in the morning."

"Just let me go." He started backing away from her. "Hell, the best I can tell, he's leading us away from Winchester. My sister and the people I trust are that way." He jerked a thumb to his left.

"Let's catch up with him and confront him about your concerns." She had a bad, bad feeling about this. "We'll figure out the best option. We're safer in a group."

Levi shook his head and took off in another direction. West, Sadie decided. She went after him. As curious as she was about whatever Flynn had in mind, Levi was the one she'd come to rescue. She had a duty to keep him safe, even when he made it difficult.

She wanted to call out to Levi but she couldn't risk that the enemy was close. The last thing she wanted was to draw Prentiss's people.

She pushed harder to catch up with him. All this

time he'd dragged behind. Apparently he'd gotten his second wind. They hadn't made it far when she heard someone behind them. Adrenaline fired through her veins. She glanced over her shoulder and spotted Flynn.

Levi ran harder. Sadie did the same. But Flynn was gaining on them.

In the next moment Sadie had to decide whether to keep going with Levi or to distract Flynn, giving the younger man an opportunity to reach his sister and help. If Flynn had no real interest in what happened to them, why come after them? Why not just let them go?

Something was wrong with this scenario.

And if Levi was familiar with the area and knew the way home, why not give him a chance to make it?

Decision made, she zigzagged, heading south once more. She held her breath until Flynn shifted his direction and came after her.

She ran harder still, determined not to make it easy for him to catch her.

She sidled between two trees; her shoulder scraped hard against one. She cringed. That would leave a mark.

Keep going.

Maintaining her balance at this speed and along this rough terrain as she plowed through brush and dodged the bigger trees was not an easy task, especially downhill.

No slowing down! He was close. Only steps be-hind her. She could hear him breathing.

Damn, she needed to go faster.

Fingers grabbed the back of her sweatshirt. Yanked her off her feet.

They went down together, rolled in the brush. A limb poked her cheek. She grimaced.

Flynn landed on top of her, his bigger body grind-ing her into the brush and dirt.

"What the hell are you trying to do? Guarantee we end up dead?"

She tried to scramble away. Screaming was not an option. If there was anyone out there on their trail, they would hear.

Better the devil she knew…

"Get off me," she growled.

He glared at her for a long moment, those silver eyes icy with fury.

Then he got up, pulled her up with him and kept a death grip on her arm. He had no intention of al-lowing her to run again.

"That little move you pulled back there, allowing your friend—your rescue target—a chance to run, likely put a bullet in his brain or worse."

Uncertainty trickled into her chest as she strug-gled to catch her breath. "He knows how to get home from here. He said you're taking us in the wrong di-rection. Is that true?"

Frustration hardened his face. "That depends on where you think the right direction is. He's going home to Winchester? To his friends?" He laughed, shook his head. "I hope he makes it, but that's highly unlikely. They have watchers in town. Those watchers will be on the lookout for all of us. The possibility that he'll make it to help before someone nabs him right off the street is about the same as Santa paying him a visit early this year. He won't make it. Do you hear me? He. Will. Not. Make. It. Which is why we're not going directly to Winchester. I have a safe place to wait for help."

That trickle of uncertainty turned into a river. "Then I have to go after him."

When she would have headed back in the direction she'd come, he held on to her more tightly.

"You're going to draw them right to us. We have to go. We've wasted too much time already. The only way you can help Levi now is by doing exactly what I say."

She stared at him, tried to see beyond that iron mask of his. "Who are you?" She had no real reason to trust this man and yet every instinct screamed at her to do exactly that.

"You already know the answer to that question. Right now, I'm the man who's trying his best to save your life."

"How can I be sure?"

She waited for an answer, held his gaze. He needed to give her something concrete. Why would a man so high up the food chain in the Resurrection organization suddenly throw everything away and run just to save her or anyone else?

"You answer a question for me and I'll answer one for you," he countered.

"Quid pro quo," she suggested.

He gave a succinct nod.

She could do that. He pretty much already knew all there was to know about her anyway. She'd owned being a federal agent. She'd made the mistake of spilling her true mission to Levi. Beyond her last boyfriend, this guy probably knew everything there was to know about her, including her favorite college professor's name.

"All right." She braced for his question.

"Why did you use the Trenton Pollard cover story? Where did you get that name?"

"That's actually two questions," she pointed out.

He gave her a look that said he was running out of patience.

"That was the name I was told to toss out if I needed more leverage in a dicey situation."

"Who gave you the name?"

"My point of contact."

More of that frustration tightened on his face. "He or she has a name?"

She nodded. "But I'm not giving that name to you until I see where this journey ends."

He shrugged. "Fine. Let's get moving."

"Wait a minute. I get a question, too."

"So ask your question so we can go."

"Why does the Pollard name mean so much to you?"

"He's a friend of mine and I don't see how you or your point of contact could know him."

Done talking, he started forward again. She glanced over her shoulder. Hoped like hell Levi knew what he was doing. She followed Flynn. If Flynn was truly on the run, her money was on Prentiss and his people coming after him first. Finding him and Sadie was likely far higher on their priority list than finding Levi.

Hopefully that would work in his favor until he reached help.

Either way, he'd made his decision and she'd done the only thing she could: helped him escape an unknown situation.

THEY WERE CLOSE. Smith was relieved. He wasn't sure how much longer Buchanan would last. She'd held up far longer than he'd expected as it was. She was strong but they were both tired.

The safe place he'd prepared wasn't far now.

"Give me a minute."

Smith stopped, sized her up as she leaned against a tree. He shrugged off the pack and removed the last bottle of water. "We can share this one," he offered, passing the bottle to her.

This last one would have been for Winters but he'd cut out on them without any supplies. Smith wondered how far he would get before a member of Prentiss's posse caught him. Not all the way into town for sure.

He watched as she opened the bottle and downed a long swallow. When she came up for air, he said, "We're almost there."

She choked out a dry laugh. "That's what you said an hour ago. I'm beginning to think you're lost, Flynn." Her gaze locked with his. "I hope that's not the case."

"Being lost is one thing you do not have to worry about, Buchanan."

He knew this place inside and out. He'd explored every square mile in his youth. Always looking for something different, something else. He'd never found it here. Leaving had been the only way to escape this life and the people he had grown to hate. His father had been the only voice of reason among the group of preppers who had started the Resurrection. When Avery Flynn had fallen ill, Prentiss had taken over and changed things without his knowledge. He'd started to dabble in criminal activities. Smith's father had never wanted to cross that line. There had been fringes of his followers who'd gotten caught up in the black marketing of weapons and even in transporting drugs, but he'd always weeded them out in time.

But when his father lost control, it all went to hell.

Smith hadn't come back to make things right. It was too late for that. Too many of the old-timers were gone and too much of the younger blood was greedy and power hungry. The extremists without conscience had taken over. He'd come back to take them down. It wasn't what his father would have wanted but his father had been wrong. Anywhere those with extreme attitudes and beliefs gathered, nothing good came of it.

Ever.

"Fifteen minutes," he assured her. "We'll reach our destination in fifteen minutes—barring any unforeseen events."

She screwed the cap onto the water bottle and tossed it to him. "I'm holding you to that."

He downed a long swallow and put the remaining water away. Before he could stop himself, he licked his lips and savored the taste of her. Sadie was different from any woman he'd ever met. She was stronger, determined, loyal. Intelligent. Unconditionally fearless. She stirred his interest in numerous ways.

Shaking off the distraction, he started moving forward again. "Let's go. We don't want to fall behind schedule since you're holding me to it."

She laughed again. He liked the sound of it. "You're a smart guy, Flynn."

Maybe. He hadn't considered himself smart in a long time. The truth was, he hadn't even considered the future until very recently. He had resigned himself to the idea that he would likely die getting this done.

Still could. It wasn't over yet.

The underbrush was thinner here in the rockier soil. Made going a little easier. Being physically exhausted, however, made just moving a chore. It had been a long day. Buchanan wasn't the only one who was beat.

They made the fifteen-minute timeline with a couple of minutes to spare. He pointed to a copse of trees that hugged the mountainside maybe ten yards below their position. The relief on Buchanan's face was palpable.

The overgrowth was thick around the cave opening. He carefully pushed the limbs aside and ducked inside first. There were times when a man should go first—like when he needed to ensure there were no wild animals, no den of snakes holed up in his safe place. Buchanan would likely argue the point with him but there were some things his father had taught him that stuck. *Always protect those under your care.*

Something else she would argue. Fiercely, no doubt.

He tugged the flashlight from its holder on the side of his pack and scanned the small shelter. Clear. No sign of animals. As often as he could get out here he sprayed the area with repellant to ward off animals but some critters weren't so easily put off. Thankfully the place was clean, no animal droppings. No snakes.

"You can come in." He held back the limbs, ensuring he didn't break any. Those limbs acted like a curtain, providing a layer of camouflage.

Once she was inside, he used his flashlight to locate his stored supplies. The cave was only about fifteen feet deep and the last five or six feet narrowed down to the point where crawling was the only option. He'd banged his head plenty of times. At the very back, he carefully moved the stacked stones he'd gathered in the immediate area. All looked exactly as if they'd always been right here in this pile. He'd gone to a great deal of trouble to ensure no one who might stumble upon this place noticed his stored goods.

Beneath the stack was a nylon bag, pale gray in color, nearly as large as his pack. It was sealed in a clear plastic over bag. Inside he kept his emergency supplies. The plastic was to better protect them from the elements and to ensure the bears and wolves didn't pick up on any scents.

His gut growled as he set the ready-to-eat packets aside. They'd only had a couple of protein bars today. It was time for something a little more substantial.

"What's all this?" Buchanan moved in next to him, sat back on her knees.

"Dinner. A burner phone. Weapon. First-aid supplies." Not so much of the latter but enough to get by in a minor emergency. A packet of blood-clotting agent, a suture kit. Antibiotic salve and a few bandages. "Water. A small blanket. Emergency light. You know, the usual."

There was also a backup plan, which he pocketed without mentioning. He tucked the nine millimeter into his waistband and loaded most of the other supplies into his pack. "You want beef or chicken?"

She studied the two packs of ready-to-eat meals. "I'll take the chicken."

"Good choice." He passed it to her and grabbed the beef.

He moved back to the roomier portion of the cave and opened up the small emergency light. He sat it on the ground. The lumens were low but he didn't want it glowing beyond the cave opening. It was enough. He tossed his guest the thin blanket. It wasn't much but it was better than nothing when one was sleeping on the ground.

"You can use that tonight. I'll use my pack for a pillow. I don't mind sleeping on the ground."

"So we're staying the night here?"

He shrugged. "If that's what it takes."

While she opened the food pack and ate, he fired up the burner phone. Once it was on, he moved to the cave opening to get better service. With a few taps, he sent the necessary message. The phone's battery was way too low. He'd charged it the last time he was here. With it turned off it should have maintained the charge. When the message had been delivered, he relaxed. He returned to where Buchanan sat and settled in for however long they had to wait.

He opened his meal pack and ate slowly, more slowly than he wanted to but it would satisfy him better that way. Buchanan did the same. She'd likely had similar training and understood the need to adapt to extreme change. Being a field agent required a degree of flexibility. That she consumed every bite of the less-than-tasty meal confirmed his conclusion.

When she'd finished, she said, "Tell me about the message and why we may be here all night."

"The message goes into a pipeline of sorts. It takes a while to get to the intended recipient. Once he has it, he'll make arrangements for a pickup. When the pickup is ready, we'll go to the designated location. There are several good options within two miles of our position."

She sipped on the packet of water. "The contact is aware of this location?"

He shook his head. "No one knows this location. It's a security precaution in case there's ever a breach in our communications. I selected this location based on my knowledge of the area and the best egress routes. We agreed upon designated pickup points. The gap allows for a degree of separation between me and any trouble that might crop up. As I'm sure you're well aware, advance preparation is key."

She nodded but then frowned. "What if you're injured? You might not be able to make it to the pickup point."

"That's where my backup plan comes into play." He patted his pocket. "I have a beacon, the same technology skiers use. If necessary, I turn it on and they can find me."

Her expression told him she was impressed. "You've got all the bases covered."

He focused on his food for a while, let the silence fill the space. It would be dark soon. Since there was no way to know what time they would have to move, it would be best to get some sleep now while they had the opportunity.

When he'd finished his meal, he put the packaging into his pack. "Sleep if you can. We may have to move again at any time."

He checked the screen on the burner phone before sliding it into his shirt pocket. With the phone on vibrate and the pack as a pillow, he stretched out for a quick nap, braced his arms over his face. He hoped like hell the charge lasted until he had a response.

He listened as Buchanan spread the thin blanket out on the ground and did the same. She lay there quietly for about a half a minute. He was surprised she lasted that long.

"What are you, Flynn? If you tell me you're just a run-of-the-mill member of that group we escaped, I'm going to know you're lying."

At this point he didn't see any reason to keep her in the dark. "I'm like you."

She rolled onto her stomach. He felt more than saw the move. "Only way different."

He chuckled and lowered his arms. "Not so different."

"Come on. You don't work for the Bureau or I would know. The ATF didn't claim you. Neither did the DEA. Since when does Homeland Security embed agents in the middle of nowhere like this?"

This time he outright laughed. "I'm not with Homeland Security. I'm with the ATF."

She lay there for a moment seeming to mull over what she'd learned. It wouldn't be unusual for an embedded agent to be denied for the purposes of protecting the mission. Like the military, need to know was the motto for most federal agencies.

Finally she asked, "How did that happen? Did someone recruit you?"

"No. I recruited myself."

She waited for him to go on but he didn't. He should have realized she would want his story as soon as she knew the truth about who he really was, but he wasn't sure he wanted to share it. It felt too intimate.

Or maybe he was afraid it would turn the *moment* into something intimate. It was essential that they stayed focused. Emotions could not get tangled up in this precarious situation.

"I'm waiting for the rest of the story, Flynn. Don't leave me hanging like this."

"I grew up in Franklin County. My father was one of them, only not like what you see today. It didn't start out that way. But I watched it happen and I hated it, hated the men who made it happen. I made my way into the ATF for the sole purpose of coming back here and taking Resurrection down. For years I pretended that wasn't my motive. I tried to be a good agent, take the assignments given. Do the job to the best of my ability—whatever that job might be. But I couldn't forget. Two years ago when my father died, I approached the top brass with an offer. They accepted and I came back to do what needed to be done."

"Wow. That's a hell of a story, Flynn. You must have incredible restraint. You've had to pretend to be one of them for two whole years."

He rolled over her comment for a time and then he said, "I've always been one of them. I'm just not like them. That's the difference."

She nodded. "I get it."

"What about you, Agent Buchanan? How did you become a rescue and retrieval specialist?"

"Growing up in Montana I always said I wanted to work where the sun shines all the time and there's no snow so I ended up in Miami. I was so new it was painful but because of my obvious Hispanic heritage, I was needed for a particularly high-profile assignment right off the bat. They wanted me to get inside and evaluate the situation with a deep-cover agent who had gone silent. Getting in was easy. I have a knack for putting people at ease and making them believe what I want them to believe."

"You do." If it hadn't been for her using the Trenton Pollard name, he could have fallen for her story. She was good.

"Not only did I find the guy but I got him out using my favorite bait-and-switch tactic. It almost never fails."

"Is that right?"

"That's right. I make the bad guy believe he's going to get one thing and then I do exactly the opposite of what he expects."

He chuckled, couldn't help himself. This was a woman who enjoyed her work.

"Turns out my target was the grandson of a former director. He was so impressed with my work, he urged the powers that be to make better use of my skill set. So here I am. This was basically a favor. An off-the-record mission."

"Well, Agent Buchanan, it's a pleasure to make your acquaintance." He thrust his hand at her.

She grinned and gave it a shake. "Ditto, Agent Flynn."

Now if they could only get themselves out of this thorny situation, maybe he'd ask her out to dinner.

A frown furrowed his brow. The beef jerky obviously hadn't done its job or he wouldn't still be thinking about food.

Then again, maybe it wasn't food on his mind.

He peeked at the lady lying so close.

Too dangerous, he reminded himself.

Maybe another time when they weren't both targeted for execution.

Chapter Ten

Monday, August 12

The way Flynn kept checking the burner phone, Sadie was reasonably confident he was worried more than he wanted her to know that there had been no response from his contact and the phone's battery was dying.

He hadn't said as much but she was no fool. There was no way a crucial reaction to a critical situation would take this long. She pulled her fingers through her hair, wished she had a brush. She shifted her position a bit—this rock was not made for comfort. Being stuck in this cave all night was even less so. She was thankful for the protection from the elements and the enemy but even when she slept, fitfully to say the least, she was aware of *him* next to her. The smell of his skin, the heat emanating from his body. Not helpful when trying to sleep. At least not when she wanted desperately to do something entirely unrelated to sleeping.

Not smart, Sadie.

The situation wasn't completely unexpected. She had been so focused on her career for years now that she'd totally ignored her personal life. Sure, she had the occasional date with some guy a friend insisted she so needed to meet. Very rarely did that develop into physical gratification. Apparently, that was an issue. She was like a starving animal now, desperate…

She rubbed her hands over her face and wished for a long, hot bath. Maybe a trip to the spa the way she'd done years ago—before her career took over her life. There, she decided, was the real source of the rub. All her female friends—the ones with whom she'd done lunch and spa days—were married. Most had children. They all thought because Sadie was approaching thirty-five that she should be doing the same. It wasn't really because they were old-fashioned or had narrow views, it was just human nature. The heightening urge to procreate as one reached thirty.

Sadie had passed thirty several years ago and not once had she thought about a permanent relationship, much less kids.

She worked. Work was her constant companion, her best friend, her lover.

Her traitorous eyes stole a glance at the man packing up their sparse campsite. But this man had her dwelling on her most basic instincts. Of all the times for an attraction to form, this was the absolute worst possible one.

The guy was a stranger—no matter that she now knew he wasn't a criminal—and their situation was dire at best.

Before daylight he'd gone outside their hiding place and checked the area. When he'd returned, she had taken a turn slipping out of the cave to go for a necessary break, as well. Flynn was good at concealing his concern but she hadn't missed his mounting tension. It was in the set of his broad shoulders, the lines across his handsome forehead.

He was worried.

Which made her worry.

It was possible, she supposed, that there had been a delay due to some unpredicted issue. But they had gone well beyond that possibility now. This was not just a delay, this was a total breakdown in the link between a deep undercover agent and his primary support contact.

When Flynn pulled on the pack, she asked the question burning in her brain. "What's the plan now?"

"No response from my contact. The phone's battery is dead. We move on. Staying here any longer would be a mistake. As well hidden as we are, the dogs could pick up our scent again."

"Agreed." For the first time this morning she thought of Levi. She hoped he had made it to someplace where he could call someone he trusted. Things would have been a lot simpler if he'd stayed with them. She glanced at the man towering over her. A lot simpler on numerous levels.

"Stay close," he reminded her, "and move as quietly and quickly as possible. We'll head off this mountain and into town via trails that keep us out of sight and away from where we would most likely run into people."

Which meant they would be hiking a lot of miles, taking the longer, tougher routes. The blisters forming on her feet ached. They weren't as bad as the ones on her hands, but they were getting there. She glanced at the bandages, considered discarding them but decided against it for now.

At the opening that would take them out of the shallow cave, he hesitated. "We'll save the backup plan for later. I have no way of knowing what's gone wrong with my communication link so I don't want to give anyone our location until we know whether the one who receives the signal is friend or foe."

So, she'd been right.

He parted the thick foliage and made his exit. Sadie followed.

Whatever happened now, they were on their own.

SMITH HAD NO choice at this point but to admit that his contact was either dead or he'd turned.

He had known the man who was his primary backup for a decade. He found it difficult to believe he could be turned. Odds were, he was dead. The mistake was Smith's. He had insisted on only one person having knowledge of his egress options. He should have known better than to rely on only one man. Humans were not immortal. Accidents happened, health issues cropped up. One or both stealing lives at inopportune moments. Things happened, infusing desperation, weakening even the strongest man.

Choices at this juncture were extremely limited but at least they still had a couple.

Smith had decided that they would keep moving. Yesterday had been spent traveling in wide circles up and then down the mountain. No express routes. Today would be somewhat more direct. He would use a scatter pattern to prevent leaving a straight-forward trail to follow. However hard he tried not to leave signs of their presence, it was impossible not to break the occasional small branch or trample plants.

Their path wouldn't be difficult for a trained tracker to follow. The dogs wouldn't need anything but their scent.

Frankly, Smith was surprised he hadn't heard the dogs at some point yesterday. Particularly after Winters separated from them.

This, too, was cause for concern.

Was Prentiss so certain he would win that he didn't bother sending a search party?

The idea hadn't crossed Smith's mind until his contact failed to come through and time had continued to lapse without trouble finding them.

Now that he considered the possibility, Prentiss

had been the one to insist Smith take Buchanan and Winters to the *others*. If he'd discovered Smith's secret, why not kill him at the compound? Was the old bastard's intent to make an example out of him? Show his followers who their true protector was?

This was more wrong than he had realized.

There was a mole all right, but it wasn't Buchanan. It was someone on Smith's home team. Someone in the ATF with clearance to this mission. Only a handful of people knew about this cleanup and infiltration detail. Still, that didn't mean someone with the opportunity hadn't found a way to access the files. The world was one big electronic filing cabinet these days. Nothing was unattainable if one knew in which drawer to look and possessed the skill to open it.

Had Prentiss turned someone with that kind of know-how?

The only way to be sure was to get Buchanan to safety and then for him to return to the compound for Prentiss. This was a finale that required an up close encounter.

He had spent the past two years of his life digging deeply into the Resurrection. He was not going to walk away without eliminating the organization, even if that meant taking matters into his own hands.

The compound had been built into the mountainside. It was completely camouflaged and protected by the earth itself. Over and over he had mentally plotted where and how the explosives would need to be planted to destroy the place—to bring down the entire mountainside. The problem was, as gratifying as that result would be, it wouldn't change anything. Some of the powers that be lived outside the compound. They hid themselves among the locals to stay aware of whatever was going on in the rest of the world. Having everyone with power, reach and contacts in the same place at the same time for elimination would be virtually impossible.

Smith had toyed with that scenario a thousand times.

Once the compound was destroyed, those who survived would go into hiding. He knew them all— every single one. But sending them to prison for their criminal activities required solid evidence, none of which he possessed outside that compound. Even lining them up for vigilante-style termination would require an army. The moment one was taken out, the rest would scatter like crows. Since he didn't have an army prepared to commit cold-blooded murder, he needed a better plan.

A laugh tugged at his gut. In two years he hadn't been able to come up with a workable strategy.

He could sever the head of the snake, Prentiss, but another one would sprout in his place.

Unless...he found a more lethal snake willing to swallow up the competition entirely.

A new plan started to form. Smith had a feeling this one might even work. But to make that happen he would need to enter the territory of that lethal snake.

It was a good plan. He thought of the woman right behind him. Rather than attempt to explain the intricate details and to persuade Sadie to go along, he decided to keep her in the dark. She would be mad as hell when she found out, but if he accomplished his ultimate goal, she would forgive him.

He hoped.

Altering his course, he headed for dangerous territory. He readied for trouble, exiling all distraction in order to focus fully on his surroundings, listening and watching. Within the hour they would cross into territory ruled by another group. They couldn't really be called an organization since they weren't technically organized. These people didn't even have a name, much less a motto. Anyone who knew them merely called them the *others*. The one thing Smith knew for certain about them was that they were dangerous. Cunning and methodical.

Maybe clinically insane. Certainly crazy by anyone's measure.

Crazy was what he needed at the moment.

All he had to do was find it without getting Buchanan or himself killed.

THEY WERE TRAVELING in a different direction now. Yesterday he had done the same. Flynn had wound back and forth around this mountain. She'd figured his goal was to make their path more difficult to find and follow. With no response from his contact and no sign of Prentiss's people or dogs, she had expected he would take a more direct route today.

Maybe not.

She wanted to ask him about his plan, but he'd reiterated that silence was particularly important today. Rather than risk making too much noise, she'd kept her questions to herself for now and followed his lead. If she had to find the way out of here they would likely end up bear bait in these damned woods.

Not that she'd spotted any bears or bear tracks but there could be bears, coyotes or wolves, to name a few predators who would present a problem.

There was the gun he'd had hidden in the cave. But she didn't have any idea how much ammunition Flynn had on him. Maybe only what was in the weapon. Maybe not enough to survive if they were attacked by man or beast.

But they had their wits, no shortage of determination and Flynn's extensive knowledge of the area.

The situation could be a lot worse.

A muzzle jammed into the back of her skull. Before her brain had time to analyze how it happened so fast without her noticing someone was closing in on her, her body instinctively froze.

"Don't move."

Somehow she had known the person—man obviously—on the other end of that barrel was going to say those two words.

Smith spun around, his weapon leveled on the threat. "Back off," he warned.

Before his growled words stopped reverberating in the air, three more men stepped forward, rifles aimed at him.

Sadie blinked, startled when she'd thought nothing else could shock her. The men wore paint, like body paint—nothing else as far as she could tell. They had melted into the landscape and only when they moved had their presence become visible. She blinked again to ensure she wasn't seeing things.

"Back off," Flynn repeated. "Aikman is expecting me."

If these were more of his friends, it would have been nice if he'd given her a heads-up before the one behind her startled the hell out of her.

One of the three fanned out around Flynn stepped forward, moving closer to him. "Drop the gun."

Sadie held her breath. Agents were trained never to relinquish their weapons but sometimes there simply was no other choice. An agent learned through experience when it was time to forget the classroom training and do what had to be done.

Flynn tossed the weapon to the ground and raised his hands. "My name is Smith Flynn. Take me to Aikman."

The guy behind Sadie shoved a bag at her. "Put this on."

Sadie took the bag and tugged it onto her head. The last thing she saw before the black fabric fell over her eyes was Flynn with the business end of a rifle stuck to his forehead.

The nearest muzzle nudged her back. "Start walking."

She did as she was told, hoping like hell she didn't trip over a tree root or a rock. No one talked but she heard the faint sounds of their new friends moving through the underbrush. She suddenly wondered if the painted guys wore shoes or boots or something on their feet. She hadn't noticed. The guy behind her was probably painted, too. He was, she decided as she recalled the arm that had thrust the bag at her.

The only good thing was that Flynn appeared to know who these people were. This Aikman, she assumed, was someone in charge. Hopefully someone high enough up the food chain to keep them from becoming "emergency supplies."

Her toe snagged on a root or a rock and she almost face-planted. Thankfully, she managed to grab back her balance. Her sudden stop to capture her equilibrium won her another nudge from the muzzle.

Sadie counted off the seconds and minutes. By her estimate, they walked for half an hour. The terrain didn't change much. Brush, rocks, moving sometimes up, sometimes down. The scent of food cooking told her they had reached a camp of some sort. She doubted it was noon yet but it was past midmorning. No matter that she'd had a protein bar very early that morning, her stomach sent her a warning that she needed to eat again soon.

And coffee. What she would give for a big, steaming cup of coffee.

She wondered if this group would have a compound built into the mountainside like the Resurrection. She had to admit, the idea had been ingenious. A hand suddenly rested on her left shoulder. She stopped, braced to either fight or run like hell. The bag whipped up and off her head.

She blinked twice, three times, and surveyed the area. There was a canopy of green overhead. A combination of trees and vines and other plant life she couldn't readily identify. Sunlight filtered through, making her blink with its brightness after wearing the bag. There were shacks made of branches, twigs and brush. This didn't look anything like a compound. These were like primitive huts that flowed seamlessly with the brush and trees. She looked upward again, spotted similar builds in the trees. The tree houses were also constructed with limbs and other pieces of the surrounding natural resources, making them almost like an extension of the trees.

Another nudge in the back and she started walking again. Flynn walked ahead of her, a painted man on either side of him. They moved deeper into the trees. Finally they reached an area that looked very much like the place against the mountainside where they'd slept last night. Brush and branches hid a narrow cave opening. They were escorted inside where two more men, these wearing dark clothes similar to SWAT gear, took over escort duty. The man who'd been behind Sadie all that time and his friends slipped back out the way they had come.

Beyond the opening, the cave widened into a room. There were lights in the cave but not electric lights. The lanterns looked like the old oil type. The cave floor was rocky. Water trickled from the walls here and there. Smelled musty. No more food smells. Whoever had been cooking, they were outside in the rustic camp they'd passed through.

This cave was far larger than the one they'd called home last night. The ceiling zoomed several feet overhead and the width of the space was five or so yards. They moved downward from there. Maybe a more elaborate compound had been built deeper in the cave.

The wide tunnel divided and they took the left fork. A few yards in they passed another wide room-size section on the left. Rows of rustic tables filled that space. Dozens of oil lamps lit the area. People dressed in white coveralls like painters and wearing paper face masks were frantically packing some sort of product.

Oh hell.

Drugs.

Her stomach sank. This was one of those things you couldn't unsee. People in this business didn't allow outsiders to see their work and walk away.

This was bad.

She hoped like hell Flynn knew what he was

doing. She also hoped he knew these people really well—well enough to share dark secrets.

Otherwise they were goners.

Once they had moved beyond the workers in the white suits, they passed a number of large round stones that sat on either side of the corridor. The lead man stopped. With obvious effort he pushed one of the stones aside, revealing a hole in the rock wall, like a large round doggie door without the flap.

Not exactly a user-friendly entrance to wherever they were going next.

"Inside." The man looked at Sadie as he said this.

She glanced from him to the hole. Was he serious? She shifted her gaze to Flynn. "I'm supposed to go in there?"

"For now. Don't worry."

He couldn't be serious.

The man with the gun waved it as if he was running out of patience.

Great. She squatted, then dropped onto her hands and knees. She poked her head far enough through the opening to see what was inside. Nothing. As best she could determine it was just an empty, small, cube-like rock room. She crawled inside. Squinted to get a better look at the space. She shifted, scanning all the way around while there was still light filtering in from the open hole. In the corner to the left of the hole she'd just entered her gaze snagged on a form. She crawled closer, her eyes adjusting to the even dimmer light.

Bones.

Not just bones. An intact skeleton.

The rotting clothing suggested the owner of the bones had been male.

She swallowed back a sound, not exactly a scream but something on that order.

The noise from the stone rolling in front of the hole once more rumbled around her. She sat down on her bottom and stared at the only exit from this new prison. A dim outline of light from the lanterns in the corridor slipped in past the stone now blocking that exit.

Her gaze shifted back to the bones. She couldn't really see them now but her brain filled in the details from the picture seared into her memory.

Whoever had been stuck in here before had died in this place.

Without water or food it wouldn't take that long.

She thought of the lack of tissue on the bones. The person had been trapped in this place for a very long time. Years. Maybe as much as a decade considering the deteriorated state of the clothing he wore.

Sadie sat in the middle of that musty, dark space and replayed the past decade of her life. She had graduated with a master's degree and some big plans. Two summer internships with the Bureau and she was accepted as soon as she reached the age requirement. Her parents had been so proud. Her mother had been a little concerned about her daughter going into law enforcement, but she'd come to terms with the decision after the first year. Maybe it had been Sadie's excitement that had won over her mom.

Sadie had ended the relationship with her hometown boyfriend before entering training. The long-distance relationship had basically been over since undergrad school anyway. They were going in different directions with changing objectives. Why prolong the misery by watching the relationship they had once believed would go on forever shrivel up and die? Strange, she never once considered when the relationship ended that it would be her last one.

Dates, never more than three, maybe four with the same guy. Her social calendar consisted more of bridal showers, weddings and baby showers for friends than dates for herself.

If she died in this dark, dank place her parents would be devastated.

A life half lived.

Not true, she decided. If she died in this place, she would be dying young, for certain. But it wasn't a life half lived. She had lived every single day to its fullest. She had loved the hell out of her work. She had helped to bring down numerous bad guys and she had rescued more than her share of good guys.

"Get over it, Sadie. You are not going to die in this hole in the ground."

She pulled up a knee and rested her chin there. She would find a way out of here. It was what she did. And she was really, really good at it...usually.

As soon as Flynn finished his meeting with this

Aikman person and was brought here, they would put their heads together and come up with an escape plan.

Flynn had a contact with these people. He hadn't appeared worried when they were captured. She shouldn't be worried, either. Then again, Flynn's record with his contacts hadn't actually been a reassuring experience so far.

Maybe it was time to get worried.

Chapter Eleven

Smith had waited a half hour. The cuckoo clock on the wall counted off every second with a loud tick-tock. Any minute now the bird would slide past its door and count off the hour: 11:00 a.m.

He forced himself to relax. He possessed as good an understanding of these people as anyone. They did things their way in their time. Making him wait was a way of showing dominance. As long as he was still breathing there was reason to believe an arrangement could be reached.

This move had been a risk. A risk he was wagering everything would work out. Unfortunately, the wager involved Buchanan's life as well as his own. If things didn't work out as he intended, her death would be on him. That was the one part that didn't sit well with him. But they were in a no-win situation. As a trained agent, she would understand the need to take drastic measures.

Smith drew in a deep breath and reminded himself to be patient. To play the game.

The tunnel where Buchanan had been secured had forked again, leading to the outside once more. Another campsite had been built against that side of the mountain. Again, using elements that blended in with the environment to keep them off the radar of reconnaissance flyovers.

Aikman's office was like any other with a desk, chairs and electricity. The electricity was furnished by a generator. The primary difference between this place and that of the Resurrection as far as Smith could see was the absence of electronics. The *others* didn't use electronics with the exception of burner phones, which they used sparingly. They stayed as far off the grid as possible.

The door behind Smith opened and Aikman entered, minus his usual bodyguards. They no doubt waited outside the door. No matter that he was well aware that Smith was unarmed, he would never take the risk of being alone in a room with a known follower of the Resurrection without backup close by.

"You got some nerve coming here after what you did, Flynn." Aikman sat down behind his desk. "I was expecting you to deliver two packages yesterday. Prentiss and I had a deal. First, you don't show, then I get word you've dropped off the grid. Now you waltz in here with only one package." He shook his head. "This is not good."

Draven Aikman was younger than Smith. His rusty-brown hair was kept skinhead short but his beard was long, at least ten or twelve inches. He wore the same dark uniform as his soldiers. He'd killed the old man who held the position as leader before him. The story was that the old man was sick, practically on his deathbed and making bad decisions. Aikman claimed he took care of the failing part for the good of the whole. Whatever his motive, he now held the highest position among this closed, clannish group known only as the *others* by the few who were aware of their existence.

Aikman propped his feet on the desk and leaned back in the chair, eliciting a squeak of protest from the base. The desk and chair, like the rest of the furnishings, might have been unwanted castoffs picked up from the side of the road on garbage day. The *others* had a reputation for living free of excessive material burdens. Survival of the coming human self-annihilation was their singular goal. Still, they were only human and not completely immune to power and greed. In any group there was always someone who couldn't resist the temptation of *more*.

"You suddenly develop a death wish?" Aikman asked. "Coming here, throwing my name around like we're friends. I could get the wrong idea."

"The deal Prentiss made is off. I'm here with a different offer."

Aikman lifted his brows. "This better be good."

"There are other names on my list," Smith warned, "but I chose to bring this offer to you first."

The other man's gaze narrowed. "What kind of offer?"

"We both know the Resurrection is your primary competition. We've blocked your every attempt to expand your operation into other areas. You've been stuck making the drugs no one else wants to make unless they have no other choice. We've pushed you out of the arms business. Basically, we've kept you down for decades."

"If you're supposed to be buttering me up for some proposition," he laughed, a rusty sound, "you're falling way short of the mark."

This was the mistake most people made. To look at the *others* and how they lived, one would automatically think uneducated, backwoods hillbillies. But that was not the case at all with the ones like Aikman. According to Smith's sources, the man had a master's degree in business administration. He was smart. Allowing you to believe he wasn't automatically put you at a disadvantage in any negotiation.

"I'm sure you get my meaning," Smith said, ignoring his dig. "I've decided it would be in both our best interests to join forces. We both have our resources. If we pool those resources, we could expand our operations and take over the Southeast."

Aikman dropped his feet to the floor. "You want me to believe that you're ready to abandon your loyalties to the Resurrection—an organization that runs in your blood? You would trample on your daddy's memory?" He grunted a sound of disbelief. "Pardon me if I don't believe you. What're you up to, Flynn?"

This was the risky part. It would have been easier for Smith to keep walking. To climb down this damned mountain and turn himself over to local law enforcement. He would have been sent back to where he belonged ASAP. The mission would have been over and the goal he'd dedicated his entire existence to for the past two years would have been lost forever.

He would have been alive, safe and free of this nightmare.

Except Prentiss would have gotten away. He and his Council of ruthless killers would have relocated and continued doing whatever they pleased with no care of the human cost. No worry about what the guns and the drugs were doing to society.

Smith was left with one option—finish this in the only way possible: light the fuse of the Resurrection's number one enemy.

Start a war.

"Prentiss sold me out," Smith confessed. That part was true. Rumor of the shake-up would get around soon enough if it hadn't already.

There was no other explanation for the trio who'd showed up behind them on that mountain road after they left the compound. Prentiss had intended to wash his hands of Winters, Buchanan and Smith.

End of story. To believe they had appeared for any other reason would be foolish. Somehow Prentiss knew. Which would also explain the sudden drop in communications with Smith's contact.

Whatever had gone wrong, Smith was on his own. He had few options if he wanted to finish his mission and this was the best one.

Aikman reared his head back and considered the announcement for a moment as if he didn't quite believe what he'd heard. He pursed his lips then rocked forward, propping his forearms on his desktop. "You actually expect me to believe that Prentiss dared to attempt a coup so he could be rid of you?"

"Believe what you want." Smith turned his palms up. "I came here to give you the first dibs on *my* coup. If you're not interested, then I overestimated your ability to see the bigger picture. I won't waste your time. I have other options."

Aikman's gaze narrowed once more. "What other options? We own this mountain. My people and yours. There's no one else."

Smith smiled. "If that's what you believe, then I really did overestimate you, Aikman."

The statement was a direct insult but it also made the other man think. "You're talking about that Hispanic gang, aren't you? They've been inching their way up the food chain for years, but they're not organized enough or financially flush enough to be more than a nuisance." He hesitated. "What is it you know that I don't?"

There was no time to go there. "We have to act fast, Aikman. We can't sit around discussing the politics of the region. Prentiss is out there looking for me right now."

Aikman scrubbed a hand over his jaw. "What is it you've got to offer?"

"You get me and my friend off this mountain and I'll give you everything you need to take down the Council. Locations, security codes. Everything. The Resurrection and all it entails will be yours for the taking."

"Where do you come back into the picture?" He shrugged. "Doesn't sound like we're doing anything. Sounds more like I'm doing and you're cutting out."

Smith shook his head. "I'll be back. There's a personal matter I have to take care of first."

Aikman grinned. "Are you referring to the woman?"

Tension slid through Smith. "I am."

Aikman scratched at his thick beard some more. "You see, that's where we have a bartering issue."

Smith's instincts stirred. "What does that mean, Aikman?"

He leaned back in his chair, his hands on the worn arms. "To tell you the truth, things get a little lonely out here from time to time. Sure there's women, but not one I've cared to take for more than a little bump and grind. There's definitely none like her. I need someone who presents a challenge. The ones I've run up on so far bore me."

Smith's gut clenched at the idea of what this bastard had in mind. The *others* were known for staying to themselves. They had no use for those who were different, whether that difference was as simple as skin color or went way deeper. The man's fascination with Buchanan would be short-lived and then she'd end up a curiosity or, worse, a sex slave.

"I don't see how that's my problem. This is business. Important business," Smith warned. "You should keep that in mind as you decide your next move."

Aikman grinned. "I'm making it your problem, Flynn. You brought this problem between you and Prentiss to my door, now I'm bringing mine to you. I want the woman. You give me the woman and we'll have a deal."

"Not happening." Smith stood. "Let's not waste each other's time with games. We'll be on our way to the next prospect if this is your final answer."

The other man stood, leaned over his desk, bracing his hands on the worn surface. "Do you really think I'm going to let you just walk back out of here?" He moved his head slowly from side to side. "This was a no-turning-back meeting, Flynn. You don't get to sit in my office and then just walk away. You think Prentiss would watch me walk away if I paid him a visit?" Aikman angled his head and studied Smith. "Then again, he might if I told him I had a gift for him. What you think you're worth to the old bastard?"

Smith smiled. "Not nearly as much as you are."

Aikman reared back, then laughed as if Smith's statement hadn't startled him. "I gave you a chance, Flynn. I guess you aren't as smart as you think. What woman is worth dying for?"

"I could ask you the same thing."

Aikman didn't flinch, but Smith saw the glimmer of uncertainty in his eyes before he blinked it away. "My people appreciate tangible proof they're being protected. With that in mind, from time to time a public display is required to keep them reassured. At dawn, we'll give them something to feel good about. Maybe the two of you will be worth all the distraction you've caused after all. You wouldn't believe what organs go for on the black market."

Smith ignored the threat, turned his back and walked out of the man's office. The guards grabbed him by the arms and jerked him forward.

Not exactly the news he'd hoped to take back to Buchanan.

SADIE HAD MOVED around the entire space and found no openings, not even a crack, except for the small round opening she'd been forced to crawl through to get in here. She couldn't help wondering if the owner of the remains in the corner had done the same thing—searched for some way to escape, wondering what would happen next—before he died here.

Whatever he'd had planned, it hadn't worked out for him.

For the first time on a mission, her mind wandered to her folks and she tried to remember the last time she'd spoken with her parents. Had she said the right things? Told them she loved them? She couldn't see her sister being there for them in their time of grief if Sadie never made it out of this place.

Don't even go there, Sadie.

Moving around the perimeter of the room once more, she closed her eyes and listened for any sort of sound. The soft whisper of words slipped beyond the crack between the stone that made a door and the hole in the wall that it covered. She couldn't say if the voices were those of the guards outside the room or people walking past in the long corridor.

The lives of these people likely revolved around the preparing and packaging of drugs. Survival. They lived to please their leader, this Aikman that Flynn asked to see. There was no logical reason why they would concern themselves with her or her survival.

Lines creased her forehead, nagging at the ache that had begun there. How long had Flynn been gone? An hour? An hour and a half? He could be dead by now for all she knew. She hugged her arms around herself, feeling oddly chilled. It would be bad enough to be stuck here with him. The concept of ending up alone in this hole—her gaze drifted across the darkness—was far worse.

Movement near the small opening drew her attention there. The rock rolled away and light poured in. Sadie stood back and waited to see what would happen. She held her breath, hoped it was Flynn and not the guards ready to drag her away to some torture chamber.

When Flynn popped up through the hole, relief rushed through her and she drew in a lungful of air.

Before he could speak, she asked, "What happened? Did you talk to Aikman?"

The stone was rolled back over the hole, blocking all but that narrow crack of light. Flynn hesitated, waiting for the guards to lose interest and wander back to their posts.

"I did. He was intrigued by my offer."

His tone told her that wasn't the whole story by any means but it might very well be the best part of it. "What was your offer?"

"The information he would need to take over the Resurrection."

No surprise there. Flynn was worried that Prentiss would get away. He didn't want that to happen. "What did you ask for in return?"

"Safe transport off this mountain."

Made sense, she supposed. If his ultimate goal was to stop Prentiss and his followers, giving away his secrets to an enemy would certainly do the trick. Not exactly the usual protocol for a federal agent, but desperate times called for desperate measures. She couldn't fault him for wanting to see his primary mission accomplished no matter that his cover was blown.

She sat down on the floor. No need to keep standing. She'd walked this space a thousand times. Exhaustion and hunger were nagging at her. "When do we leave?"

He didn't sit. Instead, he kept moving around the space as if he was agitated or frustrated. Either would be understandable under the circumstances.

"Watch for the bones on the left of the door," she warned.

Still, he said nothing, just kept moving through the near total darkness. After five minutes, his movements had grown unnerving with her sitting so still. Finally, she stood and demanded some answers. "So what's the rest of the story?"

He stopped, turned to her. She couldn't see his face, certainly couldn't read his expression, so she waited for him to explain.

"I took a calculated risk coming here. I put my offer on the table and it didn't go the way I expected."

"Can you be a little more specific?" He'd told her a considerable amount with those two statements and yet nothing at all.

"The only way he's prepared to accept my offer is if he gets *you* in the bargain."

Sadie barked out a laugh. "Are you serious?"

"Unfortunately, I am." He heaved a frustrated breath.

The idea of where they were and those bones over in the corner slammed into her midsection like a sucker punch. "How did you respond?"

On one level she could see how he might want to agree. After all, at least one of them needed to get out of here alive. It was the only way the people expecting their return would ever know what took place on this mountain. No matter that she comprehended the logic, she struggled to maintain her objectivity. Agreeing to the man's terms would be the reasonable thing to do.

At least that way Flynn could go for help. Assuming she survived whatever came after that, she could still be alive when help came.

But on a whole other level, she wanted to kick his ass for coming up with this insane idea in the first place. Fury burst through her.

As if he'd read her mind or felt her mixed emotions, he said, "I told him no way. If I go, you go."

Her heart skipped and then sank just a little. "What good does it do for both of us to be stuck here?" Or end up like the guy in the corner? She exhaled a chest full of exasperation and crossed her arms. "Tell him you changed your mind. Tell him," she added firmly, "he has a deal. You go and I'll stay."

"No way."

His hands were on his hips and she could feel his glare even if she couldn't see it.

"It's the right thing to do, Flynn. One of us needs to get down this damned mountain."

She hoped Levi Winters had found help. Maybe she would have been smarter to go with him. Except it was better that she and Flynn drew the danger away from him and let him get away. At least he could tell Ross and the others all that he knew. That was something.

"I got you into this," Flynn said, his voice low, fierce. "I'll get you out."

"How do you plan on doing that?"

He moved in closer, put his face near enough to hers that his lips brushed her ear. She shivered in spite of her best efforts not to react.

"He's not going to pass on this deal. He just wants us ready to do whatever he asks when he pretends to have a change of heart."

The feel of his breath on her skin made her want to lean into him. She pushed the idea away. "What do you think he'll want us to do?"

"He'll want us to act as a distraction while he carries out his coup."

"What kind of distraction?"

"The kind that gets captured and taken back to the compound and to Prentiss."

She jerked away from him. "What? Why the hell would we do that?"

"Because he's not a fool. He knows it won't be easy getting in even with the information I can give him. If that's what he requires, we have to be prepared to go. Are you with me?"

She wasn't so sure this plan was any better than the first one he walked in here telling her about.

But that was irrelevant.

"I'm in," she said finally. "At least we won't end up like the guy in the corner."

How had this mission turned so completely upside down?

Chapter Twelve

Tuesday, August 13

Sadie woke, her body shivering. A moment was required for her to orient herself.

Cave. Aikman. The *others.*

She sat up, scrubbed at her cheek where her face had been pressed to the cold ground. She'd been curled into a ball on the cold rock floor. She peered through the darkness, scanning the room as best she could. Listening for any sound, including breathing, she heard nothing.

Where was Flynn?

Memories of him pulling her against him in the night invaded her thoughts. She'd shivered from the cold invading her very bones and he'd pulled her against his big body to keep her warm. Several times during the night she had awakened to the feel of his protective arms around her, his shoulder like a pillow and the length of his body radiating heat into hers.

"Flynn?"

She got to her feet, dusted herself off for the good it would do. No answer. She ran her fingers through her hair. Apparently she'd slept through him being taken away.

Had Aikman summoned him for another meeting?

Her heart kicked into a faster rhythm. Maybe they'd already taken him off this damned mountain. Maybe she wasn't going anywhere.

Aikman had requested to keep her.

She chafed her arms to create some heat with the friction. Flynn would never go for it. He'd said so last night. He wasn't going without her.

Then again, it was possible he hadn't been given a choice this time.

For a few minutes she walked around, warming up her stiff, aching muscles. She really needed to use a bathroom but she doubted she would be permitted to leave her small prison. A few more minutes and she decided she couldn't wait any longer. She chose the corner the farthest away from the remains and relieved herself. The dead guy had likely been forced to do this for days or weeks before his body could no longer resist death.

Another ten or so minutes elapsed with her walking back and forth across the center of her prison cell when the stone suddenly rolled away from the opening. She moved to the wall and braced for whatever trouble might be coming. If one of the guards came in for her, she could fight him off for a while. As weary as her body was, the battle might not last long.

"Out!"

The voice was male but not one she recognized. She didn't move.

"Come out!" the man demanded. "Time to eat."

Her stomach rumbled. Getting out of here was better than staying. If it involved food, that was all the better. She pushed away from the wall and moved to the opening. On her hands and knees she scurried out as quickly as possible and shot to her feet. She didn't like being in a vulnerable position. She looked up, and two men—guards she presumed—stared down at her as if she were some sort of alien.

She blinked repeatedly to help her eyes adjust to the light. It wasn't that bright but it was a hell of a lot brighter than inside that hole she'd been stuck in all night. The two stared at her for a moment longer, then gestured for her to go to the left. Her gait was a little off at first but she soon found her rhythm. One of the guards ambled in front of her, the other behind her. They led her back the way she'd originally come into this cold, dark place. Once they were outside the cave, she squinted against the way brighter light. The sun was up but it was still early. She was escorted to one of the twig shacks and ushered through the primitive door.

A woman waited inside the shack.

"Take off your clothes and get into the tub."

She stared at Sadie, waiting for her to obey the

issued command. Her hair was long and dark like Sadie's but her skin was pale. If a bath was on the agenda, Sadie wasn't about to argue with her. She stripped off her clothes and toed off her shoes. Once she was in the tub the woman peeled the bandages from her hands and ordered her to sit. Sadie complied.

It was at precisely that moment that she considered maybe she was to be the morning kill. Maybe she was breakfast. She jerked her attention to the left just in time for a pail of water to be poured over her head. Surprisingly it was warm. A bar of soap was tossed into the tub with her and she went to work washing her face and body. It felt so good. More water poured over her and the woman started washing her hair. Sadie didn't complain. It felt amazing to have her scalp massaged. She could sit here and savor the attention for hours.

Then came more water, only this time it was cold. When she was thoroughly rinsed, the woman helped her towel off and provided a pair of blue cotton shorts and a white tee. Sadie had no idea where the clothes came from but they fit and she was glad to be out of the days-old sweats. She tugged on the same shoes she'd been wearing since her time at the compound. They were finally dry after their trek through the water. The blisters on her hands and feet were still tender but there was nothing she could do about that.

The woman ushered her over to a table and chairs and prepared food for her. The plate was metal, more like a pie tin. Scrambled eggs and toast were heaped onto the plate. A tin of water stood next to it. Sadie didn't wait to be told—she dove in. She was starving. She hoped Flynn was given food before he was taken to wherever he had gone. The food suddenly felt like a lump of cement in her stomach. She felt guilty about the nice bath and the hot food considering she had no idea where he was or what might be happening to him.

Focus, Sadie. You can't stay strong and be of any use to anyone if you don't eat.

As she forced bite after bite into her mouth, first one and then another woman came into the tiny shack and climbed into the tub of water she'd used. After five women had bathed, they shared the duty of carrying out pails of the dirty water.

Sadie understood the concept of conservation but she was immensely grateful she'd been first this morning.

The woman with the long dark hair led her back outside. One of the guards who'd escorted her from her cell was waiting. He led Sadie through the woods and to yet another shack-like house, this one larger. Once they were inside, she could see that this one was built into the mountainside and the interior was more like an actual house. A long corridor led to another door. The guard opened this door and urged her inside.

"And here she is. The woman we've been waiting for."

The man behind the desk stared at her, a grin on his face. Another man stood, rising above the chair that had prevented her from seeing him.

Flynn.

The relief that gushed through her made her knees weak. He was still here. More important, he was alive.

Rather than aim her question at Flynn, she stared directly at the other man. "What happens now?"

"Now, the two of you head out."

So Flynn had been right. This man—Aikman, she presumed—had never intended to keep her. The threat was nothing more than leverage to garner their cooperation.

"We'll take you as far as the road where you dumped the SUV. You'll be on your own from there." Aikman turned to Flynn. "As you know, I'll have eyes on you at all times. Once you're inside, I'll wait for your signal to make my move."

Sadie kept her thoughts to herself. There was no point in asking questions until she and Flynn were alone.

Flynn nodded. "On my signal."

Aikman nodded and with that gesture they were escorted from the man's office and back outside his rustic dwelling. Two all-terrain vehicles waited. One guard climbed aboard each vehicle and ordered Sadie and Flynn to do the same. Once she climbed on behind a guard and Flynn did the same with the other, a third guard dropped the black cloth bags over their heads. Aikman intended to keep their location a secret.

The vehicle bumped over roots and rocks and God only knew what else. Sadie held on tight no matter that she'd just as soon not touch the guy driving. Holding on to the enemy was better than risking a potentially fatal injury from bouncing off this rocky ride. She focused on counting off the minutes.

Half an hour later the vehicles stopped.

"Get off," the driver shouted over his shoulder at her.

Sadie reached up and removed the bag, then climbed off the ATV. The guard snatched the hood back from her as if he feared it might carry his fingerprints. She smoothed a hand over her hair as she watched the two drive away, bouncing and bumping over the terrain. When they were out of sight, she scanned the area. Woods. So thick they almost blocked the sky.

She turned to Flynn. "You're still sure about this plan?"

"I don't have an option."

She turned all the way around, surveyed the woods once more. Nothing but trees and brush. "The way I see it, we can go in whatever direction we like." Her gaze settled on him once more. "You don't have to finish this if it means you'll end up dead."

Flynn held her gaze for a long moment before he finally spoke. "You go. Stay south and you'll find your way to the main road running into Winchester.

If I still had the emergency beacon you could use that, but they took it so you'll be on your own. Keep your movements quiet and you'll be fine."

Sadie was shaking her head before he finished talking. "Either way we go, we go together."

"They have Winters," he said, his tone grave. "I have two hours to show up or he's dead."

Son of a bitch. Frustration, then fury tore through Sadie. "He should have listened to you." To both of them for that matter.

Flynn shook his head. "Doesn't matter. Prentiss had learned my identity before I left the compound with the two of you. We were never getting off this mountain without doing this or something like this."

"In that case, I guess we should get moving." Damn it all to hell. "We have a timeline we have to stick to." When he would have issued another protest, she held up her hand and shook her head.

Obviously not happy about her decision, Flynn led the way to the narrow rutted road. It split through the forest like a dusty brown snake. Sadie shuddered. She was extremely thankful they hadn't run into any creepy creatures. At least not the kind without legs.

When the silence had dragged on about as long as she could tolerate, she said, "You know, I thought you left me this morning." Might as well make conversation while they walked toward their doom.

He glanced at her. "You still don't trust me?"

"It wasn't about trust." In fact, she hadn't considered the idea of trust in a while now. She had instinctively trusted him. "I assumed you weren't given a choice. Then they took me for a bath, gave me clean clothes and fed me. The next thing I knew I was in Aikman's office with you."

His gaze traveled down the length of her, pausing on her bare legs before shifting back up to her face. "I noticed."

His attention swung back to the road. She smiled. Funny how such a simple, offhanded compliment could give her a moment's pleasure even at a time like this. But then, when you might not live beyond the next few hours it didn't take much.

As cold as she'd gotten in that cave last night, it was already hot enough to make her sweat this morning. The humidity was off the charts. Made the uphill journey even more of a slog.

Since Flynn had given her a sort of compliment, maybe she would give him one. "Thanks for keeping me warm last night." She flashed him a smile. "That was very gentlemanly of you."

"I thought you were keeping me warm."

Her jaw dropped, then he grinned. "You're a real comedian." She laughed. "Seriously, though, I appreciate it. I woke up shivering after you were gone but I remembered you keeping me warm through the night."

"You're welcome, but it was a mutual exchange."

Combined body heat. "What's going to happen when we get there?" As much as she would like to pretend they wouldn't really have to return to that damned compound, she knew there was no way around it outside the cavalry showing up out of the blue to take over the situation.

No one even knew their exact location. They were on their own and the chances of either one of them surviving were about nil. If they walked away, Levi, her target, would die. No matter that they would likely all three die anyway, she couldn't just walk away and leave him without attempting to do something. She glanced at the man beside her. She couldn't just walk away and leave Flynn to deal with this on his own, either.

"I have one sibling, a sister, and my parents." Sadie wasn't sure why she made this abrupt announcement. Just seemed like the thing to do. They might as well enjoy each other's company until they were taken prisoner again.

He said nothing for a while, just kept walking. She did the same.

"No siblings. Parents are long gone. It's just me."

So he was completely alone. "No wife or kids or best buds?"

He shook his head. "The job fills those slots."

This she understood all too well.

"Same here. Although my parents aren't going to be happy if I don't come back."

Another span of silence.

"I guess I'll have to make sure that doesn't happen."

She glanced at him again and this time he was looking back. They smiled simultaneously. It was foolish, she knew, but the shared smile had butter-flies taking flight in her stomach. "I'm sure they would appreciate that. I know I would."

The conversation waned from there. What was there to say? They both had at least a couple of choices. If they chose not to go through with this, Levi would die. If she walked away and left Flynn to go on his own and he and Levi didn't make it out, she would have to live with that decision. Levi was not Flynn's problem but he was choosing to take that responsibility. No way was she leaving him to do her job. Walking away wasn't an option.

An hour later, the road was scarcely more than a path now. They were close. Sadie remembered the terrain. The memories sent a chill over her skin. Whether it was self-preservation or utter despera-tion, she suddenly stopped.

"There has to be something else we can do." She surveyed the endless woods. "Someone who lives out here who has a phone or a vehicle."

There was no one. She was aware of this. Not any-where close by at any rate. Still, she couldn't *not* ask the question again. Being ambushed was one thing but walking into a death trap was just plain crazy. Of course, that was exactly what she'd done to get into the compound in the first place.

What did that say about the two of them? Maybe they both had death wishes that they explained away with their careers.

"There's no one for miles." He stopped walking

and turned to face her. "I understood the risk when I started this. There's no way out."

Sadie moved in on him, taking the three steps between them. "Are you doing this for you or for your father?"

He looked away from her but not before she saw emotions cloud his eyes. "Does it matter?"

She folded her arms over her chest to prevent reaching out to him. One of her instructors had warned her about a place exactly like this. The place you find yourself when you've lost all sight of the difference between your life and your work. When work becomes more important than anything else— even surviving.

"This is the job, Flynn. This isn't about you or your father. This is the job. Justice. Doing the right thing. Taking down the bad guys for the greater good, not for your own personal reasons. Like maybe revenge."

He laughed, shook his head. "Did you spend the last hour thinking up that speech or did you suddenly remember it from your agent-in-training handbook?"

She had definitely hit a nerve. "Don't be a smart-ass. I'm only trying to help. To make you see that we've both lost sight of what we were trained to do. What we swore to do when we started this journey."

"I don't need a lecture, and the only way you can help is to walk down that mountain to safety while I do what I have to do."

Now he was just being arrogant. "Levi Winters

is my target. He's my responsibility. I have just as much right to walk into this trap as you do."

He stared at her long and hard. "It's only a trap if you don't see it coming."

"We need a plan, Flynn. We shouldn't just walk into this, whatever you want to call it, without a plan."

"I have a plan."

That was the moment she remembered what Aikman said. The memory had rocks forming in her gut. "What did your friend mean when he said he would wait for your signal?"

"Let's go."

When he would have turned to start walking again, she grabbed him by the arm. "We're in too deep for you to blow me off at this stage of the game."

He stared at her, his own anger blazing in his eyes.

"It means just what he said, I give the signal, he and his people invade. I've given them the access codes along with the guard locations. Now let's get moving."

Did he really think she was going to let it go? "What's the signal?"

Since they didn't have a cell phone, beacon, flare gun, air horn or any damned thing else, just how the hell did he expect to give anyone outside the compound a signal?

The stare-off continued. Ten seconds, fifteen, twenty.

Enough. She made up her mind then and there. She grabbed him by the shirtfront and jerked his face down to hers. Then she kissed him. Kissed him hard on the mouth. Kept her lips pressed to his until he reacted. His fingers plowed into her hair and pulled her more firmly into him, deepening the kiss, taking control.

She poured herself into the kiss, into the feel of his mouth, his lips and his palms against her face. When the need for air forced them apart, he looked her straight in the eye and said, "I'm still not telling you."

The answer to the question was suddenly as clear as shiny new glass. He had no way of sending a signal.

"They have someone inside, don't they? That's the person who'll give the signal when you've done whatever it is Aikman has asked of you."

He looked away.

She shook her head. "All this time they've had someone inside. Why the hell do they need you?"

"We're running out of time. Let's go."

She grabbed him by the forearm, kept him from turning away. "No. Not until you tell me the truth."

Fury tightened the lips she had only moments ago kissed. Wanted to kiss again, damn her.

"You don't have a need to know, Agent Buchanan."

A sharp laugh burst out of her. "Don't even try playing that game with me." She held his gaze, silently demanding an answer. She saw the answer without him having to say a word. The determination as well as the resignation. Her heart stumbled. "You're going to kill Prentiss, aren't you? That's the signal Aikman will be waiting for."

He snapped his gaze away from hers and started to walk once more, but not before she saw the defeat in his eyes.

Prentiss's bodyguards would kill Flynn.

There was no way he would survive.

She had to figure out a way to turn this around.

Chapter Thirteen

Smith started walking. He could not allow her to sway his decision. She didn't understand. Aikman would have killed her after doing other unspeakable things if Smith hadn't agreed to his terms.

There was no other choice. No way out.

It was true that at this moment there was some measure of leeway. Quite possibly they could take off and maybe get down this damned mountain before they were caught. But that would be like putting a gun to Levi Winters's head and pulling the trigger. If that wasn't bad enough, Prentiss would no doubt disappear.

This—right now—was the one chance Smith had of stopping him.

"You're a fool."

He ignored her, which wasn't easy to do. She had surprised him when she kissed him. He'd felt the mutual attraction almost from the beginning, couldn't have missed it if he'd tried. The intensity of it was his own fault. It had been way too long since he'd allowed himself basic human pleasures. She made him want to indulge those ignored needs. It was difficult for a starving man to ignore a buffet right in front of him.

"This goes against your training. We both understand what needs to happen. This is a textbook example of a no-win situation. We need backup."

"You feel strongly about following the rules, is that it, Buchanan?" She was as bad as him. She'd walked into a deadly situation without so much as a blink and damned sure without any backup. She had no right to judge his actions.

"It's not the same," she argued.

"It's exactly the same."

She stopped and turned to him. He bumped into her shoulder.

"I didn't walk into that compound prepared to kill a man."

Anger clenched his jaw. He struggled to utter an answer. She couldn't possibly understand. "He deserves to die."

She nodded. "Maybe so but not because you want to put a bullet in his brain. What you're talking about is premeditated murder. Are you a murderer, Flynn?"

He bit his lips together to prevent denying the charge. Maybe he was a murderer. He had never wanted to kill another man the way he wanted to kill Prentiss.

"If you are, what makes you any better than him?"

A part of him wanted to refute her words. To explain his reasoning. But did any of it really matter? He wanted to watch Rayford Prentiss die. He couldn't wait to see him take his last breath. Equally important, he wanted the bastard to know that he—Smith Flynn, the son of Avery Flynn—had been the one to bring his ruthless reign and his life to an end.

"Nothing," he admitted.

He walked on. They were close to the compound. The watchers would spot them and send out a team to bring them in. It wouldn't be long now.

The answer he'd given to her last question kept her quiet for a few minutes. She was searching for some other rationalization for why he couldn't do what Aikman had ordered him to do. He could practically hear the wheels in her head turning. She wanted to help him.

But she couldn't.

No one could. Not at this point. It was too late.

As much as he regretted what he had become and all the things he'd had to do, if necessary he would do it all again to stop Prentiss.

"Once we're inside, give me some time," she suddenly said, her voice low as if she feared the trees had ears. Most likely they did.

"Time for what?" He asked this without looking at her. He didn't want to look at her. Not simply because she was attractive and alluring and made him want things he shouldn't. But because she reminded him of all that was good—of the reason he became an agent in the first place. She made him want the career he'd had before this journey started. She made him wish things had been different.

Could he be that man again? Did the good part of him even still exist? He had worked for two long years to erase that guy. To make him immune to the emotions that would only get in his way.

Buchanan had made a valid point. He was a murderer. He'd killed the man he used to be. What he was now was no better than Prentiss.

He doubted there was any going back.

She stopped again, moved in close to him, making his body yearn to pull her close. "Once we're inside, give me time to create a distraction. We can turn this around, Flynn, make it work for us."

The hope in her eyes made him want to believe her. Made him want to grab on to the life raft she offered and hang on for the ride.

But what if she was wrong?

"He won't be fooled so easily this time. He knows he can't trust either of us. How do you expect to manipulate him in any way to buy time or anything else?"

She was an optimist. A woman who wanted to stand by the goodness and justice she believed in. She needed him to believe, too, but he'd lost the ability to blindly believe in anything.

"Trust me, Flynn. You would be surprised at the tricks I have up my sleeve."

He shouldn't agree to the idea. He should do what he had to do and be grateful for the opportunity.

But she made him want to do the right thing.

"I'll give you as much time as I can."

She grinned. "That's all I can ask for, partner."

Despite the worry and uncertainty nagging at him, he smiled back at her. Maybe they could turn this around.

He just hoped she lived through it. He had never expected to survive this assignment, but he didn't want to be the reason she lost her life.

As they ascended the next ridge, troops came out of the trees. Seven, no eight. The group swarmed out and surrounded their position, weapons leveled on his and Buchanan's heads.

Smith held perfectly still. "I need to see Prentiss."

"He doesn't want to see you."

Smith knew this soldier. He was an ambitious man. He would want to prove he was somehow responsible for Smith's capture.

"Take me to him," he said to the younger man, daring him to argue. Smith was now listed as an enemy but there would be those who had their doubts. Those who feared turning their backs on him since it was not out of the question that he could be restored to his former position. After all, he was Avery Flynn's only son.

The soldier gave a nod to one of his minions. "Search them both."

When he and Buchanan had been patted down to the man's satisfaction, he ordered his team to move out. The soldiers stayed in a tight ring around Smith and Buchanan as they continued on to the compound.

The compound was only a mile or so away at this point. He glanced at Buchanan. Somehow he had to find a way to keep her from ending up dead no matter that she refused to cooperate.

She'd asked for time, which likely meant she had a plan. Maybe he should listen to her reasoning. She wasn't emotionally tangled up with this situation and he was. Her reasoning might be clearer than his own. He'd been guilty of a lot of mistakes over the years but he didn't have to make one today.

PRENTISS WAITED ALONE in the meeting room.

Of course he wouldn't want any of the other members of the Council present when he said what he had to say. The secrets and lies he had kept over all these years were not the sort he wanted anyone to know, particularly those who looked to him to lead them. There was not a bigger con artist alive. The man was capable of anything if it gained him what he wanted. But the other members of the Council, the followers, none of them would ever believe he was anything other than a selfless leader who protected their way of life.

Smith had barely resisted the urge to take a swing at one of the guards when he prepared to separate Buchanan from him. As two guards dragged her away she had shouted for him to remember what she said.

He did remember.

For what it was worth, he would try his best to give her some time.

Smith was shackled and escorted to a chair, where he was forced to sit before the shackles around his ankles were anchored to the floor. Prentiss didn't speak until the guards had left the room. Only the two of them would ever know the whole story if Prentiss had his way.

"Is it true?" the old man asked as if he could hardly believe the reality of what had occurred.

"What would you know about the truth?" Looking at him sickened Smith. How had he managed these past two years?

"I know enough," Prentiss warned. "I know a mole when I see one. A traitor. A man whose entire existence is a betrayal to his own people."

"Doesn't matter now," Smith mused, deciding on a delay tactic that might just work. "You're finished."

The old man's gaze narrowed. "I don't believe you. If the feds had anything on me, they would be here now arresting me and pinning medals on you." He glanced around the room. "I don't see or hear anyone coming to your rescue. Perhaps you should pray about this dilemma in which you find yourself."

Smith chuckled. "I don't need to pray, old man. I've spent two years feeding information to those feds. They have what they need, they're only waiting for the perfect moment. Believe me when I say that moment is close at hand."

"If that's true, then why were you and your friend still wandering about on this mountain? Why haven't your comrades rescued you? Or have they forsaken you as you have forsaken me?"

"I refused a rescue. I want to watch from right here." He smiled. "I want to witness them dragging you away in shackles." He shook his head. "Too bad the other members of the Council are going down with you. They are only guilty of following your orders. How fast do you think one or more of them will roll over and start spilling his guts about the executions and the shipments?"

Prentiss stood and moved toward him. He looked even older and more than a little frail in those overalls and worn boots. But there was nothing frail about this bastard. He was dangerous. Ruthless. Cunning as hell.

"I will know what you've told them," he warned as he braced his hands on the arms of the chair and leaned in close to Smith. "I will know every secret and every name you've shared. And then you will die a slow, agonizing death."

Smith allowed a wide smile to slide across his lips once more. "I shared them all. Every single name, every single secret. They know about your partners in South America. They know your next incoming shipment and the distribution channels you intend to use. They know *everything*."

"I want names," Prentiss demanded. "Who are your contacts?"

"You can't stop this, old man. They're coming and you and all this will fall."

Prentiss drew back sharply as if he feared catching some contagious disease. "Your father would be sickened by your actions. He would kill you himself."

Smith leaned forward as far as his shackles would allow. "My father was not like you. He would be grateful to me for stopping you."

Prentiss held his ground. "Maybe you're right. Avery had grown weak in his old age. He failed to see what was best for the security of our people. Progress is necessary. As is extending our reach. He was blind to those needs."

"But they followed him. Looked up to him. Not you," Smith reminded him. "You were always in his shadow."

Prentiss was the one smiling then. "And yet I'm still here and he is gone."

"How much longer do you think you can hang on when your people learn you failed to see the traitor in their midst? Or maybe they'll see you as the traitor."

"They already know what you are. You're just like your father. Weak. Shortsighted. A stumbling block to survival."

Anger ignited deep inside Smith. "My father was not weak. His vision was far greater than yours. You will never be half the leader he was."

"Before I order your public execution perhaps it's time you were told what really happened."

Smith stilled. His father suffered a heart attack. "I'm well aware of how he died."

On some level he would always believe that his decision to leave had been part of the burden that weighed upon his father, making him a prime candidate for a sudden heart attack. He couldn't help wondering if he'd secretly discovered what Smith had become, a traitor to all his father believed.

"His heart stopped true enough." Prentiss reared back, his thumbs hooked into the side splits of his overalls. "It was the only way to protect what we had achieved. He would have ruined everything."

Something cold and dark swelled inside Smith. "What does that mean?"

"It means," the bastard said, obviously enjoying the moment, "that he wanted to pull back. When he found out about my deal with the cartel, he demanded I leave. He intended to put me out after I had dedicated my life to the cause." Prentiss shrugged. "It was him or me. He was too sick to understand what he was saying and doing. So, as you can see, it wasn't me."

Shock radiated through Smith. "You killed him?"

"I did," Prentiss confessed. "Just like I'm going to kill you."

SADIE DIDN'T BOTHER STRUGGLING. Prentiss had ordered her to the tunnels. Her friend Levi, Prentiss had warned, was already there, unless he'd ended up as dinner earlier than expected.

No wonder Flynn wanted to kill the man. He was a ruthless degenerate. Every minute he drew breath, someone else suffered.

The dome was pulled back by one of her guards, revealing the ladder that led deep under the ground. Sadie went along, feigning uncertainty. She had a plan and having it start in the tunnels would work to her advantage.

When she reached the bottom of the ladder, George was waiting. He still wore those flimsy flip-flops he'd bartered out of her.

"Wasn't expecting you back," he said. "I heard you ran off."

"I missed you and decided to drop by for a visit."

He stared at her a long moment, her light sarcasm seemingly lost on him. Finally, he nodded. "Anyway, your friend is down here, too. He ain't faring so well."

"What's wrong with him?"

"I guess he don't like the idea that if an emergency happens and we run out of food, he'll be the backup."

Levi was supplies. Prentiss had enjoyed telling her that, as well. Before George could turn and start walking away, she said, "We should probably talk before joining the others."

He frowned. "You know the drill down here. What do we have to talk about?"

Sadie looked around as if to make sure no one else was nearby. "They're coming today. If all of you are still here, you'll end up in jail, too."

Confusion flashed in his eyes. "Who's coming?"

"The feds, local law enforcement. They're coming to take Prentiss and the Council to jail. They know everything about this place."

He shrugged. "They've boasted about taking Prentiss down before and it never happens. He's way too careful."

"Trust me, George. I'm with the FBI. They know everything. You were nice to me so I'd like to help you and the others down here. But there isn't a lot of time. We should get out of here while we still can."

"What?" He drew back as if her words had attacked him.

"You know how to get out. You've dug egress routes. You know where they are and how to use them. Don't pretend you don't, George."

"I think we should get to work." He started walking deeper into the tunnel.

Sadie didn't move. She stayed next to the ladder. She wasn't going anywhere until she got George thinking about how easy it would be to escape this tunnel and flee to someplace well beyond the reach of the Resurrection. Not that the group would have any power left when this was done. She decided on a new tactic.

"Prentiss and the rest of the Council are leaving. You think they're going to let you guys out of here before they evacuate?" She shook her head. "They'll leave you to die. The authorities can't question the dead."

He stalled, shook his head at her. "You're lying."

"I'm not lying, George. I have no reason to lie. I just don't want to die and that's what will happen if we don't get out of here."

He started walking again. She followed.

"The feds are coming to take Prentiss and his Council down. They'll be here before nightfall. We don't have time to waste. Prentiss and his cronies are going to get away clean and all of us down here won't."

He stopped and glanced back at her again. "If what you're saying is true, what do you expect us to do?"

"You told me about the egresses you've prepared. Let's go to the closest one and get out of here before it's too late. Before Prentiss orders any and all loose ends cleaned up."

"There will be guards waiting at the egresses," he argued. "They'll shoot us."

She shook her head. "They'll be gone. They're afraid. They're not going to hang around once word about what's coming gets around."

George kept moving until he reached the work area. Sadie trudged along behind him. Levi was there and he looked in reasonably good condition. No visible injuries. Relief rushed through her. Maybe this would be a second chance to get him safely out of here. This time she wasn't allowing him out of her sight. She fully intended to deliver him to his sister.

With his shovel in his hand, George joined the

others. Sadie wanted to shake him. Why the hell wasn't he listening? She needed something to happen soon if she was going to help Smith.

"Hey," she shouted at him. "Didn't you hear what I said? We have to get out of here or we're all going to die. Why aren't you telling these people?"

Several of the men glanced at her and then at George but made no move to stop what they were doing.

"Levi!" She waited for him to look at her. "Come on. We're getting out of here."

He looked around at the other men. Just when Sadie was certain he would keep working, he threw down his shovel and walked toward her.

Another wave of relief swept through her. "Who else is with us?"

She scanned the dirty faces. All stared at her, their expressions weary, defeated.

"Tell them, George," she urged. "Tell them what's about to happen up there. We have to run while we still can."

George stared at her for a long moment, then he threw down his pickax and stalked toward her. She held her breath, not certain whether he intended to yank her over to take his place or if he intended to join her.

When he reached her, he turned back to the others. "We'll need shovels and axes. It'll take us at least twenty minutes and if they see us on the cameras, they'll come down here and make us wish we hadn't listened to her."

"We can do this," Sadie urged, not wanting his warning to dissuade them. "We'll work faster than we ever have before."

George surveyed the men now watching him. "Grab your shovels and the axes. We're out of here."

Much to her immense gratitude, George led the way. Sadie and Levi followed. At least twelve more hustled along the corridor behind them. She glanced at the cameras placed overhead approximately every fifteen yards along the seemingly endless corridor. They wouldn't have a lot of time.

The alarm was sounding by the time they reached the closest egress. Six of the men climbed the ladders and started to dig. Six more formed a wall across the tunnel in anticipation of the guards who would no doubt come.

The sound of boots pounding on the ground echoed through the tunnel. George and his friends were shouting at each other to hurry. Sadie dragged Levi closer.

"As soon as that egress is cleared," she murmured close to his ear, "we have to get out of here and go for help."

He nodded his understanding.

Shouting in the tunnel echoed some ten yards away.

Hurry. Sadie looked from the wall of bodies

standing between the coming guards and their position to the men jabbing and poking overhead.

"Go!"

Sadie jerked her attention toward George. Sunlight suddenly poured into the tunnel. Three of the men were already scrambling out.

"Let's go." Sadie nudged Levi forward.

They rushed up the ladders and climbed out. Two guards who had been taking a smoke break suddenly turned toward them. George and the others were on top of them before they could get their weapons into position.

Others were clambering out behind Sadie and Levi.

Sadie didn't look back. She held on to Levi's hand and ran through the woods as fast as she could.

She had no idea how far they were from help but she had to get to wherever that was as quickly as possible.

Smith's life depended upon it.

Chapter Fourteen

Sadie kept a firm grasp on Levi's hand as they ran through the woods, branches and undergrowth slapping at her bare legs.

The crack of gunfire behind them forced Sadie's heart into a faster cadence.

She charged forward with a new burst of adrenaline-inspired speed. Levi managed to keep up though he was barefoot and stumbling with exhaustion. He would pay for the lack of shoes or boots later. She imagined he had blisters on his hands just as she'd had after her time in the tunnel, though hers were partially healed now.

If the guards got off a good shot, the two of them would have far more than blisters to worry about.

"This way." Levi tugged at the hand she had clenched around his.

He knew the area and she didn't. She might as well trust him. He had as much reason to want to escape this mountain as she did. Staying alive was always a strong motivator no matter which side of the equation one was on.

Levi deviated into a different direction. Plowed through the jungle of trees.

By the time they slowed Sadie could barely get her breath.

"Hold on a minute." Levi leaned against a tree and struggled to catch his breath, as well.

Sadie propped against the nearest tree and took slow, deep breaths. When she could string words together, she asked, "How far to civilization?"

"If we keep going this way—" he hitched a thumb in the direction they'd been headed, south Sadie thought "—we'll hit the valley in about a mile and a half. There are a few houses in that area. We can probably use a phone there."

Sadie nodded. Worked for her.

When they headed out again they moved considerably slower. Sadie's muscles burned from the hard run and the abuse they'd suffered the past several days. She would need weeks to recover from the way she'd mistreated her body on this mission.

Assuming she survived. She glanced over her shoulder to ensure no one was coming. Clear for now.

As they moved downward the underbrush grew less dense. Even the trees weren't so thick. Up ahead beyond the tree line an open pasture came into view. She and Levi hesitated at the edge of the woods to have a look at what lay beyond.

Sadie spotted a house and barn in the distance.

Judging by the cows in the field and the farm equipment scattered about, someone lived there. There were other houses beyond that one. Acres of open pasture rolled out between the houses. She glanced behind her once more. Moving through those open areas would be risky if the enemy on their trail caught up with them.

Sadie turned to the man at her side. "Do you know any of the people who live on this stretch of road?"

Levi shook his head. "All we need is to use the phone, right? Surely one of them will let us do that whether they know us or not."

Sadie nodded. "We'll tell them our car broke down. If we mention the trouble on our heels, they may not let us in the house. Some people don't like to get involved."

"Yeah." He surveyed the expanse of green space in front of them. "You're right. We can't tell them what's really going on."

Sadie scanned the woods behind them. She listened for several seconds. "Maybe we lost those guards."

More than a dozen people had escaped the tunnel. Most went in different directions. Hopefully, the two guards she had spotted as well as those who had come up from the tunnel had followed some of the others. Not that she wished that unlucky break on anyone, but she was only human.

"Let's try that first house," she suggested. "The sooner we get to town the sooner we can send help for Flynn." Her stomach twisted at the idea that he could be dead already. She had urged him to buy some time. To do his best to drag out the inevitable. She hoped he was successful. As long as he didn't allow his emotions to take over, he would be okay. He was a well-trained agent. Hopefully that training would kick in and keep him thinking smart.

With one last backward glance, she and Levi dashed across the pasture. Part of her braced for the crack of a weapon firing at them but it didn't come. As they neared the house a cow raised its head and stared at them.

They bounded up onto the front porch. Levi reached the door first. He knocked. Sadie kept a watch on the tree line to ensure no one came rushing out after them. All they needed was a phone. One call.

Her pulse pounded as Levi knocked again. No television sound, no footsteps moving about. The house sounded empty. Worried that was indeed the case, Sadie peered through the nearest window. *Kitchen.* There were drying dishes on a towel on the counter. If no one was home now, they had been earlier.

"Somebody lives here." She checked the tree line and pasture again.

A loud thump drew her attention to the door. Levi backed up and body-slammed it again, using his right shoulder.

Sadie winced as he slammed it a third time before it gave way and burst inward.

She exhaled a big breath and followed him across the threshold. Breaking and entering wasn't such a bad thing considering they were running for their lives.

"Phone's over here," Levi said.

Sadie went to the side table beneath the big front window. "Have a look around and make sure no one's in the shower or something. We don't need an armed homeowner thinking we mean harm to him or his property."

She sure as hell didn't want to escape armed killers only to end up shot by a terrified farmer or his wife.

Levi nodded and headed into the hall. The house was a brick rancher, not so large. It wouldn't take him long to have a look.

Sadie entered 911 into the handset. As soon as the dispatcher finished her spiel, she identified herself and asked to be connected to Sheriff Tanner.

Tanner was on the line in under twenty seconds.

Sadie sagged with relief. "Tanner, we're…" Hearing footsteps, she turned to ask Levi exactly where they were.

Gun.

She froze.

Levi stood in the cased opening between the living room and the hall, his hands high in the air. An older man wearing a cap had the business end of a rifle jammed into the side of his head. Levi's eyes were round with fear.

"I tried to tell him we need help," Levi explained.

"Put the phone down," the man demanded.

Damn. "Sir, I'm on the phone with Sheriff Tanner." She thrust the phone at the man. "We're unarmed. Speak to the sheriff and he'll explain everything."

The man backed away from Levi but kept a bead on his head. He took the cordless phone receiver from Sadie and backed a few steps farther away in order to keep them both in his line of vision.

"Sheriff Tanner, this is Cord Hawkins." Hawkins gave the address and then listened as Tanner spoke.

Sadie couldn't make out what he was saying but she heard the rumble of his voice. Judging by the way the man lowered the barrel of his weapon, he understood Sadie and Levi were no threat to him.

"I'll do it," Hawkins said. He offered the receiver to Sadie. "Sheriff wants to talk to you again."

"Thank you." Sadie took the phone and pressed it to her ear. "Tell me you're on your way. We don't have much time."

As Tanner passed along orders via another phone line, Sadie was vaguely aware that Hawkins had brought cans of cola from the kitchen. He passed one to Levi and offered one to her.

Sadie summoned a smile and murmured a thank-you. She popped the top and downed half the can before Tanner turned his attention back to the conversation with her.

"Sit tight, Agent Buchanan, we're on our way to you. We'll have that mountain covered within the hour."

Sadie ended the call and drank more of the cola. Levi leaned against the wall and slid to the floor as he guzzled his cola. Sadie closed her eyes against the weariness dragging at her. She had never been so tired in her life.

"Are those friends of yours?"

Sadie jerked her attention back to the here and now and rushed across the room to the big window. Hawkins pointed at three men running across the same pasture she and Levi had sprinted across. She peered across the distance to make out their faces. One was George, she decided. She didn't need to recognize the faces of the other two. All wore the dirty sweats and sported the greasy hair and dirty faces of tunnel workers.

"They were prisoners just like us." She turned to Hawkins. "They're not the bad guys."

His fingers tightened around his rifle. "You sure about that, ma'am?"

She nodded. "I'll go out and talk to them."

"I'll be watching," Hawkins assured her.

"Thank you."

Sadie stepped out the front door as the three men bounded up the porch steps. "Did they follow you?" She hadn't seen anyone else coming out of that tree line.

George shook his head. "We lost them."

"Hurry." Sadie opened the door. "Let's get inside. The sheriff is on the way with help."

Hawkins passed out colas to the three and dug up a couple of big bags of chips. The men ate as if they hadn't eaten in days. Probably hadn't. She kept her attention on the tree line and said a prayer for Flynn.

He was still at that compound. On his own.

"The sheriff's here," Hawkins announced.

A whole parade of official vehicles arrived. Uniformed deputies and officers poured into the house. Paramedics insisted on giving Sadie, Levi and the other three a quick check while she and George provided information about the compound, the people there and the precarious position in which they'd left Agent Smith Flynn.

Winchester's chief of police, William Brannigan, was already on the phone with the ATF. The state police and the Bureau had been notified en route. Through the window Sadie spotted Agent Ross and Cece Winters, coming up the porch steps.

"Levi." Sadie turned to the young man who had resumed his seat on the floor. "Someone's here for you."

He pushed to his feet at the same time that his sister and Ross entered the house. The reunion of brother and sister was the one good thing that had happened this day. Sadie was grateful to be a part of it.

Cece Winters hugged Sadie next. "Thank you for rescuing my brother."

Sadie glanced at Levi. "I think it was a mutual rescue."

He smiled. "Maybe."

Special Agent Deacon Ross shook Sadie's hand. "I appreciate what you must have gone through to make this happen."

"We're not finished yet," she warned. "There's a war about to happen on that mountain. The Resurrection and the *others* are going head-to-head. Agent Flynn is caught in the middle of it. He could be dead already. We have to hurry."

George suddenly stepped forward. "I know the one access road to get to that compound. Know the codes, too. I'll take you there."

The other two who had come with George echoed his offer.

They all wanted to see Prentiss go down.

No one wanted that more than Sadie.

"Ms. Winters will take you back to my office," Tanner said to Sadie.

She shook her head. "No way. I'm going with you."

Tanner started to argue but he must have seen the absolute determination in Sadie's eyes. He nodded. "All right, then, let's move out."

SMITH STRUGGLED TO FOCUS.

He hung from a hook attached to the ceiling, his feet dangling several inches off the floor. He'd been stripped to the waist and tortured for hours. He'd lost track of the time.

The beating he rode out without much more than a flinch. The shock torture had become tedious the last half hour or so. This was nothing he hadn't endured before. But it was the burns that were about to be inflicted with a branding iron he would just as soon skip.

Prentiss, the son of a bitch, watched from a safe distance across the room as the irons turned red amid the fiery coals. Smith knew the soldier tasked with the job of inflicting the torture. The man didn't appear to feel bad about having to torture an old friend. Maybe Smith had made more enemies than he'd realized during his time here. Or maybe the guy was just glad to be the one inflicting the torture and not the one receiving it.

Who could blame him?

The one thing Smith knew with absolute certainty was that providing he survived long enough he would kill Rayford Prentiss if it was the last thing he ever did.

The bastard had admitted to murdering his father.

Prentiss was responsible for the deaths of countless other people with his gunrunning and drug trade. And that was only the beginning.

As if his thoughts had summoned him, Prentiss dared to venture closer. He surveyed Smith, enjoying the blood dribbling from his mouth and nose, the swelling of his face and eyes as well as the bruises forming on his torso. All these things gave him pleasure. This bastard had tortured and murdered many. But Smith would be his last, one way or another.

Whether Smith survived this day or not, Buchanan would ensure the bastard got what he deserved.

If she had survived.

Smith closed his eyes against any other possibility. She was too smart and too determined to fail. Prentiss had been called out of the room once, a couple of hours ago. Smith hadn't been able to hear all that was said but he'd picked up on the gist of the conversation. There had been an escape. Ten or twelve people had dug out of the tunnel and evaded the posted guards.

She would be one of them, Smith felt certain.

Go, Sadie.

A smile tugged at his damaged lips. He liked her name. *Sadie.* He liked her sassiness and her courage.

He hoped he had the chance to get to know her better.

"What on God's green earth do you have to smile about, boy?"

Smith opened his swollen eyes as best he could. "I was just thinking how you'll rot in prison with all your friends. Oh wait." He managed a rusty laugh. "You don't have any friends. That should be interesting."

He'd expected Aikman to show up even though he didn't get a signal indicating Smith had taken care of Prentiss. With all the access codes and information Smith had provided him, he'd figured the man would make a move either way.

"I thought maybe you were worried about your own friend, or enemy as the case might be," Prentiss said. "Aikman, I believe his name is."

Smith clenched his aching jaw to prevent showing a reaction to the name.

"You see, I found out about his man inside. He was watching, nosing around in places he didn't belong today, so I guessed something was up. Unlike you, he sang like a bird with very little prodding. My people are on high alert. No one is getting into this compound today or any other. Strange." He rubbed at his beard. "I understand you were going to kill me. Whatever changed your mind?"

Smith smiled again, his split lip burning like fire. "I decided I'd rather know that you're rotting in a prison cell than give you an easy way out. I want you to live, old man. A very long time so you can enjoy what the future holds for you when justice is served."

Prentiss picked up one of the knives lying on the table with all the other torture instruments. He turned it over in his hand, pretending to inspect the stainless steel blade and handle.

Tension slid through Smith. He braced to lift his

legs and kick him across the room. He'd been waiting for time alone with the guy administering the torture in hopes of using that move as a means to escape, but so far that moment hadn't come. Once he attempted any sort of maneuver, if he was unsuccessful steps would be taken to ensure he was unable to repeat the effort. So he had waited. Unfortunately, his strength was waning far too quickly. He'd have to make a move soon or find himself unable to do so.

The door on the other side of the room opened and one of Prentiss's private bodyguards rushed in. He whispered something in the old man's ear. Prentiss set the knife aside. His gaze settled on Smith as he listened to the rest of what the man had to say.

It was happening. Smith didn't have to hear the words. He saw the abrupt fear in the old man's eyes.

Prentiss looked to the other man in the room. "Finish him and clear out."

Oh yeah. Either Aikman and his people were descending on the compound or the backup Sadie had gone after was close.

Either option suited Smith.

Prentiss hurried out with his bodyguard.

Smith held very still as the man who'd beat and tortured him walked toward him for the last time. Mentally preparing himself to expend the last of his physical strength, Smith waited until the man was close enough to pick up that big-ass knife from the table. His fingers wrapped around the handle and he weighed it, hoping to add a layer of tension, to build the dread.

Smith made his move.

He wrapped his legs around the man's neck and squeezed. Struggling to free himself, the bastard lifted his right hand, aiming the knife at Smith.

Smith used his whole body to jerk to the right, snapping the bastard's neck. His eyes bulged. The knife fell from his slack fingers and clanged on the floor. Smith loosened his hold and the now-lifeless body followed that route, dropping like a rock.

Swinging his legs to the left, Smith grabbed hold of the table with his bare feet. He hung that way for a moment to catch his breath and to give his muscles a moment to recover. Slowly, he used his feet to drag the table closer. When he could kneel on it, he rested another moment. Finally, he pushed upward, lifting his bound hands from the meat hook that had held him suspended in the air. He collapsed into a kneeling position on the table. A few minutes were required for his arms to stop stinging.

He scooted off the table and found his footing on the floor. Where the hell was the key to these wrist shackles? He checked the table and the items that had been flung to the floor when he'd dragged it close. No key. Then he checked the dead guy who'd wielded the hours of torture. The key was in his right front pocket. Smith pulled the key free.

Collapsing into a cross-legged position, he focused on getting the key into the lock that held an iron bracelet around his left wrist. He dropped the key, once, twice before he managed to get it into the lock. He had to twist his right hand in an awkward position to turn the key but he finally managed. The lock on his left wrist fell open. Relief surged through him. He picked up the key and unlocked the bracelet on his right wrist. When the final shackle fell free, he rubbed his wrists and dragged in a deep breath. His damaged ribs ached with the move.

Pushing to his feet, he surveyed the room for a weapon.

Depending on who had arrived, he could be in for another battle for his life. He turned over the dead guy, snatched the gun from his waistband. He checked the ammo cartridge. Full. He shoved the gun into his waistband and went in search of his shoes. He finally found them in a pile with the shirt that had been cut from his body. The shirt he could live without but the shoes would be useful.

Now to find Prentiss before the bastard managed to slip away.

Smith stalled halfway to the door and went back to the dead guy for his cell phone. It was possible Prentiss would call to ensure Smith was dead. He no doubt wanted Smith dead as badly as Smith wanted him caught. A vehicle fob fell out of the guy's pocket. Smith took that, as well.

Running footsteps in the corridor outside the door snapped Smith's attention in that direction. He started toward the door. Halfway across the room it opened.

Smith leveled the weapon on the potential threat.
Aikman.

Chapter Fifteen

"Well, well, if it isn't the man who failed his mission." Aikman shook his head. "*Tsk, tsk*, Flynn, I had you pegged for better than that."

Apparently the idea that Smith was the one holding the gun aimed at him didn't faze the guy. Aikman's weapon was in his hand but not aimed at anything other than the floor. Whoever else had been in that corridor with him had moved on to the next door. A bad decision any way you looked at it.

"I was working on it and the bastard found out you had invaded the compound. So he took off while I was still a little tied up."

Aikman glanced at the meat hook beyond Smith. "Ouch."

Smith wasn't sure whether the guy was trying to put him off-balance or if he really wasn't worried about the weapon aimed at his head just now.

"You might want to put that weapon away," Smith suggested. "I don't want to get nervous and do something we'll both regret."

Aikman smiled, made a laugh/grunt sound. "Of course." He tucked the weapon into his waistband. "We've decided we prefer these accommodations over our own. So we'll be taking over the compound."

"You planning on killing everyone here?" Smith hoped like hell backup was close.

Aikman shrugged. "There are some I'd rather have join my team." He made a questioning face. "You interested, Flynn?"

He lowered his weapon and wiped his bleeding mouth. "Why not? As long as the terms are agreeable."

Aikman glanced around the room. "Where's your little friend? I was looking forward to seeing her again."

"I'd like to know the answer to that one myself." He started toward the door that Aikman currently blocked. "I'm hoping Prentiss didn't take her with him." Smith knew that wasn't the case but Aikman couldn't know.

Aikman turned his back to Smith and exited the room first. The guy continued to surprise Smith.

"We've rounded up all the Council members." Aikman glanced at him as they moved along the corridor. "Except Prentiss and you, of course."

Dread thickened in Smith's gut. "Did you kill them?"

Aikman shook his head. "Not yet. They no doubt have information I'll need going forward. Unless you have everything you think we'll need. In that case we can be rid of them right away."

"Prentiss was careful never to give all the power to one person. Each of us had our domain. We'll need them all."

This was a lie but if it kept Aikman from performing a mass execution, that was all that mattered.

There was just one problem as far as Smith could see. He couldn't be sure which of the Council members would be smart enough to keep his mouth shut about him being an undercover agent. If any of those who knew warned Aikman, this situation would do a one-eighty in a heartbeat.

He needed that backup to arrive now.

"I have them gathered in the conference room." Aikman glanced at him. "We'll join them and start the downloading of information, so to speak."

"I'll meet you there in fifteen. I need to wash the blood off my face and change clothes. We don't want them to see any sign of weakness. We need to present strength and unity so they'll understand the shift in power."

"Smart move. Fifteen minutes." Aikman suddenly stopped and turned back. "Ollie!"

One of his followers hustled up to join them. "Escort our friend Mr. Flynn to his personal lodging. Ensure he's in the conference room in fifteen minutes."

"Yes, sir." The man named Ollie turned his shaggy head to glare at Smith. "Let's go, Flynn."

Aikman didn't trust him as much as he'd let on. That made them even because Smith didn't trust him at all.

Outside was quiet. "Where is everyone?"

"They're in the detection center."

Smith was surprised the other man, Ollie, gave him an answer but he was glad he had. As much as Smith despised Prentiss, he did not want this day to turn into a mass killing of people whose only mistake was believing in the wrong man.

Walking across the quad was eerie. No sound. No movement. Nothing. The faces in the guard towers were unfamiliar to Smith. Aikman's people, no doubt. When they reached his cabin, Ollie went in, looked around and then waited outside, leaving the door open.

"If you go in the bathroom," he said to Smith, "don't close the door."

"Got it."

Smith grabbed fresh clothes and went into the tiny bathroom. He pulled the cell phone from his pocket, placed it on the sink, then did the same with the gun. When he'd dragged on the clean clothes, he looked to see that Ollie was still outside the door. He held the phone where it couldn't be seen from the door and sent a text message to 911. He had no idea if the 911 service in the area was able to receive text messages but, at the moment, it was his only available option. He couldn't risk making a call with Aikman's man right outside.

Once he'd sent the text, he deleted it. He set the phone to silent just in case the dispatcher tried to call him back, then slid it into his hip pocket. He shoved the weapon into his waistband at the small of his back, then washed his face.

His eyes and jaw were swollen, and he was reasonably sure he had a couple of cracked ribs, but things could be far worse.

He joined Ollie outside. "I'm ready."

The walk across the quad was the same as before, too quiet. Too still. They reached the headquarters and entered. Two guards were posted outside the door to the conference room. Ollie walked right up and opened the door and entered. Smith followed him.

The scene in the room brought him up short. The members of the Council lay on the floor in a neat line. All were dead, all had been shot once in the head.

His gaze swung to Aikman, who stood in the center of the room. Behind him someone was seated in a chair but Smith couldn't see who it was since Aikman blocked his view.

"I thought we were going to interrogate them." He glared at Aikman, his fingers itching to reach for the weapon in his waistband.

As if Ollie had sensed his thought, he plucked the weapon from Smith.

"That was far too much trouble," Aikman said. "It

seemed far easier to simply go to the head and learn everything straight from the source."

He stepped aside, revealing the person in the chair.

Rayford Prentiss.

"You weren't expecting to see me, were you, *Agent* Flynn?" Prentiss laughed. "Looks like this game of double-cross is going to turn out just fine for me." He glanced up at Aikman. "New blood is always a good thing."

SADIE DROPPED TO her haunches next to Sheriff Tanner. "Aikman and his people have taken over," she said, worry gnawing at her. "We can't wait, we have to move fast. The killing won't stop until we stop it."

The text message relayed to Tanner from the 911 dispatcher mentioned heavily armed men and numerous prisoners. Dozens were dead already.

Sadie's chest squeezed. The text had to be from Flynn, which meant, for now, he was still alive. She hoped he stayed that way until they could get in there and stop the killing.

The good news was, inside those walls were the leaders of the Resurrection and those of the *others*. This operation was going to stop two of the worst kind of extremist organizations in one fell swoop.

As much as she wanted to be grateful for that possibility, she couldn't help worrying about Flynn. She didn't want him to end up a casualty. She wanted to spend time with him. Time that didn't involve a mission or a race to stay alive.

Tanner nodded. "We're almost ready."

Sadie had been able to warn them about the scouts around the compound. Strangely they hadn't spotted any outside the walls. Had to have something to do with the takeover. Several bodies had been discovered.

Tanner put a hand on her arm. "We're moving." His gaze locked with hers. "But you're staying right here until we have the situation under control."

She drew her arm away from his touch. "No way, Sheriff. I'm going in with you."

He nodded to someone behind her and she shot to her feet only to come face-to-face with two female deputies.

"Ma'am," the dark-haired one said, "we'll go in as soon as we receive the all-clear signal from the sheriff."

Anger swirled through Sadie as she watched Tanner sprint forward. He'd double-crossed her. Dwelling on the reality would only distract her so she shrugged it off and focused on the events unfolding only yards away.

The two deputies moved in close next to her. One wore earbuds to listen in to the ongoing operation. The other watched through binoculars. Tanner hadn't left these two women with her because he didn't think women were as strong as men. Sadie had noticed seven female deputies. The other five had obviously gone in with Tanner. One of the women, she noticed, was very pregnant. She would have needed to stay away from live fire anyway.

Obviously she was fearless or she wouldn't be in these woods right now.

The echo of gunfire jerked her attention forward. The exchange was happening outside the entrance to the compound that had been built into the mountainside. Aikman no doubt had the entrance heavily guarded.

The sudden silence was more unnerving than the bursts of gunfire had been.

One minute turned into two and Sadie couldn't take it a second longer.

"Sorry, ladies, but I can't do this."

Sadie took off in a sprint. The deputy who wasn't pregnant rushed after her. Sadie ran harder. She disappeared into the thick trees and underbrush that camouflaged the entrance. The entrance stood open, dead followers lying on the ground.

Inside, Tanner's deputies had fanned out and were entering buildings.

Sadie palmed her weapon and headed for the headquarters building. As she neared the entrance, Tanner and the female caught up with her.

He pulled her next to a vehicle that had been parked there.

"What the hell are you trying to do, Buchanan?"

"They'll be in there." She jerked her head toward the building that was the headquarters. "This is where all the decisions are made. Where the Council meets."

"And you're certain Flynn will be in there."

His words hit like a blow to her midsection. She wasn't certain. She was guessing. Speculating. Concluding the most likely scenario.

"It makes the most sense." Sadie suddenly felt completely unsure.

Tanner used his radio to divert resources to their position. Sadie's heart thundered in her chest. What if she was wrong?

A single shot exploded beyond the walls of the headquarters building. Sadie might not have heard it if one of those moments of absolute silence hadn't settled around them beforehand. And the entry door stood open.

Tanner was the first to move. He burst through the open entrance.

Sadie was right behind him. The other deputy behind her.

With Tanner's glance at her, Sadie moved ahead of him and led the way to the conference room where she had been questioned by the Resurrection Council.

At the door Tanner gave her the signal to wait.

His next signal had Sadie and the deputy dropping into a crouch. Tanner banged on the closed door.

The door opened and a guard walked out.

Tanner rammed the muzzle of his weapon into his temple and pulled him aside.

Another guard rushed out. Sadie handled him.

"Well, well, it appears we have the proverbial standoff."

Sadie recognized the voice. Aikman.

"Do come in," he said. "Agent Flynn and I were just discussing our next move."

Leaving the two guards under the careful watch of the female deputy, Tanner and Sadie entered the conference room.

"Drop the weapon," Tanner ordered.

Sadie moved to one side of Tanner, who had a bead on his target. When her brain absorbed the image before her, her heart sank to the floor.

Aikman had Flynn on his knees. His weapon was pressed against Flynn's forehead. Nearby Prentiss sat in a chair, the bullet hole between his eyes leaking blood.

On the floor to her left was a line of dead bodies. The Council members.

"I'll drop the weapon when I'm safely on my way out of here," Aikman argued. "I'll turn Agent Flynn loose at that time, as well. Otherwise, I'm going to do the same thing to him that I did to Prentiss and the members of his esteemed Council."

As Tanner negotiated with the man who wasn't going to change his mind, Sadie made a decision. She lowered her weapon. "Take me instead. The Bureau is far more flexible in these negotiations than the ATF. Did we mention that both are here?"

Something flashed ever so briefly across Aikman's face. Flynn's was far easier to read: he was not happy with her offer.

"Back off," Tanner muttered to her.

Aikman grinned, obviously enjoying the dissention. "Well, aren't you the brave one? Come on over here and I'll let your friend go."

Sadie stepped forward.

"Don't do it, Buchanan," Tanner warned, his attention zeroed in on Aikman.

"It won't be my first bait and switch, Sheriff." She looked directly at Smith as she said this but quickly shifted her gaze to Aikman. "I'm not afraid of this guy."

Aikman smirked. "That's an astounding statement considering the dead bodies lining the room."

It was in that moment—that fraction of a second when Aikman thought he had to prove how scary he was—that Flynn made his move.

He twisted and dove into Aikman's knees.

Sadie dropped to the floor.

As if he'd been in on the plan from the beginning, Tanner fired one shot straight into Aikman's right shoulder. The fool's weapon fell from his suddenly limp fingers as he was propelled backward by Flynn.

Flynn grabbed Aikman's weapon and pushed to his feet. Aikman clutched at his shoulder, right where that major nerve center would be, and howled.

"Good shot," Flynn said to Tanner.

Sadie pushed to her feet but her knees had gone so weak she had no idea how she would remain upright.

Tanner took over the prisoner and Flynn walked toward her.

Her breath caught at the injuries to his face or maybe just at the sight of him moving toward her.

He was alive.

She was alive.

And they were getting out of here.

Flynn wrapped his arms around her and hugged her. The weapon in her right hand slipped to the floor. Her arms went around him.

"Thanks for coming back to rescue me," he murmured against her hair.

She turned her face up to him. "It's what I do."

He smiled then grimaced.

"Your face looks like hell," she pointed out.

"Feels like it, too."

THE NEXT SEVERAL hours were filled with rounding up prisoners and getting medical attention to those injured, as well as identifying the dead.

Flynn refused to bother with being checked out until the work was done. By the time they were off that mountain, Sadie was ready to drop.

George was in the DA's office making a deal. Sadie was glad. He'd paid in that tunnel for whatever he'd done wrong. Aikman was trying to work out a deal, as well. As it turned out the remains in that rock hole at Aikman's compound were those of Jack Kemp. The FBI had waited a long time to learn this information but both Ross and Tanner assured Sadie that Aikman wouldn't be getting any sort of deal beyond the possible setting aside of the death penalty.

Aikman was like Prentiss; he didn't deserve a deal. He deserved a long life behind bars where he'd have plenty of time to reflect on his bad judgment.

Deacon Ross had accompanied Levi Winters for his statement.

The place was crawling with federal agents.

Sadie's SAIC had called and made sure she was okay. Flynn had been sequestered to one of the interview rooms for his debrief. She had called her parents just to hear their voices. There was really no reason at this point for her to stay. She had done what she came here to do. She could go home. Maybe even call her sister.

Maybe if she told herself a couple more times there was no reason to stay she would talk herself into walking away without waiting for a chance to say goodbye to Flynn. He'd already thanked her for rescuing him. Goodbye wasn't actually necessary.

Except it felt necessary.

"Agent Buchanan."

Sadie looked up at the sound of her name. Cece Winters smiled as she walked through the door of the sheriff's office where Sadie had taken refuge. It was about the only room in the building that wasn't filled with agents and deputies. Tanner had told Sadie to make herself at home.

"Hey." Sadie returned the smile. "I'm sure they'll allow Levi to go home soon. This part takes a while sometimes."

Cece nodded as she sat down in the chair next to Sadie. "I wanted to thank you again for saving my brother not once but twice."

"He did his part," Sadie told her. "He's a good guy. A little confused maybe, but a good guy."

"Deacon and I plan on seeing that he gets back on the right track."

Sounded like the two were definitely a couple. Sadie had gotten that impression.

"Ladies."

Sadie's attention swung to the door once more. Flynn stood there, still looking a little worse for the wear.

Cece got to her feet. "I should see how Levi's doing."

She slipped out of the office and Flynn walked in. He closed the door behind him. Sadie looked from the closed door to him, her pulse starting to pound.

"I was afraid you'd left already."

"I was just getting ready to go." She tried to think what to say next. "It'll be good to get home."

He nodded. "I don't want to keep you." He exhaled a big breath. "But I was hoping we could get a bite to eat first. I don't know about you, but I'm starved."

As if her belly had just realized how empty it was, she nodded. "I could eat. Sure."

"Good."

They stood there for a moment without saying more. Sadie suspected he felt as awkward as she did. Neither of them was the kind of person who did this well.

"We both live in the Nashville area."

"Home sweet home." She felt heat rush to her cheeks. What a totally dumb thing to say.

He smiled, grimaced. "Yeah. Anyway, I hoped we might spend some time together. You know, get to know each other better."

She felt certain the grin that spread across her face said way too much about how happy his words made her. "I would like that very much."

"It's been a long time," he admitted, "since I've met anyone who understood this life…who made me want to get to know them better."

She was certain it would be entirely dorky for her to say the same thing. Instead, she put her hand in his. "I'm ready."

"I could take you home," he offered. "I heard you lost your car."

She laughed. "I would love for you to take me home."

That was all she needed to say. The rest would take care of itself.

* * * * *

LET'S TALK
Romance

For exclusive extracts, competitions
and special offers, find us online:

 facebook.com/millsandboon

 @MillsandBoon

 @MillsandBoonUK

Get in touch on 01413 063232

For all the latest titles coming soon, visit
millsandboon.co.uk/nextmonth

JOIN THE MILLS & BOON BOOKCLUB

* **FREE** delivery direct to your door

* **EXCLUSIVE** offers every month

* **EXCITING** rewards programme

50% OFF YOUR FIRST PARCEL

Join today at
Millsandboon.co.uk/Bookclub

MILLS & BOON

MODERN

Power and Passion

Prepare to be swept off your feet by sophisticated, sexy and seductive heroes, in some of the world's most glamourous and romantic locations, where power and passion collide.